Five Bush Weddings

Clare Fletcher grew up in St George, regional Queensland. She studied journalism and business at QUT in Brisbane, before moving to Sydney in 2007 to intern for the Walkley Foundation for Journalism, where she remains working in communications. She lives in Sydney with her husband and daughter. *Five Bush Weddings* is her first novel.

Five Bush Weddings

CLARE FLETCHER

MICHAEL JOSEPH

an imprint of

PENGUIN BOOKS

MICHAEL JOSEPH

UK | USA | Canada | Ireland | Australia
India | New Zealand | South Africa | China

Michael Joseph is part of the Penguin Random House group of companies
whose addresses can be found at global.penguinrandomhouse.com.

Penguin
Random House
Australia

First published by Michael Joseph, 2022

Cover design by Lisa White © Penguin Random House Australia Pty Ltd
Cover images by Elizavita_21/Shutterstock and Inna Makarova/Shutterstock
Typeset in 12.5/18pt Adobe Garamond by Midland Typesetters, Australia

Printed and bound in Australia by Griffin Press, part of Ovato, an accredited
ISO AS/NZS 14001 Environmental Management Systems printer

 A catalogue record for this
book is available from the
NATIONAL LIBRARY OF AUSTRALIA · National Library of Australia

ISBN 978 1 76104 678 0

penguin.com.au

MIX
Paper from
responsible sources
FSC® C009448

*We at Penguin Random House Australia acknowledge that Aboriginal and Torres Strait Islander
peoples are the Traditional Custodians and the first storytellers of the lands on which we live and
work. We honour Aboriginal and Torres Strait Islander peoples' continuous connection to Country,
waters, skies and communities. We celebrate Aboriginal and Torres Strait Islander stories,
traditions and living cultures; and we pay our respects to Elders past and present.*

For Madge, Bec, Em and Pi: It's no regrettable bridesmaid dress, but I hope this finally makes up for me running away to get married. You'll always be my bridesmaids in my heart, if not a photo album.

In loving memory of Barry Scott and Peter Hackett, the best afternoon tea hosts of all time and lovers of a juicy morsel of gossip.

I

Six twangy notes of guitar were all it took for every man in a hundred-metre radius to unbuckle his belt, drop his pants and do a dumb dance in his undies.

Stevie-Jean Harrison sighed and clipped the lens cap back on her camera; she'd shot enough country weddings to expect this response to 'Eagle Rock'. While she loved collecting colour from the dancefloor, this was a sight that every Queenslander of a certain age already had burned into their memory. The happy couple's parents wouldn't be interested in seeing it immortalised in the wedding album.

Under an endless inky sky crumbed with stars, the groom's brother and his best friend swayed in their boxers with their arms around each other, bow ties unclipped and collars loosened. Their eyes were closed in ecstasy as they sang along with Daddy Cool, a cigarette dangling from one's lip.

At thirty-one, Stevie had seen this scene play out at weddings and wakes, eighteenths, twenty-firsts and B&S balls since she was old enough (legally or not) to hold a stubby. But it still brought a smile to her face, the literal abandon of men, young and old, dancing a shuffling two-step hobbled by the pants spilling over their boots.

Stevie recognised a cousin of the bride racing away from the dancefloor. Near the portaloos she stopped to grasp her mother's shoulder, her face sunburned under a fascinator. Her eyes filled with tears as she inspected her feet in their strappy designer heels, now caked with red dirt like chocolate truffles. Not a local, then.

'I don't know what the hell is going on over there,' she wailed, her fascinator pointing back at the dakked denizens of the dancefloor, 'but I've gotta get out of here and there's no phone service, let alone an Uber!'

Stifling a laugh, Stevie swung her camera strap around her body and followed, maintaining her eyeline strictly above the men's chests. In her summer work uniform of a long, sleeveless black dress and Blundstone boots, she was glad she'd pinned up her frizzy, dark blonde hair; the sun had long set but the heat of Queensland in late January lingered. There was barely a breath of breeze to stir the leaves of the eucalypts or the strings of coloured light bulbs stretched above the hired dancefloor. The band were clambering back onto their stage, the back of a hessian-draped flatbed truck parked on the bride's parents' property. Floodlights beamed down over the Lions Club-run bar, where clusters of people were chatting and drinking. A few kids were still racing around, hiding from their parents' attempts to put them down to sleep. Beyond the haloed lights was a darkness so thick you could almost touch it, alive with unseen creatures and swallowing paddocks and trees and channels and dams and tracks into one unfathomable expanse.

Stevie looked down at the boots she'd polished before leaving Brisbane the previous afternoon; now they were covered in dust after a long day's work. Stevie had been on location from the first bridesmaid's blow-dry and ill-advised early rounds of prosecco. She'd slunk around the cottage while the women were made up, captured the delivery of bouquets, the arrival of wedding cars, and caught the father-of-the-bride's first look at his daughter, which had everyone welling up. She'd shot the ceremony from 'dearly beloved' to the last handful of confetti, and deployed her bawdiest jokes to keep the bridal party smiling through a series of poses. Then it was back to the reception, with barely time to snatch a canapé before she had to work through dozens of configurations of family photos, then race off into the paddock for kissy portraits of the newlyweds as the sun set.

As the guests filed in to the marquee and sank into hired chairs for a three-course meal, Stevie had no such respite. She shot the speeches, the cake-cutting, the couple's first dance. Most other wedding photographers she knew ducked out after the first dance, but Stevie stayed to capture raucous scenes from later in the night. It was something she'd started doing when she was learning the ropes. Often she was shooting for friends and dancing around with her camera in one hand and a drink in the other, a tangled, glorious mess of business and pleasure. She'd caught some hilarious moments over the years, and now her clients expected it.

Having photographed more than a hundred weddings, Stevie barely had to think about her checklist of images any more. She was pretty sure she had it all, which was lucky given the flasks of Bundy rum now being passed around with increasing frequency. The 'Eagle Rock' moment usually heralded a turning point of sorts, after which her camera lens was less welcome. But she'd do one last sweep.

She ducked under the marquee, where empty wineglasses littered the long dinner tables. The candles had burned down, wax pooling amid scattered gum leaves and forgotten place cards, and Stevie clocked a quiet moment that made her lift her camera and inch silently closer, like a nature documentarian who'd spotted a big cat.

Red, the burly groom, was trying to feed his famished, tipsy bride a piece of wedding cake. It was a classic, old-school fruitcake rendered with a sturdy facade of fondant – a sign that this family was ruled by a powerful matriarch with a love of tradition and an iron fist – and Janelle was not interested.

Stevie knew this was their first moment alone as a married couple, and she also knew that Janelle's untouched plates had been cleared while she'd been circulating among the guests, downing bubbly. She was now perched on Red's lap: a generally capable and no-nonsense woman reduced to a giggling heap of tulle skirts. As Red tenderly nudged a forkful of cake between Janelle's teeth mid-laugh, Stevie snapped a frame that said more about their relationship than any of the shots they'd posed for earlier.

Satisfied, Stevie made two milky cups of tea, grabbed a piece of wedding cake and pulled up a chair next to the bride's great-aunt Mabel.

Mabel had proven herself an ally earlier in the day, when she deftly helped Stevie avoid a family faux pas while setting up the group portraits. But Stevie had recognised Mabel's role as the family fixer as soon as they arrived at the church. Mabel was the sort of woman who carried an arsenal of floral hankies to hand out at the first sign of a sniffle. She'd headed off renegade relatives as they entered the church and guided them towards neutral pews with a kind but firm hand. At the reception she had stocked the ladies' bathroom with baskets of tissues, deodorant, hairspray and perfume. She made sure the waitresses knew that Red's grandma needed a tender piece of meat, and to take their time topping up Uncle Tony's drink. She knew everybody's business. There was something familiar about her; Stevie wasn't sure if they'd met before, or if she was just such a staunch archetype of a bush woman of a certain age.

'Ooh, thanks for the tea, love,' Mabel said. She was ensconced in a plastic chair, a hefty woman stuffed into a taut jacquard skirt suit like an upholstered front-rower. From the set of her curls, it seemed she was single-handedly keeping Elnett in business. 'You've been working hard today. Have you been a photographer for long?'

'You know, I just realised this week it's been five years since the first wedding I shot,' Stevie said, blowing on her tea. 'It was always meant to be a temporary thing before the next proper job. I dipped a toe in with a few friends' weddings and here I am, still doing it years later.'

Mabel patted Stevie's arm. 'You seem like a natural. I don't have much of an arty eye, but I can see the way you see people. You have a knack for spotting the little moments that mean a lot. And you're one of us – you know the land, not like some city blow-in who'll flinch at a bit of red dust on the wedding dress and cry over a dead kangaroo on the side of the road.'

Stevie laughed. 'I guess it's one of the few times being a hopeless romantic comes in handy.'

'Hopeless, hey?' Mabel echoed, her voice rising with intrigue. 'Do you have a partner?'

'Mabel, you might think you know about drought in this district, but I haven't had a boyfriend in six years.'

'Well, in the year of our Lord 2019, I worry for the men of this country if you can't get a date with an arse like that.'

Stevie wasn't sure she'd heard that right. 'I promised myself after that break-up that I'd hold out for a grand, glorious, perfect love story.' She added drily, 'Still waiting.'

Mabel set down her cake fork, and Stevie, anticipating a lecture about being picky, prickled.

'I've put myself out there, I've dolled myself up, I've tried everyone's advice and met all the nephews and friends they wanted to set me up with. I swear I've met every eligible bachelor on the eastern seaboard. When you're single at a certain age, everyone thinks it's because there's something wrong with you, but so much of it is just luck.' Stevie jabbed at a slab of fruitcake with her fork. 'Maybe it's time to give up on the big love story and just embrace spinsterhood.'

Mabel huffed. 'Why is "spinster" such a dirty word when "bachelor" is practically a compliment? You're preaching to the choir, darl.'

In that moment Stevie felt the weight of all she'd done since 5 am pressing down on her. Not to mention all the all-nighters and dud dates and solo Sunday nights she'd endured for years. 'I think maybe I've been waiting for my real life to start once I found the person I'd spend it with. And he's not coming. Time to back myself.'

'You could do a lot worse,' Mabel said gently. 'And not just in a "you'll meet the love of your life when you least expect it" way. Be the love of your own life. If you're still treating this job, which you're obviously great at, like a temporary gig, maybe that's a good place to start.'

'Am I going to have to start acting professional?' Stevie moaned. 'Get a proper website and start using hashtags on my Instagram posts? Stop dancing at wedding receptions and say no to the after parties? Mabel, this doesn't sound like much fun.'

'Oh, you've got to have a bit of fun in your life. But stability, security, contentment? They don't get enough credit. They're too important to leave to chance – or to expect a husband to sort out for you.'

'You're sounding a lot like my mum.'

'Point taken! But while I'm giving out advice, I'm a bit of a connoisseur of love stories myself, even if I am an actual old maid. If you're looking for perfect, you'll always find a reason to give up on people. And that includes yourself. Everyone deserves a second chance sometimes.'

Stevie swallowed a yawn and sipped her tea.

'Well, I could chew your ear off all night,' Mabel said, 'but I think there's someone else who'd rather be talking to you. Have a good night, love.'

Stevie looked up as Mabel heaved herself out of her plastic chair, and there was Johnno West. She had thought she'd spotted him in a back pew at the ceremony, but it had been so long she didn't quite believe it.

'G'day, stranger.' His voice was low, his face cracking into the grin she remembered. The chipped front tooth was still there, a curl of dark brown hair falling into his eyes as usual, but this Johnno seemed somehow more at ease in his skin than the rumpled friend she'd known at university.

'You rascal. I thought you were in London!' She scrambled to her feet.

'Got back last week. Time to face the future at Mum and Dad's.'

'If you ever posted anything on social media, I'd have known to look out for you,' she said, punching his arm.

'Ah, I like to keep you on your toes. C'mere.' He put down his beer and wrapped her up in a bear hug. Stevie sank into it.

'I can't even remember the last time I saw you,' she exclaimed, breathing in cedar against his neck. *Hmm. Glad to see Johnno's finally graduated from Lynx body spray.*

'I remember exactly the last time I saw you, Stevie-Jean: six years ago at the Black Dog Ball at the St Lucia golf club. You must have just got your camera – you were taking it everywhere then. It just about flew across the room when "Hey Ya" came on.'

That brought the memory rushing back. The camera was her best friend Jen's 'get-over-it' gift after Stevie's atomic-level break-up. 'Well, I get paid to take the pictures now.' She raised the camera to her eye and he pulled a James Bond pose.

'You're doing well, Stevie. I love following your photos.'

'You're on Instagram?'

'Just to creep on a very select few. I don't have your thousands of followers, that's for sure. You've always had a fun way of seeing things. That photo you got of the couple in the cotton field with the emus popping up was amazing.'

'Ah, it's all good lighting and great timing.' Stevie laughed, but it was definitely one of the shots she was proudest of. 'Who knew you were so into weddings, Johnno. Are you back at your folks' place? How are Penny and Rod anyway?'

'They're good. Ready to put me to work on the place. Mum's relieved I didn't bring a Pommy girl home, but I reckon she's already putting together my application for *Bush Bachelors*. You know they're desperate for you to settle down when they turn to reality TV girls.'

'That's desperate, all right.'

'So, no bloke on the go for you either?' Johnno fished.

'Nope.'

'Give it another year and I'll have to remind you of the pact we made at uni to get married if we were both still single at thirty-two.'

'You mean that night we broke in to every pool between the RE and college?' Stevie feigned forgetfulness; they both knew exactly the night he was referring to. A classic steamy Brisbane pre-dawn, after their favourite pub had shut and they'd somehow lost all their other friends. It remained a confusing memory for Stevie, who still wasn't quite sure who'd initiated the kiss at the second pool. She'd put it down to a moment of madness and they'd wordlessly decided it was better to keep it between themselves. Particularly given Johnno was best friends with Stevie's on-again, off-again boyfriend at the time, Tom.

'Have you knocked off yet?' Johnno asked. ''Cause that dance-floor is calling.'

Stevie had already spent much of the night there, capturing candid moments. Red and Janelle had been bashful for their first dance, but they loosened up once everyone else spilled back onto the dancefloor. Stevie had ducked and scooted her way in between spinning couples and high-kicking, rum-drunk yahoos, her camera strap wrapped around her wrist, allowing her to shoot one-handed. She had kneeled for low angles and shimmied out of the way just in time to avoid a zealous young man dipping his nervous partner dangerously close to the floor. In the slow numbers, Stevie hovered around the edges waiting for tender moments between the bridal party and parents, grandparents and little kids.

But now, with her work well and truly done, all it would take was the opening bars of some B-52s or Neil Young to get Stevie on the dancefloor in seconds. No matter how compelling the conversation she was in, no matter how hard-fought the spot in the bar queue, certain songs begged a response.

'I took the liberty of making a request,' Johnno said, as 'Love Shack' started up. Stevie grabbed his beer with one hand, his hand with the other, and ran towards the music.

The drink in her hand might spill; let it. She shook her hair, whipped her skirt around, gyrated briefly in an attempt at sexiness. In the end she just jumped up and down, shouting all the words.

'Ah, you don't see moves like that in London.' Johnno beamed before breaking into a series of school dance specials: the sprinkler, the shopping trolley, the lawn mower.

The years fell away, six years of separation overpowered by a cover band playing the hits of the nineties, and once again they were just two kids who were really, really bad at dancing.

The Bush Telegraph added you to the WhatsApp group 'Neighbourhood News'

Bush Telegraph: Toodle-oo, my gossips and gadabouts. After the recent disappointing news that the Darling Downs Sentinel won't be renewing my column contract (something about defamation risk), I've decided to take matters into my own hand-held device – thanks to my young nieces for helping me set up this group. I'll be sharing my usual tidbits of news here and I welcome your tips. Please invite your friends to join the group and follow along. You know the drill – keep it clean and respectful, please. Everyone knows everyone in this small world, and the person you're sharing about will probably see what you post. That's what DMs are for!

I met a lovely young photographer at a wedding outside Dalby last week – can you believe she's giving up on men at the ripe old age of 31? Something tells me our single snapper won't stay that way for long. Check out her Instagram @StevieJeanLoveStories.

LOL, Mabel

2

Stevie's eyes cracked open. There was light streaming in through an unfamiliar set of blinds. A pounding in her head resolved into a shrill point of focus: her phone alarm was bleating. Everything felt foreign. Stevie tried to piece it all together: single bed, cheap sheets, undies on (phew), mouth like a desert . . .

'For the love of God, make that stop.' A voice came from the neighbouring single bed. Stevie added that to the spluttering air-con unit and terrifying carpet; they'd made it back to the pub in town. Phew.

'What time did we get back here?' Stevie asked the voice, which she eventually recognised beneath the panda eyes and moaning as belonging to one of the bridesmaids, Ally.

'Girl. I couldn't tear you away from the dancefloor in time for the courtesy bus, and then Heath brought out a bottle of Scotch that you had to partake in. We were on the verge of walking the seventeen kays back to town when an angel appeared in the form of Red's Aunty Kim and her Toyota Corolla. She drove us back here about four.'

'Ugh . . .' Stevie tried to tally the number of drinks she'd consumed around the camp fire after her dance-off with Johnno. She wasn't going to be able to drive home until she'd killed a few hours, showered and found a greasy breakfast.

'I need bacon,' Ally bellowed. 'No, a bloody mary. Not sure they know how to make them here, but recovery starts at 10 am, thank God.'

Stevie gave a silent prayer of thanks to bush tradition. For those hungover after a bachelors' and spinsters' ball or a wedding in the sticks, any host worth their salt also offers a recovery the next morning after a remote event requiring hours of driving. From a barbecue breakfast to another full day's partying, recoveries ran the gamut to get you safely on your way home again, even if it wasn't until the following day. In this case Red and Janelle had booked out the closest town's single pub for their guests, and had organised a big fry-up breakfast rolling into lunch. They'd even made space in the beer garden for musical family members to jam.

Stevie dragged her weary bones and her toiletry bag to the shared bathroom. As she creaked along the hallway, she heard the moans of sore heads and a cacophony of farts greeting the morning. The hot water was life-giving, shampoo and soap erasing hours of camp-fire smoke and dust, and the ghosts of cigarettes and spilled drinks. The hotel towel was scratchy but clean.

She combed her wet hair into a thick messy bun and pulled on a well-worn pair of Levi's and a holey Magic Dirt T-shirt. She felt much better, though when she unfogged the mirror she was reminded: *You're not twenty-five any more, Harrison. Where's the bloody eye cream?*

Another job, another hangover. Much as she might have felt nineteen again doing the nutbush with Johnno at 1 am, these mornings-after were getting harder. *And right on cue, here comes the self-loathing. How much has really changed since the old days of sessions with Johnno,* she thought, *except the wrinkles?*

Ten years ago, Stevie had imagined herself as a professional success by thirty-one – published author, perhaps, or award-winning filmmaker – with a serious haircut and, let's face it, a husband. The reality was much more thrown together, both job and hair, and a lot more single. *What am I doing with my life? I dreamed of big love and telling big stories; the best I'll do today is a big sandwich.*

Life goals notwithstanding, the thought of a big sandwich was encouraging, and Stevie resolved to tackle the day. Backing out of the bathroom with her hands full, Stevie collided with a hunched form clad in footy shorts and little else.

'Johnno, I didn't see you there. Get a bit of sun yesterday, did you? You'll have to invest in some sunscreen now you're home, my delicate English rose.'

'Give a bloke a break, Stevie,' he muttered, rubbing his red nose. 'I'm a bit fragile today.' He seemed dazed, but she took in the bloodshot eyes and sleep-mussed hair and chalked it up to a hangover. 'You staying for the recovery?' he asked.

'See you down there,' she said, drifting back to Room 24, already thinking about which of yesterday's shots to focus on for the first Instagram post. There was so much editing to do once she got home, and a three-hour drive before that could start . . .

She was too lost in her thoughts to notice Johnno scratching his head in her wake.

Stevie glanced at her watch. She should kill another hour before fuelling the Pajero and hitting the road. Considering how many kilometres she had to cover to do her job, it wasn't worth the risk of losing her licence for blowing over the limit.

The breakfast barbecue had hit the spot and even if the coffee was instant, it had helped. Stevie's bags were packed and her car was parked on the main street outside the shady Victory Hotel. She pulled up a stool in the front bar and asked the publican if he'd charge her phone.

'How'd it all go last night?' he asked, plugging in the battered iPhone and introducing himself as Bluey.

'Big night, but the ceremony was lovely and the party was fantastic.'

'Glad to hear it,' he said. 'We sent six kegs out and I don't expect there was a drop left over. Even today we've put on extra staff in the kitchen and the bar to cater for everyone recovering.' He gestured at the dining room, a hub of activity, and continued. 'You wouldn't believe the difference a party can make for the town. Visitors drinking our beer, staying in our rooms, eating our food, fuelling up at the servo . . . Do you know, that's the first wedding we've had in that beautiful church since about 1992?'

Stevie was surprised, given how picturesque the little church was, neat red brick with white accents like a gingerbread house of God; she'd taken some shots of all the guests outside it that she couldn't wait to see on her big desktop screen. But then again, she'd seen many times how a wedding could wake up a town, bring it to life. People prepared for months to get their lawns green and gardens perfect. Everyone pulled together, stocking the caterers with local meat, donating the best blooms from their gardens to decorate tables, assembling teams of local teens to serve drinks and help with food. It was hard work but rewarding for the families who made it happen.

It happened enough to keep Stevie in business, shooting

country weddings mostly in Queensland and New South Wales, but she was surprised more people didn't go the country route for their big day. She supposed the dominant trends on Instagram and in the wedding magazines looked pretty different: rows of perfectly matching chairs, gauzy white fabric drapes, immaculate flowers, rolling green lawns and ocean views. A far cry from the red dirt, flies and whatever glassware could be supplied out here.

Stevie had shot plenty of those perfectly symmetrical city and coastal affairs, but they almost felt too easy. To her, there was so much more heart in a wedding that guests had to plan and drive for. Where things quite often went pear-shaped, and the only option was to improvise with what was on hand. Stevie felt lucky to be part of that.

She ordered a chicken parmy from Bluey and another ginger beer, and walked out across the lawn of the beer garden where Red's little sister Grace was singing a Fleetwood Mac song accompanied by her acoustic guitar. Toddlers twirled, and more than one grown-up might have been snoozing behind their sunglasses.

She made eye contact with Johnno, who was looking much less dishevelled in a striped shirt and his akubra; he smiled and patted the empty seat next to him. He stood as Stevie reached the table and she caught a breath of his smell, soap and sunshine, as he pulled out a chair for her.

'How can you possibly be drinking beer, Johnno?' Stevie asked.

'Stevie-Jean, a hair of the dog is saving my life right now, and I urge you to do the same. It's science.'

'No way. Some of us have a long drive ahead today.'

'You still living in Brissie?'

'Yep. Jen and I are firmly in old-married-couple territory. Except now she's stepping out on me with a man. Good thing he's boring or I'd worry it's getting serious.'

'Good old Jen. Say g'day for me. Well, I have a long drive too. But I at least have the promise of one of Mum's famous Sunday roasts at the end of mine.'

'You'll need a nice long stick to beat away the girls when they find out you're living with your parents,' Stevie said sweetly.

'Mmm, yes, all the gorgeous single ladies tucked away across the Darling Downs who've been waiting patiently for my return. Much as Mum wants to start planning my wedding, I think Dad and Kate have some more pressing jobs they want me to do around the place.'

'That's right, you're a farmer now,' she teased, and he let out a sigh.

Another one bites the dust – literally, Stevie thought. *I hope he can keep that sense of humour intact.*

'So you're taking over from Rod?' she asked. 'I can't quite imagine him lounging by a pool in retirement with his holey old akubra and his sock tan.'

'Right?' Johnno laughed. 'He set this deadline so long ago. If I had a dollar for every time I've heard him say, "John, I am retiring the day I turn sixty-five", I'd be rich enough to hire someone else to take over.'

As Johnno explained, it wasn't enough to just turn up on his Dad's sixty-fifth birthday, either. A year earlier, Rod had begun needling Johnno about the handover process and whether he had his flight home booked.

'There's power in getting to choose when you step down,' Stevie said. 'Look at all the best rugby league retirements. And the worst. Or Mum.'

'How is Paula?' Johnno asked.

'She's good.' Stevie sighed. 'Better. But she never got to choose when to say goodbye to our property. Given the choice, she never would have left at all.'

'So what does retirement look like for her?' Johnno asked.

'Oh, a little flat in town, lots of trips to the library, a dog-eared meals-for-one cookbook,' Stevie said breezily. She didn't mention the laundry drying on a folding rack in the living room, a tenth the size of the Hills hoist it'd have once flown on. Or the looks Paula got from other women her age while serving at the grocery store check-out. Or the fact Paula wouldn't be retiring from that job any time soon. 'Last I heard she was considering a pottery class. Actually, I can imagine Rod up to his elbows in clay, turning out some nice chunky mugs.'

'I'll let you know if that's what he's plotting.' Johnno smiled. 'In the meantime, all roads lead to the lawyer's office on November twelve to sign the succession papers. It's all in red on the kitchen calendar. Haven Downs, the next chapter.'

'And now you've got the rest of the year to prove yourself?'

Johnno shrugged. 'Truth is,' he said, 'my old boss in London already emailed begging me to come back. Said she can keep a role for me until the end of the year. So at least I have a back-up option.'

Typical Johnno, Stevie thought. *One hand on the escape hatch in case things get too hard.*

'Last night I felt like we were nineteen again. But this morning I felt so, so old. Can you imagine what our nineteen-year-old selves would make of this,' Stevie said, gesturing between them.

'I would have been pretty happy to know I'd be still spending hungover mornings with you more than a decade later. And we've only gotten better-looking.'

Stevie laughed. 'But we had such high expectations for ourselves. And here we are, both single. You're living with your parents. If you'd asked me at nineteen, I would have said I'd have knocked over a masterpiece and a marriage by now.'

'Hmm,' Johnno said, swallowing his beer. 'And how is the masterpiece going?'

'Non-existent. Can't fail if you don't try.'

'Ah, but you're capturing love stories for the ages.'

'It's hardly great literature, is it? I dunno, I just thought I had a big story in me. But if I was really any good, I wouldn't keep giving up, would I?'

'Looks like it's time to knuckle down for both of us. Actually, I'm pretty sure we did have this conversation when we were nineteen and hadn't studied for our exams. We're not great at adulting, are we?'

Stevie moaned and buried her head on her forearms. Johnno clapped her on the shoulder. 'Orright, Stevie, I'm going to the bar. Beer?'

'Nah, mate. I'm trying to sober up here.'

'Go on. Just one Goldie won't hurt you. It's basically beer-flavoured water.'

Stevie thought about how cold and fizzy that one, harmless little schooner of XXXX Gold would be, how she could make it disappear before the glass even stopped sweating. Grace was singing a Courtney Barnett bridge with her eyes closed and her toes curled in the grass. Home and work felt a long way away. 'Just one then, you bastard.'

Stevie caught her eyes wandering from the road and cursed Johnno and his 'harmless' little schooner. The sun was low enough to blind her in the rear-view mirror; she'd barely snatched defeat from the jaws of the Victory and had set out for home much later than her best-intentioned plans.

Her ringtone suddenly cut through the music she was blasting.
'Stevie?'

'Speaking. Who's this?'

'It's Alex.'

'Alex! What's on your mind? I don't have you and Steph in my calendar for a few months yet, right?'

'Yeah, not 'til August, don't fret. But we've had a bit of development on the wedding and I wanted to run it by you. You got a second?'

'Shoot,' Stevie said, welcoming the distraction. This last stretch of the drive home, highway stuttering into suburbs, was always the worst.

'So I know we talked about a low-key wedding at Mum and Dad's, but Network Six dangled a carrot too big to turn down. They're footing the bill for the wedding of Steph's dreams, in return for full access to shoot a reunion special.'

Stevie laughed. 'I thought you'd had enough of the spotlight.'

'"The *BB* Dream Wedding",' Alex said, groaning.

'So you need me to bow out and let the pros do their thing?' Stevie asked.

'Well, that's what the network wants. But we really want you to do it.'

Stevie and Alex had been friends since college, and she had ribbed him mercilessly a few years earlier when she found out he was going to be featured on a new reality television show called *Bush Bachelors*. But the joke was on her – Alex had met his fiancée and become one of the few enduring success stories of *BB*, which was now a flagship Network Six program.

In season, *BB* was appointment viewing for bush and city girls alike, who tuned in to see a cast of daggy farmers paired off with potential wives. The blokes ranged in age and looks but they were all as hapless at romance as the boys Stevie had grown up with. The women were another species, selected by the producers for maximum drama, so the less they knew about life on a property, the better. Over a series of challenges, the number of women was whittled down to the final contenders, supposedly soulmates for the bush bachies. Exotic dancers would strike out with steely potential mothers-in-law; squeamish vegan dental nurses would drop out when required to go roo-shooting. The bachelors – from Tasmanian oyster farmers to top-end ringers, pig breeders and wheat barons – would try to cop as much action as they could along the way.

Each season would climax with an emotive finale as the farmers chose between their final fillies, egged on by producers to drop a knee for a rash proposal to boost ratings. These unions would eventually fizzle out and the gossip mags would reset for the next season, while the bachelors would slink back to their local pubs and try to live down the ridicule of their peers.

As the seasons progressed, the producers had to work harder to find the unpolished gems that had made the show's debut season such a hit. There were still plenty of mums nominating their oblivious sons, but there were an equal number of fame-hungry bounders eager to grab their fifteen minutes in the spotlight.

Before season one, Alex's sister had sent in his application, and the producers couldn't believe their luck. Alex's property, Athelton, was a remote and vast Far North Queensland cattle operation, complete with helicopter mustering, weekend polo matches and tennis tournaments on the antbed court next to the stately homestead. Plenty of babes had vied to go home with strapping Alex, whose collars were always snug around his rugby-formed neck. But from the premiere, Alex only had eyes for Steph, a nurse from

Melbourne who'd also been dobbed in by her sister.

It had been increasingly excruciating for the other girls as Alex and Steph fell in love on camera, the producers working overtime to create plotlines to keep the other girls from walking. To their despair, Alex didn't propose in the finale. Instead, he and Steph waited for the camera crews to decamp and then attempted to date in a vaguely normal way. She found she loved the endless vistas and the aching greens of the wet season; he let himself believe it was really real. And when they did get engaged, they called Stevie to shoot the wedding.

'Look, Stevie,' Alex was saying, 'as part of the deal, *Ladies Day* has the rights to publish the first images from the wedding. But we have a bit of leverage – we could go in to bat for you to still be involved. You'd just have to work around a bit of showbiz silliness and a bit of paperwork.'

Stevie had a feeling Alex was underselling both the amount of silliness and the paperwork. But if this was her time to back herself, she wouldn't get a better opportunity to raise her profile. 'So it could be my shots in *Ladies Day*?' she asked.

'I don't see why not,' Alex said.

You're not even properly trained as a photographer, Stevie's brain taunted her. *You think you can haggle with magazines and TV networks and do a better job than the professionals they work with?* Then she thought of her bank balance, or lack thereof. Of how many people would see those photos and what opportunities it might bring. *Back yourself. Fake it till you make it.*

'I'm in. But I don't want to be tripping over other photographers while you're walking down the aisle – I want to be the main photographer.'

'All right,' Alex said, sounding pleased. 'Let's make it happen.'

3

The red dust kicked up in the Landcruiser's wake as Johnno steered through the gates, onto the straight-shot driveway to the Haven Downs homestead. The sun was low, blinding him, and he'd had to take the last hundred kilometres at a crawl as kangaroos massed thick and unpredictable at the sides of the road, nibbling the green pick in the cool of the evening.

He'd had one too many beers with Stevie and left the recovery far later than intended. He caught himself dreading how disappointed his parents would be, and then reminded himself he was a grown man. *No point going in with your tail already between your legs.*

He checked the dashboard clock: 6.30 pm. Cutting it close. His mother would be taking the Sunday roast out of the oven any minute. His sister, Kate, and her husband would be there for dinner too. Johnno was looking forward to catching up with them properly, after a week of distracted snippets of mid-work chat. He decided he'd breeze in and get everyone swept up in conversation and gossip before they had a chance to rouse on him.

As the verandah-wrapped house came into view, nestled within Penny's beloved garden, Johnno turned down the stereo. He met his own eyes in the rear-view mirror. Not as bloodshot as he'd worried they might be, but he was no oil painting. He felt suddenly self-conscious thinking of how he'd bailed up Stevie at the recovery, all fresh and glamorous in her sunnies while he'd slouched under his hat with this sunburnt face.

Ugh, pick your battles, Johnno. There was a tougher crowd waiting inside. He straightened his collar, ran a hand through his hair, pulled in around the back of the house and shut off the engine.

'Ah, the prodigal son returns,' came Cameron Stone's warm throaty drawl, along with a back-slapping hug that left Johnno slightly winded. Kate's husband was a bear of a bloke, as tall as Johnno and twice as wide, especially since Johnno had taken up running.

Cam was still in shorts and socks, his filthy work boots shucked off on the verandah, but he had donned a clean checked shirt as a concession to Penny's hostessing. Penny would no doubt have words with Kate at some point about it being unironed. Cam flicked the cap off a frosty stubby and Johnno took it gratefully.

'How's the forecast looking, Cam?' he asked.

'Beautiful one day, perfect the next. Dry as a bloody bone.'

Johnno heard his father clear his throat before he emerged through the screen door, ruddy and freshly scrubbed in one of his 'good' shirts. Cam wordlessly handed him a beer. Rod would never admit it, but Cam was much more like him than his own son.

'Bit late, isn't it, mate?' Rod needled Johnno, who cursed himself for not getting out on the front foot.

'Yeah, too many people to catch up with,' Johnno said. 'Mabel Peters sends her regards to you and Mum. And Stevie Harrison, too.' He willed his voice to remain casual, distracting himself with pulling off his boots. Cam tousled Johnno's hair on his way inside, and a waft of roast lamb drifted out from the kitchen, rich with rosemary and garlic.

'You'd better get in and wash up,' his dad said. 'Your mother's just about ready to serve.'

Johnno washed his face and hands in a bathroom still steamy and Old Spiced from his father's shower. In his room he threw down his bag and surveyed the damage, decided his jeans were clean enough for dinner.

'You right, Johnno?' Kate asked, her blonde ponytailed head peering around the doorframe.

'Yep, just changing,' he called, not turning his eyes from the closet. It offered only checks, stripes and old rugby jerseys.

'Kate,' came a voice from the kitchen.

'Mum's getting fidgety – get your arse into gear, hey? Bloody hell, you need to clean up in here. It's like a museum of your awkward years.' To give themselves some space, Kate had renovated the cottage that had once been their grandparents' when she and Cam moved back to Haven Downs after their wedding three years ago. She had chosen neutral colours that echoed the red dust and warm wood of the land. When he was given the tour upon his return, Johnno hadn't missed the details, particularly the spare room off Kate and Cam's master bedroom. What used to be an office was now full of soft fuzzy rugs and a restored rocking chair, cleared for potential additions to the family.

'I'm getting to it,' Johnno grumbled. 'I've only been back a week, and Dad had me straight to work. Interior decorating wasn't quite on the agenda.'

Kate sniggered. 'Interior decorating is an extremely generous way to describe all the bar mats and glasses you flogged from pubs when you were eighteen.'

'Kate, can you set the table, please?' their mother pleaded.

Kate rolled her eyes and threw a shirt at Johnno as she left the room. He almost missed her muttering, 'Nothing ever changes here.'

When Johnno West arrived into the world, in a small-town hospital ward in 1987, he was the answer to his parents' prayers. A longed-for son after three girls in six years, he was their golden child, their future. But the crown never quite sat right with him. Faded photographs on top of the piano showed Johnno and Kate, who was just eighteen months older, forever side by side in childhood photos with matching grins that made their eyes disappear. While their elder sisters, Emily and Sandra, played with Barbies and left for boarding school, Johnno and Kate caught tadpoles and yabbies in the dam. On swim club nights they raced goggle-faced until the lights were turned out at the town pool, then fell asleep on each other's shoulders in the back seat on the long drive home.

They'd slept out in their swags under the stars in the backyard, planning the horses and cattle they'd have when they were grown up. They were inseparable, equally matched in strength and stubbornness, a dynamic they'd never outgrown. And while Kate had the edge on him in a footrace, Johnno had a lifelong trump card: he was the baby, he was the boy, and one day the property would be his.

At seventeen he'd known Penny and Rod would indulge him a certain amount of mucking around. Now he had tested their patience through a protracted degree and then all the way to London and back. But it had been made very clear that it was time for him to come back to Haven Downs.

He pulled on the polo shirt Kate had pegged at him, a Christmas gift from his mother that he knew she thought brought out his blue eyes. *Yep, breaking out the big guns.*

Johnno sauntered into the kitchen and kissed his mother on the cheek. She flushed and shooed him to the table, untying her apron. Kate was setting out the last of the cutlery around the heavy farm table they'd eaten from their whole lives.

'Turn off that TV, would you, John?' Penny asked. There was a day-night match underway, and Johnno found the remote and turned down the volume while leaving the screen on. Cam shot him a thumbs up. Penny set down the roast and handed Rod the carving knife and fork.

Kate took her place, Cam beside her, Johnno opposite. There was a flurry of napkins shaken into laps and the squawks of chairs pushed back on the polished floorboards, all of them unconsciously performing their steps in a dance they'd perfected over many years of Sunday roasts.

As Rod sliced the meat, Penny set out steaming bowls of crispy roast spuds, burnished pumpkin slices and peas flecked with mint from the garden. There was a jug of gravy, a pile of buttered white bread. Cam uncorked a bottle of shiraz and poured it around the table, one eye on the cricket. Johnno met Kate's gaze and they grinned at each other.

'Bet you missed this in London,' she said, passing the peas.

'Like you wouldn't believe,' Johnno said. 'A pub roast just doesn't compare, although I'd take a bit of snow over this heat today. Mum, this looks outstanding – thanks so much.'

'Bess Childs came over from next door for a cuppa this

morning,' Penny said. 'I wish you could have been here to say hello, John. Young Sarah was looking lovely, and she's been such a help around the place for them.'

'Managed to complete an ag science degree and bring her skills back to the family business as soon as she graduated,' Rod said gruffly.

'Point taken, Dad,' Johnno said.

'To be fair,' Kate interjected, 'I studied agribusiness at the same uni as Sarah, and from personal experience I reckon she probably got all the hijinks out of her system there that Johnno had to go to the UK to seek out.'

'Mmm,' Cam added around a mouthful of potato. 'Johnno definitely spent his university days focused on academia. He failed those units on purpose so he could spend a couple of extra years in the hallowed halls.'

'But we're so pleased you're here now,' Penny said, smoothing things over.

'Could have used another pair of hands fencing the east paddock earlier,' Rod said, uninterested in being smoothed.

'What's the plan there again, Rod? Winter crop of barley?' Cam asked.

'Only with steady rainfalls in the next couple of months, I'd imagine,' Kate said.

Johnno let the work chat wash over him. He'd barely been back at Haven Downs for a week, and while some of the rhythms hadn't changed since Johnno was a boy, he was still settling in. Particularly with Kate and Cam on the place; he was getting used to their role and wanted to make sure he didn't disrupt their systems.

As well as helping out Rod and Penny, Kate was managing the books and wages for her and Cam's earthmoving business, which took him away more often than he was at home. But what they really wanted was land, their own patch of country to develop. Johnno knew it grated on Kate that for all the work she did on the property, all that she and Cam invested into it, Penny and Rod had never even considered offering her a stake or factoring them into the succession plan. There wasn't enough to split. It was all Johnno's, signed and sealed when he was delivered, screaming, red-faced, with a penis.

'What do you think, Johnno?' Kate's voice interrupted his thoughts. He had no idea what they were talking about.

'Yeah, sounds like a great idea,' he said, hoping it was.

'I'd be waiting for the agronomist's advice, Dad.' Kate frowned. 'If the weather's like last season, we'll spend more on spraying than the crop is worth.'

Rod grunted into his wineglass.

Underneath every conversation, Johnno could feel them all holding their breath, waiting to hear his plan for their future. And he just didn't know. As far back as high school, when he'd tried to picture his future as the master of Haven Downs, it had stayed out of focus in his mind's eye. Now here he was, *a big lump of a man*, as his mother would say – thirty-two, single, and with little more to show for the past decade than some stamps in his passport.

His mind went to Stevie again. She knew what it was like to live in this world without the expected partner. She was the first to joke about it, not bitter but weary, determined to get in first with self-deprecation before anyone could judge her. That judgement was partly what had kept him in London so long. But he'd just delayed the inevitable.

'So, how was the wedding, John? I hope you gave our best to Janelle,' Penny said.

'Of course,' Johnno answered. 'She sends her love. It was a great ceremony.'

'Heard your old girlfriend Stevie was there.' Kate smirked. Johnno kicked her shin under the table.

'She was looking very well when I saw her a few months back,' Penny said.

'Easy, Mum, we're just mates.'

'Der.' Cam laughed. 'She's got better options than this clown.'

'Well,' Penny fussed, 'that's her loss.' Which only made Cam and Kate crack up more. This was not turning out at all the way Johnno had hoped. For a moment he imagined the next ten years stretching ahead of him, nothing but monotonous farm work, watching the weather forecast and enduring merciless ribbing from Cam.

No, he'd need more than that. His boss's offer felt like a sweet escape compared to the expectation in this room. He hadn't told anyone but Stevie about it; he still had time to decide. Better to give things here a real go first. He'd have to get established in the town again, join some committees, get involved with the rugby club.

There'd be social events to look forward to – he had four mates' weddings to attend before the year was out. No doubt Stevie would be at a few of those too. He'd liked seeing her shooting. Lost in her work, she'd moved with a lightness and purpose that made him happy to see. Especially after how she'd been in the later years with Tom. She still held some of that self-doubt, never quite carrying her tall frame and broad shoulders with the pride he thought she should, but he found her as beautiful as ever. He'd forgotten how he was always somehow aware of where she was in a room, the way her cheeky smile could light him up.

'How's the Cockies' preseason going, Cam? I thought I might drop in this week and put my name down,' Johnno said, hoping to steer the conversation in a different direction.

'Can always use an old boy,' Cam answered. He really never missed a chance to niggle. 'You can show the young blokes how it's done. Probably going to be a rough season – lot of first-timers now the Bakers and the Campbells have left the district. Greeny's the president now. I'll let him know to expect you.'

'Thanks, mate. Dad, I thought I might offer the Rotary guys a hand – maybe the tennis club too.'

'Just don't be in and out of town every night, John,' came Rod's stern reply. 'Fuel's not cheap.'

4

The evening sky was just turning pink over the jacarandas as Stevie's Pajero rattled down her gravel driveway. The car panted with heat even after she killed the engine.

Lugging her bags up the stairs to the Queenslander's latticed front door, Stevie ran a mental inventory of where her keys might be and came up blank. But she was in luck: the lock rattled from the inside as her best friend and housemate, Jen, opened the door and their mutt, Fred, waggled past her to jump up on Stevie.

'Sorry I couldn't take you this time, Fred.' Stevie knelt down to scratch all around his face, and Jen sniggered as his eyes rolled back and his tongue lolled in pure pleasure. Stevie was flooded with the same feeling she'd had when they'd gone to the shelter to adopt him as a wonky little pup a few years earlier: *my family*.

'Stevie-Jean, I was just about to open a bottle of wine,' Jen said, her red hair dishevelled and her petite figure swamped by a worn university jersey that indicated she'd spent her Sunday cleaning. 'Got time to debrief, or are you straight into it?'

'Lots to discuss, but I do need to smash out a post first. I'll meet you on the verandah?'

Jen nodded. 'I'll feed this guy.'

Dropping her gear bag on her desk, Stevie unpacked the bare minimum, putting her battery packs on to charge and arranging her lenses on a shelf. As well as her workhorse camera bodies, she had a small collection of second-hand film cameras: a beautiful silver Leica, a Polaroid and even a Holga, and some plastic cameras from an experimental phase.

She avoided eye contact with the twelve-month calendar pinned above her desk. With upcoming weddings and their associated travel blocked out with highlighter, there wasn't much white space to be seen. Even if Stevie didn't take herself seriously as a photographer, the quality of her work was enough to deliver a steady stream of word-of-mouth enquiries. Which had landed her here: staring down the barrel of working almost every weekend for six months straight, and a weekday shoot most weeks as well.

Shooting a wedding was only half the job. What the calendar didn't show was the clients whose images Stevie still had to finish editing, upload to websites and package into albums. Photoshopping flies off brides' faces was a part-time job in itself. Her heart rate quickened as she wondered how many of those sweet brides were arriving home, newly tanned from their honeymoons, and barraging her inbox, wondering when they could expect their full set of photos.

She shook off the thought, planted herself at the desk, powered up her computer and opened Lightroom. She wouldn't tackle the full set tonight, but she could earmark the highlights and pick one for a first look on Instagram. Stevie's follower count had been steadily growing and half her client enquiries now came from the platform, so she knew she should be posting more consistently. She also got a kick out of sharing the first image from a wedding and imagining it instantly curing the bride's hangover. She scanned the options.

Janelle and Red facing each other on the railway bridge: it was nicely composed with the creek running below.

The couple under the string lights for their first dance: Janelle's back was to the camera and Red's hand was at her waist protectively, their faces turned towards each other with a smile as he whispered something funny in her ear. The faces of the crowd around them weren't in focus but you could tell they were all grinning.

Mabel, sneaking some cake; Stevie would save that one for later.

Johnno, posing with finger guns; she should send that to him.

Aha – that's the one. The couple kissing outside that adorable little church, Janelle's veil catching the breeze as Red dipped her, and the air festooned with confetti frozen in flight as all the guests cheered. Stevie was impressed at how symmetrically she'd caught the moment. She imported the image and applied a preset that would give all the photos a uniform palette, in this case accentuating the blues of the skies and Janelle's eyes. She pumped up the saturation on the reds just slightly, so the confetti and the church's bricks popped against the cloudless sky. Then she straightened the horizon, adjusted the white balance and opened Instagram.

Time to make some magic.

'Janelle and Red . . .' she typed into the Instagram caption.

Stevie padded out to the back deck where Jen had her feet up on the wooden table next to a half-full glass of wine, and her phone in hand.

'Finally. The pic looks great,' Jen said, passing Stevie a glass of wine. It was the kind of unconscious gesture that came with more than a decade of friendship. 'I've got to stop doing this,' Jen muttered to her cigarette as she lit it.

'Ah, but it makes you look so cool,' Stevie said. 'Would we be here together today if you hadn't been a rebellious teen smoker?'

Stevie and Jen had attended rival girls' schools but had crossed paths at sports carnivals, dances and debating competitions. They were both overachievers who were too cynical (and socially functional) to go full nerd, and Stevie would never forget their first non-rebuttal interaction. Stevie had wandered out the back door of the St Mary's auditorium during a break between debates and spotted Jen leaning against a brick wall. Jen had lifted her head, red curls escaping from under the brim of her straw boater and blue eyes sparkling. She then reached behind the ornate crest of her blazer and pulled out a crumpled pack of Benson and Hedges, wordlessly offering one to Stevie before lighting her own. They'd smoked in silence for a minute.

Stevie pulled up her long socks, something she seemed to spend the entire five years of boarding school doing, like a tic.

'Why don't any hot boys ever do debating?' Jen had finally asked.

'Rugby,' Stevie had grunted in response. 'All we get are the dweebs building their extracurriculars and the flamboyant boys in search of an audience.'

They'd laughed together, made a bet on whether any of the St Mary's boys were straight, and then gone back inside where Jen had demolished Stevie's team in the debate.

'You didn't fall for me straight away, though, did you?' Jen said.

Stevie shook her head. 'Too intimidating.'

Grudging respect at school became obsessively close friendship when they moved into the same residential college at university. But for the first few weeks they were prickly, each thinking the other was too cool. Finally they'd been seated next to each other at an inexplicably Mexican-themed formal dinner. Together they polished off two bottles of wine under their sombreros and fake moustaches while bonding over music and judging people, and the rest was history.

Tom had made his move on Stevie not long into that first year. She never thought she'd be one of those girls who coupled off straight away, but Tom had rolled straight into boyfriend behaviour. Stevie had liked the way all their friends saw them as the perfect couple: classic college sweethearts who were going to get married, take over his family property and have a brood of cute, gingham-clad kids. Jen, meanwhile, was terminally single, narrating every disastrous hook-up for Stevie's entertainment. *Quite the contrast to our current dynamic*, Stevie thought, with a pang of nostalgia for the days before it was her own tragic love life they laughed about.

Jen had studied social work at UQ while Stevie went to QUT for her business degree. After graduation Jen had moved into volunteer work and clinical placements, while Stevie followed Tom out west and picked up work in a bank. In the years that followed, they'd have blowout weekends when Stevie visited, sleeping head-to-toe in Jen's bed after devouring greasy pizza slices on the stagger home from the Valley.

After Stevie broke up with Tom and blew up her life, she'd turned up on Jen's doorstep. Jen had taken her in like a stray puppy, and when Stevie finally emerged from her depression doona with a sudden energy for reinvention, Jen had surprised her with her first DSLR camera. Stevie had scraped up enough for a round-the-world ticket and skedaddled. Eighteen months later she returned with a swag of stories and a mountain of credit card debt. When Jen's flatmate kicked up a stink about Stevie still sleeping on their couch four weeks later, Jen had reminded him that it was her name on the lease, and he'd given notice.

They'd been living together ever since. In the midst of a shared man-drought, Jen had finally capitulated to Stevie's begging that they should adopt a dog.

'You have to promise to walk him and feed him and pick up his poo, Stevie. God, listen to me. What am I, your mother?'

'You'll be a wonderful mother to our dog. And I promise, you won't have to do a thing. Please, please, please, please, please?'

'Fine. Just promise me never to call him a "fur baby".'

They called him Fred.

'So, how was the wedding?' Jen asked. 'I know you have gossip, because you were supposed to be home much earlier than this.'

'It was fun, but I did stay up a bit too late.'

'You sly dog. Get a pash?'

'What are we, fourteen?'

'Um, neither of us was pashing anyone when we were fourteen, so no.'

Stevie had to concede this was accurate. 'No, I did not get a pash. But Johnno was there.'

'Johnno West?' Jen sat up a little straighter. 'I thought he was in London?'

'Yeah, I think his folks were putting the pressure on to come home,' Stevie said nonchalantly.

'Interesting,' Jen said, drawing out each syllable as she studied Stevie's face.

'Oh, stop it! You know nothing ever happened with Johnno,' Stevie muttered. 'How was your weekend?'

'Quiet. Andrew booked our Europe flights, so we've been planning out the trip.'

'Good old Andrew. How many spreadsheets has he made already?' Stevie teased.

'Just one,' said Jen, before adding quietly, 'although it does have multiple tabs and colour-coding.'

They burst out laughing, and Jen topped up their glasses.

Checking the reaction to her Instagram post, Stevie noticed a direct message request from an account called @BushTelegraphMabel.

STEVIE IT'S MABEL GREAT TO CATCH UP AT THE WEDDING PHOTO LOOKS GREAT KEEP IN TOUCH LOL MABEL

Something about being over a certain age led people to text like they were shouting a telegram, all capital letters and no punctuation, but Stevie's favourite touch was always when older people thought 'LOL' stood for 'lots of love'. She flicked through to Mabel's profile, a prolific record of weddings, christenings, race days, wakes and school fetes around the state. She replied: *Great to see you on here, Mabel. Now I can keep up with all your adventures.*

Almost immediately, Stevie saw that Mabel was typing a response.

THE GIRLS AT BINGO GOT ME ON IT LOVE SEEING WHAT ALL THE YOUNG ONES ARE UP 2, MUCH BETTER THAN FACEBOOK ... U GOING TO BE AT THE MACE WEDDING IN MARCH? GET A DEPOSIT UP FRONT I HRD THERES TROUBLE IN PARADISE

Old Mabel was quite the social media butterfly. And Stevie was indeed booked for the Mace wedding. She'd have to check over the paperwork. Trust Mabel to have the juicy goss.

'Got a hottie sliding into your DMs?' Jen asked.

'Nah, my new friend Mabel. She knows the dirt on everyone. Check it out – The Bush Telegraph.'

Jen peered at Mabel's profile. 'Stevie, I've heard of this lady. Celeste said when her sister had that terrible affair with the married farmer near Thargomindah, her parents found out about it from some nosy old lady and shamed her into breaking it off. She spends all her time volunteering and going to social events – a one-woman rumour mill. Apparently she's quite the matchmaker, too.'

That rang a bell for Stevie. But all those times her mum had told her to rein it in at the races and rugby days with threats that the Bush Telegraph would trash her reputation, Stevie had assumed it was just a figure of speech.

Scrolling back through Mabel's posts, Stevie realised what a boon technology was to the ancient art of gossip. From carefully worded insinuations about suspect Fashions on the Field voting (the only competition more plagued by corruption was the Roma Agricultural Show's 'best six classic scones' category), to baby bumps and punch-ups. It appeared no shotgun wedding went off without Mabel knowing every scandalous detail. The Bush Telegraph knew about every estate sale before the bankruptcy had been declared; she knew about every highway prang and drug bust. But what she seemed to love more than anything was weddings, and matchmaking to make them happen. The posts spanned Queensland and delved into New South Wales; one old lady couldn't be covering all this ground, Stevie thought. She probably had a network of contacts sending tip-offs and photos.

'*Gossip Girl*, eat your heart out,' Stevie said. It might seem like trivial meddling, but there was an element of it Stevie respected deeply.

She'd seen how small communities live and die by the next generation of young people who commit to them, so often at the whims of whether the right person meets and falls in love with a local. 'She gave me some good advice, actually.'

'Mabel?'

'Yeah. We were talking about how you can't wait for around for a man to make your life perfect. She said I should be the love of my own life and start taking my work seriously.'

'Stevie, I've been saying the same thing to you for years. But hey, I'm glad the message is getting through, even if you had to hear it from some random old lady at a wedding. So what's the plan? Get a business coach? A financial adviser to sort out your credit card debt? Freeze your eggs?'

'I'm still figuring out the finer details. But I'm going to work on growing my profile, see if I can build more momentum on my Instagram. And Alex and Steph's wedding in August is going to be on national TV, so I'm going to make the most of that.'

Jen nodded. 'Sounds like a good start. You've got so much talent, Stevie. I reckon once you start actually trying to make a go of it rather than just letting things happen, you'll be amazed what you can do. I'm glad you're thinking about the future. We're not teenagers any more, you know?'

A possum squawked in the jacaranda tree above them, showering them with mauve blossoms and prompting a growl from Fred, who was keeping vigil below. Stevie's rapidly disappearing glass of rosé was sweating a ring onto the wooden tabletop and Jen blew smoke from her rollie absent-mindedly into the sky.

Stevie's phone didn't ping but some ominous instinct made her look over at the screen, face up on the outdoor table, as a new email preview flashed up. Lily Taylor . . . Why was that name so familiar?

Stevie clicked on the email and a flash of recognition opened a trapdoor in her guts. She let out a groan.

'What is it, babe?' Jen blew a nonchalant smoke ring, but she sniffed drama.

Stevie handed the phone over, draining her wineglass in one gulp and reaching for a refill as Jen read aloud.

'Dear Stevie, I hope this finds you well. We haven't met but I think you know my FIANCÉ Tom Carruthers. We literally got engaged an hour ago and I am desperately hoping we can book you in to shoot the wedding! I'm a huge fan of your Insta and I know you'd do such a perfect job of making us look beautiful with no cheesiness. Whatever it costs, we'll pay it. The date we have in mind is coming up fast – we want to get married at the property on Tom's mum's birthday, October 10. Can you fit us in? Please, please, please say yes. Lily Taylor.'

'I suppose I should be grateful she didn't attach a photo of the ring, but I bet that rock is huge,' Stevie said.

'Bet she just happened to have a fresh manicure, too,' Jen egged her on.

Stevie wasn't sure how she'd momentarily forgotten her ex-boyfriend's new girlfriend. Picture the platonic ideal of the last woman you'd want your ex to date after you, and Lily was worse. A gorgeous 22-year-old law student and part-time yoga instructor, she followed a photogenic daily routine: working out in matching activewear with her abs bared; a green smoothie; studying with other over-achievers with rich-girl hair; and a procession of cocktail parties.

Stevie knew all this because she'd spent a night or six tumbling down Lily's Instagram grid. She'd once scrolled so far she drifted off into a self-loathing sleep and accidentally double-tapped a picture of Lily from three years earlier on a yacht somewhere. A deep like of deep shame that she had hastily undone but felt certain Lily had noticed.

'God, she makes me feel like such an old heifer,' Stevie moaned. 'She's so perfect and tiny and dainty. It's just rude.'

'I know she's awful,' Jen started, 'but you were so much happier after you broke up with Tom. Eventually. And obviously you don't have to shoot their wedding.'

'It's not that I want Tom back . . . I just hate being followed by the literal younger model. And it's the *Sliding Doors* thing. If I'd stayed with him, my life would be totally different now. We'd be married, with kids, on the property.'

'Yeah, but that doesn't mean you'd be happy. You were together, what, six years? That relationship peaked when you were at uni – you're both different people now. Never forget Celeste's wedding.'

Stevie inhaled sharply. Jen was invoking the bleak memory of a friend's nuptials in 2013. Their college friends were going down like dominoes: it was the fifth wedding she and Tom had attended that year. They had the routine nailed – dress up, church, drink, dance, recovery – but Stevie still felt like she was play-acting at being a grown-up.

Sweating in the church, Stevie had found herself doing the equation she always did at weddings. Celeste had met Rob in their third year at university. After three years of dating, they took the standard trip to Europe and Rob proposed in Paris. Nine months to plan the wedding and there they were, right on schedule. Stevie steeled herself for the inevitable patronising 'you'll be next' comments. It drove her crazy, the uncomfortable looks as other people did the maths and came up short with her – six years and still no ring? *I'm only twenty-five*, she'd thought. But a voice inside her did wonder, even if she couldn't actually picture herself and Tom living together as a married couple: what was holding him back from asking?

'You knew that night it was over with Tom,' Jen reminded her.

After the wedding, Stevie had lain next to Tom, his rummy breath smelling like Christmas. 'Tom?'

'. . . Mmm?'

Her voice was small. 'Do you ever think about getting married?'

There was a long pause. 'Yeah, sure,' he'd finally said. And the silence had stretched out again, growing louder with every second until Stevie's ears rang with it, hanging heavy over the bed, suffocating her. What was he thinking? Why couldn't she think of anything to say? She became aware of Tom's slow breathing. Was he . . . asleep? While she was having some kind of panic attack?

'Night, babe,' Tom muttered, rolling over, already half asleep, patting her hair limply. 'Is your face wet?'

'*Is your face wet?*' Stevie mimicked to Jen back in the present. 'Ugh.'

'Emotional intelligence wasn't his strong suit,' Jen allowed. 'But you were only in it for the "college sweethearts" storyline, and that's not enough to sustain a relationship. You freed each other to find better partners.'

Stevie snorted. 'One of us is still searching.' But her brain was already flicking through her mental calendar. She'd felt a ping of recognition at the date Lily mentioned because a client had cancelled for that date only two weeks ago. (Very juicy, classic broken engagement with a twist: the groom had discovered that his fiancée's newfound commitment to 'shredding for the wedding' was motivated by an unusually close relationship with her personal trainer.)

Lily did say she'd pay whatever it cost . . . Stevie could get that new drone she'd been eyeing, set up some gorgeous sweeping shots in the long paddock at sunset. She knew that property like the back of her hand; even with it so dry, the colours would be achingly good. *Back yourself.*

Could she really shoot her ex's wedding?

'Shall we go catch up with Jessica?' Jen offered. Stevie nodded, and they headed inside to curl up on the couch. They'd been watching *Murder She Wrote* together since college, enough to know all of Jessica Fletcher's sassy quips by heart, but they continued to choose it over newer series. Jen was asleep before the first twist, while Stevie's racing thoughts kept her awake. She threw a blanket over Jen and switched off the TV. The usual comfort she found in neatly solved murders was no match for the Lily conundrum.

Instagram post by @StevieJeanLoveStories:

JANELLE & RED, January 2019: These two know how to party – I should know, I was there until the bitter end. But the joy in this image is an instant hangover cure. Right, Janelle?

I've noticed some new followers, so I wanted to say welcome and introduce myself. I'm Stevie-Jean Harrison. I live in Brisbane but I shoot around regional Queensland, where I grew up, and beyond. I have a great dog called Fred and I'm single – but don't let that put you off. I know weddings. Especially bush weddings. I've been photographing them for five years and we've been in drought the whole time. There's something profound about being there for the rare chance people get to let their hair down. It's a small world, which has its pros and cons, but I feel lucky to be part of it. This year I want to take my career to a new level, so I will be posting more yarns here, both the picture-perfect moments and the behind-the-scenes, which can be less glamorous! Thanks for following – buckle up, it's going to be a big year. xo Stevie

5

Stevie was sneaking a beer from the fridge when she heard Jen's keys in the door.

'Jesus, Stevie, it's a brothel in here,' Jen called before she'd even kicked both shoes off. Her cheeks were flushed after a hot commute, her Cue suit looking worse for wear. Shucking off her jacket, Jen threw a manila folder of client notes on the table and asked, 'Are you going to get me one of those? Man's not a camel.'

Stevie sunk a stubby into a holder and passed it over. 'I was just about to tidy up, honestly.'

'Sure,' Jen said. 'Big day of editing?'

Stevie had got distracted writing a vignette of all the Chinese restaurants she'd tried in small towns, ubiquitous and idiosyncratic, but posting it to her Instagram had left her with enough momentum to tackle some actual work.

'Finally finished off a few jobs. I just have to package up the printed albums tomorrow and mail them out – get a few newlyweds off my back.' Stevie sighed, straightening the chairs and folding some laundry. Jen was shuffling through a pile of mail Stevie had been ignoring, and handed her some envelopes that looked worry-ingly like speeding fines.

'I'll put these new bills in the spreadsheet, Stevie. Just transfer me your share by the end of the month. We have rent next week too, remember?'

'Yes, boss.' Stevie bowed, trying to lighten the mood, but she caught a split-second wince from Jen. They'd lived together for six years, so long Stevie couldn't imagine living with anyone else. But, increasingly, domestic resentment was simmering on a backburner under their old married couple dynamic. She changed topic. 'Jen, it's time.'

'What time?'

'You told me to tell you whenever the situation arose again. And I'm telling you, the situation has arisen. It's all hanging out. It's time for action.'

In the bathroom, Jen tilted back her head as they both peered at the mirror.

'Oh God,' Jen said. 'How did it get this bad?'

'Sorry, mate, it's on me. I'm just not often at an angle to see your nose hair.'

'I've never regretted having a tall best friend more,' Jen lamented. She took the nail scissors from the cabinet and thrust them at Stevie. 'Help me!'

'Are you sure you don't want to try doing this yourself?'

'I get too nervous, my hands get shaky. It's a vicious cycle. You have to do it for me.'

'There's a part of me that loves that you'll always rely on me for this,' Stevie said, placing one hand at the back of Jen's head for steadiness. 'Now, hold still.' She went in for the trim. To distract Jen, she continued, 'No Andrew tonight?'

'He's got a games night with his boys,' Jen answered. 'Finally got him to stop insisting I come along and watch them play stupid board games.' Both girls laughed.

'Why don't you try online dating again?' Jen asked Stevie.

'Look, just because it worked for you and Andrew doesn't mean I'm that basic.'

'Thanks a lot.'

'You know what I mean. Where's the story to tell your grandkids about how you met? Where's the grand romance?'

'I'm remembering why I dreaded telling you I was dating Andrew.'

'Yeah, remind me of the fireworks of those lustful early days . . .' Stevie teased, knowing full well that Andrew had taken Jen to dinner at a restaurant too fancy for a first date. She remembered Jen's ambivalence after she got home, how he'd rambled about his accounting job, misunderstood Jen's literary references and sharp jokes, and administered a dry kiss on the cheek to end the night.

Stevie had assumed that was it for Andrew – if there was no chemistry at the start, why bother wasting a minute more? She only realised Jen was still going out with him when he turned up for dinner weeks later. When Stevie answered the door, he introduced himself and handed Stevie a mid-range bottle of red wine before taking off his boat shoes and lining them up neatly at the front door. A year later, Stevie still fought the urge to yawn when he tried to make conversation, but she had to admit her best friend seemed happy.

'He irons his own shirts, he can cook from a recipe—'

'Even if he gets hung up on following every instruction to the letter,' Stevie interrupted. 'I don't think he's ever improvised a thing in his life, Jen.'

'Probably not,' Jen conceded. 'But he's punctual, he's polite to my parents, he plans things. He talks about our future instead of pretending nothing exists beyond the present moment, like every other bloke we've pashed in the past decade.'

Stevie knew Jen was increasingly ready for that future: dreaming of her own practice, buying a big Queenslander, a couple of kids. All the clichés she'd joined Stevie in mocking over the years didn't make her laugh any more.

'I'm going to stay at Andrew's tomorrow after work,' Jen told Stevie, brushing nostril trimmings off her blouse. 'When I get back, this place better be shipshape.'

Stevie saluted.

At midday the next day, Stevie rinsed the last wineglass and snapped off her rubber gloves. Every utensil they owned was dripping and gleaming on the drying rack. Stevie's approach to cleaning was much like her approach to everything: all or nothing. She liked to think of it as binge cleaning.

She barely had a chance to exhale and admire her handiwork when the music in her headphones gave way abruptly to her ringtone. 'Mum, I was just about to call you,' she answered.

'Of course you were, darling,' came the response, laced with a sardonic smile Stevie could actually hear. Just when she was starting to feel like a functioning adult.

'What's for lunch?' Stevie asked, flopping onto the couch and scratching Fred behind the ears. She'd got into the habit of making sure Paula was eating after her dad left. There had been a lot of long calls with not much said in the early days, long silences where Stevie could hear the tears rolling down her mum's cheeks.

Now that Paula and her appetite had bounced back, Stevie asked the question more out of curiosity.

'Well, I have all this fennel coming up in the garden, so I had a very fennelly salad, which really just leaves one looking for something else to eat.' Stevie pictured Paula leaning against the kitchen counter in baggy linen pants, taking off her glasses and rubbing the bridge of her nose with her eyes closed. 'But darling, there's something else I wanted to talk to you about.'

Stevie tensed; she could hear that Paula was nervous.

'Oh God, there's no easy way to say this. I set up a profile on eHarmony.'

'*Mum!*' Stevie cracked up out of sheer relief. 'Send me a link *right now*. I hope you used a good photo.'

'Is that safe?' Paula asked. 'I haven't actually added a photo yet. I don't want some psycho to hunt me down and kill me in my bed.'

'Mum, they can't find you from a photo. Besides, no one will go on a date with someone who doesn't put a picture up. They'll assume you have a deformity.'

'A date! Darling, I never even went on a date with your father. I wouldn't know what to do.'

'One step at a time, hey? First you have to start talking to someone. And that's not going to happen until you have a picture,' Stevie said.

'What about the picture from Stacey's wedding?'

'Come on, Mum – you can't use a picture you have to cut Dad out of. Tell you what,' Stevie offered. 'If you can wait to meet your Prince Charming, I'll be coming through town in a couple of weeks after the Mace wedding. Get *lots* of wine, I'll sleep over and we can workshop this together.'

Paula murmured her assent.

'By the time I'm done with you, the eligible men of the region will be beating down your door. In a non-home-invasion way.'

The next day, Stevie was a thousand miles away, her eyes drinking in the azure waters of Greece, when knuckles rapped on the other side of the glass. In a daze, she looked up from a travel photography book to see Johnno grinning through the bookstore window.

'Fancy seeing you here,' he boomed, striding into the tiny shop. Broke hipsters paused reading the imported magazines to scowl at him over their glasses, and the clerk huffily rearranged the architecture titles.

'Keep it down, champ,' Stevie said. She'd been so deep in her reverie she still felt a little bit entranced. She held up the page she'd been looking at. 'A far cry from the old brown snake, isn't it?'

'Bloody oath. Are you getting itchy feet again, Stevie-Jean?'

'Always. Holding out hope for some good destination weddings for the European summer – you never know. Did you ever get to the Mediterranean?'

'Of course,' he said. 'Did my Croatian drinking tour – I mean sailing tour – like any self-respecting expat. You've probably seen more of Europe than me, though.'

'I bet you've seen more culture than you're letting on,' Stevie replied. 'But what are you doing here? I feel like it's twelve years ago and you've busted me wagging a lecture.'

'I would have been the one wagging, not you!' He laughed. 'You managed to actually graduate on time at least, unlike me straggling back after you and Tom had moved on.' He looked at his watch. 'Bugger. I'm on a strict time line of errands and I'm late for my suit fitting.'

'Keen Brothers?' Stevie asked.

Johnno nodded. 'And if I don't get there soon, the old bastard will definitely stick me with the pins "accidentally".'

'Want some company?' Stevie offered.

'Yes, please.'

They strolled through the city laneways, out of pace with office workers scurrying about on their lunch breaks.

'Thought you were in a rush,' Stevie said.

'This is me rushing,' Johnno said. 'Can you imagine racing around like a blue-arsed fly every day in between sessions in a fluoro-lit cubicle? City life is not for me.'

Stevie had been thinking the same thing. 'There's a lot to be said for living outside the nine to five. Weren't you an office drone in London, though?'

'Technically, yes, but I managed to get into one of the forgotten departments with a few crusty old researchers in a suburban branch. They still had a tea lady bringing around sandwiches on a cart. It was like going back in time.'

Stevie could just imagine him, in his element with a cohort of crotchety old blokes in elbow-patched tweed, flirting with a pensioner pushing a tea trolley.

'I can see what you're thinking, Stevie-Jean, and I'll have you know Doris was the one flirting with me.'

She was still laughing as Johnno grabbed her elbow to guide her into the narrow shopfront of Keen Brothers Tailors. It was ten degrees cooler than the baking city streets, all dark wood with rows of hanging blazers and stacks of shirt boxes.

'You're late, John.' The old tailor was scowling, but his face lit up when he saw Stevie. 'Ah, pretty lady, you sit over here. At least someone will appreciate my craftsmanship.' Nudging Stevie into a velvet armchair, he pushed Johnno into a dressing room with a suit and whipped the curtain closed.

A minute or two later, Johnno pulled the curtain back with far less energy. 'Let's get this over with,' he muttered. Stevie had forgotten this quirk of Johnno's: he had no shame in making himself the clown of any situation, but as soon as he was the centre of attention for anything serious, he was desperately uncomfortable. Like someone gritting their teeth through a crowd singing them happy birthday.

Stevie thumbed through one of her new books as the tailor began his work, measuring and pinning the hems of Johnno's suit. She pretended to read but couldn't help noticing how much leaner Johnno was. He was surely subsisting on a healthier diet than he'd favoured at uni: the unholy trinity of beer, two-minute noodles and hot-box fried foods. That Johnno would have looked ridiculous in a tux. This one, though, could wear a suit.

'After years of rentals, this tight-arse is finally buying a proper tuxedo from me,' the tailor teased, giving Stevie a lopsided grin around a mouthful of pins.

'I've got that many weddings this year I'd be mad to keep renting,' Johnno fired back. 'Although what you're charging me for this is still daylight robbery. Stevie, do these shoulders look right to you?'

She looked up from her book. 'Shoulders look good. You should try the pants taken in a bit.'

'I told him this,' the tailor agreed.

'Dad'd have a heart attack if I started swanning around in tight duds,' Johnno said, shaking his head. 'Got to give the family jewels room to breathe.'

'You hurt my heart, John, but the customer is always right. I will finish these adjustments in two weeks. Can you pick up the suit? I don't think the couriers deliver to your country house.'

Johnno was back behind the curtain. Stevie could hear him pulling on his boots. 'I won't be able to get back, mate,' he said.

'I'll be home for a gig in a couple of weeks, if you could get it from me there?' Stevie said.

'She is an angel,' the tailor said.

'I'd better take you for lunch then,' Johnno said. 'You free?'

'I should be doing some work at home, but how often do I get shouted lunch? Let's do it.'

'Oh no, you wouldn't!' Stevie squealed as they approached Harry's Fine Food, the site of many a greasy 3 am D&M. 'I've never been inside Dirty Harry's in daylight and I don't intend to start now.'

'Easy tiger, we're not there yet,' Johnno said. 'Counter lunch at the Cakko?'

'Classic,' Stevie nodded in approval. The Caxton had had a much more chic fit-out since the days Stevie and Johnno had frequented its dancefloor.

'My shoes are barely even sticking to the floor,' Johnno said in wonder as they found a table. 'We're moving up in the world.'

As they waited for their steaks and chips to arrive, banter again flowed like no time had passed.

'How come we never crossed paths in London?' Johnno asked, slicing his steak. 'You were in Europe more than once.'

'Well, I try to get off the beaten track. I was looking for adventure, not half my graduating class, so London was a bit too obvious.'

'Oh, so you think I'm basic?' Johnno laughed.

'Completely. But I did try to meet up with you once, remember? You were supposed to meet me at the mummies in the British Museum.'

'I can't believe you're bringing this up, Stevie. I did go, and you weren't there.'

'You were late! How was I to know you were going to turn up at all? So when a very handsome Spanish backpacker invited me for a jamón sandwich, what was I supposed to do? I was hungry.' *Oh, Alejandro,* Stevie thought wistfully. A few weeks later they'd reconnected in Barcelona. A rapid-fire montage of memories surfaced: whizzing through back lanes on the back of a Vespa, eating pintxos and drinking vats of cheap wine, making out on cobblestoned streets. That was a more fun flashback than remembering the protracted email row she'd had with Johnno, trading blows every time she had some wi-fi.

'I think we'll have to agree to disagree about that, again,' he said. 'How'd you get into wedding photography anyway? When I last saw you in Brisbane, you'd just got your camera and you were about to leave the country.'

'That was my first trip overseas. A glorious year, but I came back with a massive credit card debt, so I bunked in with Jen and kept on with the hodgepodge of jobs I'd been scraping by on overseas – bar work, nannying, bits of freelance writing and photography. A friend asked me to take photos at her wedding. I gave it a go and realised I had a knack for it. Word got around, I got busier. Somehow it became my full-time job.'

'And are they always bush weddings?'

'Well, I get a lot of gigs through personal connections, and people seemed to like the stuff I shot in the dust . . . and people definitely know how to have the most fun at bush weddings. So yeah, mostly.'

'Living the dream,' he said.

'Am I? I just kind of fell into it, and now it feels like a ride I can't get off.'

'You were always going to be a storyteller, though.' He said it like it was obvious, but it had taken Stevie years to come to the same conclusion.

'I thought I'd be telling bigger stories by now.' She sighed. 'Don't you feel like this switch flicked when you turned thirty? All these decisions I made in my twenties about who I am suddenly feel like a trap. Everyone else has settled down and that kind of life feels so far out of my reach.'

'Ah, you're feeling like an old maid.'

She threw her napkin at his head.

'No, I know what you mean. I've been dragged back by my parents to face reality and all my mates are getting married this year. We're not as young as we used to be. But we're not dead yet.'

'Is it really what you want to be doing, though – Haven Downs?'

'Gotta grow up some time, I s'pose,' he said with a shrug. 'I don't really know what I should be doing. Why not be a farmer? Kate can't wait to see me stuff it up.'

It was classic Johnno, joking around about the stuff expected of him. Only it wasn't a missed assignment or a failed exam, it was his family's livelihood. Stevie's mum's voice rang through her head. *Land is a privilege, Stevie. The only way to live on the land is to give it your whole heart, and ask for help when you need it.* They'd seen what could happen when someone didn't take it seriously.

Like he was reading her mind, Johnno asked, 'How's your mum going?'

'She's good,' Stevie said. 'It was a big adjustment for her, getting used to living in town. But she's okay.'

'I'm glad to hear it. I remember how it was hard on you, your dad walking out,' he said gently.

'Ancient history,' Stevie said, keen to change the subject. 'Now, more details about your romance with the elderly tea lady, please.'

The beers were flowing as easily as the conversation, and Stevie felt the warm glow of effortless chat with an old friend. She was unravelling the parts of Johnno's life she'd missed. And the years of shared jokes and history before that meant there were plenty of mutual friends to gossip about and nostalgia to bathe in together.

The afternoon sun was dipping low across the beer garden. Stevie caught herself drinking in the sight of Johnno, the planes of his face softened in the golden hour light, his hands not yet tattooed with dirt from farm work, his shirtsleeves rolled up at the elbow and his bare, capable forearms on the table.

She felt like she'd never looked at him straight, never let herself really see him. All those years when he was her boyfriend's best friend, it wouldn't have been right. They'd trafficked instead in sidelong glances. Next to Tom, he had always been out of focus. Just as tall, but never as trim or well groomed, Johnno was always a bit untucked and woolly around the edges. In those uni days, blokes could get away with scruffiness. But this Johnno had finally started to take care of himself, learned how to iron his own shirts and get a decent haircut.

And this haircut, she had to admit, was decent. It made the most of his neck, a little bit pink from the sun, against his shirt collar. It was just long enough at the front that he occasionally had to nudge a strand out of his eyes. Stevie caught herself wanting to do it for him. And suddenly Stevie realised she was staring. As if floating above the scene, she saw herself. Was she actually crushing on Johnno? Could she just brush a hand across one of those fore-arms, lean in closer to that neck . . .?

Oh boy, Stevie-Jean. Time to sober up. Granted, you're in a hell of a dry spell, but this is still Johnno. The scruffy bogan who's never taken himself or his future seriously, and who's seen you at your absolute worst. Your ex-boyfriend's best friend. And he's just given up life in London to move in with his parents in the middle of nowhere. Nup, no way, can't happen. No more thoughts about kissing Johnno.

'You okay there, Stevie? You've gone a bit quiet.'

'Fine, fine,' she said. 'It's your shout, you tight-arse.'

Some time later, Jen strode in jingling her car keys. 'I thought you were going to meet me outside, Stevie-Jean?' she said, round-ing on the table, as Stevie dimly recalled texting Jen to pick her up.

'Jennifer!' Johnno sprung up and tackled her in a hug.

After a minute, Jen pulled back. 'Let me get a look at you, stranger.' She shot Stevie a meaningful look, along the lines of 'you didn't mention this glow-up', over his shoulder.

'Wait till you see my new suit,' he said. 'You're looking well yourself.'

'Now, Johnno, as much as I'd love to catch up, I'm illegally parked. Has your mate here told you I'm taking her home, or is she leaving you in the lurch?'

'I should call it a night, anyway,' Johnno said. 'Or will you have one more drink with us for old times' sake?'

Stevie could see Jen was tempted, but before she could agree, an unholy shout rent the room.

'As I live and breathe, the Salmon has returned!'

A small but very loud man Stevie had last seen doing a keg stand at St Leo's College some eight years ago was advancing towards them with a manic glint in his eye.

'I can't remember the last time someone called me that,' Johnno said, but he was already in a mismatched hug with their old friend Agro.

'Nothing good ever comes of it,' Stevie said.

'I can't believe you're here, you bastard.'

'Me either, Agro. How are you?'

'You missed my wedding! And I have two daughters now.'

'You have been busy,' Johnno said, as he and Stevie exchanged a look.

'Forget that. It's time for one of those legendary Salmon sessions. Let me get you a drink. Hang on, let me see if they have a beer bong behind the bar.'

'Oh no, that's our cue,' Jen said, pulling Stevie behind her. 'See you next time, Johnno. Agro, always a pleasure. Give my best to Marie and the girls.'

Stevie stumbled into the hallway behind Jen and sat down to cuddle Fred, trying to make it look intentional.

'Stevie-Jean, I do believe you have the wobbly boot on,' Jen teased. 'To what do we owe this luxurious return to the land of the long lunch?'

'Jennifer, roll me a cigarette and I might regale you.'

Jen dutifully produced her Tally-Hos and pouch of tobacco as Stevie uncapped two stubbies. Leaning across the overflowing ashtray on the back deck's grotty table, Jen proffered the rollie. 'Quid pro quo, madam.'

'Look, don't be weird about it. I ran into him while I was shopping in the city and he took me to lunch.' Stevie tried to get this out in an uninterested monotone, but she still felt that weird fizzing in her stomach. She kept sneaking glances to gauge Jen's reaction in a way she hoped was subtle.

'Oh, Johnno took you to lunch?' Jen repeated nonchalantly. 'How nice,' she continued, her voice slowly building in intensity and volume. 'Why would I be weird about you having a friendly catch-up with the recently returned from years overseas, long-lost enigma from our salad days, whom you are clearly destined to marry?'

Stevie choked on her beer. 'Jen! I knew you'd do this, you maniac. Johnno and I are mates, have always been mates. No one's marrying anyone.'

Jen puffed on her own rollie like a modern-day ginger Sherlock Holmes. 'Are you maintaining your story that you've never touched Johnno West's penis?'

'Christ! I can categorically deny any contact with that specific dick.'

'But can you be as emphatic in denying that he has ever touched your boob?'

'We've played unprofessional team sports together and done a lot of sloppy drunken dancing, so there's probably been some incidental contact,' Stevie admitted. 'Look, are you going to go through all the body parts? I'm telling you, like I've always told you, nothing ever happened.'

'The fact that you've always told me this merely corroborates the undeniable sexual tension that has always existed between you two. I know you've never given me the full story.'

'Jen, I dated his best friend for six years. Even if there was a tension, it could never withstand that.'

'Maybe not for you.'

Stevie wasn't quite sure what to say to that.

'So, how was it today? No dick-touching, I take it?'

'All pants stayed present and correct,' Stevie said. 'He bought me a steak at the Caxton, we talked about old times, got a little tipsy. He's going to be the best man at half the weddings I'm shooting this year, so please don't make this awkward.'

Jen put up her hands in surrender and they drank their beers in silence.

'So Johnno's home for good then?' Jen asked. At Stevie's nod, Jen said, 'You seem disappointed.'

'No, it's great that he's back. When we're talking it's like no time has passed. I just don't know if the whole Haven Downs legacy is for him.'

'What does he say about it?'

'He's cagey. I don't think he knows what he wants to do. But it's clear what his parents expect him to do. And then there's his sister, who's been putting in the work on the property all this time he was away.'

'Kate?'

'Yeah. Apparently his old boss in London is begging him to come back, so he's got that option in his back pocket. I don't reckon he'll last out there.'

'Would be a big change from London,' Jen agreed.

'I don't know how anyone could go back to that life after living in a city like London. All that culture and action, so many choices you can make all day every day, and then suddenly you're stuck out in the middle of nowhere, no one to talk to but your parents and some dumb cows, all your choices made for you by the weather and the bank . . . It's a recipe for disaster.'

There was a long silence where Stevie could feel Jen psycho-analysing her. 'Just because it was a disaster for your dad doesn't mean it will be for Johnno,' Jen finally said, carefully.

'That's not what I meant,' Stevie started. But the thought of Johnno forcing himself down a path he wasn't sure about left her with an uneasy feeling.

6

'I've been thinking a lot about Arcadia lately,' Paula said. Stevie had called her mother to plan a visit and could tell there was something on her mind.

Arcadia. The name still held a mythic place in Stevie's heart. The first home she ever knew; in retrospect, perhaps the only one. A name that, when she learned its meaning, now seemed a little on the nose. But as a kid it was just home, hope – everything. The word after her name when her friends addressed postcards and birthday cards to her.

'You know I joined that online workshop about genealogy,' Paula was saying. 'I've been working on a proper history of our family. And so much of it goes back to the property there.'

'Of course,' Stevie said, wondering where this was going.

'I took what I could after the sale, the old ledgers and maps, but I wasn't in the best state then.'

No, you weren't, Stevie thought dully. *Which is why this doesn't seem like a good place to revisit.*

'But I'd love to go just one last time, for my research. There are still old graves out there, and the original homestead was built by my great-grandfather. There are lean-tos and sheds that date back to when the family first took ownership.'

'I don't know, Mum. This seems like it could all be very painful. Is it the best project you could be throwing yourself into?'

'We could go together, Stevie. You could take some photos for me? Just once. A proper goodbye.'

'I'm pretty busy,' Stevie hedged.

'We can do it whenever suits you. Next time you're out. Only I've heard on the grapevine it's going on the market soon, and you never know what the new owners will do to all those little bits of our history.'

Stevie could hear in her mother's voice that this was a plan she wouldn't let go of easily. 'Okay, sure. Can I stay the night after I do the portraits for Joe and Connie next week? We can go out the next day.'

Stevie had a midweek family portrait session for an old friend from her hometown. Joe's wife, Connie, had recently had their second child and since she was adamant their family was now complete, Joe had booked Stevie to immortalise the moment.

Stevie and Joe had crossed paths in overlapping social circles at boarding school and university, then lost touch after Joe finished his degree and moved to the UK. Given he'd worked in finance in London, Stevie had been surprised he and Connie had settled down in town rather than taking a lucrative job and riverside house in Brisbane.

Joe answered the door with baby Gus on his hip and three-year-old Susie raced up, twirling to show off her fairy dress. There were toys everywhere, sunlight streaming in. Fred's nose sniffed at baking smells wafting from the kitchen. Susie grabbed him for a hug.

'Could you take Fred out to the backyard for me,' Stevie asked, and Susie nodded solemnly.

Joe kissed Stevie on the cheek. 'Can you go talk to Connie? She's having a bit of a meltdown.'

Stevie found her in the bathroom.

'Stevie, the house is a tip.' Connie was wild-eyed, frantically trying to straighten her hair and apply eyeliner at the same time. 'I had grand plans of the kids dressed in earth tones, like those Byron Bay mums on Instagram. I even bought a white silk blouse, which already has Susie's breakfast on it. This is a disaster and we haven't even started.'

'Connie, breathe!' Stevie laughed, taking the straightening iron from her hand. 'First: screw the Byron Bay Instagram mums. They're full of it. We're going to take some photos you can pull out at Gussy's twenty-first and not see dead-eyed robots in matching outfits like a boy band. I want you to be able to look back at these pictures and remember how your life was right now – chaotic and colourful and full of love. So finish your make-up. I'll grab you a cup of tea.'

Connie exhaled. 'You sure?'

'Absolutely,' Stevie said. 'We'll get some standard posed pictures in your backyard, but I was also thinking we could get action shots at the store. Let's capture everything that makes this time in your life so good.'

Connie wrapped her in a grateful hug. 'You're mad, but I trust you.'

An old-fashioned bell tinkled as Joe guided Stevie through the door of their store on the main street.

'This was the fruit shop when I was a kid,' Stevie marvelled. 'You still have the old scales.'

Joe smiled proudly and lifted Gus onto them. Susie was sneaking cherry tomatoes from a basket and Connie was pretending not to notice. Stevie shot a few frames before directing Joe and Connie behind the counter for some action shots.

'So how do you go from London to this?' Stevie asked.

'After we'd moved back to Brisbane, it started just with weekend visits,' Joe explained. 'I was filling in on the rugby team, wanted my folks to get to know Connie.'

Joe had convinced his parents to trial some different food crops in one of their fallow fields – blueberries, gooseberries, kiwifruit. 'The locals loved them, so we agreed to move out for a year or so to scale up the operation,' he continued, checking the display produce. As he'd dealt with the town shops to set up distribution, they'd met other small-scale growers. 'There were guys with blocks of pumpkin vines, hobby gardeners with zucchini gluts, people growing more garlic and tomatoes than they could eat. It just seemed crazy that quality local produce was being given away, while locals were paying inflated prices for watery tomatoes and limp lettuce delivered to the grocery stores three times a week.'

Meanwhile Connie had volunteered and charmed her way into the local social scene. She won over Lorraine from the town cafe by cutting her produce costs by a third, after supplementing her orders with local fruit and vegetables.

'We'd been in town for twelve months, and I felt a reckoning coming,' Joe said, glancing at Connie, who was wiping Gus's face. 'I kept waiting for Connie to get bored of small-town life and say it was time to get that city mortgage and settle down.'

Instead, she had presented him with a hastily sketched business plan. 'I told him we should invest in this town,' Connie said. 'Why blow our savings on an apartment in the city when we could get a beautiful big house here for half the price, and start a business the town was crying out for?'

'Nine months later, we had the shop – and Susie.'

Along with Lorraine's cafe, they had become part of a growing string of small businesses that appealed to grey nomad tourists caravanning through town. After great success selling a local artist's works displayed in the store, Connie had encouraged some friends from the Arts Club to set up a small gallery, and they'd been pleasantly surprised by the number of local makers and artisans who had come out of the woodwork with crafts, paintings and ceramics to sell.

'She's trying to talk me into running for council now,' Joe teased. He put his arm around Connie and Stevie snapped another portrait. 'It's funny, isn't it? I thought I'd escaped this town as a teenager. Came back grudgingly in my twenties. And now it's the place I can see us growing old together.'

Scores of weddings had toughened Stevie's hide, but this comment from Joe pierced right through to her heart.

Back in Connie and Joe's backyard, Stevie was perched on the trampoline. She was taking overhead shots of Joe with Susie and Gus in the grass, when the side gate creaked open.

'Uncle Johnno!' Susie squealed, racing over to tackle his legs.

Johnno winked at Stevie as he tumbled over. 'Help, I've been attacked by the Susie monster!' He writhed around in the grass while Susie, giggling, jumped on his stomach, and Fred howled.

'I'm so weak, I can barely summon the strength, but I must . . . TICKLE MY WAY OUT.'

Even little Gus was enthralled by Johnno's antics, commando-crawling across the lawn towards the melee. Stevie took a few quick shots of Johnno with the kids and Joe reaching down a hand to pull him up, then snapped the cap back on her lens.

'You're lucky we were just finishing up, Johnno,' Stevie said, packing up her gear.

'Wouldn't dream of interrupting your work,' he replied, throwing Susie over his shoulder.

'To what do we owe this pleasure?' Connie asked. 'And how long can you keep this up? I'd love to chug a glass of wine without a child holding on to me for a few minutes.'

'I'm collecting my new suit from your photographer,' he said. 'And I'm free all afternoon. Why don't you and Joe go to the pub for lunch? Stevie and I can handle things here for a couple of hours.'

Excuse me? Stevie raised an eyebrow, and Johnno beamed back at her. Connie's face had lit up and Joe was already pulling on his shoes.

'Hell yes,' Joe said, grabbing Connie by the hand and sweeping her towards the front door. 'There's expressed milk in the freezer, bottles in the dishwasher. Gus should go to sleep shortly and he'll need a feed when he wakes up. Susie will just talk your ear off until we get back. Are you guys okay with nappies? Great, see you soon.'

Connie gave Stevie a little wave as she and Joe raced towards the pub, hand in hand.

'I've seen Olympic walkers move slower than that,' Stevie said. '*Are* we okay with nappies?'

'How hard can it be?' Johnno said. In a show of comic timing far beyond his tender months, Gus chose that moment to audibly fill his nappy.

'You're about to find out.' Stevie said with a smile. 'Susie needs to show me her tree house.'

Stevie was surprised how quickly Johnno had managed to deal with Gus's blowout; she'd barely finished the cup of flower tea Susie had served her. They spent the afternoon rolling around the lawn with Susie after Johnno put Gus down for a nap. Johnno's goofy personality made him irresistible to kids, Stevie realised. He had always been shameless in debasing himself for a laugh and he had found his perfect audience.

'Thanks again for bringing the suit out for me,' he said as Susie cast spells on Fred. 'I wasn't quite sure how detailed a plan we'd made after our session at the Caxton.'

'How did things end up?'

He groaned. 'Agro called in the cavalry.'

'And you went full Salmon?' Stevie asked. He nodded. 'Regret it?'

'I dunno. The boys were all egging me on and it felt like it was going to take more effort to explain that I've grown up a bit since the old days than to just step into that character again. And, you know, people love the Salmon.'

'Yeah, but it's a bit tragic.'

Johnno lay back on the grass, arms draped across his face to block out the sun. Stevie found herself mesmerised by the wiry blond hairs on his tanned legs. Once she would have known the story behind every scrape and scar. Now they were a mystery to her.

'Stop checking me out, you perve,' he said.

Stevie snorted. 'You've got old man legs now.'

'They'd still scrub up all right with the right treatment.'

'Bloody hell, how long did it take you to shave them that time?' Stevie laughed.

It was a perfect metaphor for Johnno's university career – he'd never found time to do any homework, but at the suggestion of donning a netball skirt for a college revue sketch, he'd gone full drag and choreographed a dance routine.

'About three hours, by the time I'd mopped up all the blood. It was like the *Texas Chainsaw Massacre*. I don't know how you girls do it.'

'That's why I like winter so much. No one sees under your jeans, so you don't have to bother.'

Johnno sat up and raised an eyebrow. 'There must be plenty of people who'd want to see under your jeans.'

She threw a toy at him. 'Why isn't everyone hounding you to grow up? I can't walk into a room without people speculating about my ovaries.'

'I don't have any ovaries, for a start.'

'I hate that blokes get it so much easier. You can take the piss for another fifteen years, then turn around and decide you're ready to have a family and find some fit younger woman. I don't get a second chance.'

'You've got plenty of time, Stevie.'

'That's what I thought. Twenty-seven, twenty-eight, sure – most of them were married, but I could still pull a group of girls for a big night out. Then the thirtieth birthdays start and see ya later. One by one they're pregnant or breastfeeding or too tired out with the toddler. And when I dare to want to have a good time, everybody's judging me. It's not like I made an active choice that I didn't want to settle down. But I'm suddenly on a different path just because I haven't met the right guy. And on these Saturday nights when there's no one keen to go out, you have a bit too much time to comb through all the past decisions you got wrong that landed you here. You know, if I'd never broken up with Tom, we'd probably have three kids by now?'

'You wouldn't have much time for soul-searching then.'

'The worst thing is Jen is getting sucked into it too. She's settling for the most boring man on earth just so she doesn't get left on the shelf.'

'I thought she seemed happy with Andrew?'

'I've met socks with more personality than Andrew.'

'No one's asking you to go out with him.'

Fred wandered over, and Stevie scratched behind his ears.

'Are people really that invested in your choices?' Johnno asked quietly. 'Or is it possible you're the one judging yourself?'

Before Stevie could figure out how to respond, Susie was screaming across the yard to crash-tackle a groaning Johnno. *Good thing I worked out there's no romantic possibility here*, Stevie thought to herself, watching Susie ride Johnno like a recalcitrant pony, *or this might have been a bit confusing*.

An hour later, Stevie watched Johnno change Gus's nappy and give him a bottle after he woke from his nap. There was still no sign of Joe and Connie. 'Better get some dinner going for these kids, hey?' he said.

'Should I order a pizza?' Stevie asked.

'I'm sure we can rustle something up,' Johnno said, rummaging through the fridge. 'Can you put Gus in the highchair and wash Susie's hands?'

Stevie followed his directions and got the kids settled as he scrambled eggs, cut the crusts off toast and sliced fruit. Fred loitered, sensing food.

'That's bloody teamwork,' Johnno cheered as Stevie caught the banana Gus launched from the highchair.

When Joe and Connie returned hours later, cheeks flushed and arguing about who had won a game of pool, they found Johnno asleep on the couch, Gus napping on his chest. Stevie was sporting a face of dramatic make-up applied with Susie's heavy hand and six glittery barrettes clipped throughout her hair.

Connie laughed. 'I love this natural look for you.'

'I think I've aged ten years since you left,' Stevie said.

'Looks like you managed okay.'

'Actually, I can't take much credit,' Stevie admitted. 'Who knew Johnno was such a baby whisperer?'

'Oh, he's obsessed,' Connie said. 'He's here all the time. We can't get rid of him.'

'I think he'd take any excuse to get away from Haven Downs,' Joe interjected, stumbling a bit as he pulled off his shoes. Stevie raised an eyebrow.

'He's figuring it out,' Connie said, shaking her head. 'Why's it so hard for you to believe our Johnno just loves kids?'

'The weight of precedent,' Stevie said. 'The loosest unit in the history of St Leo's College doesn't change his spots just like that.'

Johnno gave a loud snore, which startled Gus awake. Gus farted so loudly he scared himself and burst into loud wails. Stevie grabbed her gear bag and beckoned Fred as she backed out, waving as the house went from silence to chaos in ten seconds flat.

—

'Okay, Mum, I'm nearly done editing these pictures. I'm going to give you six options and you have to choose three, okay?'

Stevie was spending the night at Paula's before shooting a wedding in Inglewood and had finally taken the portraits she'd promised to shoot for Paula's online dating profile.

'Fine. Should I get some more of that cheese out?'

As she got up, Paula dug out *Tusk* from her shelf of vinyl and leaned it against the stereo in readiness. Stevie cropped an image of Paula in a white linen shirt in front of pink and mauve sweet peas, straw hat and secateurs clasped in her hands and a smile on her lips. Stevie also had one of Paula gesticulating with a glass of wine in front of the bookshelves; it was darker but lively. And one sitting on the verandah with her hat-clad head down, reading. Now Stevie crept out towards the kitchen and caught Paula shaking her hips and assembling a cheese platter. *I'd date that.*

'Darling, should I put on more lipstick?'

'Nope, you're perfect – I'm done. Get in here and pull up your profile. Let's get to work.'

Together they workshopped a version of Paula that was single and ready to mingle. Trying to get Paula to sell herself was like pulling teeth, but Stevie hoped her temperament would show through in the way she talked about her love of gardening, books and life on the land. They gossiped as they worked, but they pointedly didn't talk about Mark, Stevie's dad, or the latest girlfriend to move in to his bachelor pad in Brisbane. Paula ticked the boxes, narrowing down the men she was interested in to those who were regional or rural.

'Are you sure you're looking for someone that old, Mum?' Stevie asked, trying to get Paula to be a bit more specific.

'Oh, I don't mind, darling. I really just want someone to chat to.'

Stevie couldn't decide if it was sweet or tragic, but either way it seemed important to top up their glasses. The next hour flew by in a haze of giggles and wine as they filled out Paula's profile. What was she looking for in a man?

'Conversation, an open mind, and I quite like a solid set of forearms . . .'

It was eye-opening for Stevie, not just to see her mum as another single woman looking for companionship and comfort, but to consider the strength it took for Paula to open up to the possibility of meeting a nice stranger. To put herself out there after thirty years of marriage and another few of being dumped, divorced and dissected by the town gossips. Stevie felt a rush of love and reached over to hug Paula. Why was it always the women who ended up alone in their later years, while the blokes all seemed to take up with younger women or die from heart attacks in their fifties?

Late the next morning, Paula turned her car off the highway and idled at the gate. Out of habit, Stevie was already unclipping her seatbelt and opening her door to jump out when she heard Paula utter a shocked 'Oh'.

She took in her mother's face, drained of colour, and followed her eyes to the gate. 'Oh,' she said herself.

'They've put in a new gate. Of course,' Paula said, as if convincing herself this was no big deal. It was a shiny aluminium gate, secure and practical, which would no doubt unlatch easily and swing open smoothly. Everything you could want in a gate you had to open every time you left or returned home, and a far cry from the rusted one Stevie remembered forcibly dragging through the dust. It was the time she most regretted being an only child, the moment the car would slow into the driveway and she had no one to shotgun into opening it for her. The perfect new gate had a shiny new sign, laser-cut metal with lights inside to illuminate the property name for travellers arriving at night: Avalon. Stevie hated it.

'Are you okay, Mum?'

'I'm fine.' Paula took a deep breath. 'I wonder if they threw away the old sign,' she finally said in a small voice.

The old sign had been hewn from a tree that Paula's great-grandfather felled in his first month on the property. He'd cut the wood into planks, cured them, then shaped a piece for the sign. He had painstakingly carved into the surface the six letters he and his wife had chosen for their piece of earth – 'Avalon' – white paint following the paths of the letters, rustic and daggy and irreplaceable.

When a new baby was born, the family would hang blue or pink streamers from the sign to let the neighbours know the news. There was a photo of Mark and Paula right at this spot, grinning into the glare with newborn Stevie a bundle in their arms.

'Why don't we ask about it while we're here,' Stevie said gently. 'But I think you should brace yourself for lots of changes like this, Mum. It's not your place any more.' Paula blew her nose. 'Ready?' Stevie asked. Paula nodded, and Stevie jumped out to open the gate. It swung open without a squeak, *the bastard*.

They drove up the driveway in silence, but Stevie could sense her mother registering every new bit of fencing, every cleared patch. If you zoomed up to the clouds and took an aerial view of the property, Stevie suspected it would somehow be a perfect map of her mother's heart. Meandering natural creeks, geometrically carved dams and channels, and the wells of long-ago sunk bores were the vessels that circulated the lifeblood of the place. Even when they'd dried down to a trickle of a puddle, these bodies of water were ringed with life – the grasses and plants they sustained and the ani-mals that flocked there. The country was unrelentingly flat, with rocky outcrops here and there. Fence lines and well-worn tracks vivisected the landscape, while trees, gums standing lonely sentry or copses of scrubby mulga, clouded the land with patches of life-giving shade. It had been a few years, but Stevie had no doubt Paula could still draw every inch of Avalon from memory.

I've got to get that drone, she reminded herself.

They sat in silence as Paula's tyres ate up the rest of the drive-way. Rather than pulling in at the homestead, Paula parked at the work shed nearby where she'd arranged to meet the manager.

Stevie had her gear bag open in the boot and was clipping a multipurpose lens into her camera body when a dusty pair of Blundstones walked up.

'You must be Paula,' a man's warm voice said.

'George. Thank you for having us.' Paula smiled.

'No worries. It's nice to meet you properly.'

Stevie emerged around the side of the car to see her mother caught in a lingering handshake with a man perhaps ten years younger. He was stocky, wearing a stained work shirt and shorts. Where he'd pushed back his well-loved Akubra, his grey hair was light against his deep tan, and his blue eyes were fixed on Paula's. When the handshake showed no signs of ending, Stevie coughed.

'Oh. George, this is my daughter, Stevie,' Paula said. 'She's going to take some pictures for me.'

'Hi, George,' Stevie said. The handshake he gave Stevie was much more perfunctory.

'Run me through what you wanted to see, again, Paula,' he said.

Stevie watched her mother fumble with a notepad, then reel off her sites of interest.

'You've probably got work to do,' Stevie said to George. 'You can leave us to it – we know our way around.'

'I'm sure you do, love. But I've got plenty of time, and the owners would prefer if I stayed with you. Besides, Paula might have questions for me about the work we've done.'

They walked around the machinery sheds and the old shearing shed and the dongas. Stevie took shots as they went: the juxtaposition of state-of-the-art vehicles alongside archaic old tractors and parts; the ghostly outlines of tools drawn on the workshop wall; the windmill lazily turning, looking down over everything. The classing table still stood in the woolshed, even though the shears had hung lifeless for years now. Stevie had seen dozens of sheds like this converted into wedding venues – with a good clean, their high ceilings and rustic bones lent themselves to a romantic atmosphere – but here every surface was faintly greasy with lanoline and dust. Only a faint, musty trace remained of that telltale smell of the shed in full swing: wool, dust and shit.

As a child, Stevie had found the raucous energy of a shed full of shearers both intriguing and intimidating: the buzz of the shears, the shouts of the sweating men, the sheep scrabbling free down the race after their haircuts. She'd insist on helping Paula carry down the slices and biscuits for the shearers' morning tea, and then hide behind her mother's legs when a kindly contractor tried to talk to her. Soon enough the break would be up, the shearers and roustabouts throwing the tea dregs out of their enamel cups and heading back to work. Paula would look on, in her element, and sometimes the men would egg her on to get involved. Stevie had a vivid memory of Paula's face alight with pride as she expertly threw a fleece over the classing table. Then she'd shoo Stevie out of the way as the furious dance of shearing, gathering, classing and pressing went on.

And to think, in those days they had a fraction of the sheep and shearers that would have passed through Arcadia in the '50s.

Stevie remembered playing by herself under the raised floor of the shed long after the shearing teams had moved on. Sometimes she'd find stubby lids and playing cards in the dust and wool fibres that had drifted down. She didn't remember her dad being around for the shearing days, except maybe when the beers came out at the end of the day.

Looking up, Stevie realised her mum and George had wandered off ahead of her, and she raced to catch up. They were deep in conversation about bores, from what she could tell. *Has anything ever been more aptly named?*

The homestead was always on the periphery of their view, but George didn't offer to take them in and Paula didn't ask. Too many memories, and Stevie didn't think either of them was up to a chat with the new owners, but she was surprised to feel a dash of disappointment along with her relief.

Behind a vast pepperina tree was the little graveyard. Paula had been gathering a fistful of everlasting daisies as they walked and now she knelt at the newest pair of headstones.

George doffed his hat and ducked away. 'I'll give you some privacy.'

Stevie took photos of each of the graves. Her grandparents and *their* grandparents rested alongside sisters, brothers and cousins, and even some of the most beloved family dogs. Some had lived out their days until old age, while others had been cut down too early; all were reduced to names and dates carved in stone.

'It never feels right to leave them here,' Paula said. 'I'll always feel like I failed them.'

'Come on, Mum. It doesn't help to think like that.'

George eventually came back to find them and offer a cup of tea, but neither Stevie nor her mum felt much like staying after that. Paula thanked George and he saw them back to her car, leaning at the driver's side window to say goodbye.

'You don't know what happened to the old property sign from the gate, do you?' Paula asked him.

'Nah, there's piles of junk all over the place here,' he replied.

'It's quite special to us,' Stevie said. 'If it turns up, could you let us know?'

'I'll keep an eye out,' he said.

Instagram post by @StevieJeanLoveStories:

CONNIE & JOE: When I stopped by to take some portraits of this beautiful young family, I was so struck by what they bring to the small community they've returned to. A new shop that has helped other local businesses and provided fresh produce and support for local growers. Two new kids who will go to local schools. There's a real sense of promise in the air, even as the traditional industries of the town have ground through a long dry spell with the drought. They'd never take any credit, but I don't think it's a coincidence. What a stroke of luck that these two met and decided to try a different path. Some people think weddings and relationships are trivial, but I think they're missing the point. Small communities live and die by the next generation of young people who commit to them, which is so often at the whim of whether the right person meets and falls in love with a local. If that's not worth celebrating, what is?

7

Johnno was in the tractor when the call came through. The Johnny Cash warbling over the engine suddenly gave way to his ringtone and made him jump.

'Johnno, it's Tom.' His best mate's voice was all around him on the tractor's bluetooth speakers.

'What's happening, Tommo?'

'I'm hoping you might be free tonight, mate. I'm just driving through Bogga and plan on spending the night at South Star. Can we catch up for dinner, a few beers?'

'Mum and Dad would never forgive me if I let you stay at the Royal. Come and stay with us – join us for dinner and Mum can make up the spare room at the homestead,' Johnno said.

'Oh, I couldn't impose. Can you check with your mum?'

'I don't need to, Tom, I know she'll squeal as soon as I mention your name. What time will you get in?'

'Round five-thirty,' Tom said.

'We'll see you then,' Johnno said, hanging up. Once he finished clearing he'd call Penny to tell her the good news. She had always had a soft spot for Tom. Most mums did, or perhaps it was just women in general. Back when Rod and Penny had dropped Johnno off at Toowoomba Grammar for Grade 8, suitcase full of stiff new uniforms with his name sewn into the collar, they'd shaken hands with Tom's parents.

From the earliest, sniffliest nights of boarding school they were allies. They complemented each other. Tom was serious and studious, while Johnno was the genial class clown. Johnno smoothed the way socially for Tom, whose reserve could read as hostility; Tom kept Johnno in the good graces of their teachers and dorm masters. Tom was the guy everyone picked first for teams because he excelled at sports, and Johnno was the guy everyone picked second, because he was the last person you wanted sledging you.

In Year Twelve they went through a stage of double-dating; the girls always seemed to come in pairs. Tom would flirt with the pretty ones, and Johnno would disappoint their friends. At college, when Tom got together with Stevie, Johnno would be left with her on the sidelines at Tom's rugby games, or waiting for Tom to get to the pub after matches. Stevie and Johnno spent a lot of time together in her first year, waiting for Tom.

The next year Johnno had to pull back. He could sense his crush on Stevie was making him mean, and spending time with either Tom or Stevie made him resent them both. So he buried himself in college life. Johnno became a mythical figure at St Leo's, his name handed down reverently to later generations of boys as one of the true legends. He could outdrink anyone, played the best practical jokes, told the best yarns, and stayed on a year too long after his contemporaries had moved off campus. That took some recalibration, academically, and so Johnno found himself still trying to graduate while Tom and Stevie moved out into real life.

To this day, Johnno felt confident Tom had no idea of the depth of the feelings he'd had for Stevie back then. And Tom certainly didn't know that Johnno's crush might be forming again now. Even Johnno wasn't sure about that. Besides, Tom was dating a knockout babe in her early twenties.

Johnno chuckled, imagining what Stevie would make of Lily. Tom had introduced him to Lily over a few beers at the Regatta not long after Johnno's return from London. Johnno had watched his friend, smitten and disbelieving, wear Lily on his arm like an expensive watch, sneaking constant glances to make sure she was still there. But Johnno had walked away impressed with Lily. She was young, but she wasn't silly.

That night was an emotional reunion for Johnno and Tom. They hadn't seen each other face to face since a friend's wedding reception in 2013, when Johnno broke a table full of glassware attempting the worm and Tom had walked away exasperated after trying to reason him into taking some responsibility. Not long after that that night Tom and Stevie had broken up for good.

From their inseparable schooldays, they'd drifted apart to the point that Johnno had had to ask a mutual friend for Tom's number when he heard about Tom's dad. Whatever your differences, you reach out to a mate when he loses his old man. Unfortunately, in this part of the world, there were too many men who wandered out to the shed and never came back.

After that first stiff phone call, Tom mute with held-in tears, they'd caught up more regularly over Skype. Johnno told Tom all about the bright, fresh green of London spring and made Tom laugh with tales of terrible dates; Tom reminded Johnno of the landscapes of home, bleached straw in baked paddocks.

So Johnno was glad to have the prospect of a few beers and a catch-up with his mate ahead of him that evening. There was a one-dayer on, and they could sit side by side in companionable almost-silence until Tom felt like talking. If Johnno could get through the evening without dropping Stevie's name – it seemed to be constantly hovering on his lips lately – so much the better.

Johnno killed the engine and dialled the homestead. 'G'day Mum. What have you got in mind for dinner tonight?'

Johnno was pouring precious greywater over Penny's roses in the homestead's front yard as Tom's Prado roared up the driveway. Johnno hadn't had a chance to shower but he had an idea.

The two men met halfway and squared up into a back-slapping hug.

'How's your arvo?' Johnno asked.

'Long,' Tom admitted. 'I'm parched.'

'Dam beers?'

Tom matched his smile.

'Mum said dinner will be a while, so we've got time. Come in and say g'day.' Tom followed him into the homestead and Penny did indeed squeal, pulling Tom in for a hug.

By the time Tom emerged from Penny's cosseting, Johnno was waiting on the four-wheeler with an esky. The sun was just starting to dip but there was plenty of heat left in the evening. Tom jumped on the back and they tore off down a track they both knew well, for one of their treasured traditions. When they reached the dam they shucked off their boots, shirts and shorts, prancing through the mud with beers held aloft until they could sink into the water. The cows barely looked up from their drinking at the sight of two heads bobbing above the surface. Johnno sunk his toes into the silt to find the cool, and felt the glancing traces of yabbies.

'This is living, hey?' Tom said. Johnno raised his beer. The cicadas began to strike up their evening dirge.

'So, what's the story?' Johnno asked.

'Had to check out a harvester down south – they're going to drive it up to us next week. But I was hoping to see you, too.'

As every visible square inch of Tom blushed, Johnno exclaimed, 'Mate, what's happened?'

'I asked Lily to marry me, and she said yes,' Tom said, no longer able to keep a straight face.

Johnno splashed him with dam water the colour of chocolate milk. 'That's great news – congratulations.'

'I'm gonna need a best man . . .' Tom started.

'Is that you asking?' Johnno asked. 'You sure know how to make a bloke feel special.'

'There's no one else I'd rather have there with me, Johnno. Just go easy in the speech, okay?'

'I'd be honoured, Tom. Hang on . . .' and Johnno raced awkwardly out of the water to fetch a couple of fresh tins. 'To you and Lily,' he said, and they clinked cans again before sinking into comfortable silence. The cloudless sky slowly darkened and the stars twinkled on. 'When did you know? That you wanted to marry her?' Johnno asked.

Tom laughed. 'You've seen her, mate.'

'She is a fine-looking woman, no doubt. But seriously – when?'

'I felt like my life had turned some invisible corner after the first time we met,' Tom said quietly, and Johnno quashed the urge he felt to make a joke. 'She's so still, you know? She really listens. I was so nervous, that first dinner, but she was so calm. Just kept asking me questions and before I knew it the plates had been cleared and I'd eaten an entire meal without even noticing.'

'I don't think I could say the same for many other 22-year-olds,' Johnno said.

'I told her from the start my future's on the property. Mum's been slowing down, and I'm keen to take over from the manager. I thought she'd bail when she realised I couldn't live in the city.'

'She didn't, though?'

'I've never been so tired, driving up to Brisbane every weekend to see her. But it never felt like a choice. I knew I wanted her as my wife.'

'Wow,' Johnno breathed.

'The real test was taking her home. I figured that would be a wake-up call and she'd realise she couldn't live out of the city. When I took her out to Mossdale and introduced her to Mum, it was the first time I'd seen her nervous. Not that you'd know it – she was cool as a cucumber. She didn't ask me what she should pack, or what she should wear, and I know how much she likes to be prepared. But she was watching and listening and learning the whole time. The whole drive out, she was reading a brief, but she kept looking out the window when she thought I wasn't watching. Taking it all in.'

Johnno laughed. 'I bet you were packing it.'

'Completely,' said Tom. 'Waking up next to her that first morning in the homestead, I was so nervous about whether she'd be able to love the place. I woke up with that feeling – you know when you're a kid and you have a whole Saturday full of adventure ahead? She smiled and she said, "Show it to me." And I knew I'd be asking her to marry me, no matter what Mum thought of her.'

'So what's the plan, for the wedding?' Johnno asked.

'We're going to have it at home,' Tom answered. 'October, round Mum's birthday. I'm stoked Lily's happy to do it there. She's got a whole vision.'

'I'll bet she does.'

'There's a whole app, mate, did you know? For girls to save pictures of every tiny thing they've been dreaming about for their wedding? I've learned more about flowers in the last two weeks than I ever wanted to know. Anyway, I'm gonna need your help to get through this thing. We'll get some good cigars, a nice bottle of rum, have a great weekend away for the bucks, no bloody cummerbunds.'

'Unless Lily wants cummerbunds . . .' Johnno said.

'Yes, unless Lily wants cummerbunds. Then we'll wear what we're told.'

'Well, I'm in,' Johnno said.

'More beef, love?' Penny offered.

'I've got more than enough here, thanks, Penny,' Tom said. 'What a beautiful meal.'

Happy silence settled over the table as Tom, Johnno and Rod all tucked in to the elaborate beef Wellington Penny had put together that afternoon.

'What did you say brings you up this way, Tom?' Rod asked.

'I had to look at some machinery we're keen to buy,' Tom said, before breaking into a beaming smile. 'But I also wanted to ask Johnno if he'll be my best man. Lily's agreed to marry me.'

Penny dropped her fork with a clatter. 'Oh, Tom! Congratulations.'

'I'll get a better bottle of wine out,' Rod said, rising stiffly from his seat and clapping Tom on the back before shuffling off in search of an appropriately aged shiraz. Once he'd charged all their glasses, Rod made a toast to Tom and his bride-to-be.

'Well, tell us all about it,' Penny urged him. 'How did you ask her?'

'It was pretty simple,' Tom said. 'We'd been out at Mum's for a nice weekend. I'd been carrying the ring around for months and I just couldn't wait any longer. Stopped the car halfway out the driveway and went around to the passenger side and dropped a knee.'

Penny was beaming. 'You old romantic.'

'Hardly,' Tom said, although he couldn't resist returning her smile. 'But she didn't seem to mind that it was a bit rustic.'

'Well, your mum must be delighted. Have you set a date?' Penny asked.

'October, at home,' Tom said. 'It's pretty soon but that's fine by me. Lily really wanted Stevie to do the photos and she happened to be free then, so we set the date.'

'Stevie's going to be your photographer?' The words left Johnno's mouth before he could stop them.

Tom shrugged. 'It was all Lily – she's obsessed with Stevie's photos on Instagram. Emailed her right after I proposed, before she even called her mum.'

'Won't it be weird?' Johnno said, imagining what Stevie would make of Tom proposing to a girl ten years their junior.

'She wouldn't have said yes if she didn't want to do it. It's been years since we went out. Water under the bridge, mate.'

'You saw her recently, didn't you, John?' Penny interjected.

Johnno grunted in response. It might have been years, but it would raise awkward questions about a long portion of their friendship if Tom got wind of Johnno's little crush. But Tom, now gathering up the plates from the table to Penny's delight, didn't appear to have noticed the effect Stevie's name had on Johnno.

'Tom, don't forget your other surprise for John,' Penny said. 'I left it in the laundry for you.'

'I was just about to grab it.' Tom grinned, disappearing with the plates. He returned carrying a bundle of cloth with both arms, and deposited it in Johnno's lap.

It was an ancient Rabbitohs jersey, somehow warm and squirmy. When Johnno inspected further, he realised it was a puppy. She woke groggily in his arms. First one liquid eye and then the other blinked open at him, from a teeny face of soft chocolate brown and tan fur.

'Kelpie border collie cross,' Tom was saying. 'They were just about giving them away when I picked up the harvester, and I figured you could use some company.'

She'd be a great working dog, Johnno thought, although he'd have to spend the next few months training her. He should come up with a serious name that suited the tenacity and intelligence of the breed. But she was far too cute for Johnno to have a manly, rational reaction. He called her Rabbit.

8

Stevie was six years old when she attended her first wedding. Family friends were getting married in the town's little brick church, and Paula had had a dress made specially for Stevie. It was pink, with a print of tiny flowers, and Paula gathered up Stevie's curls with glossy satin ribbons.

Stevie couldn't stop twirling in front of the mirror. On the car ride to the church she sat carefully, smoothing the skirt in her lap, and Paula glanced back at her from the front passenger seat with a smile.

After that, weddings were little Stevie's obsession. At school, the older kids held lunchtime weddings in the sports equipment shed. Chantelle Mullins, a leggy blonde who ruled Grade 6, was on to her fourth husband of the year. Stevie was a fervent front-row guest at every one, holding a bouquet of weeds from the playground.

At home, pushing peas around her dinner plate, Stevie begged her parents for details of their wedding. 'What was your dress like, Mum? Did you have a flower girl? Was your priest fat? What song did you dance to first? Were there lots of people there?'

Her dad chuckled and shuffled off to his study, saying he had reports to write.

Paula pulled down a leather-bound photo album and Stevie sat on her lap to look at the pictures. Under cellophane were yellowed images of her parents smiling out from the same church steps.

'Was it the happiest day ever, Mum?' Stevie asked.

Paula thought for a moment. 'It was really nice. We were happy, even if my parents were still not quite sure about your dad. But I think the happiest day was when you came into our lives, Stevie.'

Stevie smiled. 'I wish I could have been there for your wedding. Did you dance all night?'

Paula laughed. 'We stayed up pretty late.' She turned the pages and pointed out the wedding guests. Her grandad was there, looking stern, and her petite grandma. Stevie remembered them only in snapshots. They had both died when Stevie was little, leaving Paula an orphan and their property for her to run. They had known Paula would need more support, especially with a husband who had no experience of the land and didn't want to give up his role as principal at the local primary school. But with Paula being an only child, they had no choice. She had hired a manager and Stevie had adored her childhood weekends spent on the property. As Stevie was finishing primary school, though, Paula was spending more time at Avalon, while Mark and Stevie stayed at their house in town for the school weeks.

When Stevie was about to start boarding school, Mark insisted he could help Paula run the place, and she couldn't say no. It was the point from which everything started to fall apart, Stevie now realised, but at the time all three of them had put on a brave face about their new starts.

On a steamy afternoon, Stevie threw her keys down in the entryway with a clatter, shrugging off a sweaty gym towel.

Oh no. The Buena Vista Social Club album was playing, a dead giveaway that Jen and Andrew were in the kitchen pretending they could cut it on a reality cooking show. *Yeah, right,* Stevie scoffed. No producer in their right mind would select a couple that boring for television.

Jen's face peered into the hallway. 'You're home. Are you staying for dinner?'

'Yeah, but I can just make a toastie if you guys are having a romantic dinner,' Stevie offered.

Andrew popped out in a 'Kiss the Cook' apron – *the dork* – with a pair of tongs in his hand. 'We're making fajitas,' he said, pronouncing it with a hard j while Jen shuddered. 'You've got time for a shower if you like.'

'Thanks, Andrew,' Stevie said, slinking off to the bathroom, wondering how terrible her hair looked. She dawdled in the shower, imagining the pair of them out there in their aprons, a daggy little team. Things had got decidedly more boring since Stevie had become the only single girl in the house.

As she sat on her bed to comb her wet hair, her phone buzzed, an old photo of her dad flashing up on the screen. It was as close as she got to him these days, and she silenced the call.

Back in the kitchen, Andrew made a show of pulling warmed plates out of the oven, laying them out alongside cutlery and folded napkins. *Bet he had his protractor out to make sure everything was at perfect angles,* Stevie mentally grumbled. But her rumbling tummy betrayed her and as Andrew brought out a sizzling hot plate of capsicum strips, onion and marinated chicken, Stevie had to sigh in appreciation.

'Can I do anything?'

'Pour some wine,' Jen said, nodding her head towards a bottle of shiraz on the counter as she carried a bundle of warm tortillas to the table.

Stevie topped up the waiting glasses and helped herself to a steaming dinner. 'This is fantastic, guys,' she said, mouth full, and Jen and Andrew exchanged a look.

'So what have you got on this week, Stevie?' Andrew asked, slicing off a bite of fajita with his knife and fork.

'Just use your hands, honey,' Jen said quietly.

'Well, I'm still processing the shots from my last two weddings,' Stevie said. 'I'm down in Tamworth on Friday for another one, nice little civil ceremony and dinner, and back to Inglewood for a Saturday afternoon church shebang.'

'That's a lot of driving. How's your car holding up? You know you can claim wear and tear on your tax return since it's a work vehicle,' Andrew said.

'Yeah, yeah. Tax is the last thing on my mind. Unlike you, Andrew.'

'You're doing your quarterly BAS though, aren't you?' he asked, his voice rising. Stevie grunted in response, reaching to make another fajita.

'Is there any more wine?' Stevie asked.

'Honey, are you okay?' Jen said, resting a gentle hand over Andrew's fingers shredding the label off the wine bottle.

'Did you master chefs make dessert?' Stevie asked, pushing her plate away, having mopped up every last bit of juice with a final tortilla.

Stevie was walking Fred along the river path when Paula's latest dating dispatch stopped her in her tracks. Fred tugged at the lead while Stevie picked up the phone she'd dropped, checking for more cracks before she put it back to her ear.

'You can't be in love, Mum.'

'Stevie, we've been chatting constantly, about anything and everything. It's wonderful.'

Stevie sighed. 'You've been talking on the phone?'

'No, typing on the iPad. In the app,' Paula said.

'Have you got any plans to meet up?'

'He's all the way in Mungindi, and he can't get away for a while.'

'Red flags, Mum. You've let the chat go on too long.'

'We're just getting to know each other. I think he might be a poet, the way he writes. Such beautiful observations about nature . . . He thinks I'm beautiful.'

'Try not to let your imagination run away with you, Mum.'

'Growing up as an only child out on a property breeds quite an imagination, you know that. It's the only company you get, the people you make up.'

Stevie remembered vividly the innocent joy Paula took in showing her the places she'd played as a child – the hollow trees that had been her cubbies, the fairy potions she'd made with bore water and everlasting daisies, the rocks that had been stand-ins for friends. It was something they shared deep in their bones, the creativity of the lone child in the bush, which grew into a dreamy romanticism as an adult. *Bit sad that I'm more cynical than my mum now, though.*

'The conventional wisdom is that you should try not to chat too much online,' Stevie said. 'Just meet the guy as quickly as you can and see if there's any real chemistry between you. It's too easy to hide behind the keyboard and pretend to be something you're not.'

'Oh, but Harry seems so natural. Just let me have my fun, Stevie.'

'Okay, but don't say I didn't warn you. Can you show me his profile? I want to see what he looks like.'

Paula sent through some screenshots. The pictures were pixelated, but Harry was quite ruggedly handsome and seemed very well dressed. There was something oddly familiar about him, but Stevie couldn't put her finger on it.

Paula was sighing happily. 'Well, darling, was there anything else you wanted? I'd better go and do some jobs.'

'You're just itching to chat to him again, aren't you?'

Paula was all fluttery. 'It's just nice to have something to look forward to, you know?'

The longing in her voice plunged Stevie straight back to being fourteen and flirting for hours on MSN chat with boys who were always vague friends of friends. You were never quite sure what they really looked like. But with the buffer of a hulking beige school library monitor between you, the imagination could really run wild.

Sure, Stevie might have embellished her descriptions of herself along with the stars and hearts in her username, but she never outright lied. Not like that charlatan *~BundyBear69~* who, when he actually came to the dorm during one Sunday afternoon's visiting hours, was a full head shorter than Stevie, emblazoned with acne and sweaty of palm. The worst betrayal wasn't the disappointing sight of each other in the flesh; it was the excruciating awkwardness of face-to-face conversation. Gone was the witty repartee, the snappy one-liners and sending song lyrics to hint at emotional depth. Instead she was just a girl, standing in front of a boy with Twisties breath, asking him to take his hand off her training bra.

'Let me know how it goes, Mum. Love you.'

Paula was actually giggling as she hung up. *Bless her*, Stevie thought. *If there is a God, please protect a sweet lady's heart.*

God must have been otherwise occupied. A few days later Stevie was cleaning the bathroom (at Jen's insistence). While carrying a bundle of old dunny-reading magazines down to the recycling bin, she tripped and lost her grip. As she sprawled on the driveway, a Rivers catalogue fluttered down in front of her face like a mildewed butterfly, landing open on a spread where a ruggedly handsome older gent modelled a series of knitwear against a rural backdrop. It was 'Harry'.

'Should I tell her?' Stevie asked Jen. 'She was so happy.'

'Maybe they can keep things at penpal level and live happily ever after,' Jen mused.

Stevie nodded. 'I'd be comfortable with that.'

That Sunday after the Inglewood wedding, Stevie called in to South Star to break up her drive. Johnno and his new mates from the rugby team were propping up the bar at the Royal. A 'quick beer' soon turned into a college-style Sunday session and Stevie realised she'd better do the right thing and book into a local motel for the night.

As the sun set, Johnno's teammates egged her on to play pool with them. Stevie wished she was one of those girls who could coolly pick up a cue and dominate, but in truth she'd never got the hang of it. Her confidence that maybe this time would be different rose with each additional schooner, though, and soon she was deep in an interminable game of doubles. Her partner, the Cockies' gregarious scrum half Curly Stanton, was now deeply regretting inviting her to join him.

The carpet was sticky, the air thick with the TV commentary of the Sunday afternoon rugby league game competing with

Pearl Jam on the jukebox. And Johnno West was keeping her glass topped up.

'So I can't find a date for the life of me, but my mother's started online dating and she's bloody inundated,' Stevie was loudly regaling Curly. 'If you want to feel single, try giving dating advice to someone in their sixties who immediately has more success than you.'

As he delivered her a fresh round, Johnno said, 'I hear you're shooting Tom's wedding.'

Stevie threw up her hands. 'And I'm going to photograph my ex-boyfriend's wedding.'

Curly shook his head with a laugh before lining up his shot.

She turned to Johnno, dropping the act for a moment. 'Is it weird? It's weird, isn't it?'

'Well . . . it's a bit weird,' he agreed. 'But you're a professional. He said Lily's stoked you said yes.'

'Have you met Little Miss Yoga?' Stevie asked, regretting her tone almost immediately.

'I have. She's a bit younger than us, but she's very sweet,' Johnno said. 'Quite proper, but there's a dark sense of humour under the surface.'

Stevie was chastened. 'I mean, I shoot weddings all the time for people I know,' she said, talking herself into it for the hundredth time. 'And I know the property so well. That was the main reason I said yes – I can picture some of the shots already. It'll be gorgeous. A little awkward, but gorgeous.'

'You and Tom are fine now though, right?' Johnno asked. 'There's nothing there to worry about?'

Stevie thought about the last time she and Tom crossed paths. It had been at a race meet in the small township close to where

Tom grew up. Stevie was taking social snaps for the Town &
Country pages as a favour for a journo friend from *Country Life*
who had the flu. She and Tom had made stiff small talk and she'd
wondered if the politeness was worse than asking all the needy
questions she wanted to, to tally up the ledger of who had come
out on top.

'It'll be fine.' She sighed. 'It's just my age paranoia again. He's
clearly won the break-up and I just need to accept my place and eat
humble pie while his beautiful wife smiles for my camera.'

'Well, I'm on best man duties again for that one. So I look forward to seeing you grovel through it all.' Johnno smiled. 'And for
the record, I disagree with that score line on the break-up. Could
you have built your life around a job that lets you travel and be creative and party most weekends if you'd stayed with Tom? He never
understood what you were capable of.'

This last sentence was delivered quietly, with Johnno avoiding
direct eye contact. Stevie's beer was frozen halfway to her mouth.
She had no idea what to say. They'd exchanged plenty of vague flir-
tation in the past few weeks, but there was no plausible deniability
on a statement like that. Was Johnno making a move?

'Stevie. Stevie!' Curly called. 'It's your shot.'

'Oh God,' she blustered, attempting to line up a simple shot
and barely grazing the ball. 'You boys have outgrown nudie run
rules, right?'

The minute hand had pirouetted around the clock face many times
now, getting a little more rambunctious each time – but maybe
that was Stevie's imagination. Or the beers, which had turned into
gin and tonics an hour or so ago. The chat was rowdy, their group

had full control of the jukebox, and the hits of 2006 were going down a treat.

But suddenly it was midnight and the bar staff were herding them out into the night. The town's one taxi was working overtime and people were saying goodbyes and walking off singing into the night.

'Johnno,' Stevie called, clawing his attention back from his attempts to bum a cigarette from one of the boys.

'Yo!' He giggled, throwing an arm around her. 'What's next?'

'I'm staaaarving,' Stevie moaned. With a ten-beer delay, she watched his eyes light up and a grin split his face. She could just about see the light bulb flash on above his head. 'What?'

'I have just the thing. But we have to sneak off – I don't want the word to get out.' He grabbed her hand and marched off into the darkness. They crept down the main street, turned down a side street, until they reached the bakery.

'Der,' Stevie said, gesturing at the locked door and unlit windows. 'Nothing doing here, mate.'

Johnno led her down the driveway at the side of the building. It was pitch black, and a dog barked at them through the neighbouring fence.

'Johnno, what the hell?' Stevie was starting to worry he was lost. And then a faint light grew brighter as they reached the end of the driveway, and Johnno pulled her around the back of the building. The lights were blazing inside and the radio was playing the late-night insomniacs chat show.

'Millsy!' Johnno whisper-shouted.

Dressed all in white, a kid of no more than eighteen shuffled over towards them in unlaced Dunlop Volleys. He wiped floury hands on his apron. 'Jeez, Johnno, you didn't tell anyone about this, did you?' he said, glancing around. 'Damo left me in charge and if all the drunks start turning up at his door when he gets back from holidays my apprenticeship'll be in strife.'

'Nah, don't worry, Millsy. This is Stevie – we can trust her. Now, got any pies?'

Millsy rolled his eyes. 'I got potato pies, tomato and onion, or beef, cheese and bacon. Cash only, though.'

Johnno proffered a twenty-dollar note. 'One beef, cheese and bacon, one potato, and whatever the lady's having. And keep the change.'

'Potato,' interjected a delighted Stevie. Millsy pocketed the cash, shuffled off and returned with three white paper bags, each with a steaming hot pie in its little silver tray.

'Now rack off. I've gotta get back to work,' Millsy said, shooing them away.

'I'm going, I'm going,' Johnno said, already about to bite into one of his pies.

'That's gonna burn . . .' Stevie warned, but Johnno was already cursing.

'Every bloody time,' he said. 'I never learn. But they're the best pies in the world – I swear I've never had better. I used to dream of them in London.' He looked at his pie like a lover, blew on it gently and went in gingerly for another bite.

They crept back out the driveway and Johnno paused before they reached the street. 'Stay here a second,' he whispered, checking the coast was clear before directing her to follow him. Stevie could still feel the pressure of his hand on her sternum where he'd pushed her gently to stop. They walked slowly back towards the motor inn where Stevie was staying that night, devouring their pies and trading gossip from the evening and memories of the town landmarks they passed.

'Well, this is me,' Stevie said. They crunched into the gravel car park, under the pooled neon light of the motel sign. Stevie paused at the back of her Pajero, her pie bag scrunched up into a ball in her fist. Johnno still had his second pie, saving it for the walk back to his car, he'd told her.

'Fun night,' Johnno said.

'One of the greats.' Stevie smiled. The streetlights flickered and she looked up for the first time since leaving the pub. 'Bloody hell, look at that,' she marvelled, wheeling slowly around beneath the velvet blanket of the sky, sprayed with stars so thick in places they looked like dust. The moon hung low, skinny as a fingernail.

Johnno's face was as awestruck as hers, but his sights weren't set so high. He steadied himself, stepped in and gently cupped a hand beneath her jaw, fingers threading into her hair. Her gaze snapped down to lock eyes with his, surprised.

Before she could speak, he ducked his head and drew her in to a kiss.

It had been more months than Stevie cared to count since someone had kissed her, and after a few seconds of shock her brain switched off and she melted into the sensation of it. Johnno kissed her deeper, and her hands found his waist, his back. Stevie was vaguely aware of a papery thud and then his arms were all around her. *Damn, Johnno's got moves*, she registered vaguely. *Wait . . . Johnno . . . pies . . .* and a giggle bubbled up from within her.

'What?' Johnno asked, pulling back and panting a little. She read concern all over his face.

'Did you drop your pie?' She giggled again and he looked blankly at her for a moment before his brain caught up, and they looked down at the wreckage on the ground. The white paper bag was turning translucent where grease and mince mingled. Looking back at each other they both laughed.

'Fuck the pie,' he said, for the first and probably only time in his life. With one hand at Stevie's waist and the other in her hair, he pulled her in again. It was a searching kiss, and his hands were asking questions too, hinting at the hemline of her shirt and brushing over her buttons. And Stevie's body was answering yes, her hands asking some questions of their own, while her brain tried to diagnose exactly why this was a bad idea.

'I've had enough small town pashes to know we're not being discreet enough right now,' Stevie said breathlessly. 'Where are you sleeping tonight, again?'

'I'm in no state to drive home, was just going to bunk in the back of my ute,' he said, trailing kisses in a line from her earlobe down towards her clavicle. 'Got a better offer?'

'Mmm . . .' Stevie's moan turned gradually from pleasure to pain. She could already feel the hangover starting, and waking up next to Johnno would bring a whole lot more confusion than she'd be capable of handling. She vaguely remembered having decided this was never going to happen. 'I don't know if this is the best idea,' she started, although her lips were seeking out his again.

'I think it might be the best idea ever,' he said, but his breath was slowing. Silence grew awkwardly between them. Finally, his hands gently wrapped her shoulders into a hug, and into her ear he said quietly, 'If you're not feeling sure, let's not push it. Just a bit of fun.'

'Yeah,' Stevie said, trying to muster some conviction. But he'd taken the tentative out she'd given him, hadn't he? It obviously didn't mean much to him. 'A moment of madness between old friends, high on nostalgia and the best pies in the state.'

'Best pies in the world, I'm telling you,' he said, and she could feel his walls going up along with his jokes. 'Better let you get some sleep then,' he said, bending down to scoop up the mess of splattered pie.

'Night, then,' Stevie said, pulling the motel key from her pocket. She swung in to kiss him quickly on the cheek and hurried off to unlock Room 14. Johnno watched her silently, making sure she got in. Once she clicked on the lights, she heard his laconic footsteps recede through the gravel, starting the walk back to his ute parked at the pub.

Stevie leaned back against the locked motel door, closed her eyes and felt a dull ringing in her ears. What the hell had just happened? She pulled off her boots and flopped onto the bed, reaching out blindly to switch off the lamp. *Just a random make-out session with an old friend,* she thought hysterically, *nothing to worry about. A few too many beers and feeling like we were twenty, no harm done. He would have tried it on with anyone.*

But as she drifted into the welcome void of sleep, Stevie kept hearing the papery thud of a pie dropped from waist height onto a gravel surface, and it sounded suspiciously like devotion.

9

It was a miracle, frankly: it was a Saturday evening and Stevie was attending a wedding without her camera. She was a guest at a black-tie affair at Customs House, no expense spared, and Stevie felt like a schoolkid on the first day of holidays.

Before the reception, Stevie stepped outside the venue to call Paula, who was on her way to a date. She'd been chatting with a divorced dad from Dalby and, given their shared interest in local history, they'd agreed to meet up for an old-fashioned bush dance at Jondaryan Woolshed.

'I suppose it takes the stress out of deciding what to wear,' Stevie teased, 'when you're dressing up in period costume.'

Paula was nervous. 'What if he wants to kiss?'

'You decide if you want to kiss him, and do it,' Stevie said.

'I haven't kissed anyone since your father.'

This was reassuring, so why did it still feel like too much information? 'Mum, I believe it's one of those skills like riding a bike – you can't really forget how to kiss. Just let it happen. If you want it to. The same goes for . . . full bike riding.'

'Oh, I'm not ready for that,' Paula said.

'Well, you don't need to share all the gory details with me when you are,' Stevie said, and wished her luck.

As she hung up the phone, the sun was setting over the brown snake of the Brisbane River, the magical golden hour that made even that muddy waterway look beautiful. She'd treated herself to a floor-length silk gown from a boutique in the Valley. It was a deep hunter green, the open back laced with thin straps, and her curls were loosely pinned up with a pearl clip. She felt almost giddy passing through the ornate doors. Grabbing a champagne flute (*French? Nice*) and checking the seating chart, she felt like she might float away: dangerously unencumbered.

Jen and Andrew had been invited, but they'd pulled out to spend a weekend in Melbourne after Andrew attended a work conference. So Stevie was flying solo and feeling fine about it – particularly since the seating chart had confirmed her hope that another confusing run-in with Johnno West wasn't in the stars. She still hadn't told Jen about the kiss; she wasn't quite sure why. She pushed the thought of him out of her mind. There were plenty of other faces she recognised from college, mutual friends of the bride and groom.

Evie and James both came from old money. They'd paired off as freshers and hit all the required milestones – law, honours, clerking, house in Teneriffe, a photogenic pair of purebred puppies with their own Instagram account. Saturday night coke binges followed by Sunday morning green juices and yoga.

There had been one striking face at the ceremony that Stevie didn't recognise, and now she was quietly hoping he too would be on the singles table. This mysterious stranger was a half-head taller than her, and his tux emphasised a lean frame. Dark eyes with a twinkle, hair slicked impeccably in that hipster pompadour style. You could tell he knew exactly how good-looking he was.

Traipsing to the back corner of the ballroom, Stevie slowly traced her way around the table looking for her name card.

'Stevie?' And there he was, pulling out her chair. She took it gratefully, and he sat next to her, switching his card and placing 'Lou Dylan' on the opposite side.

'I'm so glad to see you,' he continued, like they'd known each other forever. 'Evie warned me there were some scary single girls in attendance. Can I appeal to your chivalrous side to protect me? Perhaps we could pose as a couple, and protect each other?'

Well, hello. Stevie thought, but she made a show of squinting at his name card. 'Well, Charles . . .'

'Charlie, please.'

'Charlie. I know for a fact there are some very strong hockey players who'll be rounding out our table tonight and I don't want to get on the wrong side of them. My shins still bear the scars of our run-ins at university.'

He whimpered.

'Clearly you're not from around these parts,' she fished, 'so I'll lend my local knowledge to your predicament and act as your bodyguard. But I'm going to need your total commitment. Follow my lead: when I drink, you drink. When I dance, you dance. And when I start making up stories about how we met, you roll with it.'

He raised his flute to hers and gave a devilish wink. 'Deal.'

As the rest of the guests filtered in, Stevie and Charlie decided not to come up with a backstory. They figured it was more entertaining to improvise, a seat-of-the-pants ad lib. Whenever she looked around the room, Stevie noticed pairs of female eyes angled their way. She bent closer to Charlie's ear with relish and quietly commented as their table filled out.

'That's James's rugby mate, not-so-secret gambling addiction . . .

Melanie, also studied law with these guys, loves her cats . . . Ah, the hockey girls. There's Carla, and that's Lou with the tattoos . . . Newly single uncle, definitely on the prowl, coming in hot – quick, stroke my arm possessively.'

Charlie went for extra credit and leaned over to silently press a kiss to Stevie's shoulder. It was the kiss heard round the world, or at least the ballroom, as bridesmaids and hockey players alike recalibrated their hopes for the evening. Stevie felt a shower of stars in her tummy that was only partly champagne-driven.

'I've been wanting to do that all afternoon,' he said in a low voice, and took her hand under the table.

Stevie cleared her throat. 'Well, the bridal party will make their entrance any moment. What do you think they'll play – gangster rap or cheesy pop?'

'Umm . . . cheesy pop?' Charlie guessed.

'It'll be gangster rap. The filthier the better. Rattle the nannas' pearls – these rich white kids love that stuff. Now, we know the maid of honour and the best man are fellow law students, overachievers, so my money's on them having choreographed a little dance for their entrance. Then we'll have the sexy bridesmaid and the awkward brother of the groom, then the burnouts who know all the words to the song. And then Evie and James will come out to bloody Ed Sheeran, because deep down they are basic as hell.'

At that moment the house lights dropped and Snoop Dogg clicked and boomed from the speakers. Charlie's eyebrows raised as each of Stevie's predictions came true, one by one. 'How did you do that?' he asked, awestruck.

Stevie pointed to the black-clad wedding photographer slinging two camera bodies, one from each shoulder, as he crawled backwards to capture Evie and James's entrance. 'That's me. I'm a wedding photographer. But I'm usually on my own, not flanked by a sidekick and a videographer. Some serious bank has gone into this show.'

'I thought I'd been to a lot of weddings, but I know when I'm beaten,' he said. But Stevie was just warming up.

'Dinner will be a beef and fish alternate drop. The cake will be fruitcake because Mum insisted, but they'll have a trendy dessert. Doughnuts are a bit played out now – maybe macarons? And they'll serve cocktails after the first dance, negronis or espresso martinis. First dance – John Legend or Johnny Cash, I'm not sure yet. But before that, speeches. Everything's going to run a little bit late because the bridal party keep sneaking off in twos and threes to the loo. The mother of the bride will have a meltdown, the father of the bride will make a pointed joke about how much this all cost, the best man will tell some dark stories, there will be tears after the bouquet toss comes to blows, and you, my friend, are going to spin me on the dancefloor until they put the ugly lights on, and sell this fake relationship like it's your job.'

'I wouldn't dare argue,' Charlie responded.

'Ugh, get a room, you two,' Lou sneered across the floral centrepiece. Charlie winked at her sweetly.

'Ladies and gentlemen,' began the MC. Charlie kept hold of Stevie's hand.

It all played out as Stevie had described, from the speeches to the cluster of weepy bridesmaids as the final strains of 'All the Single Ladies' faded out. By that point Stevie and Charlie had been laughing and whirling around the dancefloor for so long Stevie was out of breath.

'This is insane.' She grinned at Charlie, who pulled her hips closer to his.

He smiled back at her. 'Gonna be a great story to tell our kids, about how we met.'

Now that's insane, Stevie thought, but she couldn't deny it was a meet-cute worthy of Nora Ephron. 'Oh, sure, little Betsy and Ricky are going to love hearing this as their bedtime story. The chivalrous way you protected me from the pervy uncle, the groomsmen's coke binge, the two Macca's cheeseburgers you're going to watch me eat when they kick us out of here . . .'

'That's right, babe,' he said. 'It's all about visualising the future.'

'You keep picturing it, I'm going to visit the little girls' room,' Stevie said.

In the bathroom mirror she was flushed, but not as dishevelled as she'd worried she might be. She reapplied her lipstick and made eye contact in the mirror with Lou as she emerged from a cubicle.

'Props, Stevie,' Lou said, washing her hands. 'That boy is fine. Who the hell is he?'

'You know, I have no idea. Some distant cousin or friend of Evie's? I think he might have just moved up from Melbourne.'

'Well, seal the deal, because he is looking at you like all his Christmases have come at once. You owe it to every other single woman here tonight, goddamn you.' As Lou left the bathroom, she gave Stevie a not-lighthearted punch in the arm.

Stevie thought about how long it had been since she'd spent the night with a bloke. Long enough for her to joke with Jen about whether she was a born-again virgin, nine months ago. Too long. Why not have some fun? And how often did she get the opportunity with someone who wasn't already entangled in her world? Someone who didn't know her parents, hadn't known her as a gangly schoolgirl or tipsy uni student or Tom's girlfriend?

She strode back out to the dancefloor, taking in Charlie's grin as he watched her approach, like she was the only girl in the room. After the next song faded, he held out his hand for hers and pulled her gently towards a nondescript side door. Then they were in a stairwell, climbing the stairs hand in hand, and Stevie supposed he was heading for the roof. Her entire body was suddenly very aware that they were alone.

'I don't know anything about you, Charlie, besides the stuff I made up,' she said.

'What do you need to know?' he asked, looking intently into her eyes.

They'd reached a landing and he was pushing her backwards, gently but firmly, until the bare skin of her back was against the cold stone wall and he was against her, kissing her hard and deep. The pure physicality of his weight and the sheer arrogance of the move thrilled her. Time lost all meaning and her hands were moving beyond the control of her brain, roaming his back and his hair, and one fingertip beginning to investigate where his crisp shirt disappeared into his waistband at his hip.

Eventually he pulled back and leaned his forehead against hers. They were both breathing hard. 'Sorry,' he said in a blatantly unapologetic tone. 'I've been wanting to do that all night.'

Even if it was a lie, the sense that she had somehow rendered this man powerless in his desire was intoxicating. 'I know I promised you could watch me eat a cheeseburger,' she began.

'Actually, I think you said two.'

'Well . . . could you hold out for breakfast at my place instead?' she asked.

Silent seconds waiting for his response felt like an eternity. Her heart was suddenly pounding in her ears. Could she have misread the signals? Finally, he looked up at her again, and there was that smile like the sun breaking through clouds. Was there anything more bloody annoying that a good-looking bloke who knew it?

'I agreed to follow your lead tonight, Miss Stevie, so lead the way.'

'Just a second,' she said, and with a hand at his jaw leaned in to kiss him again. Eventually she pulled herself away, with considerable effort, and led him towards the exit. 'Now, don't get any ideas. We're just going to have a cup of tea, listen to some records. Actually, I've got a jigsaw puzzle I've been stuck on for ages.'

'Mmm, lucky for you, I'm very good at puzzles,' he said as they climbed into a cab, although she had her doubts about his commitment to the jigsaw cause as he was now tracing the silk shoestring straps crisscrossing her back. 'Does it all come off when I pull this?'

10

It was after 2 am, a week later, when Stevie let Fred into her mother's tiny backyard and crept in with her spare key. She found Paula dozing on the couch with the lamp still on and a historical romance open on her lap. She'd been working a wedding close enough to her hometown that she'd been able to drive straight from the reception back to her mum's place.

Paula yawned as she put the kettle on for tea.

'Come on, Mum – you still haven't told me how your date went.'

'It was okay,' Paula said, busying herself with the tea bags.

'Don't make me do a full interrogation,' Stevie said.

'It wasn't that we didn't have anything to talk about – there were no awkward silences,' Paula explained. 'But he didn't really ask me anything about me. It was all about him.'

'Ah, one of those,' Stevie said. 'But what about the kiss? Did he lean in?'

There was a long pause before Paula finally said, 'He did.'

'And did it all come back to you?'

'I'm not sure.'

'What do you mean, you're not sure?' Stevie exploded.

'Well, it was a bit like the conversation,' Paula said. 'I didn't really get to have a go. It didn't seem like he cared if I was there, he was sort of kissing *at* me.'

'Oh dear.'

Paula gulped her tea. 'I'm not sure he's ever had a proper grasp of how to ride a bike, if you know what I mean.'

'Mum. You didn't go naked bike-riding with this man, did you?'

'Oh no. I sort of had to extricate myself . . .' Paula described how, fortunately for her, her date had made his move as they said goodnight in the car park. 'I just backed away and got into the car. Thank God you only need to press a button to unlock a car these days. It was like fending off a very weathered, persistent octopus.'

It was the kind of post-disaster-date debrief that reminded Stevie of the table-banging, snort-laughing sessions she used to have with Jen before Andrew came on the scene. Paula wasn't really laughing, though.

'I'm sorry it wasn't what you hoped, Mum,' Stevie said. 'It's a jungle out there. Sounds like you handled yourself well, though.'

Paula let out a sigh. 'It's not easy, is it? This putting yourself out there?'

'No,' Stevie agreed. 'You've just got to laugh when you can and hold out hope that every dud gets you one step closer to the big prize. Hang in there, okay?'

'I'm going to turn in,' Paula said, pulling Stevie in for a good-night hug. 'You sure you're okay on the couch? I'm sorry I don't have anything more comfortable for you. God, what a role reversal, hey? I'm your mum and I've got no comfortable place for you to crash, and you're giving me dating advice.'

—

Now the midmorning sun was streaming in through the filigree gaps in the lace curtains. Stevie smelled fresh tea brewing and stretched her limbs in her cocoon of floral sheets. She could work from Paula's for a couple of days, catch up on sleep and get some editing and admin done. And since nothing was open in town on a Sunday, she could spend the whole day right here.

With a rush of blood, Stevie had a sudden, visceral flashback of the previous weekend: Charlie tugging at the straps of her silk dress, his lips at her throat. The kind of handsy make-out session in the back of cab that leaves you blushing the next day. Fumbling keys in the Queenslander's front door and saying a silent prayer of thanks that Jen was interstate with Andrew, before Fred bounded across the living room and spent a bit too long inspecting Charlie's crotch. Taking turns choosing songs to play before Charlie really applied himself to the puzzle of her dress straps, and two nightcaps of bourbon left forgotten on the bedside table long after their ice cubes had melted.

She'd woken the next morning with her sheets in a tangle, a distinct hangover, and a note on the pillow where Charlie's head had been. If not for the sweetly scrawled lines, she would have assumed the whole adventure had been a dream.

Sorry to leave you, babe – had early plans today I couldn't wriggle out of. Let me make it up to you with dinner soon. PLEASE call me.

Stevie had re-read those ten digits so many times she had just about committed Charlie's number to memory. It was a horrible pressure to be the one in control of starting the conversation. Should she be funny? Flirty? Play hard to get? Should she text him immediately, or did people still wait three days?

Somehow she'd been so indecisive that a week had passed and she was still composing the perfect opening message. *Idiot.* Now it was too late and she'd never be pushed up against a wall and kissed breathless by him again. *Mmm.* She let her mind wander and stretched slowly, minutely conscious of the cotton sheets against her skin . . .

'Morning, darling.' Paula's voice came bustling in from the kitchen. Stevie sat bolt upright and resolved to text Charlie today, even if 'sup' was the best she could muster. Fred was one step behind as Paula came in and sat next to Stevie on the couch. He was always Paula's shadow whenever he got the chance to visit, knowing she was a soft touch and would drop food if he so much as licked her hand.

'I've made some pikelets for my morning tea, but they can be your breakfast. You'll have to do a blind taste test of Trish's latest jams – she's taking her entry for the show very seriously this year.'

'Thanks, Mum,' Stevie said with a sigh.

Stevie had managed to get some good work done, a solid first Instagram post on yesterday's wedding and some invoicing she'd been putting off. After lunch Paula slipped away for her customary afternoon nap and Stevie pulled out her phone. The reception was patchy but that was no excuse.

Charlie? This is Stevie-Jean. You might remember me from such roles as your stunt girlfriend at a recent wedding. Not to get all 'dog ate my homework' but I found your number on a note in Fred's bed so I hope this is you and not someone trying to crack on to my dog.

She took a deep breath and hit send. She felt calm and relieved that she had finally dealt with the situation for all of two minutes. And then a whole new level of craziness descended. She paced around the yard until she heard a telltale ping.

I was really hoping to take Fred out for dinner but when I didn't hear anything I figured I'd been used.

'Ha – banter, Fred,' she said. He wagged his tail, clearly wishing she'd keep scratching behind his ears, but she was already turning her attention back to that phone. 'I can do this.'

'Look, Fred's a bit of a cad. I see this happen a bit and you should probably just let it go. Maybe go out with someone else, distract yourself?'

'I see. Well, I don't know a lot of people in Brisbane yet. Would you meet up with me to give me some advice?'

'I'm out of town at the moment but back Tuesday afternoon. Take me out Tuesday night?'

'It's a date. I'll hit you up with a plan Tuesday. X'

Was this what it was like to meet someone and have a truly blank slate? If so, she could get used to it. She tried to read, but the words kept getting jumbled.

'Come on, Fred.' She clipped on his lead and they headed out for a brisk walk along the river.

'I saw Johnno West the other day,' Paula said as Stevie returned from the kitchen with a bottle of wine. It hit the table with a louder clunk than she intended.

'Really? I've bumped into him a few times, too.'

'I think all that time overseas was good for him. He looks well,' Paula said. 'I bet Rod and Penny are just beside themselves to have him home, finally ready to take over Haven Downs.'

Stevie felt she didn't know enough to confirm or deny this. She'd got the impression that Johnno didn't feel strongly about his future on the property and it was creating tension with his sister. The vagaries of succession planning rarely kept everyone happy and often created fractures that never mended.

'He asked about you, Stevie. Is he keen on you?'

'No, Mum, we're just mates,' Stevie said, ignoring the inconvenient memory of a pie hitting the ground in a motel car park. 'Mates who seem to end up at a lot of the same weddings. It's like he's everyone's best man.'

'Well, he's going to make some girl very happy one of these days. You could do a lot worse.'

'I think we know too much about each other. He's seen me at all the worst parts of my life . . . and that includes in October when he'll be the best man while I'm shooting my ex-boyfriend's wedding to a teenage supermodel.'

'Are you really?'

'Yep.'

'I'm glad to see Tom settle down. For a young man he's always been very traditional, hasn't he?'

This was insightful from Paula, but she had got to know Tom quite well over the six years he and Stevie were together. They'd always liked each other; sometimes Stevie felt like the third wheel when they were all together. Tom was a bit of an old soul, or at least an old man in a young man's body.

'Okay, Stevie-Jean, what's going on? You've been distracted.'

'I might have a date on Tuesday . . .'

'A date! Are you on eHarmony too?'

'No, it was quite old-fashioned. We met at Evie's wedding last weekend. Very flash do – I was on the singles table and so was a tall, dark stranger. There was quite a bit of interest in him actually, but we pretended to be a couple to . . . Well, it doesn't make that much sense, now I think about it.'

'Sounds wonderful. What does he do? Where are his people from?'

'I actually don't know much about him at all. We were kind of playing characters the whole night.'

'Barb was telling me you can find anyone on Facebook. Should we have a snoop around? I'd love to see a picture of this chap who's taking you out,' Paula urged.

Stevie grabbed Paula's iPad and pulled up Evie's profile on Facebook. She already had some wedding pics posted and Stevie conceded that the photographers had done a solid job, if not the most creative. In the background of one of the wedding shots she caught a distinct glimpse of a dark green dress and a hand squarely on its buttocks, and she navigated away quickly before Paula could identify anyone. She pulled up Evie's friends list and searched for Charlie, then Charles. Stevie wasn't sure of his surname but regardless, there was no sign of him. Weird. Maybe he was one of these unplugged hipsters who took pride in having no social media presence.

'No luck. Sorry, Mum. I'll give you a full rundown after the date, promise.'

'All right. Make sure someone knows where you are, stay in a public place. Barb's been giving me all the tips,' Paula shared sagely.

'Come on, Stevie, we're going into town,' Paula called the next morning, jolting Stevie from her latest Charlie-themed reverie. Paula was bustling around the house, putting on lipstick in the hallway mirror and tidying her hair. She had one of her good cake tins in tow.

'You look nice,' Stevie said, admiring Paula's linen dress. 'Is it a special occasion?'

'Something like that,' Paula replied and, taking in Stevie's more dishevelled appearance, said, 'Could you pop a dress on? And you'd better bring your camera.'

When Stevie got into Paula's car, Springsteen was playing. 'So what's the plan?'

'Just heading in to see Nina and Trish for morning tea. It's their anniversary – I thought it might be nice for you to do a portrait for them,' Paula said.

'That's a lovely idea, Mum. Thanks for thinking of it.'

Nina was an old friend of Paula's from her schooldays. They'd both married around the same time, not too many years out of high school, and had children around the same time. But when Nina's youngest graduated high school, Nina had quietly moved out of the family home and the town. And after spending a couple of years around Bellingen, she moved back to town with Trish in tow.

The town gossips had been beside themselves. While Stevie had been at uni and distracted with her burgeoning adult life at the time, she knew Nina must have faced a rough few years as she re-established herself in town with her new partner. She and Trish had met in Sydney, and while they'd had a wonderful time at Mardi Gras and on some cruises where it felt safe and unremarkable to be surrounded by other gay women, this town was where they'd built a life and made their home.

'You don't mind taking some photos, do you, Stevie? I wanted to surprise them with something to mark the occasion, but I haven't told them you're here, so you don't have to.'

'No, I'd love to,' Stevie said. 'They can't be any more reluctant to pose than you were last night.'

'Ha ha,' Paula said mirthlessly. 'Nina's just been re-elected to the council, so she's more than ready for her close-up after all that campaigning.'

Nina and Trish's place was one of the larger blocks on the edge of town. Paula turned the car down their driveway past a stunning collection of local flowering gums, acacias, banksias and ironbarks.

Dotted throughout the undergrowth were hand-built wooden bee boxes. Since moving to the district, Trish had turned her bee-keeping hobby into a thriving small honey business, and she'd also recently branched into natural beeswax candles, which were in high demand online.

'Maybe we should do the portraits out here in the trees,' Stevie thought aloud as their progress down the driveway startled rosellas, kookaburras and wrens from the trees.

'Don't forget the garden,' Paula reminded her, parking.

They approached the house through a cloud of climbing jasmine and wisteria, while narcissus and daffodils carpeted the ground around the verandah. Beyond the cottage was a small orchard of citrus and other fruit trees. Stevie breathed deeply. The air was alive with bees and fragrance.

'Tell me that's your famous carrot cake,' came Nina's voice as the screen door squealed. 'Good thing you take that driveway so slowly, Trish already has the kettle on. And Stevie's here!'

Nina had been a teacher at the high school for as long as Stevie could remember. While she'd weathered a few complaints from parents after coming out, Stevie knew Nina was keenly aware how vital it was for the local young people to see a grown-up who wasn't straight. In Nina's own high school days there had been no tolerance for being a little different. She'd come home from school to parents who never acknowledged her bruises and red eyes, just as they never acknowledged her 'roommate' while she was at teachers' college, so Nina had followed expectations and settled down.

But in this new phase of her life Nina refused to be cowed by the town's bigots. It was a point of pride for her to stay, buy a house, serve on the council, and equally for Trish to stand beside her. And as often as they were disappointed by someone's narrow-mindedness, another person's acceptance would bolster them. Nina and Trish gave more back to the community than most, and finally it felt like they were being properly recognised for it.

Stevie happily submitted to a hug. 'Mum tells me it's your anniversary. Congratulations.'

'Ten years together,' Nina said proudly, as Trish came out and took her hand.

'We wanted to give you something special,' Paula said.

'Can I take some portraits for you?' Stevie asked.

It took some convincing, but eventually the couple agreed to sit for Stevie. She tried a few set ups: inside the cottage in front of a wall hung salon-style with paintings and photos of their families and friends; walking hand in hand amid the fruit trees and natives; and finally, seated on a bench in the garden, manicured beds and hedges before them and the wildness of the bees' domain in the background. Stevie kept them talking the whole time, bringing out memories of their civil service in Byron Bay a decade ago, the story of how they met and the things they'd learned over ten years.

Stevie was struck by the contrast with the young couples she usually shot at weddings: no jitters, only the ease and care of an intimacy built over years.

Instagram post by @StevieJeanLoveStories:

NINA & TRISH, June 2019: These anniversary portraits
are a departure from the fresh-faced young couples I usually
shoot. They were just as shy in front of my camera, but once
I distracted them with questions about their ten years together,
their true love shone through. There was none of the nerves or
bravado or stiffness of young lovers trying on their newlywed
roles like the suits and dresses they'd never worn before. This is
love that has softened to fit, tested and stretched by adversity
and change. It's not without a few loose threads and tears, and
it mightn't be the latest fashion, but it will last a lifetime.

'You dirty dog.'

'Excuse me, Jennifer?' Stevie said, barely inside the front door. Fred whimpered in protest.

'You've had a MAN in here.'

Stevie tried to do a mental CSI, scrambling to remember what evidence she'd left of her tryst before heading off last week. Two whiskey glasses? Sheets still drying on the clothesline? An errant item of clothing torn off in the heat of the moment and never recovered?

'Ha!' Jen pointed at her like an old TV detective. 'I thought I was right, but your guilty face confirms it. Get in here and tell me everything.'

Stevie kicked her bag through the doorway and followed Jen in, Fred skittering across the polished floorboards behind her.

'Imagine my delight when I returned to our abode, Stevie-Jean, to find the signs of a wanton sexfest. You might have thought you'd hidden the evidence when you took off to your mum's, but you can't fool me. Exhibit A . . .' Jen turned to the living room coffee table, holding a plastic cricket bat akimbo as a pointer while Stevie tried to keep a straight face. 'The jigsaw shows signs of attempted progress, but very sloppily, almost like it was just a ruse to lure a gentleman to your lair under the guise of intellectual stimulation. Little did he know just what kind of stimulation you really had in mind.'

'Jen. Rein it in,' Stevie wheezed through uncontrollable giggles.

'Exhibit B,' Jen called with a flourish, venturing across the living room. 'Signs of a struggle . . . with a bra clasp.' She pointed first to an overturned vase, then hooked the tip of the bat under a lacy bra and hoisted it triumphantly.

'I'm afraid that's where your case falls apart, Detective,' said Stevie. 'Because I wasn't wearing a bra.'

'Damn, that's one of mine. I was wondering where that went. Moving on.' Jen strutted past Stevie's bedroom. 'Too obvious. Ah, here we are, the bathroom.' She pointed towards the sink. 'I can always tell when someone else uses my toothbrush, Stevie. I'd like a replacement asap. Oh, and there's a condom wrapper in the bin. I rest my case.'

Stevie gave her a slow clap, and Jen curtseyed.

'Very entertaining, Jen. Can you at least find me some food before I tell you the story?'

'Fine,' Jen retorted, 'but only because I'm hungry too.'

In the kitchen, Stevie filled Fred's water bowl and shook out some dry food before sitting at the kitchen island. Jen sliced cheese and carrots and celery, and poured two glasses of wine.

'My angel,' Stevie said with a grin, and they clinked glasses. 'Well, where to begin? As you know, I went to Evie and James's wedding solo, since you and Andrew had better places to be.'

'Sorry about that,' Jen said. 'Andrew really wanted me to go with him to Melbourne for his conference. He'd made a whole weekend of it. It was lovely – and it sounds like you did just fine without us.'

'It was just one of those nights . . . Not that I've had one in ages,' Stevie continued. 'You know when you make eye contact with someone and you just know it's on?'

Jen nodded. 'So who's the bloke?'

'His name's Charlie. Charlie Jones, I think? Hot. So hot. Like, every girl in the room was shooting me daggers hot. Tall, dark hair, olive skin, nicely cut suit . . . No one quite knows who exactly he is – I think he's a cousin of Evie's? Anyway, we were on the singles table together and vowed to protect each other, and spent the whole night pretending we were a couple. And then we were.'

'I love it. Show me pictures.'

'I tried to find him on social – Mum was asking a lot of questions – but he doesn't seem to be online.' Stevie shrugged.

'Bollocks,' Jen said. 'Give me a bottle of wine and his full name and I'll find him. Any plans to see him again?'

Stevie relayed the text exchanges and the fact he was taking her to see a band on Tuesday at eight.

'As in tonight?' Jen squealed. 'What are you doing? Go get dressed! What are you going to wear? Is he picking you up?'

'You don't think these jeans will cut it? I'm meeting him in the Valley. I'd better get a move on.'

Stevie walked into the Bowery twenty minutes late and Charlie was standing from his seat at the bar before she even saw him. He kissed her on the cheek, a hand low on her back guiding her to the stool next to his. Even after his fingers left her torso, she felt heat there, and he was just as disconcertingly handsome as she remembered. Her nerves turned to flutters of anticipation; she hadn't imagined the chemistry.

'What are you drinking?' Stevie asked, feeling the usual nostalgia that kicked in at the bar that had been her favourite since uni. The boys slinging the drinks were still wearing the same bow ties and hipster good looks, but these days she was older than them.

'Old fashioned,' Charlie replied, tilting the glass towards her, offering a taste. It was cold and bracing, and she was grateful to have so many forms of Dutch courage to choose from.

'I need tequila, maybe mezcal,' she said, running a finger down the list and settling for a paloma.

'Thank God these guys were touring. You're really testing me with a Tuesday night date,' he said.

'I keep telling you, Tuesdays are the new Saturdays. Did you have trouble getting tickets?'

'No trouble at all. I'm not sure the rest of Brisbane knows about Tuesdays yet.'

'You're not from around here, are you?' Stevie asked. 'Since we spent our first night together pretending to be entirely different people, we've got a bit of ground to cover.'

Charlie admitted he'd moved up from Melbourne a few months ago, and she could tell he wasn't crazy about the cultural change of gears. Over a bowl of olives and a couple more cocktails they traded the basics: uni, career, travel, family. Charlie asked lots of questions and seemed genuinely engaged. He paid the bill and held the door for her as they left the bar. Stevie felt her head buzzing as they waited to cross Ann Street, and that was before Charlie slipped his hand in hers.

They queued on the stairs of the Zoo to exchange their tickets for wrist stamps, Charlie one step behind her. He was still tall enough to rest his chin on her shoulder. 'Your hair smells nice,' he murmured, and Stevie thought her knees might buckle. Luckily it was their turn with the door bitch, who fluttered her rockabilly-lined eyes at Charlie and took her sweet time stamping his wrist. They bought beers and found a spot near the stage as the support act did their soundcheck.

'I thought about doing this kind of photography,' Stevie said as they watched a young woman scooting in the press run in front of the stage, shooting the lead singer from each side. A true frontman, he was acutely aware of the lens and subtly turned to give her his best angles as she moved around.

'Really?' Charlie answered. 'It's a far cry from weddings, isn't it?'

'I was so hungry to learn when I was getting started. I'd just got out of a long relationship and packed in a desk job I'd had for-ever. Getting behind the camera gave me a new way to see the world when I had lots of new time and freedom. Still, it took a few months to realise I might actually be able to make a job of it. I shot a few gigs here, actually,' she said.

Charlie raised his eyebrows. 'I looked at some of your wedding shoots online and it seems a lot more'—he cast about for the right word—'more rural than this kind of scene. I wouldn't have picked you for a Penny Lane type.'

'I think I've been waiting most of my life for someone to describe me as a "Penny Lane type". Didn't everyone watch *Almost Famous* and decide to become a music journalist?'

'Or a groupie,' Charlie offered. But Stevie was already chasing her thoughts down another path.

'I reckon it might go back to my mum and dad,' she said.

'Very Freudian.'

'No, I mean being comfortable in two worlds. Mum is bush through and through – she'd never leave the land, or my hometown at least. When she and Dad got together they were quite the odd couple. He'd only been in town teaching for a year, a real Johnny-come-lately round those parts, out from Brisbane. I think it was always a sore spot for them, coming from such different back-grounds, but they complemented each other. For a while, at least.'

'So you got the best of both worlds?' Charlie asked.

'Something like that,' Stevie answered. 'Going to boarding school really threw me in the deep end, but I think I needed that prod to develop some social skills. By the time I was at uni and had learned how to talk to boys again, I didn't want to be anywhere but the city, although I did always love to visit my friends at ag college.'

'And your ex lured you back to the small-town life?'

'Tom was always going to take over the family property, so that was the package deal: get married, get the place, have some kids, happily ever after. Neither of us could pull the trigger though. It really all worked out for the best. I'm going to shoot his wedding later this year,' Stevie finished brightly.

'How very evolved of you.' Charlie laughed. 'Well, I don't think we would have crossed paths out west, so I'm personally very glad you straddle city life as well as the bush.' He pulled her close, one hand at her hip and the other in her hair, and kissed her.

When Stevie pulled away, the door bitch was glaring. She turned to face the stage and Charlie held her to him. Turning back, she asked, 'So you haven't spent much time in the bush?'

'Not yet. Will you take me out and show me the ropes?'

'I think that can be arranged.' Stevie smiled, and they swayed together as the band struck up their first song.

A bleating unfamiliar phone alarm jolted Stevie from sleep at 6 am. She could feel her eyes encrusted with last night's eyeliner and the faint beginnings of a hangover. Charlie was pulling on his socks and jeans and, sensing her stir, he turned his muscular torso towards her. Propping himself above her on lean arms, he kissed her. 'Good morning, babe.'

'It's so early,' she moaned. 'Want me to make you a cuppa?'

'Nah, gotta run. Some of us have to work today,' he said, grinning and tucking her back in. 'Let's do this again soon, okay?'

'Okay.' She smiled, already drifting off as he eased himself out her bedroom door with his immaculate RMs in hand.

It could only have been minutes before Stevie was awakened again by Jen jumping on her bed. 'I met the stud!' she crowed.

'What time is it?' Stevie whined.

'Six-thirty,' Jen chirped. 'I was just doing my morning yoga when who should creep through the living room on a walk of shame but one Charlie Jones, who introduced himself very graciously given the circumstances. Want me to bring you a tea?'

'I'd rather keep sleeping,' Stevie muttered. 'But since that doesn't seem to be an option, yes, I'll take a tea.'

Jen ran out and returned with a steaming ceramic mug. Stevie cupped it with both hands, inhaling.

'We didn't wake you up when we got home last night, did we?'

'Oh no, I slept like a baby and was blissfully unaware of your antics until that strapping specimen let himself out this morning,' Jen said. 'He's easy on the eyes, isn't he?'

Stevie grinned.

'But what do we know about him?' Jen continued. 'Where's he from, who are his people?'

'You sound just like Mum,' Stevie said, wrinkling her nose.

'He's moved up from Melbourne in the last couple of months. Accountant? Something in finance. I don't really know, we were mostly talking about me.'

'I'll get Andrew to see if anyone in his network knows him. I've done a basic Facebook search and you're right, there's not a trace of him. No Twitter, no Instagram, no LinkedIn that I could find.'

'He said he'd looked at my photos online,' Stevie said.

'Hmm, probably running a finsta,' Jen pondered. 'I'll look into it. But judging by his level of grooming, our Charlie isn't short on vanity. It just doesn't add up that he's not on social media. Does he have any weird conspiracy theories, a criminal past? Mention anything about wanting to be off the grid?'

'Relax, Jen. It's too early for detective work.' Stevie saw Jen's expression turn downcast; she loved a mystery to solve. And then a cartoon light bulb may as well have pinged on above her head.

'That's it, Stevie! This could be beyond my capabilities, but I know who we can turn to. The Bush Telegraph!'

12

There were certain dates on Stevie and Jen's shared social calendar that they still honoured more than a decade after they'd formed these traditions as tipsy teenagers. Some they'd outgrown: it was far from flattering to attend B&S balls at their age, or the revelry at Mooloolaba around Australia Day, when certain motels on the Sunshine Coast became hubs for families attempting to even out their farmer's tans. But some things had become unquestioned habit. Specific country race meets; an early December Sunday session at Merthyr bowls club that always marked the real beginning of summer holidays; a January weekend at a beloved holiday house on Stradbroke Island; and the Blue Tongues rugby club's annual Ladies' Day.

Stevie had managed to uphold this last tradition even amid all her wedding travel over the past five years. This year she'd worked it in with a Sunday ceremony at a property ninety minutes out of town. She'd have to get an early start the next day, but that was unlikely to pose a challenge. Things tended to peak early on Ladies' Day.

She and Jen had spent Friday night with friends in Toowoomba and got up at an ungodly hour for the four-hour drive out. At Paula's they cracked a bottle of bubbly and freshened up. The local set of next-gen yummy mummies would be there in their uniform of floppy felt hats and oversized sunglasses, chunky rose-gold jewellery tinkling as they pushed their double-strollers. Stevie threw on her akubra and a scarf in the Blueys colours.

The widescreen sky was achingly blue, one of those crisp and cloudless days of winter sunshine. Perfect conditions for day drinking, gossiping and maybe even some footy. The first-grade game was a few minutes in when Paula dropped them off. Stevie had stumped up for a table in the 'VIP' section, where ladies were served complimentary bubbles and cheese all day. A rope was all that separated them from the home team's sideline, where Stevie was delighted to see one of the local lads already smoking a durry on the interchange bench.

The crowd roared as a Blueys flanker made a break for it, but he couldn't sustain his pace and was chased down by the visitors' fullback in a crunching tackle.

'Is that—' Jen started.

'Johnno?' Stevie finished. He really was settling back in, she thought. As the scrum reset she looked around the ladies' enclosure, just as Kate West walked into the VIP section and caught her eye.

'Stevie!' Kate exclaimed, and headed towards them.

'Pull up a stump, champion.'

Kate dragged over a plastic chair and plonked her beer on the table. She'd brought her own stubby holder, a move Stevie always respected.

'How's your brother holding up?' Stevie nodded towards the field. 'I'm impressed he's playing first grade; it's a struggle playing contact sport at our age.'

Kate giggled. 'He's locked in this silent power struggle with Cam, both of them trying to outdo each other with athletic pursuits. It can only end with one of them in hospital. Good thing Cam's out for the season with a back complaint.'

'Kate, you remember Jen, don't you?'

'Of course.' Kate smiled. 'Are you girls out for the weekend?'

'Stevie's shooting the Lord wedding tomorrow, and I've got Monday off work so we'll drive back then. We haven't missed a Ladies' Day in twelve years,' Jen said. 'Will you and Johnno stay in town tonight, or are you driving straight back to South Star?'

'TBD, mate.' Kate shrugged. 'We've got the swags with us just in case. The boys are due a win, I'm sorry to say for you Blue Tongues fans.'

Just then the grandstand erupted again. Even Lewis on the bench dropped his ciggie as the Blueys busted through for a scrabbling try under the posts.

'We'll see about that.' Stevie winked at Kate. 'How are things at Haven Downs? Must be an adjustment having Johnno back there?'

'The golden boy has returned, all right,' Kate muttered darkly. Stevie raised an eyebrow gently, and Kate sighed. 'Oh, it's not Johnno. He's actually been very patient. Keeps Cam and I involved in all the decisions, took the time to let us show him what we've been working on. But Penny and Rod just get tunnel vision when he's around.'

'That must be tough,' Stevie said.

'Drinks?' Jen got up to get a round and Stevie smiled up at her for giving them space.

'How long have we known each other, Stevie?' Kate asked. 'I know you and Johnno crossed paths in college, but I don't think I met you until his nineteenth.'

'That seems about right,' Stevie said. She didn't remember a lot about that party. She'd procured a bottle of Bundy Rum somehow, and got a crash course in the nectar's narcoleptic properties. She *did* remember being struck by the invitation when it arrived during uni holidays, Johnno having tracked down her address and printed it in his blocky scrawl on an envelope. 'I guess where I really first remember you was when we carpooled with the boys to Gunnedah for New Year's.'

'That dates us, doesn't it? It's been a good ten years since they stopped having the B&S there,' Kate said.

'I remember racing around with you like a couple of schoolgirls, teasing the boys. Didn't we choreograph a dance or something?'

Kate shook her head. 'That is a question better left unanswered, Stevie-Jean.' Neither would admit it, but both could have performed that dance to this day, given the right music and a critical mass of alcohol.

'I've bumped into Johnno a few times since he's been back,' Stevie said, 'and I've been trying to put my finger on what seems different about him. He's grown up in a lot of ways, but he still seems as dreamy and aimless as he was in college.'

Kate looked thoughtful. 'I know what you mean. I love having him back home, but I'm still not sure what it means for us. Mum and Dad intend for him to take over, and that's a lot of pressure for him. Sure, he grew up with Dad showing him everything, but he's been away from the land for years. He's trying so hard to get everything right. I can't quite tell what he's thinking about for the future – if he'd just come out and say he's taking it all on, Cam and I could cut our losses and try to find something of our own. Anyway, it's only been a couple of months. I guess he's still thinking it through.'

'That's generous of you to see it from his perspective, when it must be tough to have your own future so uncertain,' Stevie said. 'And his job offer back in London doesn't make it any easier.'

'What job offer?'

'With his old boss?' Stevie said, realising she'd put her foot in it. 'Maybe he already passed on it. Maybe I had the wrong end of the stick.'

Kate's face darkened. Stevie tried to change the subject. 'Well, the local girls must be delighted to have some fresh blood in the dating pool, at least.'

'He hasn't really been putting himself out there, but there are definitely a few interested parties,' Kate said. 'You know what it's like around here – you pash someone at a party and suddenly the whole district knows about it. So he's treading carefully, much to Mum's frustration. She keeps begging Johnno to take out Sarah Childs from next door. He's held firm so far, but Penny can be persistent.'

Stevie's exposure to Johnno's parents had been pretty limited to milestone birthday parties at their property and the occasional chat at a wedding, but she vividly remembered Penny's steely eyes and unassailable manners.

'You weren't fishing there, were you, love?' Kate asked.

Stevie laughed off the idea, but Kate was serious. 'I think we both know he's always had a soft spot for you, Stevie-Jean.' Stevie shook her head, mortified. *Surely Kate didn't know about the night of the dropped pie?* 'Well, he's single for now. But between Penny and his age, I wouldn't expect him to stay that way for long.'

Thankfully Jen was finally back with plastic flutes of cheap sparkling wine. Stevie clutched at one and downed it without pause.

'Kate, what have you done to her? She's like a beetroot,' Jen exclaimed, and Kate laughed. Cameron was waving to her from outside the enclosure.

'You're off the hook, Stevie. I'm going to head out with the plebs. Catch you after the game,' Kate said as she left their table. Jen gave Stevie a searching look; Stevie shook her head, cutting off any explanation. If she told Jen now about the kiss, it would only turn into a bigger thing about why she'd kept it secret. *Just forget about it.*

'I need another drink, or four,' she said. 'Back in a sec.'

'I'll hold the table,' Jen said, looking disappointed to have missed the gossip. Stevie felt slightly bad about leaving Jen out of the loop, but it wasn't worth the merciless teasing she'd be subjected to if Jen got wind of any kind of crush between her and Johnno. She trudged to the bar, grabbed a flute with each hand, and was just on her way back to Jen when a voice called her name.

And there, regally spilling out of a plastic chair like it was her throne, was Mabel. She had gone all out for the occasion, with a flimsy fascinator perched atop her freshly set hair; it made a delicate contrast with her heavy frame. A coterie of retirement-aged women sat around her, all looking expectantly at Stevie.

'Nice to see you, Mabel.'

'Girls, this is my young friend Stevie. She's a wedding photographer. This is Gladys, Peggy and Dolores.'

Stevie smiled at each of them, thinking it was only a matter of time before hipster mummies started naming their daughters after them.

'You must be out for the Lord do tomorrow?'

Stevie nodded. 'Will you be there?'

'Wouldn't miss it. I set them up, you know.'

'Remind me to get you to tell me the story when I have a camera in my hand rather than two glasses.'

'Will do. I also need to chat to you about your beau – I've been looking into him.' Mabel's nonchalant tone was undercut by razor-sharp eyes.

'Charlie?' said Stevie, thrown. 'How did you know about that?'

'I always have my ear to the ground, Stevie-Jean, you know that. When I heard you'd been seeing a young man I wanted to make sure he was worthy of you.'

'And how exactly did you do that?'

'I have to admit, this one really tested my skills. As your friend Jen noticed'—*Damnit*, Stevie thought, bloody Jen had tipped her off—'he's not on any of the social media sites. I had to go old-school.'

'The suspense is killing me, Mabel.' Stevie rolled her eyes.

'Well, I don't know if I have enough yet. But something's not quite adding up,' Mabel continued. 'Just be on your guard a bit, until we know more.'

'I think you know quite enough, when it's really none of your business,' Stevie snapped.

Mabel drew back into her chair. 'All right, love, no hard feelings.'

'I've got to go,' Stevie said, cutting off the conversation and walking away as the half-time siren sounded and the players rushed or limped into the sheds. She didn't notice Johnno's wave as he passed.

—

By the back end of the second half, the sun was disappearing and the score was locked at 18-all. Johnno steeled himself. His fitness had been improving, but he still found himself exhausted by the final minutes of the game. Subbing off was not an option; with planting a number of boys hadn't been able to make the trip and their one-man interchange bench had been wiped out by a hamstring strain shortly after half-time. Johnno knew he had to rally and take his boys with him if they were to have any chance of getting the final critical points on the board.

He jogged around the back line, trying to control his breath and bring his heart rate down. As he passed his teammates, Johnno gave them pats on the back and words of encouragement. The Blueys were tiring, he told them, desperate to believe it himself. 'We've got this, lads. I will personally buy beers all night for the bloke who goes over the tryline.'

They ground through the next few phases, just barely holding the opposition off their line. A spat between two players nearly blew up into an all-out brawl, but it gave them the breather they needed. As the Blue Tongues tried to reset, Johnno called for a wide pass and handed it off immediately. The winger was already sprinting, took the ball square on the chest and wrong-footed the defender easily. With only the Blueys' fullback looming, Johnno darted up and called for the inside pass just as the fullback had committed to tackling the winger.

Johnno was lined up squarely between the posts with just metres to go. His tiredness evaporated with the promise of glory within his reach, and the final steps felt like slow motion. The crowd was so deafening he barely heard the footsteps racing up behind him, or the full-time siren; he leaped out, arms outstretched to take the ball over the tryline, and he grounded it with his whole body sliding along the grass behind it. Johnno felt like Superman. For a split second he wondered whether Stevie had seen it, before the defender, an enormous front rower, crashed over the top of him and knocked him out.

The Blue Tongues players were all on their knees or backs on the field, heads hung in the universal posture of defeat. The Cockies had found the energy to sprint to the in-goal to get around Johnno, and it took a few moments for the crowd to realise that he was still face-down and motionless on the ground.

Stevie found herself running onto the field. As she reached the posts, Kate and Cam were there too. The team doctor had rolled Johnno carefully onto his back and was checking his neck and speaking to him quietly.

'Yeah, but did we *win?*' Johnno sat up groggily. He was surrounded by the battered and sweaty faces of his teammates, grinning their confirmation that he'd won them the game.

'God, you scared us.' Kate's voice cut through the noise of the crowd. Johnno smirked back at her, and then at Stevie, who was having none of it.

'You bloody drama queen,' she shouted, her voice shaky. 'You stupid idiot! I'm taking you to the hospital.'

'All the health care I need is in a sixpack in the sheds,' he joked.

'I'm not taking no for an answer,' she said.

'Stevie, mate,' Kate said, 'you can't drive.'

'I'm calling Paula. You'—she pointed an accusing red fingernail at Johnno—'don't move.'

Paula arrived in ten minutes, and they pushed Johnno into the front seat, clutching an icepack to the growing lump on his head.

'I'm fine, you're being silly. Can I get a beer for the road? I don't know if you noticed, but I just won the game.'

Stevie silently clipped in his seatbelt and slammed the door closed.

'Are you coming, Stevie?' Paula called.

'Mum, I don't think I can make that trip without murdering him,' Stevie muttered. 'Can you take Kate with you?' She could feel herself acting terribly and couldn't work out why her rage was directed at Johnno. It wasn't his fault the whole bloody region was gossiping about her love life.

'I've got this, Stevie,' Paula said. 'You and Jen go on to the pub and grab some dinner. We'll meet you back there in a bit. You need to start sobering up.'

As they watched Paula's car disappear up the highway towards the hospital, Jen put an arm around Stevie. 'You okay, mate?' she asked. 'What's got into you? You know Johnno will be fine, he's just a bit concussed.'

Stevie sighed. 'Yeah, I don't know what's wrong with me. I freaked out a bit when he didn't come to. It's not his fault he got smacked in the head, obviously.'

'You were just worried because you *looove* him,' Jen teased.

'Not this again!' Stevie cried. Jen waggled her eyebrows suggestively at Stevie until she cracked up. 'I had a weird chat with Mabel that rubbed me the wrong way. Did you get in touch with her about Charlie? That's messed up, Jen.'

'It was just a bit of fun – we talked about it,' Jen said. She looked surprised at Stevie's reaction. 'Maybe not as fun as I thought. Sorry. But did she find anything out?'

Stevie scowled. 'Just a bit of baseless suspicion with no evidence – some "keep an eye on him" nonsense.'

'Is that such bad advice?' Jen asked. 'We don't know very much about him. I texted Evie to ask why they'd invited him to the wedding, and all she said was that her mum had insisted on it, one of those random family friends.'

'God forbid something happens that isn't public knowledge for every busybody in the district,' Stevie ranted. 'I'm so bloody sick and tired of everyone knowing everything about me. I'm so bored of them all trying to set me up with their weird nephews, trying to set up me up with bloody Johnno, everyone acting like my 31-year-old vacant womb is a crime against nature.'

'Okay, babe,' said Jen, eyes wide.

'I'm just a bit tired of my business being everybody's business. Maybe I want a bit of mystery, maybe I *need* a bit of mystery. And if it comes in a package as hot as Charlie, I'm willing to risk it.'

'I can't argue with that,' Jen said.

A shout went up behind them, where the football players were still scattered across the field, drinking cans of beer, congratulating each other and catching up. The boys were lining up for the traditional post-match boatrace, a kind of demented relay where, one after another, they'd scull a beer and the fastest team won. Stevie and Jen had participated in past years, but wouldn't be throwing their hats in the ring this time.

'How about we head over to the pub and order some dinner?' Jen asked gently. 'Your mum and Johnno probably aren't too far away.'

—

Paula hovered close by with her arms crossed as the doctor shone a light in Johnno's eyes and asked him to count backwards from twenty. Kate and Cam had disappeared in search of vending machine Twisties, and Paula's maternal instincts had kicked in.

The doctor released him but told Paula to try to stop him from getting drunk that night; there was unlikely to be any lasting concussion damage but his judgement wasn't 100 per cent. Paula texted Stevie that they were on their way back, and texted Kate to meet them in the car park. Johnno was walking slowly, childlike and vulnerable, not sure if it was the win or the head knock making him feel giddy.

'Where's Stevie?' he asked Paula.

'We're going to meet her for dinner. I don't think she liked seeing you get hurt.'

Johnno smiled at this. 'Always liked your daughter, Paula. Tom was never the right one for her. Makes me so happy to see her loving her work,' he babbled, and Paula laughed.

'She's great at it, but I think sometimes it's a bit hard for her – spending all her time telling other people's love stories. She thought she would have found hers by now, I think.'

'Oh, we're still young, Paula.'

'I know that, Johnno. Well, she seems very taken with this Charlie chap. Do you know him?'

Johnno turned to her. 'This is the first I'm hearing about it. Have you met him, Paula?'

'God, no. They met at some wedding in the city. I don't think he's got any connections in Queensland; no one seems to know much about him except that he's very handsome, apparently. Oh, are you all right, Johnno?'

He was squeezing his eyes tight, trying to shake the fuzziness from his brain. Charlie. Some mysterious stranger. A handsome mysterious stranger. Bloody hell.

'What'd we miss?' Kate slid into the back seat with a rustle of chip packets. 'Let's get some dinner, I'm starving!'

New post in 'Neighbourhood News' from The Bush Telegraph:

IT'S A KNOCKOUT: Our favourite prodigal son's rugby team got a come-from-behind win on the siren in St George – was that our favourite not-so-single snapper rushing into the fray when he scored a concussion along with the winning try? I'm not convinced there's nothing between these two, though they both protest. The snapper insists she's saving all her love for the mysterious Charlie Jones. I can't find out a thing about him, so I'm calling on you, my faithful friends, to send me any and all intel about where this chap came from and why he's not locking down our girl. LOL, Mabel

13

Johnno straightened his collar and checked his hair in the rear-view mirror one last time. He'd parked outside the Royal, having arrived ten minutes early for his date with Sarah Childs, and he was struggling to find the momentum to get out of his car.

His mother had been pushing him to take Sarah out for months, and despite the kiss that haunted his dreams, his crush on Stevie felt more futile than ever. So when he and Sarah had been drawn against each other in the social tennis competition the previous week, Johnno had found himself asking if she'd like to go for a counter meal some time as they shook hands over the net.

Sarah had blushed to the roots of her honey-blonde hair and, after turning her face upwards to thank the umpire, had graciously accepted. They'd made plans in a series of stilted texts. Johnno had ironed his shirt, shaved, and shone his dress boots. And now he was staring down the barrel of at least an hour of awkward chat with only a few mid-strength beers to numb the pain, since he had to drive home.

He sighed, heaved himself out of the cab and walked into the pub. A roar went up at his entrance; you could always count on a handful of regulars propping up the bar each evening, but Johnno had forgotten it was poker night. Almost his entire footy team was already here and charged and, judging by the cheers, they knew he had a date. Great.

'Pot of Gold, thanks Woody,' Johnno said, laying out his cash on the bar mat.

Woody poured Johnno's beer into a frosty glass with the practised ease of a lifelong publican. 'Heard you're expecting company, Johnno. I've reserved you our best table, next to the window, away from the pokies.' Woody was so tickled with his own wit he wheezed from breathy laughter into a coughing fit.

'Cheers,' Johnno said glumly, unsure how everyone knew about his date. He'd barely taken a sip when an eerie silence blanketed the previously boisterous bar room. It was like a scene from a western, when the baddie walks through the swinging doors into the saloon and the piano player stops mid-song. Johnno turned towards the Royal's door to see what had stunned the blokes.

And there was Sarah Childs, tottering on heels she'd clearly never tried to walk in before and poured into a tiny black dress. Alongside her was her friend the local beautician's apprentice, Jacinta, who looked very proud of her afternoon's work.

Johnno had known Sarah since she was running around naked under the sprinkler in his mum's yard. He'd only seen her break her uniform of jeans, work shirt and a stained cap for tennis matches. Now she was manicured, bronzed, blow-dried and lip-glossed, blinking back false lashes and faltering on her heels like Bambi.

Right on cue, some larrikin wolf-whistled, and Woody cleared his throat meaningfully and nodded his head towards the entrance. Johnno scrambled off his bar stool and towards Sarah.

Jacinta rattled her car keys in her hand. 'You gonna be right to get this one home, Johnno? You're neighbours, after all.' She laughed and headed for the door, Sarah throwing her one last desperate look.

'Sarah, you look stunning,' Johnno said, taking her arm. 'I should have gone to a bit more effort, I'm sorry.'

'God, Johnno, it's a bit much, I know. Jacinta just got on a roll and I couldn't stop her. Thanks for holding me steady,' Sarah said as they minced towards Woody's best table. Johnno pulled out her chair and she sank into it gratefully.

The waitress appeared, a Finnish backpacker Johnno had met at the pub after the last home game, though he couldn't for the life of him recall her name. She sullenly handed them menus, each a single laminated page.

'Any specials tonight, er . . . ?'

'Helmi,' she finished pointedly. 'Nice to see you, Johnno. The fish of the day is barramundi, and there's also a special of crumbed brains.' She shuddered. 'Would you like some drinks to start?'

'I'm going to need a Cruiser,' Sarah said, while Johnno shook his head. They each stared at their menus as Helmi moved away to get Sarah's drink. Unfortunately, there was not going to be enough reading material there to get them through the meal.

'I'm going for a steak,' Johnno said. 'Get whatever you like, my treat.'

'The salad looks okay.' Sarah squirmed.

'Sarah, you don't have to eat rabbit food on my account.'

'It's not you I'm worried about, Johnno. I'm concerned I'll explode out of this dress,' she whimpered.

'Look, I've got a jacket in my ute if you need the coverage. But relax, you look lovely. You've really raised my standing in the rugby team – I'll be hearing about this for months,' he joked, sensing her feel more at ease.

'Thanks, Johnno. I s'pose this is new territory for me. Never been on a "date" before. If I'm lucky some townie would invite me out roo-shooting on a Friday night and try to stick his hand down my pants on the way home. But I bet you went on loads of fancy dates in London.'

'You'd be surprised.' He smiled. 'I'm not very experienced at this either. Dating in London was pretty cut-throat. I had friends who were out with Tinder matches every night. They had this whole routine down pat – a script, just about. I have a bad feeling they were logging it all in some spreadsheet and calibrating it with every date to try to hack the perfect seduction. That's just never appealed to me, you know? I'd rather just try to pash a pretty girl before clos-ing time at the pub.'

'That's about all the moves I've got too,' Sarah said with a laugh.

Helmi returned with Sarah's bright pink drink and took their orders, and Johnno was pleased to see that Sarah had relaxed enough to order a schnitzel.

'Let's just get this out of the way, okay?' Sarah said. 'I know this whole set-up was our mums' idea. It's mortifying. But I just want to be clear that there's no pressure coming from me. It can just be a friendly dinner.'

Johnno smiled at her gratefully. 'Thanks, Sarah. That's kind of you. I don't think I'm very good boyfriend material, but let's see how it goes. I've already seen you naked under my mum's sprinkler, so we can save a bit of time on icebreakers.'

'Oh my God, that is not appropriate at all,' Sarah shrieked. 'You were what, eleven? And I was three. Your mum was baby-sitting me, you dirty perve.'

'I think that's partly why this feels so weird. I always felt like a big brother to you. Do our mothers really think this is a good foundation for an alliance?'

'They might be thinking more of the properties than our hang-ups,' Sarah said. The girl next door was a cliché, Johnno had to admit, although in this part of the world she lived half an hour away.

'Enough of that,' Johnno said. 'Tell me what it was like going to high school in town – I was always curious.'

'Ah yes, little Lord Boarding School wondering what he missed at the local state school. Would you like to hear about the teen pregnancy rate? Or I could teach you how to make a bong from an apple?'

'I heard there were lots of fights,' he said. 'I mean we had plenty of jumper-pulling and the odd punch-up, but didn't a guy throw a desk out a second-storey classroom window once?'

Sarah laughed. 'Oh yeah, that was a great day. Aaron got suspended and then graffitied all the school buildings that night with his own initials, the bright spark. You must have been finished uni by then. When did you go to London?'

'I graduated at the end of 2012, and went to London a year later. I hope you're not imagining something out of a Hugh Grant movie, all billowing white shirts and manicured parks. I was living in a squat with eight other Aussie blokes in Shepherd's Bush and it was a smelly time in my life. Worked in bars, cafes, eventually got a research job and moved into a much more civilised share house with only three other blokes. Ate a lot of curries, drank a lot of pints – not sure I ate a vegetable for about three years.'

Sarah had drained her Cruiser and was looking around for Helmi, who had just three other customers and really could have stepped things up. Finally, she emerged from the kitchen with their enormous dinners, piled high with chips and swimming in gravy. It wasn't fine dining, but they both tucked in happily. Sarah drank steadily and Johnno found himself increasingly relieved of the responsibility for carrying the conversation.

'Should we do shots? A little Baileys for dessert?' she slurred, fluttering the ludicrous lashes towards Johnno. He couldn't help thinking how much they reminded him of a Muppet – was it Mr Snuffleupagus?

'Johnno!' Sarah slapped his arm to get his attention.

'Righto, Sarah,' he said, scraping his chair back. 'I'm afraid I have an early start with Dad tomorrow and we have a bit of a drive home ahead of us. Do you mind if we make a move?' He went to the bar to pay the bill with Woody.

'Get us some roadies,' Sarah stage-whispered across the room. The attention of the boys from the footy team, which had been absorbed in the poker game, was suddenly back on Johnno and Sarah.

'Yeah, get us some roadies,' Sandy Gibbons, who Johnno had never warmed to, called. 'Bitch drinks for all.'

Sarah looked crestfallen and Johnno guided her out of the Royal and into his ute. He started the engine and opened the glove box to pull out a family-sized block of Dairy Milk.

'Break that up so we can share it on the drive, hey?' he asked Sarah, who was looking at him with deep affection.

'Johnno West, you're the best,' she said. 'Ha! A poem. Do you have any Dixie Chicks?'

After about fifteen minutes of fighting over the stereo and polishing off half the block of chocolate, Sarah fell asleep. She snored gently, her forehead leaving a smeary trail of foundation on his passenger-side window, and Johnno cast his jacket over her bare legs with his left hand. An hour later, as the engine slowed at her parents' driveway, Sarah woke with a start.

'Is it possible I'm already hungover?' she moaned. Johnno turned down the volume on 'Dreams' by Fleetwood Mac, a song that always made him think of Stevie; it felt wrong in this context. 'Ooh, I love this song,' Sarah said. 'Maybe I'm still drunk.'

'Thanks for going out with me, Sarah,' Johnno said, unbuckling his seatbelt and jumping down from the cab to walk around and open her door. 'I had a great time.'

Sarah was fumbling with her seatbelt, so Johnno reached over to help her unclip it. Before he could lean back, she tilted her face up to his, grabbed the back of his head and went in for a pash. Johnno was so taken by surprise, by the sudden mouthful of her, that he kissed her back for a moment before gathering his wits. He pulled away slowly. He could already see she felt self-conscious, and tried to smooth the situation with a joke.

'You *are* still drunk, you wild thing. You'd better get home before your parents think I'm taking advantage of you. Give them my best, hey?' And he helped her down from the cab, gave her a hug and nudged her towards the house.

He watched her totter to the front door, made sure she got in and waved to her mother when she answered the door. The roos hadn't been too bad, so he should be able to make it home within half an hour. When he started up the engine, Stevie Nicks was singing about loneliness like a heartbeat, a feeling he knew well. It hadn't been so bad with Sarah. She was sweet and funny, and it made sense – they'd both be building their futures here. But Johnno still wasn't sure it was the future he wanted.

Right on cue, loneliness pulsing in his veins, he wondered where Stevie was and what she was doing. Then he remembered she was probably with Charlie and she certainly wouldn't be wondering about him. Johnno punched out a finger to skip to the next song, and put his foot down.

After his day's work, Johnno raced by the homestead to grab his boots and a change of clothes for rugby training before heading into town. It had been a long day. A pump had given out in a distant paddock, which he, Rod and Cam had seemingly fixed with some tie wire and prayers. Johnno spent much of the drive on the phone with his dad about what they'd need to do the next day.

So when Johnno swung the Landcruiser into the red gravel driveway of the town oval, he hadn't given any thought to the last time he'd seen his teammates. Racing in to the change room, he pulled on his jersey and hastily strapped his ankles before lacing on his beaten-up boots. The boys were already on the field when he arrived, with the exception of a few stragglers still making their way in from the farms. As Johnno jogged out, their coach, Slim (the town carpenter, whose beachball beer belly belied his salad days as a handy halfback), limply blew his whistle to gather the team in.

As they noticed Johnno's entrance, one smart alec's slow clap soon gave way to a full wolf-whistling, knee-slapping standing ovation.

'Johnno! Pants man. Tell us about your date, mate. Did you get lucky?'

'Jeez, Stanton.' Johnno shook his head. 'Isn't Sarah your cousin? That's no way to speak about a lady.'

Stanton looked contrite and the boys gradually quietened down as Slim fought for their attention.

'Right, lads. Dynamic warm-up. Johnno, since you're the team hero apparently, you can lead it.'

Johnno sighed and corralled the team into two long parallel lines. He led them through lunges, sumo squats, skips, grapevines and a series of half-hearted sprints.

Slim lit a cigarette in disgust. 'You blokes are hopeless. You got bloody lucky with that win against the Blue Tongues, and they'll be ready to thump you when we host them in August. Don't think I didn't notice how busted you all were with a full twenty minutes left on the clock. I'd better see more focus from you tonight or I'll have you all doing time trials until you spew.'

It was enough to scare the lads into submission through a series of passing and kicking drills. For the final session they broke into smaller groups to focus on rucking, tackles and goal kicks.

As he'd warmed up, Johnno was glad to feel the soreness his muscles had carried since St George ease. Physical as his work was, it felt so much better to run around, to push his body into some speed. And once his teammates settled into a rhythm, it was satisfying to feel their quick passes connect and kicks find their targets. They were all breathing hard by the time Johnno wordlessly led them through a sequence of cool-down stretches. In the chill night air, steam rose from their tousled heads, ghostly under the floodlights as sweat cooled on their skin.

Someone passed around cans of Gold from a carton and they drank contentedly in silence. Their thoughts all turned to dinner then, and a plan formed to head to the pub for parmy night.

'Oooh, I could murder some chips and gravy,' Stanton moaned. 'Who needs a ride? Let's get a move on.'

'Yep, shotgun,' burly Bill Thompson called. 'I reckon I'm in with Helmi, been putting in the groundwork for months and she knows my name now.'

'Good on ya, Bill.' Curly Stewart laughed. 'She's just trying to get you to settle your tab, you goose.'

They piled into Stanton's Nissan shitbox and took off for the pub with an explosive backfire.

'Coming, Johnno?' Greeny, the taciturn frontrower and captain, asked.

'We'll see, mate. Gotta hit the showers or I'll be sore before I even make it home,' Johnno said with a chuckle, jogging back to the change room with a wave. His stomach was rumbling but dinner at the pub would mean getting home closer to 11 pm. Not to mention all the questions he'd face about Sarah.

He had questions of his own; his polite text thanking her for the evening had gone unanswered. He was sure she would have woken with a sore head the next day, but another two days had gone by with no response. He hoped she wasn't beating herself up about how things had ended. Johnno made a mental note to text her something funny the next day, to try to diffuse any tension before tennis.

The change rooms were empty but for forgotten socks, clumps of strapping tape full of ruthlessly ripped-out leg hair and a flat football. Johnno stripped off and was soaping himself blithely in the shower when Slim staggered in under a giant net bag of balls, fag in mouth.

'Good effort out there tonight, Johnno,' Slim said out one side of his mouth while maintaining staunch eye contact with any part of the room that wasn't Johnno's body. Johnno swivelled sideways, mortified, thankful he had such a lather up. 'Thanks for trying to get the boys to focus.'

'It's like herding cats, but you know that,' Johnno replied. 'I do think we have more wins in the team, but you're right, they won't come without a big improvement in fitness.'

Slim sucked deeply on his Winnie Blue and exhaled thoughtfully. 'Short of showing up with a stockwhip, I don't know how to force them into it. They should be running on their own time, but the only thing that could get half of those blokes off their arses is the kind of sheila we just don't have around here. If only we could get Claudia Schiffer to trot around the oval a few times, I reckon we'd have 'em all doing four-minute kays in no time.'

Johnno smiled as Slim stared off at a particularly hairy strip of discarded tape, clearly painting in the details of his Schiffer strategy. Johnno wondered if Stevie was planning any visits. He reckoned having her lead the way in her old 501s might be pretty good motivation for some fitness work. He had every inch of those faded jeans committed to memory.

Now it was Slim's turn to catch Johnno lost in a reverie. He stubbed out his cigarette on a bench. 'What about young Sarah Childs? If we could get her running in the dress she wore for you the other night we might be in business.'

Johnno turned off the taps and reached for his threadbare towel. 'Not you too, Slim! Can't a bloke get a break? Mum's been at me to take her out for months. I just took her for a pub feed, nothing to it.'

Slim laughed gutsily, like a donkey with emphysema. 'Easy, mate, just taking the piss. You could do a lot worse.'

'She's a lovely girl,' Johnno agreed. 'I'm just not sure she's the girl for me. I'm pretty confident I'm not the bloke for her.'

'I don't know about that,' Slim said. 'She might be shy, but she's smarter than most give her credit for.'

Johnno raised an eyebrow to probe for more details as he stepped into fresh footy shorts and a holey Powderfinger T-shirt.

'Well, she went all through school with my Jessie,' Slim explained. 'I'd help out at the school every now and then – working bees and serving grog at the fete, obviously, but I'd also go along to chaperone on the odd movie sleepover night, camping trip. Now, Johnno, a mob of teenage or, God forbid, pre-teen girls is a terrifying thing.'

They both chuckled. 'One movie night they did in the Year Seven classroom. It was me and one of the other dads in charge, and while we were distracted the little turds got into the teachers' whiskey stash in the staffroom. Had 'em puking all over the place, crying when we busted 'em, turning on each other. But Sarah always had her head screwed on, never got involved in that kind of thing. She never ratted anyone out, either.'

'Fair enough, Slim. If you're telling me to let her down gently, I've got the message,' Johnno said, zipping the last of his stuff into his bag. He started gathering up the rubbish and detritus around the change room.

Slim moved to the door, lit another cigarette and waited with his finger hovering over the light switch, keys in hand. 'Strike me roan, Johnno, I'm telling you not to let her down at all. Take her out again, do something where you're not both just sitting at the pub together. Give her a chance. She might surprise you. You might surprise yourself.'

Johnno nodded, chastened, as Slim locked up the room. They parted quietly in the car park, Johnno promising to think about it, and he did. He thought about it as he drove past the pub, oblivious to the raucous conversation of his teammates inside. He thought about it all the way home, via a stop off at the BP for a scalding broccoli bomb from the hotbox. He thought about it as he trudged into the homestead at 10 pm, Penny and Rod already in bed, a foil-wrapped plate in the oven for him, Rabbit snoring on her towel nest in the laundry. As he wolfed down

Penny's chicken curry, he composed and recomposed a text to Sarah Childs.

'Fuck my brown dog!' The pliers bounced into the dust as Johnno winced away from the barbed wire and shook his hand to ease the pain. The song blaring from the open door of his ute suddenly felt too loud, and his head throbbed inside his hatband. The winter sun beat down, relentless, and as he wrenched off the radio, the noisy silence of the paddock swelled around him: cicadas, crickets, the groggy croaks of crows.

Eleven am, and he'd left the homestead at 5.30 to get these fences done before the sun got too high. He should have been done by now, and knowing that his father would express this in no uncertain terms kept him from the sensible retreat to Penny's tea and scones.

Johnno took a long slug from his water bottle and replaced his hat as he resolved to finish this paddock and the next before heading back for lunch. Throughout his years in London, the akubra had been waiting for him on his designated hat peg in the mud room. Having worn it in his late teens, Johnno wondered if somehow the felt was messing with his brainwaves, returning him to an adolescent mental state. Maybe it was just being back at home. But he felt as uncertain about his future, his purpose, as he'd done when school finished.

There had to be more to life than this. The daily drudgery of fencing, watering, feeding, moving stock from point A to point B and back to A again. Things breaking down from heat and overuse, figuring out how to fix them with wire and duct tape until you had to bring in a paid professional (always the last resort). He'd only been in this grind a couple of months and the days felt endless, but Johnno could feel them slipping away into years and turning him into an old man. And for what?

He'd watched the grim set of his father's mouth turn to something stony and permanent after decades of this. Years of Rod tracking the Bureau of Meteorology's updates and forecasts like others gripped their racing form guides, waiting for the big win that was going to clear the slate of all their failed bets. Years of weighing insurance costs against the rains that had to be coming. Years of debt compounding, of long sunburned days and weary nights when he could hang his hat and take off the dusty work clothes, but there was so much that wouldn't wash off in the shower.

Rod wore the weight of all the unpaid bills and long-range forecasts and what-ifs on his shoulders, a heavy blanket that would wake him in the middle of the night, suffocating. He was far from the only man in this position: around the country there were hundreds like him. Some of them had wives they could share their blanket with in bed at night; others carried theirs alone, by choice or otherwise, until they could see no way out but to walk away. Or worse. Like poor Tom's dad.

Johnno swung the gate closed and drove off to the next empty paddock. Against everything he'd been taught all his life, he'd left the gate open while working in it. There was no urgency any more, since there were so few beasts. As the drought limped on, Johnno's parents had gradually destocked until they were down to hand-feeding their breeding stock. The daily work shrank along with the headcount but the bills, the weight, never seemed to lift. Some properties let go of their managers to cut costs, but then where would those good men and their families go? They'd leave the district and never be back. So the Wests had kept theirs on, until he couldn't handle the tension and announced he was moving his family to the coast.

These days Johnno had noticed his dad's anger finding a growing outlet in outrage about the greenie hippies in the city. Bloody vegans, weak and feeble-minded, and their silly protests. Didn't they know where their food came from? Didn't they understand the decades of inherited knowledge and care he and his family had poured into this land? How he had all but bankrupted his family to ensure no animal suffered starvation, how his heart broke every time he found a broken beast moaning with pain or disease? All this bulldust from pampered city boys with man buns, ruining the good name of the honest grazier, all in the name of 'climate change'. He knew more than anyone about the climate of this land, his home, his livelihood.

Johnno knew better than to try to argue or reason with Rod those evenings when he was under the influence of his third beer, exhaustion and dubious patriotic Facebook groups. The trouble was, Johnno could see both sides. Cam would never let him hear the end of it.

'You've been too long in the city, mate – it's made you soft. Both can't be right. No good wearing a barbed wire fence like a G-string. Pick a side, and you know how welcome you'll be here if you choose the greenies.'

It just made no sense to Johnno. There shouldn't be two sides at all. If you cared about the environment, agriculture was one of the industries that could make the biggest difference to sustainability. And if you wanted to make a living from the land long-term, you had to work with the changing environment and take advantage of all the latest science and technology to protect your investment.

It was a central value of his family that they were caretakers of this land. So why did it so often feel like they were battling against it to extract an income? And that was without digging into the Aboriginal heritage of the region, where generations of barely veiled slavery and massacres and missions had divorced the most experienced caretakers from the land that was so sacred to them. Surely there was some way to bring all these threads together, to learn from history, to listen to the land itself, and to look to the future and technology to find a way forward that wasn't such a constant struggle?

He made a mental note to head into the library in town and see if the books he'd requested on regenerative agriculture and Aboriginal land management had come in. Maybe he could chat to the local elders about what they knew about long droughts in the past. If his contemporaries could embrace drones for monitoring their vast properties, GPS-driven and remote-controlled ploughing and planting, surely he could propose some new ideas to Rod and Penny.

The thing was, farming didn't look like it used to. His generation were largely university educated in agronomy and agribusiness. Technology was changing all the time, from equipment to seed engineering and breeding genetics to mapping weather trends. The days of the long-suffering silent bloke running the farm and his little wife focused on feeding him and raising their kids were long gone. Women were running farms, running their own side businesses or juggling professional careers along with their properties. At this point in the drought, many of them were the ones keeping income flowing into their households. And amid all the despair, people were still marrying and having babies and moving to the district. Their experiments with what had once been ridiculed as hobby crops were, with the power of ecommerce and smart social media, taking off into viable businesses.

Just through the grapevine at tennis, Johnno had heard about a family selling top-notch extra virgin olive oil, women farming native flowers, people blending artisanal teas and reviving bush tucker native foods, two sisters cultivating buffalo to experiment with milk and cheese. He knew there were men crafting wooden toys and plaiting leather belts in their idle hours who could find delighted customers across the country if they could just get a crash course in using Instagram.

Johnno clipped the last bit of fence wire and pulled off his gloves. His head was reeling, and when he took off his hat and rubbed his hands through his hair they came away sweaty. God, it was quiet out here. He'd forgotten how rusty his mind got when he didn't have someone to talk to. Soon Rabbit would be obedient enough to come along, so at least he could talk to her on these endless days. He drained the water bottle and gunned the ute towards home, feeling like he'd made some small progress, if only in his mind.

14

'How on earth did you find this place?' Stevie asked. She should have suspected it when Charlie told her to bring a pair of socks for their next date, but she hadn't put the pieces together then, or when he drove her deep into the northern suburbs. Now she was lacing up a daggy pair of hired tenpin bowling shoes and trying not to inhale their aroma.

'I'll never tell,' Charlie teased, making a show of warming up his arms and bouncing around.

'I haven't bowled in years,' Stevie said happily.

'Well, if you can beat me, I'll take you for a fancier dinner than the fast food here.'

'Challenge accepted.'

The only other people at the lanes were young families, so Stevie and Charlie had a little corner to themselves. The decor was vinyl in various shades of orange and brown, the lighting was relentlessly fluorescent, the music was terrible, the beer was served in plastic cups, and they were having a blast.

'Read it and weep, Stevie,' Charlie crowed, pointing to the scoreboard after bowling yet another strike.

'Weird, it's like you want to have dinner here,' Stevie said. 'I know how you feel about pineapple on pizza and I don't think it's within that kid's pay grade to pick it off for you. Or nachos? I think I saw they have that liquid cheese they can pump out of a bottle straight onto your food—'

'Stop! I'm going to be sick just thinking about it,' he begged, ever the food snob. 'Surely we can find some vaguely authentic dumplings or noodles around here.'

'Mmm, dumplings,' Stevie said, realising the bowling alley beers she'd been pounding had gone to her head.

'Finish your last frame and we'll get out of here,' Charlie said with a cheeky pat on her bum.

Half an hour later they were grinning at each other across a plastic table loaded with steamed pork dumplings, Chinese broccoli, crispy shallot pancakes and BYO beers.

'Where's the last place you travelled to?' Stevie asked him.

'You mean aside from my trips scouting the strangest spots in Brisbane's suburbs for our dates?' he asked. Stevie nodded. If his face kept doing that thing with the dimples she was going to have to switch to sitting on his side of the table, it was too distracting. 'I was in Europe last summer. Well, European summer, you know.'

'Of course. One would never bother with Europe in winter.'

'Spoken like someone who's never had a hot chocolate at the Christmas markets in Geneva, or seen Paris lit up in the snow . . .'

'Only seen Paris in the spring, like a yokel,' Stevie admitted.

'Don't worry, I'll take you on a real winter adventure.'

'Sounds great. So where did you go on your summer trip – Greek islands?'

'They're gorgeous, but so overrun with tourists, you know? Even Croatia is a zoo these days, but there are some fantastic

beach towns and lake resorts in Slovenia that the idiots haven't discovered yet.'

'I've just booked a destination wedding on a Greek island in a
couple months. Have you been to Sifnos?'

Charlie hadn't heard of it, which was satisfying. But the entire
evening had once again been thrilling for Stevie – she couldn't
remember the last time she'd been able to talk to someone where
everything was new and unknown. Even trading the simple details
of growing up and daggy first jobs was fascinating. At no point had
he mentioned a school or workplace or town where she could ask if
they had common acquaintances. They had no social overlap what-
soever, and he had no preconceived ideas about who she was. *That
might be the best part*, Stevie thought: with Charlie, she could actually be the person she'd always wanted to be.

'Where would you love to go that you haven't been yet?' he
asked, changing the subject.

Stevie thought for a minute. 'I haven't been to South America at
all, and I love the sound of Argentina – and Cuba. Have you been
there?'

'Not Argentina, but I did do Machu Picchu a few years back
with some mates. Great people in South America, if you can stomach all the tourists.'

'I've also never been to Italy, which seems like an oversight given
my interest in pasta and pizza.'

'I once rented a villa in the countryside in Tuscany, which was
divine. We had a local chef give us a cooking class and spent our
days biking around the local villages. You wouldn't believe the produce in their markets – the best tomatoes you'll ever eat.'

'Sounds amazing.'

'You'll love it, I'll take you there, too.'

'Can't wait.' She giggled.

'You don't think I'm serious?'

'I mean, it's our second date. But I'm game. When do you want to go?'

'It'll take some time to plan, and I figure you're pretty booked up for the rest of the year, right? Wouldn't want to go before May – make sure it's nice and warm over there.'

'How do you know you'll still want to hang out with me in May next year?'

Charlie stood up and moved around to slide in next to Stevie. He held her face with both his hands and stared intently into her eyes. Stevie prayed she hadn't slopped oyster sauce on her chin.

'I can't imagine not wanting to hang out with you, Stevie. You feel this too, don't you?'

Thankfully he didn't wait for an answer before kissing her tenderly. Stevie wasn't sure what exactly they were feeling, but it was intoxicating.

'Have you had enough to eat?' he asked. 'Because I want to get you home, immediately.'

'Yes, sir,' Stevie said, and he kissed her again before sweeping off to pay the bill.

Later, in her bed, Charlie asked her if she planned on continuing her work on bush weddings.

'Well, I love it, and there's enough demand for me to fill the next couple of years,' Stevie said.

'Have you ever thought about staying closer to the city? I'm going to go crazy with you away every weekend,' Charlie murmured, stroking her hair.

'I've thought about it . . .' Stevie trailed off.

'It must be exhausting, all that travel.'

'It is. But you travel for work too.'

'Sure, but they're neat little plane trips to other capital cities and four-star hotels. How many hours are you driving on an average weekend? Are you getting paid extra for that time? And what about when you have kids?'

He was asking all the questions she asked herself when she woke up sweating in the early hours of the morning. She didn't have the answers then, and she didn't now.

'What do you think I should do?'

'It's not up to me. But you're so talented, you shouldn't limit yourself. You could do anything. You could be a photojournalist, or open a portrait studio, or start a gallery and have exhibitions, or publish a book.'

Stevie laughed.

'Why not?' he asked.

'Why not?' she repeated. Her heart felt like a caged animal that had finally found some space to stretch for the first time in years. Why not indeed?

'Think about it,' Charlie said. 'You'll be amazing at it, whatever you decide to do. And I'll be right beside you cheering you on.'

'Hey,' she said, feeling brave. 'Are you not a fan of social media?'

'Did you try to stalk me?' he joked.

'Not exactly,' she said, laughing. 'But if I did, would I find you?'

'No, I'm not on social media. It's kind of a long story, and I don't want to freak you out.' He let a dramatic silence hang before continuing. 'I had an ex-girlfriend who got a bit intense when things ended between us. She was pretty persistent in trying to make contact when I'd made it clear that we were over, and it just didn't feel right or safe to have an online presence where she might find me, or even just torture herself looking at what I was up to. So I just shut it all down. It's pretty liberating, believe it or not.'

'Wow. I'm sorry you had to deal with that,' Stevie said. 'Sounds a bit scary. Is everything okay with her now?'

'Yeah, nothing for you to worry about.' He yawned loudly, making it clear the subject was closed, and snuggled in to spoon her. 'G'night, babe.'

'He has a stalker?' Jen squealed. 'Oh, this is so juicy.'

'He didn't say she was a stalker, exactly,' Stevie said. 'Just that it was better – maybe he even used the word "safer" – for him not to have a presence online.'

She and Jen were having a back verandah debrief, Jen smoking while Stevie threw a tennis ball into the yard for Fred, who was growing tired of having to climb the stairs to return the ball each time. It had been nearly two weeks since Stevie's bowling date with Charlie but between her work and Jen spending time at Andrew's, this was their first chance to catch up about it.

'It's a bit convenient though, isn't it?' Jen ventured.

'Is it convenient to have a stalker? I wouldn't have thought so,' Stevie said.

'No, you're right, I'm being silly. So it's all going well then?'

It was indeed going well. Stevie mightn't have seen Jen in weeks but Charlie had been relentless in demanding her attention. She detailed for Jen the other dates they'd been on, the sweet texts he'd sent, and just a choice selection of the compliments he'd lavished on her.

'He's smooth, I'll give him that. And his taste is obviously good if he's picked you.'

'I know he sounds a bit too good to be true. Believe me, I pinch myself all the time. But maybe this is the big romance I've been waiting for. Maybe I deserve it.'

'Of course you deserve it – more than anyone. I'm happy for you, I'm just looking out for you. Has he introduced you to any friends or anything?'

Stevie sighed. 'Jen, enough with the suspicion. Ask him yourself, if you want, because he's coming over tonight.'

'I'll be polite, don't worry. God, you're so in love it's ridiculous.'

'Shut up!'

After the unsuccessful date and the fake photos, Stevie hadn't pushed the subject when Paula stopped giving regular updates on her escapades. A small part of her felt a little vindicated that she wasn't the only one to struggle to find a real connection through the apps, a feeling quickly chased by a rush of guilt. Didn't her mum deserve to find some happiness?

Instead, Paula was throwing herself into family history research, judging by the multiple follow-up trips to Arcadia she'd sheepishly admitted to.

'Mum, you're not being a pest, are you?' Stevie asked gently. She was sitting at her desk struggling to focus on edits, so she'd called Paula for a distraction.

'Of course I'm not.'

'Do you just keep turning up there unannounced?'

'If you must know, George has been inviting me. We've been . . . seeing each other.'

'The manager?' Stevie was reeling. She had a flashback of her mother giggling on their trip to the property, and the lingering handshake George had given her. 'How long has this been going on?'

'Stevie, don't take that tone, like I'm your wayward teenage daughter. We're two consenting adults getting to know each other—'

'Consenting adults! Mum – are you . . .?'

'Well, let's just say you were right about the bike riding,' Paula said breezily. 'It's not something you forget how to do.'

'Oh God. Are you being safe?'

Paula snorted. 'For the first time, I can say that being this age does have some perks. Thank goodness I've been taking those yoga classes, though, and got a bit of fitness back. The . . . bike riding has been quite vigorous.'

'Goodbye, Mother. I'm off to bleach my ears.'

'Love you,' Paula trilled.

'Love you too,' Stevie grumbled before hanging up and hurling the phone across her bed.

That night Charlie came over and kept Stevie and Jen's wineglasses topped up while they cringed and laughed at *Bush Bachelors*.

'I can't tell, do you girls actually enjoy this reality TV stuff or do you watch it as a post-feminist gag?' Charlie asked in one ad break.

'Truthfully, a bit of both,' Jen admitted. To Stevie's relief she had kept her word and refrained from interrogating Charlie, and he seemed to be winning her over. When he left the room to find them chocolate, Jen hissed, 'Fine, he's a dreamboat.'

Jen ignored Charlie massaging Stevie's shoulders and playing with her hair, but said a hasty goodnight as soon as the show's closing credits started to roll. Charlie kept up his attentions until things suddenly, urgently, needed to be taken to bed.

Later, as he slept beside her, Stevie wondered if it was crazy to be in so deep with someone she'd known so briefly. Sometimes she thought she might have conjured him up, everything was so perfect. Recounting the actual events of their relationship to Jen had sounded like a montage from a romantic comedy. He always seemed to know exactly what she needed.

There was the time he showed up while she was deep in an editing binge, just to drop off a hot coffee and lunch, and told her he'd be back to make her dinner that night.

Or the way he'd stopped to pluck a flower and tuck it behind her ear as they walked through New Farm Park, on a sunny morning of kissing in the grass in between reading the papers with takeaway coffees.

Or the night he'd somehow tuned the dusty guitar in the living room and serenaded Stevie with a song, his voice low and clear. It was incredibly romantic. So why, when Charlie closed his eyes to hit a high note, did Stevie find herself stifling a giggle? When he opened his eyes again and locked them on hers, she didn't know where to look.

When Charlie got like this, with the dizzyingly romantic acts, it was easiest just to kiss him and let things run their course. Later, while he slept beside her, she'd find herself staring at the ceiling, thinking of Johnno of all people, and how hard he'd laugh if he'd been a witness.

Johnno with a guitar would be an entirely different kind of performance, the kind that would leave her rolling on the floor laughing rather than rolling her eyes. He started every speech and thought with his tongue firmly in his cheek, forever self-deprecating, putting everyone around him at ease even if it meant making himself the butt of the joke. Charlie wasn't big on jokes. But then, Johnno had probably never sent a girl flowers. He would never presume to buy her a dress and have it fit perfectly. 'Romantic' was not a word in his vocabulary.

Stevie sighed, turning onto her side in search of a cool spot on the pillow. Charlie's arms immediately wrapped around her again, lean and muscular, smelling vaguely of expensive sandalwood. How ridiculous, to be thinking of her bogan friend Johnno while this spectacle of manhood was spooning her.

A very handsome, gainfully employed adult male was not only continuing to pursue dates with Stevie, he was showering her with affection, gifts and orgasms. After how many years now of bad dates, dud blokes and dry spells? Not to mention the stares from other women whenever they walked into a room together. She was lucky; she should be blissfully enjoying the romance.

It was perfectly normal to feel a bit disbelieving after all her years in the wilderness, she reasoned. But it was time to stop over-analysing and worrying about what might go wrong, and just enjoy the moment. She snuggled back against him and tried to slow her breathing into sleep.

Maybe she was the weird one, and she should be coming up with romantic gestures for him? God forbid he got bored with her. Someone that good-looking would never be short on offers. Stevie knew the girls would be lining up as soon as Charlie was back on the market.

A gift? He was so assured in his style she wouldn't know where to start. He said he had no time for books, and while a home-cooked meal might be nice, Stevie was no Nigella.

Maybe it was time to take him out west? They could have a little road trip adventure: she could make a great driving playlist, show him all her old haunts. Even introduce him to Paula? Christine and Gavin's wedding was coming up out that way.

Charlie stirred and rolled away, and Stevie finally felt cool air on her skin. With the beginnings of a plan, Stevie's mind slowly started to unknot and her body to relax, and finally, mercifully, she fell asleep.

15

On Thursday afternoon, Johnno's drive into town passed quickly. He had unearthed a dusty case of burned CDs that had been his pride and joy in the early years of uni. It was amazing the power music had to transport you back in time. Singing along to Weezer and Offspring and Elliott Smith, Johnno felt the same strange mix of insecure and bulletproof that had been the hallmark of his early twenties. If he avoided his eyes in the rear-view mirror, specifically the crow's feet around them, he could pretend he was cruising back to college after a weekend at home. Wondering what would be dished up at the dining hall, who'd pashed who at the party he'd missed. The bubble of hope in his throat that Tom and Stevie might be off again for good this time; the deflation when they weren't.

He realised with a start that Sarah Childs was the same age now that he'd been when he made some of these later mixes. After Year Twelve graduation she'd headed straight to UQ's agriculture-focused campus at Gatton, and knocked off her ag science degree in the allotted three years. No time-wasting for her, and she'd gone straight back to the Childs' property to get to work afterwards.

No wonder Penny and Rod thought the sun shone from the rear of her Wranglers. She was everything they'd hoped he'd be.

While they weren't drawn to play each other's teams, Johnno knew Sarah would be at tennis that evening. He felt an odd stirring of nerves at the prospect. They'd been texting steadily for the past twenty-four hours. Johnno had broken the ice with a gag about Rabbit's snoring, and Sarah had sent back long strings of emojis.

On a summer evening the sun would set late, the nets casting long shadows across the astroturf, but this was midwinter and the floodlights were on before Johnno arrived.

'Hi, Johnno,' chorused the club secretary and her bestie.

'Evening, Lorna, Doris. Perfect night for it, hey?'

'Oh yes. Nice and crisp, no wind at all,' Lorna agreed.

He signed in at the clubhouse, where the older ladies had already set out Arnott's assorted biscuits, giant tubs of Nescafé instant coffee and tea bags next to a steaming urn. The cups were the same mottled ceramic blue and green ones Johnno remembered from childhood, when he'd play in the clubhouse with the other kids while his mum had her weekly hit.

'Bickie?' Doris offered.

'No, thanks. Gotta change before the first round,' Johnno said.

'Ah yes, you've got Doctor Don first, then your mixed doubles,' Lorna read from the draw sheet. 'Sarah's already out there for her first match.'

Good news travels fast, Johnno thought. He went to the bathroom under the grandstand to change. It appeared Penny had shrunk his shorts in the wash, but since the only other pants he had with him were jeans, he had no choice but to head out and start warming up in this extremely short and tight pair.

Johnno danced from foot to foot, bouncing a ball with his racquet as he waited for Doctor Don to take the court. He hoped that constant movement would render him a blur to anyone paying attention, and the fact he was smuggling budgies would pass unnoticed.

Finally Don, the 'new' locum (he'd only been in town eighteen months), jogged onto the court and took up his position opposite Johnno, swiping showily to warm up his arms. They played a quick set of singles, Doris scoring as Johnno handily beat the puffing doctor. Only after they'd shaken hands across the net and the women from their teams walked on for their singles match did Johnno realise he'd attracted something of an audience.

'Looking good, Johnno,' Lorna sang out, raising her mug of instant coffee in salute. Her coterie of old biddies snickered and he could have sworn he caught the phrase 'puppies fighting in a sack'. But he didn't have a chance to heckle them back; no sooner had he latched the gate than Johnno found himself face to face with Sarah Childs.

Compared to the last time he'd seen her, she was blessedly fresh-faced. Her blonde hair was scraped into a high ponytail, all the better to display the blush that swept from her neck across her face like a weather pattern.

'G'day, Sarah! How'd your first game go?' he asked, clapping her on the back in a way he hoped wasn't too brotherly but just brotherly enough.

She grinned. 'Smashed Rebecca Burton, didn't even let her win a service point.'

'Ruthless. I love it,' Johnno said, offering his palm for a high five. Sarah lunged to oblige with such force that her hand barely grazed his, before continuing its trajectory all the way to Johnno's snugly wrapped crotch. The slap prompted a fresh round of cheers and jeers from Lorna's lusty old friends and Johnno wondered, not for the first time, whether there was more than Blend 43 in their mugs.

Before Sarah could sputter out an apology, he burst out into a deep belly laugh, and she soon joined in. 'Well, that's one way to break the tension,' Johnno said.

Sarah rolled her eyes at him. 'Shut up. I've been so bloody nervous about seeing you again, it's ridiculous.'

'Nothing to be nervous about,' Johnno said, despite the queasiness he'd felt on the way into town.

'Did I . . . sing the Dixie Chicks when you were dropping me home?' she asked, eyes fearful.

'Just a few songs,' he said. 'You wouldn't even take requests.'

'Urrrgh,' she grunted, rubbing her face in embarrassment. 'Same stunt I pulled when Tyler took me out. Bloody Drunk Sarah! I'm gonna have to ask the people at the pub to start refusing me service of Breezers, Cruisers – hell, any drinks stronger than a Fourex Gold.'

Johnno chuckled and tried to figure out why he felt a stab of jealousy that a townie, and God knows who else, had experienced Sarah's drunken alter ego before him.

The rest of the night had passed quickly. Johnno and Sarah's chat was cut short when her next match came up, and then it was time for Johnno's mixed doubles game. It was nearing 10 pm by the time they had another chance to talk, and to Johnno's chagrin all the biscuits were gone.

'I've gotta make tracks.' He shrugged apologetically. 'Early start.'

'Me too,' Sarah said. 'No stress. But hey – have you got a two-way in that Cruiser of yours?'

'I do. What have you got in mind?'

Sarah looked at her feet for a moment, then visibly summoned her courage and met Johnno's eye again. 'Well, we're going the same way for nearly the whole drive home. We don't have to be in the same cab to have a chat.'

It was so simple, and yet it would never have occurred to him. He smiled. 'You're on.'

'Channel two,' she called over her shoulder as she swung into the high cab of her Prado. 'The truckies tend to be on a different channel, so there shouldn't be too many people listening.'

The Prado had no chance to idle; she'd no sooner turned on the ignition than she was roaring out of the gate. Johnno gunned the Cruiser and caught up with her just as she hit the bridge to leave town. His stereo was still blaring the hits of 2002 and while he'd decided to let Sarah take the lead, he turned down the volume so he wouldn't miss her when she did come on the two-way radio channel.

Darkness had fallen hard, and Johnno drove for a while with the window down. The night rushed in, sharp and cool, drying the sweat on his skin. Beyond the beams of his headlights and the glow of Sarah's tail lights ahead, there was only navy blackness and the humming of cicadas. It was prime time to hit a kangaroo, but if one did veer out onto the road and catch him unawares, the bull bar on the high-set Cruiser would prevent any damage to the vehicle. The roo would not be so lucky.

Moths and dragonflies flung themselves at Johnno's headlights, the age-old doomed romance between filament and fly. Above, the moon was waxing, a fatty yellow, and a faint ring of cloud around it gave every farmer a glimmer of hope that rain might build up the next day.

'Night Cruiser, you on channel?' the two-way radio crackled. 'This is Dixie Chick, come in, Night Cruiser. Over.'

Code names? Cute. Johnno picked up the handset.

'Yep, this is Night Cruiser. Roger, Dixie Chick. You're making good speed there, you maniac. Over.'

'I would have thought you'd be in more of a rush to get home to your little Rabbit. Who's taking care of your bunny girl tonight, Night Cruiser? Over.'

It was a great ploy, he thought. Teasing him mercilessly in a conversation that could be overheard by anyone who happened to be tuned in to the same channel. If anyone was listening, odds on it would be a bloke – a truckie on the late run, a lonely farmer listening out for human contact – and she was making him look like a big softie. His mum was looking after his puppy in his absence, but it wasn't the kind of thing he wanted to admit to in this context.

'Ah yes, Dixie Chick, I had to knock her out for the evening while I was away. Sprinkled a little crushed-up valium on her dinner. By the time I left she was sprawled out on her back, snoring gently with her tongue hanging out. Over.'

'You sure know how to treat a lady, Night Cruiser.'

They drove in companionable silence for a while, and Johnno was starting to think she'd tired of the conversation when the two-way roared to life again. Sarah was pumping a Taylor Swift chorus on her stereo. When that cut out, he countered with some particularly crude Bloodhound Gang that happened to be playing on his mix. The silence stretched out again, and he began to worry that he'd offended her. But no – there was Miley Cyrus at a party in the USA. He'd have to make this chick a mixtape if they were going to have any chance of a relationship.

As Sarah's turn-off approached, Johnno picked up the receiver again. 'Dixie Chick, you on channel? Over.'

'This is Dixie Chick. Go ahead, Night Cruiser. Over.'

'You got any plans this weekend? Over.'

'I was going to go roo-shooting – Dad's been having some issues in the top paddock. Over.'

'Want some company? I haven't been out shooting for ages. We could take out some food, couple of beers. I can play you some decent music . . . Over?'

A loaded silence dragged out for what seemed an eternity. Johnno felt like a massive idiot. Or maybe that was exactly what she wanted him to feel.

'Jesus, Sarah! Say yes and put him out of his misery,' came a deep voice that cracked into a guttural belly laugh. *Bloody Cam.*

'Just messing with you, Johnno.' Sarah laughed. 'Meet me at Mum and Dad's place at nine on Saturday night.'

'Yippee hoo-bloody-ray!' Cam hollered.

Penny's dessert, an old-fashioned jam roll served with custard, was so good it obliterated any conversation after the Wests' Sunday night family dinner. Only as spoons scraped the final morsels from their bowls did anyone start to verbalise thoughts again.

'So good, Mum,' Johnno moaned, leaning back in his chair and rubbing his tummy like a satisfied toddler.

'Bloody delightful, Penelope,' Cam said, and Kate nodded her agreement.

'Well, you lot can wash up,' Penny said. 'I've got the new Rachael Treasure and I'll be reading it in the bath.'

After she left the room, Rod added, 'And I'm not missing this opportunity to catch up on *Top Gear*. See yas tomorrow.' He practically skipped off.

Kate reached for the wine bottle and drained the dregs into her glass.

'Well, in that case . . .' Cam turned away from the table, rummaged through a bag and emerged holding aloft a bottle of OP rum.

Johnno said a silent prayer that he'd be able to prise himself away after one round. The alternative, and the hangover that would go with it, was too grisly to countenance. He got up to fetch three glasses and ice from the kitchen, planted one in front of each of them, praying Cam would let him pour his own.

'Bloody beautiful,' Cam said, slopping four fat fingers of rum into all three glasses.

Kate laughed. 'Hun, it's a school night.'

'Oh, old Night Cruiser here doesn't let a little thing like work in the morning stop him from indulging his appetites. Eh, Johnno?'

And there it was, the dig Johnno had been waiting for all night. Cam had been shockingly discreet all through dinner, even as Penny pumped Johnno for details about his date with Sarah and their trip roo-shooting the night before.

Johnno had arrived home in the small hours of the morning, after a night he had to admit was a lot of fun. He hadn't been shooting in years, and once he'd got used to the rifle's kick back into his shoulder, and got his eye in under the spotlights, the satisfaction of executing an old skill had washed over him.

He'd felt content in a way that he hadn't since returning to Haven Downs, like he knew what he was doing. And with a task to focus on, he and Sarah fell into an easy rhythm together: one of them navigating the ute and directing the spotlight as the other took aim. Slim had been right. Without the pressure of having to look at each other across a table, they teased out each other's histories in short stories. And after a while, they were doing a lot more talking and drinking than shooting.

This time it was Johnno's turn to wonder if he'd put his foot in it at the end of the night. He'd felt himself staggering a bit as he got back into his own ute outside the Childs' homestead, insisting he was fine to get home on the back roads. He hadn't tried to kiss her, he knew that much, but there had been a moment when he knew he could have. And as long as it had been since he'd had any intimacy, it was his newfound respect for Sarah – her simplicity, her earthy sense of humour, her sweetness – that stopped him from initiating an easy hook-up he'd have to walk back later.

Of course, the recap Penny got was much briefer. But it was enough to have her fluttering around, planning what work the garden would need to host a wedding reception next spring. And Johnno knew Cam would have more to say about it. So now, with the sharp Christmassy smell of the rum tweaking his nostrils, Johnno changed the subject.

'Have you ever heard of anyone breeding donkeys out this way, Kate? I was reading how some blokes in western Queensland are using them to protect their stock from wild dogs. Might be a bit of demand given how dog numbers just keep going up.'

'I feel like I've heard Dad talk about having a donkey when they were kids,' Kate said, stretching out her words as she searched her memory. 'You'd have to ask him where they got it.'

'Yeah, I will, cheers.' Johnno steeled himself for another sip.

Cam was already topping up his own glass. 'Did you ask Johnno what he reckons about the Droughtmasters?' he prompted Kate.

'We haven't had much chance to chat, have we, Kate?' Johnno said, acknowledging all the time he'd been spending in town.

'Don't worry, Dad will be onto you about the fuel any day now.' She smiled. 'But I was going to see what you thought about trying some Droughtmaster stock in the spring, especially if these forecasts hold and we don't get any rains. I've found a bloke out past Moree who can give us a good price . . .'

Johnno realised she was nervous about making this suggestion. Rod had traditionally run the softer European Angus, but the changing weather had meant the tougher, locally bred Droughtmasters might be the smart way forward.

'Kate, you're the one who's been to ag college – you're way more of an authority on this than me. I think it's a great idea. Have you raised it with the old man?'

'You know he won't listen to us,' Kate said quietly. 'If it comes from you, he'll at least consider it.'

'I think you should talk to him,' Johnno said. 'Why let me take the credit for your good ideas?'

'Because he doesn't give a stuff about our ideas,' Cam said gruffly. 'Haven't you picked up on that yet?'

Kate laid a hand on Cam's arm, and both men turned to her as she gathered her thoughts. 'It's hard, Johnno,' she said finally. 'To see how much faith he puts in you, how ready he is to let you have a go. When we've been suggesting things for years, and he always says it's not the right time, or to wait and see. We've been waiting. And now we're still waiting, for you to make up your mind about what you're doing, and it seems like you're more interested in rugby and books and Sarah bloody Childs.'

'It's not that I'm not interested, Kate,' he pleaded. 'I just don't know what I'm doing. I need a bit more time. I know . . .' He could see both their shoulders tense up when he talked about taking more time. 'I know you're both sick of waiting for me to work out what

I'm doing. I just think there has to be a better way, for all of us. Just let me think about it a bit longer.'

'Think about it right up until you piss off back to London again, you mean,' Kate said sharply. 'Wonder why you've kept that one close to your chest. You've got choices, and we just have to wait for your crumbs, hey? Well, we can't wait around forever.' She grabbed Cam's glass and stalked off to put it in the kitchen. 'Come on, Cam,' she called over her shoulder. 'Mummy's boy can handle the washing-up.'

16

Stevie was kicking herself. She hadn't booked flights, and now she was stuck doing an eleven-hour drive to her next wedding in Black-all. She hadn't booked flights because Charlie was supposed to go with her, but he had pulled out at the last minute. He had a perfectly reasonable explanation. But it stung that they wouldn't get to have their outback adventure. And it really stung that she now had no one to share the driving with. She did have company – Fred was farting up a storm in the back seat, with Jen away on her Europe trip with Andrew – but Fred never pulled his weight on their road trips.

Finally she turned the Pajero in to the motor inn. Her room was far bigger than she would have booked for just herself, and she cursed Charlie again as she flopped ruefully across the king-size bed. She had a few hours before the rehearsal dinner to do recon around town for locations. Her phone had buzzed solidly when she finally reached town and its reception, but it was mostly Insta-gram notifications, panicky dating site screenshots from Paula and a dutiful email from Jen about the sights she and Andrew were see-ing in Scotland. At last Stevie found what she was hoping for, a text from Charlie.

It was sweet but short, and no substitute for his actual presence. She swiped away to another app, disappointed, but returned to the text. She read and re-read it, turning it over, searching for the kind of tenderness she'd become accustomed to. He must have been having a bad day.

Stevie dragged herself off the bed; if she went to sleep, she'd be going into the next day unprepared. Instead, she hauled her tired bones into the shower. Over the running water she heard a text ping, and fought the urge to leap out to check it. She fantasised about a declaration from Charlie – *I miss you, I made a mistake, I'm getting on a plane.* She imagined picking him up from the airstrip at sunset, him grovelling for her forgiveness and showering her with kisses, before charming everyone at the rehearsal dinner. And then making proper use of the stupid, enormous, overpriced bed.

But when she'd towelled off and padded back out to her phone, it wasn't a text from Charlie. It was a cheesy selfie, snapped in the cab of a Landcruiser in the afternoon sunshine, an adorable chocolate and tan kelpie and Johnno with his work hat pushed back off his grinning bloody face. *Look at Rabbit*, it said. *She's already a better working dog than Fred.*

Johnno's text infuriated Stevie for some reason, but her rage gave her the energy she needed to drive around town looking for potential locations for the next day's shoot. She had a list of addresses – where the bridesmaids were getting ready, where the groomsmen were staying, the church, the reception venue – and she just needed to time how long it took to drive between each and scout for good backdrops for photos of the couple and the bridal party.

It was Stevie's first time in the town and her overwhelming initial impression was of its flatness. It would make for some dramatic wide shots, especially if the weather was cloudy. Stevie couldn't remember if the bride was wearing a veil, but that could make for a good visual feature if there was wind. The ceremony was at 2 pm, so they'd be doing bridal party shots in the afternoon sun. Flat light like that wasn't ideal, but if she could drag it out they could get a couple of shots in the golden hour before sunset.

Stevie had had some initial conversations with the bride, Millie, but they hadn't given her much to work with. Some brides had been planning their big day for decades and had every shot of the wedding album visualised. They sent Stevie bound documents and Pinterest boards of inspiration, along with precise details of the dress, the make-up, the hair and the floral arrangements. Some brides knew their best and worst features and – she was seeing this more and more – had a hard time letting someone else take the shots when they had their own preferred selfie angles. Sometimes it wasn't the bride – it was the maid of honour, the sister, the mother of the bride, sometimes the mother-in-law or a really domineering grandmother who would be the one to spell out for Stevie what they were going for. Very rarely it was the groom who had the vision. But all Millie had been able to tell Stevie was that she wanted to look pretty and natural. Millie was young, twenty, and so was her husband-to-be, Blake. They had a limited budget and Stevie knew they'd invested a large portion of it into her services. So she was determined to do a good job, and it was refreshing to have a client with few demands.

The public pool was promising – lots of primary colours and the ubiquitous sans serif lettering that all mid-century Queensland public institutions seemed to sport. There was a historic mural at the Black Stump that might make an interesting backdrop. There was also a giant ram monument, which could be fun if the bridal party was up for some jokey shots. Millie and Blake didn't strike her as a humorous couple, but you could never discount the influence of a few wild ones in the bridal party to liven things up. Stevie noted a public park as a possible backup; even the bowls club could be okay. But the best thing would be to chat to some locals about picturesque spots just outside of town, where she could play up the colours of the landscape, that huge sky, and get Millie and Blake to relax without townsfolk gawking.

The 'rehearsal dinner' was a mass counter meal at one of Blackall's pubs, a chance for all the visitors to catch up with the local guests. Stevie introduced herself to the publican, who pointed out Millie and her parents, and that led to a round of introductions to various family members. Stevie tried very hard to retain people's names, since it helped disarm people in front of the lens, but when all else failed, a warm 'mate' usually did the trick.

'Miss Stevie-Jean,' a loud voice called from across the bar. She whirled around to see an unexpected familiar face.

'Father Lachlan! Fancy seeing you here.'

The priest had been one of her favourite customers during her stint pulling beers at the Argyle Hotel in Dalby. He had a penchant for poetry, and not just biblical verse. After a certain number of rums, he was renowned for reciting long runs of Banjo Paterson and Henry Lawson. And if one was very lucky, Father Lachlan might share his own brand of earthy bush poetry. 'Aren't we a bit far afield from your parish?'

'Yep, I had to find a replacement for all my sermons this weekend. But I did a few years out here as a young deacon, and Millie's family were very good to me, so when they asked me to do the wedding, I jumped at it.'

'I'm so glad to see a familiar face, and one that knows the area,' Stevie confided. 'I'd love your advice on good spots for me to take portraits tomorrow.'

'Of course,' the priest replied. 'There's a nice little clearing near the creek about ten minutes out of town where people like to picnic, that might work well. And . . . Oh well, I suppose that's a silly idea.'

'No such thing, Father. What were you thinking?'

'Well, it could just be my nostalgia. See, Millie and Blake were just tiny little Grade Twos when I first met them. But the playground at the convent primary school could be a bit of fun?'

Stevie beamed at him. 'I think I owe you a rum, Father.'

'Glory be.' He smiled.

Later in the evening, after both sets of in-laws had given stilted but heartfelt welcome speeches, after the plates had been cleared from the long, joined-together tables in the bistro, and as Father Lachlan was approaching the critical mass of rum consumption, the night turned to conversation. Stevie spent some time with Millie and Blake, who were sweet and silly and chaste. They weren't at all hung up on the ceremony itself.

'Talk me through how you two met,' Stevie said.

'You know, I can't even remember,' Millie replied. Her cheeks had flushed after a half-glass of bubbles earlier and, with the golden ringlets that had sprung around her face in the humid evening, she reminded Stevie of a cherub from a toilet paper ad. 'It just feels like we've known each other forever.' She giggled.

'Our families went to the same church,' Blake explained. 'I remember Millie in her little dresses, sitting so prim up the front in the classes they'd do for the kids while the adults were at the start of the mass.'

The angelic demeanour was mainly for the nuns' benefit, apparently, because as soon as they were out of sight, Millie had dakked Blake and stolen a stash of lollies from the nun's desk.

'And that was love at first sight?' Stevie clapped with delight.

'Oh no, she bullied me relentlessly for most of primary school,' said Blake, and Millie nodded earnestly.

'But then he had his growth spurt in Grade Seven and I realised he was cute!'

Stevie subtly pushed a glass of water towards Millie. 'So did you make a move, or . . .'

'I knew something was up because she suddenly started ignoring me,' Blake said.

'I couldn't talk to him, I had such a terrible crush,' Millie said. 'We had our end-of-term disco, and I was dying for him to ask me to dance. But I think he thought I was messing with him.'

'I left the hall and was sitting on the swings out the back in the playground, and next thing Millie came out and sat on the swing next to me. And . . . I don't know what came over me. I just gave her a little kiss.'

'And that was it,' Millie said.

Stevie had heard they'd dated all through high school, but this was even cuter than she'd expected. Father Lachlan's suggestion about the playground was perfect, but she'd keep that as a surprise for the next day.

Stevie went to say goodnight to the priest, who was chatting with Blake's mother about the readings for the ceremony. Waiting to catch his attention, Stevie pulled out her phone – still nothing from Charlie. She reopened the text from Johnno, and tried to remember what had got her so annoyed about the picture of his adorable puppy.

'Is that Johnno West?' came Father Lachlan's voice over her shoulder. 'I heard he was back from overseas. Can you say hi for me?'

'I'll do you one better, Father. Let's send him a pic,' Stevie said, and pulled him in for a selfie. She sent it off to Johnno with a quick 'Look who I found', then drained her drink.

'Well, I better head home. See you at the church, Father,' she said, and they hugged goodnight.

When Stevie's alarm went off at 6 am she groped for her phone as if through mud, disoriented in the unfamiliar motel room. She put on the kettle to make instant coffee – those tiny motel mugs somehow always made her wish she still smoked – and as her brain slowly awakened, she scrolled through her phone.

Text from Charlie: *Babe, good luck for the wedding today, not that you need it. I'm so sorry I'm not there with you. I'll make you dinner tomorrow night when you get back to the city, and make it up to you. xx*

Text from Johnno: *Is that Fr Locky?! I need video of any poetry recitals please.*

Email from Jen: *Just ate a meal that was 90% butter. I love Prague even if Andrew can't shut up about how everything is overpriced. What was the name of that street you mentioned, with the antique stalls? How's Blackall? Don't forget electricity bill due Tuesday. xx*

Stevie walked around the town, a playlist of dreamy electro in her ears. She wanted to get a feel for the day, the light and the temperature. Eventually she found herself in the playground of the

Catholic primary school. There were moveable mini grandstands for tiny people to watch assemblies, in striped primary colours. There were brightly coloured forts and activity playgrounds, a huge sandpit blanketed in a tarp to protect it over the weekend. And in a corner near the school hall, framed by jacaranda trees, an old-fashioned swing set. *That'll do nicely*, Stevie thought.

She snapped a quick selfie, fired it off to Charlie: *Game time. Missing my assistant. xx.*

The day passed in a flash, refreshingly low on drama. Millie was true to her word about being unfussy, and any potential power struggles were avoided by Millie yielding immediately to any opinion expressed by anyone else. A bridezilla she was not. Her dress was simple and modest, sewn by her mother. A wreath of baby's breath around her strawberry blonde curls added to her angelic look. And while Millie would have been satisfied with no makeup at all, her maid of honour managed to talk her into some blush, mascara and lip gloss.

Mille and her maids and mum were settling down to a very civilised pot of tea when Stevie left them to check in on the groomsmen. There, too, the proceedings were unusually dignified. In fact, it was only when Stevie looked back at her shots to check some composition of group shots of the lads and dads doing up one another's ties that she realised not one of them was gripping a stubby or can. Was this . . . a dry wedding?

There was a first time for everything, Stevie supposed, but she'd honestly never expected to see the day she shot a wedding with no alcohol. Beer, wine and rum were the lubricants that greased the gears of Queensland social life and, particularly in rural and regional areas, a few drinks went hand in hand with letting one's hair down. But it tracked, both with Millie and Blake's tight budget and their churchgoing families, that drinking wasn't a priority for them. Stevie wondered what it would mean for her usual chaotic dancefloor photos after the reception. What would this crowd do for 'Eagle Rock'?

Millie rode to the church with her parents, their freshly detailed sedan festooned with white ribbons. Nobody ran late, nobody was tempted to 'speak now or forever hold your peace'. Stevie tiptoed cautiously around to get her shots during the ceremony, feeling God's attention on her more than usual. All eyes in the church were moist as Millie and Blake beamed at each other, both looking freshly scrubbed and not so much older than when they'd met here as kids. Father Lachlan brought the house down with his homily, connecting the bond Millie and Blake had shared as kids, the faith their families raised them in, and the way their new family would become the next generation of the church's community.

As the ceremony wound down to its conclusion, Millie and Blake having solemnly made their vows and exchanged rings, Stevie took her position for the kiss. She found this the hardest thing to predict about couples: who would chastely peck, who would go for the big Hollywood kiss, and which couples would just go for it and scandalise the nannas with tongues and groping. If Stevie's theory about Millie and Blake saving themselves for marriage was correct, this one could really go either way – would it be nerves and decorum, or years of lust on the verge of spilling over?

'I now pronounce you husband and wife,' Father Lachlan boomed, ever the showman. 'You may kiss the bride!'

Blake took Millie by the shoulders and gently put his lips on hers. Millie melted into him, and Stevie thought she might detach her jaw and swallow Blake whole. She dropped her bouquet in order to get a grip on Blake's backside, and might have gone for a full straddle if Father Lachlan hadn't cleared his throat loudly and handed back the bouquet. Millie looked dazed as they triumphantly walked out of the church.

Stevie knew she'd have to get her shots of the bride and groom at the reception early, because these two were going to be retiring for their wedding night as soon as the knife hit the bottom of the cake. She'd have to see if Father Lachlan wanted to take a bet on what time they'd bail.

The reception was held at the very school hall where Blake hadn't asked Millie to dance all those years ago. Stevie was very excited to see a trestle table heaving with sweets, from pies and pavlovas to tiny tartlets.

'Good thing there's dessert, 'cause none of us are getting sauced tonight, eh, Stevie?' came the unmistakable croak of the Bush Telegraph.

'Can you believe it, Mabel?' Stevie said. 'I thought dry weddings were just a myth! I've got no idea how I'm going to get any colour shots when everyone's sober.'

'We'll be all finished here by nine, you mark my words,' said Mabel. 'And that won't be a moment too soon for our newlyweds.'

Stevie gave an earthy laugh before she realised a group of older women setting out teacups were staring at her. 'I'd better circulate, Mabel. Gotta work fast if you're right.'

'Of course, love. Don't go without saying goodbye.'

It was barely dark before the speeches were done. In contrast to the many brides she'd seen trashed on an empty stomach, Stevie watched Millie clean her plate at record speed. She was ready to cut the cake before some of the guests had even been served their mains. The girl had an appetite.

Finally, the couple took the floor for their first dance, to a sweet country song. Stevie could see Blake quietly crooning the words in Millie's ear, an adorable moment she could capture forever. She was careful to crop the shot from the waist up, though, editing out the investigation Millie's hands were doing around Blake's waistband. The second the song ended, Millie squealed and threw her bouquet, and started dragging Blake out the door without so much as a backward glance at the young woman who'd caught the flowers.

'What a turn up for the books,' Mabel said, giggling, as Stevie sat down with a plate of pavlova. She'd tried to take a video of the car's headlights fading off into the night with the bride and groom, but Millie had taken the driver's seat and left the church with an acceleration that would leave Formula One fans begging for more.

'Young love,' Stevie sighed, digging in to her dessert.

'It's really in the air,' Mabel said, clearly itching to share some gossip.

'Go on then,' Stevie said. 'Let's hear it.'

'Well, I usually get tips over the phone, but my old two-way came in handy a few weeks ago when I heard a young couple flirting. It's a match that will make both their families very happy, but maybe not you, Stevie.'

'What are you talking about, Mabel?'

'Johnno West and his young neighbour, Sarah Childs! They've been on a number of dates, and by all accounts things are really heating up. His mother had been on at me for years, wishing and hoping Johnno would pay Sarah some attention, but he never seemed to notice her. Well, finally things are looking up. And you know, she's an only child. It would be a huge coup to unite the properties. Oh – but didn't he used to have a soft spot for you, Stevie? I hope I'm not speaking out of turn.'

Stevie could feel Mabel's eyes boring into her. She just needed to swallow this bite of pavlova, but it was like a wad of cardboard in her mouth. What was this reaction? Was she jealous? Of Johnno and some kid?

'Of course not, Mabel,' she finally managed to choke out. 'Johnno and I are just old friends, although this is the first I'm hearing of this. I'll have to ring him and get all the details. Would you excuse me? My boyfriend's calling.'

'Oh, is that Charlie?' Mabel's eyes grew wide, but Stevie was already bolting from the room with her phone pressed to her ear, praying it wouldn't ring while she was faking a call.

Instagram post by @StevieJeanLoveStories:

MILLIE & BLAKE, July 2019: 'It feels like we've known each other forever,' said these young lovers. Forever's not such a long time when you're not long out of school, where these two met. It wasn't quite love at first sight, but now they only have eyes for each other. Judging by their passionate wedding, they couldn't get started on the rest of their lives fast enough.

New post in 'Neighbourhood News' from The Bush Telegraph:

DESPERATE & DATELESS: I recently attended a lovely wedding in Blackall – a beautiful young couple who couldn't wait to lock it down. Bumped into an old friend, our not-so-single snapper, taking photos at the reception, very much on her own despite a supposedly red-hot romance with her new beau. Trouble in paradise? LOL, Mabel

17

The robotic bloops of the Skype ringtone filled Stevie's room. She'd been trying to get hold of Jen for the past few hours, desperate to dish on Johnno and Charlie developments.

'Stevie – is everything okay?' Jen's concerned face filled the screen, her hair mussed up into a bird's nest. Andrew moaned next to her and pulled a pillow over his head.

'What time is it there?' Stevie asked, realising Jen must have been worried to Skype her from bed.

Jen squinted at the phone. 'Six am. This better be good.'

Was it good? Oops. All the urgency suddenly deflated out of Stevie, despite the two hours she'd spent working herself up into a state. 'Sorry, Jen. See, this is why I need you; I feel calmer already,' she said.

'But you're okay? What day is it – did you just get home from Blackall?'

'A couple of days ago. Yeah, I'm fine. In fact, I should never have woken you up, I'm sorry.'

Stevie had spent a restless night in the oversized hotel room after Millie and Blake's reception, and checked out at 4.30 am to start the long drive home. Eleven hours was too long to spend alone in a car with one's flatulent dog and thoughts. Especially when one's current love interest was being elusive, and the old friend you didn't think you were interested in was suddenly very interesting because you'd just learned he was going out with someone else.

'Come on,' Jen said, holding the phone ahead of her as she got out of bed. 'Tell me what's on your mind. How was the wedding? How did Charlie go in the outback?'

'Charlie didn't go anywhere near the outback, for a start,' Stevie said, pouting. 'He bailed at the last minute, so I got to enjoy the 22-hour round trip by myself.'

'Sorry, hun, that sucks,' Jen said, poking around in the pantry – for tea, probably. 'Did he give you a good reason?'

'There's always a good reason, and then I feel like an arsehole for being disappointed,' Stevie said. 'And then I think I'm going crazy, looking for something suspicious when maybe I should just trust that he's being honest.'

'Have you seen him since you got back?'

'Yeah, he cooked me a gorgeous dinner the night I got back, rubbed my feet, blah blah blah. I was a total bitch to him.'

'But things are good again?'

Stevie thought of how she hadn't been able to fully relax with him. '. . . Yeah.'

'That's not a good pause.'

'It's fine, I'm just overthinking it. Anyway, enough of my petty drama. You're on the trip of a lifetime. How's London?'

'It's great. I've always loved the summer here. It's weird though, I had all these places I wanted to show Andrew, the secret spots and off-the-beaten-track experiences and . . . he just wants to ride in double-decker buses and look at Big Ben and stuff. And that's been fun. I guess it just reminds me that the touristy stuff is great for a reason, I don't have to be a snob about everything . . .'

'But I love when you get all snobby and possessive of your hipster bars,' Stevie teased her.

Jen giggled and Stevie saw her glance towards the bedroom, where Andrew was hopefully still fast asleep.

'But I do want your Paris tips, please. We'll probably split up for a day there, so I can go to as many bookshops as I want and smoke way too much at cafes.'

'No worries, I'll email you some links. So, can I tell you something weird?'

Jen's eyes lit up at the whiff of imminent drama. 'I'm going to have to light a fag for this one, hold on,' she said, carrying her teacup out onto their Airbnb's tiny balcony. Stevie waited for the click and flare of Jen's lighter, the inhale and sigh. 'Okay, go.'

'So, I had another run-in with the Bush Telegraph at the Blackall wedding. You remember Mabel?'

'I remember,' Jen said. 'Wait, is this doubt about Charlie coming from what she said?'

'Well, it certainly didn't help. She didn't have much to say about Charlie this time. But she went out of her way to casually mention that Johnno's going out with someone.'

'Aw, Johnno. I wonder how his poor little head is,' Jen said. 'Is it serious? Who is she?'

'It's the bloody girl next door. Did you ever meet Sarah Childs?'

'Was she the one at Johnno's twenty-first?'

Stevie had a sudden flash of memory of Sarah as a coltish teenager, hovering around the edges of the party Penny and Rod had hosted. Horsey, sweet, the kind of girl they'd love him to end up with. 'Yeah. What do you remember about her?'

'Thinking she'd be one of those women who never has to worry about getting fat.'

'Ugh. Well, the parents are all very excited about it, apparently.'

'Do you think she's not good enough for him?'

'I honestly have no idea. And I can't figure out why I can't stop thinking about it,' Stevie said.

'Really?' Jen deadpanned. 'You've got no idea?'

Stevie avoided Jen's pixelated eye on the screen.

'Stevie-Jean. There's a vibe between you two, and you know it,' Jen said. 'He's always had a thing for you. And now he might have moved on and, what – you're sad you don't have your back-up plan any more? All while you're already dating someone tall, dark and handsome. Stevie?'

'What? Jen, I think I'm losing you.'

'Bull, Stevie.'

'Sorry, it keeps breaking up. I'll have to call you back another time.'

'You know it's true.'

'Love you!'

'Love you too.'

It was a Wednesday afternoon, the kind of time when Stevie should have been knocking over some admin tasks, preparing for the weekend ahead. Instead she had thirty-seven tabs open in her browser to various online shopping carts and half-read *New Yorker* articles, realising bleakly with every minute that ticked over that she had wasted an entire day putting off the invoicing and editing she'd sat down to do at 9 am.

A heavy dread sat on her chest, which compounded every time

her phone vibrated to life. One bride, from a wedding three months earlier, had grown impatient enough to see her final gallery that she was calling Stevie multiple times a day. Stevie knew screening the calls was not helping, but she couldn't bring herself to face her.

It was her worst habit, procrastinating, and it could get out of control very quickly. She knew nothing was going to make her feel better until the work was done. She knew she could do the work well, and the bride would ultimately be delighted. She knew the exact steps she needed to take to get this work done. And yet still she put it off.

'Right,' Stevie muttered, walking away from the desk. *Time to reset.*

'Fred,' she called. The poor mutt had grown so accustomed to her ignoring him he barely moved even when Stevie grabbed his lead. 'Come on, mate. It's time we got outside.' Fred realised it wasn't a mirage, roused himself from his bed and shook himself to life.

As soon as they were out on the footpath, Stevie felt better. The winter evenings were mild in Brisbane, and she guided Fred towards the pathway along the river, breaking into a jog. The moon was hanging heavy and low, bobbing above the chopsticks bridge, and Stevie felt like she could run all the way to New Farm.

Two minutes later she pulled up, red-faced and sucking in gulps of air. She had a sudden flashback to a path not far from here. A February day back in college, when she had Johnno had for some reason made a New Year's fitness pact. It had lasted all of two days, and they'd done the same pathetic attempt at running, going too hard too early until they had to stop, gasping and panting. Before they could even breathe properly, they'd caught each other's eye and were overcome with laughter, prompting a coughing fit from

Johnno. They'd both said 'Bugger it' at exactly the same time, walked to the nearest pub in their shorts and joggers, and spent the rest of the night getting silly drunk and dancing to a cover band.

And now the bastard was a runner. He looked a lot better for it, and his heroics on the footy field at Ladies' Day suggested he was in better shape than most of his teammates. How did he do it? They'd spent hours that night proclaiming all the ways that running was ridiculous. Boring. Repetitive. Pointless. But he'd cracked it. Stevie again felt the urge to text him, as she had multiple times in the past few days.

'Good thing we left the phone at home, hey, Fred?' she said, scratching behind his ears as he drank from a doggie dish under the water fountain. Over the river, the sky was blushing and the first stars were flickering on. Stevie knew darkness would fall quickly, and Fred would need his dinner.

'Okay, mate, better head home,' she said. The walk had done what she needed it to, shaken loose the stuck feeling. She could get home and start tackling tasks . . . or she could binge another series on Netflix. Why was she so useless without Jen around?

A few days later, Stevie raced up to a chic cafe on James Street. She had come straight from a yoga class in a sweatshirt she'd owned since college, her dirty hair scraped back into a bun of desperation. She was pretty sure her car was illegally parked, but she was so late she couldn't look for another option.

It was the perfect storm of circumstances in which you'd least like to meet your ex's new fiancée. Stevie barrelled up to the hostess, jittering her keys into her bag and catching her laptop just before it fell. 'Sorry – hi – I'm meeting someone . . .'

Even if she hadn't been stalking Lily on Instagram for months, even if Lily wasn't now waving serenely at her from a prime table, Stevie would have been able to pick her based on how inadequate she made Stevie feel.

Lily was seated in a leafy corner, where a beam of sunshine seemed sent from heaven itself to illuminate her immaculate bone structure to perfection. She was cool and poised in a beige linen dress, the kind that would make Stevie look like a Depression-era depressed housewife. Stevie knew this because she had ordered a dress just like it after seeing it on an Instagram influencer, and returned it a day later. Lily's shiny hair fell straight and sleek, past simple gold hoops in her ears. As she stood to welcome Stevie with a kiss on each cheek, Stevie clocked the gigantic heirloom diamond on her left hand. The pride of the Carruthers family, Granny Violet's rock. *It could have been mine*, she thought before she could stop herself.

'Thanks so much for meeting me, Stevie,' Lily cooed as Stevie tried to pull her chair closer to the table and knocked all the glasses off balance. 'I'm sure your schedule is crazy, so I really appreciate getting the chance to start discussing the vision for our big day. Can I order you a drink?'

'I'd love a coffee. Cap, full fat.'

Lily gestured to the waitress. 'We'll take a full-cream cappuccino and a green tea – is that organic?' Lily asked. The waitress assured her it was.

'Could I get a chocolate croissant as well, please?' Stevie looked pleadingly at the waitress.

'Sure. Anything for you?' the waitress asked Lily.

'No, thanks, love. Intermittent fasting,' Lily said, faintly glowing with smugness. 'Stevie, I can't tell you how thankful I am that you could fit us in.'

'It was a lucky break,' Stevie admitted. 'The weekend had just opened up when you emailed me.'

'And thank God. Planning a wedding in only eight months is stressful enough. I might have lost it if I didn't know we at least had the photographer of my dreams locked down.'

Against her will, Stevie felt herself blushing and was grateful for the interruption of the waitress plonking a pastry in front of her. 'So, do you have any ideas for the photos and the wedding in general?' Stevie asked through a mouthful of croissant. 'A theme?'

Lily sipped her tea, then reached down to her designer handbag and pulled out a book bound in creamy leather. 'I'm a bit old-fashioned,' she said, opening the cover to reveal page after page of heavy paper stock collaged exquisitely with images of dresses, flowers and cakes. 'I love a mood board, but I can't get into Pinterest. So basic, you know?' She wrinkled her nose.

'Ugh, totes,' Stevie said thickly, before gulping her coffee. She made a show of wiping her hands on her napkin before reaching for the book. 'May I?'

'Of course,' Lily said, turning it to face Stevie. 'I haven't found The Dress yet, but I want something classic, a Carolyn Bessette-style slip, probably. Simple hair, probably just down, maybe with some flowers, minimal make-up. I'm trying to talk Tom into a Tom Ford suit. I want everyone in black tie, no matter how rustic the setting is. A proper party!'

There was something unguarded and joyful in the way Lily said 'proper party', something childlike, that made their age gap feel even more vast to Stevie. This girl would have been pulling up the socks of her school uniform while Stevie and Tom were muddling through their mid-twenties together. And here she was, at the same age Stevie had been all hangovers and mascara tear stains, all grace and ease and green goddamned tea.

Stevie was struck by the realisation that both Tom and Johnno were with girls ten years younger. Girls who no doubt carried much less baggage – and cellulite. What was left for the likes of her when the blokes her age were faced with these girls, so taut and full of energy and desperate to please, not messy and demanding? They were chalk and expensive cheese sitting on either side of a cafe table, and only one of them was wearing the Carruthers diamond.

Trying to still her racing mind, Stevie flipped through pages dedicated to table settings, floral arrangements and lighting. Lily was still talking, about fireworks and string lights and long tables in the paddock. 'I love black-and-white, and the palette I'm going for is fairly monochrome, but we'd need a few shots in colour given all the work Tom's mum is putting into the garden. I don't want anything too posed, you know? I like how you tend to capture more candid moments, when people are their real selves, not fake smiling . . .'

Stevie had to admit Lily's taste was impeccable. Alongside photographs from Truman Capote's black-and-white ball and Helmut Newton fashion shoots, she recognised a few shots from other great wedding photographers, clipped from high-end magazines. And, to her delight, she recognised a few of her own that Lily must have printed off from Instagram.

'I'm a bit of a fangirl.'

'Lily, this is amazing. I can see you've got a really clear picture of what you want the day to be like.'

She sighed. 'I'm a lawyer – I get off on the details. I had a four-tab spreadsheet going within two hours of Tom proposing. It's just what helps me feel in control. Obviously, there will be plenty that

I can't control, so I'm just trying to organise what I can and make peace with the rest.'

'Yeah, try not to think too much about Johnno's best man speech.' Stevie laughed and then choked as concern swept across Lily's face. 'I'm kidding! He does a beautiful speech.'

Why the hell did you bring that up? Stevie chastised herself. Now they were going to have to address the elephant in the room and she was thinking about Johnno, tanned and laughing in his tux, right when she needed all her wits about her. 'Lily—' she started.

'Look, Stevie, I'm obviously aware of the history between you and Tom,' Lily said, her unflappable calm finally seeming almost the tiniest bit flappable. She took a deep breath. 'He speaks highly of you, and your work speaks for itself, so it's not an issue for me, as long as you feel comfortable working with us. But it will be an emotional day, so if you think it could be a problem, I'll understand if you want to pull out.'

Was she actually being patronising, or was Stevie just hyper defensive? Either way, something clicked in Stevie's brain. There was no way she was backing out now. 'I don't see there being any problems,' Stevie said. 'I've shot more than a hundred weddings, and I'm going to make yours look beautiful. I was thinking it's actually an advantage that I know the property so well. I'll know what to expect in terms of the light and locations, so we can really make the most of it.'

Lily sighed in relief. 'I'm so glad. Thanks, Stevie. Now, did you get the deposit okay?'

'Hang on, sorry.' Stevie could have sworn she saw Charlie walk past on the street. The same Charlie who'd begged off yoga that morning, saying he'd had to fly down to Melbourne for an urgent client meeting. She raced out of her seat and past the hostess. 'Charlie? Charlie!'

The man's shoulders might have tensed up by a millimetre, but he didn't turn around, striding on down James Street and out of sight. Couldn't have been him.

'Sorry about that,' Stevie panted, sitting back down across from Lily. 'Thought I recognised someone. False alarm.'

'Same thing happened to my girlfriend just the other day,' Lily sympathised.

'Look, I can't really stay much longer,' Stevie said. 'You can send me visual references whenever you like. I'll give you a call a few weeks out to talk through timing for the day and any last questions you have.'

'Sounds perfect.' Lily stood, but Stevie was scooting away before she could be pressed into any more perfumed kisses.

'So,' Stevie asked, manoeuvring the Pajero back towards home. She'd dialled her mum to distract herself from the parking fine she'd found on the windscreen. 'How's George?'

'He's good,' Paula said. Stevie could hear the smile in her voice. 'He cooked me dinner last night. It's quite refreshing dating a younger man, Stevie, they don't have the same hang-ups about—'

'I'm going to stop you there, Mum. I'm happy for you, but there are some things I'd rather not know.'

'—division of domestic labour, is what I was going to say, Stevie-Jean. Anyway, I've barely seen him for weeks. He's been flat out now they've finally listed Avalon for sale. He told me last night he's planning to make an offer himself.'

'Wow,' Stevie said.

'I know,' Paula replied. 'He said he's always loved the place – he's worked there for years now. But he said seeing my connection to the property took it to a new level.'

'What does that mean for you?'

'I don't know. George is quite serious. He said he'd like me to be involved. It's crazy – it's the kind of thing I dreamed about, being able to go back somehow. Now I have the chance, I can't quite believe it.'

'You've only been going out a couple of months,' Stevie said. She couldn't parse her feelings – incredulous? Jealous? Her mum had only been dating for a few months and had found someone who wanted to build a life with her. *What's wrong with me?*

'George says when you know, you know. And it will be another few months before the sale goes through, anyway, if he even makes a successful offer. No use fretting about it just yet. How are you? How's Charlie?'

That's right, Stevie thought. *I have Charlie.* So why wasn't that thought comforting?

Stevie had been meaning to look up when Jen and Andrew's flight home was landing, so she could offer to pick them up from the airport. But the week had sped by in a blur of editing and a mid-week trip to shoot some family portraits, and now Jen and Andrew were due home any minute. Stevie was not at the airport waiting for them. Instead she was still ignoring calls from a pushy bride, and also screening calls from her accountant. There was an email in her inbox from him with a scary red exclamation point, which always seemed a tad overdramatic, and she was waiting until she felt calmer to open it.

'I can go over your books for you,' Charlie had offered the previous evening when she complained about the accountant's pursuit. Stevie didn't have the heart to explain that her 'books' were non-existent and her tax records and invoicing were months behind.

He had resurfaced after his Melbourne trip, and he liked to have all of Stevie's attention when he was around. So she'd spent the evenings leaning on the kitchen island with a glass of wine while he cooked, or wondering if she could pick up a book while he serenaded her with his guitar.

Their involvement had plateaued in recent weeks. Stevie found herself relieved that things weren't escalating at the same wild pace of their early dates. Charlie had become so intense so quickly, it was unsustainable. At that rate, she'd been worried he'd propose within weeks. As it was there was poetry, singing, cooking, dancing in the kitchen: an effusion of affection in every possible medium. She swallowed love spelled out in blueberries in her pancakes, drank love foamed on top of her lattes. Bouquets of love dropped their petals across her house. Her phone lit up with strings of love emojis like haiku.

She had romance, drama, all the grand gestures she'd ever dreamed of. Charlie left her in no doubt of what he was feeling, and Stevie thought that might be the most confusing part. Had years of entanglements with the emotionally stunted men of western Queensland left her stunted herself? What was she, a romantic bonsai? Why would she second-guess the most emotionally available babe she had ever hooked up with just because no other man had ever been able to express his feelings with her? And there was no faking their chemistry between the sheets. So why did she have this niggling feeling that she couldn't let her guard down?

You're a head case, Stevie-Jean, she had told herself, self-administering tough love in the absence of her best friend. *Just let yourself enjoy it.* She thought of Charlie leaving for work that morning as she dozed, brushing his lips to her temple and, when she stirred, whispering, 'Don't move, I want to remember you just like this.' It was perfect. *He* was perfect. She'd just been starved of romance for so long that such a rich, indulgent helping wasn't sitting right. She just had to readjust, like someone coming off a fast.

Between psyching herself up about Charlie and frantically trying to log her expenses in a spreadsheet, Stevie didn't hear Jen's keys in the door. She didn't hear the suitcases rolling down the hall, or even notice Jen's tired but beaming face peek around the doorframe of her room until Jen yelled her name.

'Thank God you're back!' Stevie jumped out of her chair and wrapped Jen up in a hug. She could even have hugged Andrew, but he was already rearranging the mess in the kitchen.

'Busy day?' Jen asked, waiting for Stevie to ask some questions about the flight, or their last few days in Paris. But Stevie was already back in front of her screen.

'I met up with Lily. Can you believe she had the audacity to ask if I was going to be too emotional to shoot the wedding? Nothing like being patronised by a 22-year-old wearing a giant diamond that could have been mine. And my phone just will. Not. Stop. Ringing. Gah!'

'I guess I'll leave you to it. I'm going to take a shower, unpack.'

'We'll have a cuppa later, catch up,' Stevie said, without taking her eyes off her screen as Jen dragged her feet away down the hall.

18

Stevie and Jen had been dreading this afternoon, but they couldn't get out of it. Liz had planned the baby shower for a weekday specifically so Stevie could attend, so she couldn't use work as an excuse.

Celeste was hosting the do at her Queenslander in Ascot, all polished floorboards, high ceilings and white walls that even her toddlers didn't dare stain. It was a beautiful home, presented with the same effortless snobbery as the platters she wafted out from the butler's pantry. Stevie could only dream of entertaining like this, and she didn't have two kids.

The decorations were aggressively tasteful: white flowers, eco-friendly confetti, absolutely no pink or blue. When someone made the group play the game where you eat Nutella out of a nappy with a spoon, Celeste seemed quietly incensed at the tone being lowered.

To Stevie, it didn't feel that long ago that these women had danced on tables and held each other's hair back in the bathroom stalls of Brisbane's finer establishments. Now they sat like a jury on Celeste's impeccable leather sectional, peering over their pastel-clad bumps as if Stevie was a hopeless case: the single and childless 31-year-old woman.

'You really don't know what love is until you have one, you know?'

'Little Otis said the most precious thing the other day . . .'

'No soft cheese for me, thanks.'

Stevie felt compelled to share her wildest single stories, only a little embellished, just to see some shock on their faces. While they bemoaned their sleepless nights, she flaunted her freedom to stay out and sleep late. When Stevie sensed an eye roll coming on so big she couldn't blink it away, she dragged Jen into the laundry for a moment of privacy. Even this room smelled of lavender and fresh cotton, as Celeste's top-of-the-range appliances blinked at them.

'They should serve stronger drinks at these things,' Stevie whined, draining her champagne flute and brandishing a fresh bottle she'd swiped from the kitchen. 'At least we don't have much competition for this. Sorry, did you want to go outside for a smoke? I haven't seen you have one in ages.'

Jen shook her head, pointing to a patch on her arm. 'Quitting.'

'Ah, that's why you've had a face like a smacked arse since you got back. Well, good for you, babe.' Stevie topped up both their glasses. 'Thank God we can walk away from this and keep living like lesbian aunts in peace,' she muttered.

'Stevie, I have to talk to you about something,' Jen started.

'And what's with wearing activewear to a party? They're all in the same bloody puffer vest and pearl earrings, like they've just come from Pilates.' Stevie's Instagram was one long procession of these women swinging their ponytails over designer strollers and take-away coffees in parks with their angelic toddlers, who had no doubt been eating dirt or screaming minutes earlier. 'God, the judgement in that room. Just dripping with disdain that I'd dare to be single.'

'If anything, you're the one judging them,' Jen said when she could finally get a word in.

'That's ridiculous.'

'Stevie, for someone who spends so much time thinking about what other people think of you, you're spectacularly unconcerned about how your behaviour makes other people feel.'

Stevie laughed, still catching up to the conversation's change in direction.

'I'm moving out, Stevie,' Jen said.

'What?'

'Andrew asked me while we were in Europe.'

Stevie's mind reeled. 'But you got back a week ago!'

'I've been waiting for the right moment to tell you,' Jen said, not quite meeting Stevie's eye. 'You've been so busy and distracted.'

Jen, her best friend, had been slinking around the house they shared, unable to find the words to tell her she was leaving her. Stevie felt the back of her eyes prickle with the hot threat of tears. Was she that much of a mess that Jen felt bad leaving her? How would she handle the house on her own? She'd need to advertise for a housemate . . . In her thirties and incapable of living like an adult, and the person she'd thought was her ally was leaving her, vaulting towards the Game-of-Life milestones like everyone else. 'What about Fred?' Stevie asked.

'Andrew doesn't have permission for pets at his place, so you're going to have to take full custody for a while,' Jen said.

'Oh, Jen.' Stevie sighed. 'You could have told me. I mean, you could have just blurted it out without having to strategise how to manage my stupid feelings.'

'Stevie, it's a big change for us, and I know it's a bit of a sensitive spot for you. It's dumb that I feel like I'm letting you down by just living my life, but there it is. I can't put off normal progress in my relationship, in my life, any more, just to make you feel okay about your choices.'

Jen's tone had risen and her cheeks were flushed. Stevie couldn't remember the last time Jen had spoken to her like this. She was wringing her hands, fiddling with her fingers in a way Stevie suddenly realised she'd been doing since she and Andrew had got back from the airport. Stevie grabbed Jen's left hand.

'Is this an engagement ring?' The words were out before Stevie realised she was shouting.

Jen was crying now. 'You didn't even notice!'

'God, did he get down on one knee in front of the Eiffel Tower? Or a gondola in Venice? How clichéd.' Stevie hated every word spilling out of her mouth, hated herself for how she was reacting to this when she should have been joyful for her friend, but she couldn't seem to stop.

'You know what, Stevie? It was really nice. He'd thought of everything, because he cares about me. He'd planned it all, and he stuck to the plan even when he had food poisoning and I was being a bitch about the crowds. Maybe it was clichéd, but it made me so happy. And I couldn't share it, I couldn't even post a lame bloody Instagram that every other person in my life would be happy about, because I knew you'd take it as some kind of slight against you. How ridiculous is that?'

In a moment of ashamed silence, as Stevie desperately tried to think of something to say to make things right, there was a fluttering noise outside the door. Every woman in the house was straining to hear their drama.

Jen wiped away tears and smudged mascara. 'I'll have my stuff out of the house over the weekend. I'll stay at Andrew's tonight until you go away on your next job tomorrow, and email you about the bills and paperwork.' And she walked out.

Stevie stared and stared at Celeste's lacquered floorboards, but despite her best efforts they did not open up and swallow her.

Stevie picked up the call and Paula didn't wait for her to say a word. 'Stevie! He got it!'

'Hi, Mum.'

'George, he got Avalon,' Paula crowed. 'Not only that, he found the old sign. He invited me out for dinner last night, and he'd set up a picnic in the back garden, and he gave me the old sign. Said he'd found it a few weeks ago but wanted to clean it up.'

'That's very sweet,' Stevie said. *Another engagement on the way, I suppose.* 'Sorry, I can't really talk right now.'

Less than a week later, Stevie parked her car after a long drive home from Maleny in end-of-the-weekend traffic. She dragged her bags up the Queenslander's front steps, searching for her house keys as always. She could hear Fred snuffling in the backyard, but the lights were all out and in the gloom it took her three tries to get the right key in the lock.

Finally inside, she switched on the hallway light and immediately wished she'd just stumbled in blindly in the dark. The floor was freshly mopped, the walls bare of Jen's art prints. The house even sounded different, somehow both ringing with the silence and echoing in the newly empty spaces where Jen and her stuff had been.

Stevie had last seen Jen as she was walking out for the Maleny wedding on Saturday morning. She had no doubt the timing was intentional. Andrew glared at her as he passed her in the hallway, a stack of packing boxes under his arm. Stevie didn't know what his problem was; he was the one who got to keep Jen.

Jen was trying to stand casually at the door, waiting for Stevie to exit.

'I can't stay, I'm sorry,' Stevie started, trying not to tear up again.

'I know,' Jen said. 'We'll be out of here soon. I'll leave my keys here on the hallway table, lock Fred in the backyard and leave him plenty of food to last until you get back.'

Everything felt wrong, but Stevie was running too late to put it right. She would regret not trying to hug Jen then.

'Drive safe,' Jen called down the stairs, and Stevie barely held the tears until she got the driver's side door open.

Over the weekend Jen had sent a guttingly courteous email listing the bills she had transferred into Stevie's name. She had paid her share of the rent for the next two weeks and said she'd be in touch when she was ready, and not to call or come to Andrew's before then.

Stevie's footsteps reverberated as she looked in Jen's empty room, then the living room, stocktaking all that had departed along with her. On the kitchen bench was a bottle of red wine and a small wrapped gift. Stevie opened it to find a lewd decorative corkscrew. A card read, *'Found this in Paris and knew it had to be yours. Here's some wine so you can make sure it works. x J'*.

Exhausted down to her very bones, Stevie fed Fred before uncorking the bottle and pouring a large glass. She raised it in a silent toast to Jen's unwavering thoughtfulness and started drafting an ad for a housemate.

The last thing Stevie wanted was a stranger in the house. Actually, that was the second last thing. The last, *last* thing Stevie wanted was to have to talk through a series of interviews with randoms, putting on a front like she was fun to live with but also very responsible, clean and quiet. Housemate interviews were like job interviews or blind dates, but without the promise of money or sex. But putting out a call to friends on Facebook would raise too many questions she didn't have the heart to answer.

She'd written two very lacklustre sentences. *Hmm, wineglass is empty.* Stevie heaved herself out of the kitchen chair she'd slumped into, realising from her stiffness that she'd been sitting for a long time, and discovering once she was vertical that she hadn't eaten anything for hours and was quite drunk.

It seemed insurmountable to start downloading the photos from the Maleny wedding. Much better to do it in the morning when she was fresh. She opened the fridge door, suddenly ravenous, but of course Jen hadn't left her any food. (Never mind that the only food of Stevie's in the fridge was mouldy.) Pizza! Yes, she needed pizza. *Where did all those coupons go?* No coupons. Bugger them. What if she called Charlie? Then she could get dinner and dessert delivered, *heheheh*.

'Charlie. Charlie?'

'I'm sorry, I can't talk now.' His voice was muffled, like he'd stepped into a wardrobe to take the call. Stevie thought she heard a voice in the background asking who he was talking to. 'Look, I can't really go into it now, but I'll get in touch in the morning, okay?'

'But Charlie, I need pizza and my house is so empty,' Stevie wailed until she realised the thudding in her head was a dial tone, and Charlie had hung up some time ago.

'I am an independent woman capable of getting my own pizza,' Stevie said sternly to her reflection in the microwave door. She pulled her boots back on and was halfway out the door when she realised the walk to the pizza cafe would be much better if she had some wine on the way. She poured what remained of the wine into a sports drink bottle and headed down the stairs, holding on to the banister just to be safe.

It was only three blocks from Stevie's house to the pizza shop, but it felt like an epic journey. The sports bottle had got her thinking about more athletic pursuits, and Stevie decided that like any exercise, some music would help. Her headphones were pulsing with her favourite British girl-band pop songs from her workout playlist, which really put a spring in her step. She mouthed the words subtly, or at least that was what she thought she was doing, but those who passed her would definitely have heard the whisper-screamed lyrics of Girls Aloud.

While it felt like the wee hours of the morning to Stevie's starving stomach, in reality it was 8 pm and, in a neighbourhood full of uni students and young couples, it was prime Sunday dinner date time. The bouncy grooves of S Club Seven luckily kept Stevie feeling positive, and distracted her from the scowls she wanted to direct at every hand-holding twosome she passed.

Finally, the pizza shop loomed before her, the pimply youth behind the counter angelically bathed in the store's fluorescent lights. Stevie paused her one-woman silent disco to order a pepperoni pizza and some garlic bread.

'So, ya havinagood night?' Despite Stevie's best efforts at conversation, the kid was not up for a chat. When her third attempt at tapping her card finally succeeded, she turned to realise the shop was now full of queuing customers, all glaring at her. Shrugging,

Stevie sat down to wait at a plastic table facing out onto the street, and resumed her tunes. Accidentally meeting her own reflection in the shopfront window brought a harrowing sight: a wild-haired, wild-eyed woman bopping vacantly, her face haggard in the blue-grey cast of her iPhone.

Stevie shuddered, and an even worse vision swam before her: what looked like a freshly barbered Johnno, with a young, lanky blonde holding his hand. Great, now she was hallucinating her own version of *A Christmas Carol*. But the Johnno apparition was still there, and now waving. Oh God, it was not a ghost at all. He was coming in. *No, no, no, no—*

'Stevie, I forgot this was your local.'

'Hi, Johnno. What the bloodyhell are you doing here?' she asked, trying not to slur and surreptitiously lowering her drink bottle to the floor behind her. *Really*, she thought, *why are you here?*

'I've been doing some research and wanted to meet a bloke at UQ to ask a few questions,' he replied. 'We figured we'd make a weekend of it, do a bit of shopping and go out for dinner some-where other than the Royal. You remember Sarah?'

How could I forget? Stevie glowered.

'What's that?' Johnno said.

'Yes, I think I remember meeting Sarah at your twenty-first,' Stevie said, wondering if she was just verbalising all her thoughts with no filter now. 'And now you're all grown up. Nice to see you.'

'Hi, Stevie,' Sarah said shyly.

'You pull up okay from that concussion?' Stevie asked Johnno.

'Yep, no worries. What's a few more brain cells after all the ones we killed at the RE?' he chuckled.

Paula's voiced popped into Stevie's head, a singsong 'If you can't think of anything nice to say, don't say anything at all'. *Good idea,* she thought. The conversation ground to an unceremonious halt and as the awkward silence lengthened Stevie seriously considered leaving without her pizza. 'Are you guys going to order, or . . .?'

'Oh, we're going for dinner,' Johnno explained. 'Just saw you in the window and wanted to say hello. But you're right, we should make a move. Early start in the morning to drive home, you know.'

Sarah smiled awkwardly.

'Pepperoni and garlic bread for Steven,' the pimpled youth called, his voice cracking as he repeated, louder, 'STEVEN?'

'I think that's me.' Stevie leaped out of her seat. 'Well, I'll see you lovebirds around. Have a good time in the big smoke.'

'See you, Stevie,' Johnno said. He started to go in for a hug, then shifted, offering his hand instead. Stevie shook it awkwardly, then offered Sarah a handshake as well.

'STEVEN? Pepperoni?'

Truly the worst day ever, Stevie thought, glumly walking the three blocks home, the pizza box sweating in her arms. But at least there was pizza.

—

Sarah and Johnno were holding hands, swinging their arms as they walked down Coronation Drive after dinner. Johnno hadn't realised what a novelty sushi was for Sarah, but there was no Japanese restaurant in South Star, just a greasy Chinese. He forgot sometimes that she hadn't ventured far beyond their hometown – and she hadn't had much time to. At any rate, she'd given the chopsticks an admirable go. She was positively buoyant as they left the restaurant, though she hadn't been that way initially.

'I don't think Stevie likes me very much,' she'd said after they ordered. The waitress opened their BYO beers and Sarah sipped hers thoughtfully. 'I can't think why though. She met me when I was a kid.'

Johnno reached across the table and placed his big hand over her fingers, which had been fidgeting with her beer label. The gesture made Sarah look up and beam. 'Don't worry about Stevie,' he said. 'She wasn't herself this evening.'

He'd been trying to untangle the threads of her performance in the pizza shop. Obviously she wasn't sober, but she'd shown a mean streak he'd rarely seen from her. Underneath all that bravado and wine, she just seemed sad. Maybe something had happened with the bloke she was seeing. He hated to see her like that, but there was no reason for her to take it out on Sarah. That had hardened him, to see her scowl at innocent, sweet Sarah.

'Is there a bit of history with you two?' Sarah asked, clearly choosing her words carefully on a topic she'd been giving some thought to.

'Me and Stevie? No, she went out with Tom for years. Off limits!' He laughed awkwardly.

Sarah smiled, her relief palpable. 'Just seemed like she might be a bit jealous.'

'No way,' Johnno said. 'And if she got wind of you making comments like that, she would probably try to fight you.' They laughed together. Their food arrived, and the meal passed lightly in the way Johnno was becoming quite used to.

Which brought them to Coro Drive, holding hands. It still felt a bit like they were auditioning for something, playing the role of the happy new couple. Swinging their arms, Johnno felt like they were kids playing. And he did love that about Sarah, the way she made him feel light and young. At least until he was reminded again of their age difference, or the very real ties between their families that were not things to be played with.

There was also the matter of the double bed back at the motel they were booked into. Last night they'd had too much to drink and Johnno had passed out in his jeans as soon as he flopped onto the bed. But tonight there would be no such excuse. Johnno still wasn't sure how to handle it.

She was a beautiful girl, uncomplicated and hungry to be seen and desired in the way of 22-year-old girls. It would be easy to sleep with her, probably fun, and he did crave the closeness. But he was thinking all of this through very rationally, whereas if Stevie was the one lying next to him on a motel mattress, his nerve endings would all be live wires straining to connect with her. *That's the weight of history, though, right?* He also sensed that, much as Sarah wanted Johnno to want her, it wasn't necessarily the specifics of him that she was drawn to.

His thoughts were interrupted by a buzzing at his thigh, and Johnno unwound his fingers from Sarah's to pull the phone from his pocket.

'It's Kate,' he said to Sarah, surprise in his voice. 'She's barely spoken to me lately. I better take this, sorry.'

'Go on,' she said.

'Kate,' Johnno answered.

'How's the big smoke?'

'Fine. Busy. We'll be back by lunchtime tomorrow. How's everything there?'

'Well, that's why I'm calling.' Kate's voice was clipped, tired and cranky. 'Cam's been called away to drive a loader down south – another bloody useless worker's quit. We're going to need you back as soon as you can get here.'

'Like I said, I'll be back by lunchtime,' Johnno repeated, with a note of exasperation he immediately wished he'd controlled.

'I'd hate to cramp your social life,' Kate seethed, 'but unfortunately cattle still need to eat and be moved around even when you've got a hot date.'

'Understood. I'll see you tomorrow, early as I can. Text me if you need me to pick anything up on the way, okay?'

She grunted and hung up, and Johnno wondered if they'd ever fix this rift between them.

Instagram post by @StevieJeanLoveStories:

CHRISTINE & GAVIN, August 2019: Love and loss can't exist without each other, and this was a truly special ceremony that made space for both.

Have I mentioned how much I love wedding speeches? They're not the most dynamic part of a wedding to shoot, but the speeches are one of my favourite parts of the job. I'm endlessly impressed by how often you strike upon masterful orators in the bush. Sure, some just love the sound of their own voice. But others bring an eloquence that belies the dusty ways they spend their days. They might work with their hands, but their minds roam far and wide, thirsting for ideas and literature. Maybe it's the spirit of the bush poets lingering on. And the poems might be even better than the speeches – both memorised Banjo Paterson classics and meandering odes penned for the occasion and studded with inside jokes. The classic bush after-dinner speech is a blend of eloquence and earthy humour, emotion always seasoned with humour to make it easier to swallow, and a rousing finish to get everyone on their feet with glasses raised. Cheers!

19

Stevie was ready when the cream Mercedes arrived at the church. Christine's dad opened the passenger door and as he took his daughter's hand, the pride in his eyes started both of them tearing up. Stevie caught it all. Within seconds they'd wiped away the tears and lifted Christine's four-year-old son Sebastian out of the car. Stevie raced backwards to capture their walk into the church, hand in hand in hand.

This wedding was an emotionally charged one, Christine's second. Her first husband had died when Sebby was barely a year old, felled by a wicked melanoma that wrapped black tentacles around his organs. By the time they knew he was sick, they had just a month left with him.

Christine met Gavin at a school dance. He was a high school English teacher, delightedly brandishing a 30-centimetre ruler to separate teenage couples as had once been done to him; she was chaperoning a young niece. They got talking over plastic cups of red cordial. Maybe it was the fug of adolescent hormones, maybe it was the filthy R'n'B music, but she'd agreed to a date.

Now Gavin too had tears shining in his eyes, as Christine advanced up the aisle flanked by the other men in her life. Gavin was four years younger than Christine, and his friends had been surprised how easily he slipped into the father role with Sebastian. The change had been confronting for Gavin's best man, one Johnno West, who was currently trying not to stare at Stevie's rear preceding Christine up the aisle. As Stevie scooted sideways to capture the moment Christine's dad gave her away, Johnno caught her eye. They both looked away quickly.

'Dearly beloved. We are gathered here today,' the priest began.

Stevie scanned the guests; just as Christine had told her, her former husband's parents were there next to Christine's mum and dad, the two mothers holding hands. Stevie marvelled at the bonds love built.

A few pews further back, Stevie spotted Tom and her heart gave a minor lurch out of muscle memory. Of course all the boys from college would be here for Gavin. Next to him, Lily looked predictably stunning and offered a nod of recognition when she noticed Stevie staring. Stevie checked the rest of the guests, just in case, but Jen had made good on her threat to pull out at the last minute. *I really could have used someone to find the funny side of all the awkwardness that's no doubt coming this evening,* Stevie thought ruefully.

But there in a back pew, making up for his Blackall no-show, was Charlie. *At least someone here is on my side.* He looked gorgeous in his suit, not a hair out of place, and he offered a smouldering wink as he saw her looking at him.

'One, two, three,' Stevie screamed for what must have been the sixteenth time. These crowd shots were always more trouble than they were worth – it was a nightmare trying to fit all the guests on the front steps of the church while parents chased wayward toddlers, hats flew off in the breeze and stubborn gossipers refused to stop chatting. And she had to do it all while balancing precariously on a chair to get a high enough angle to keep everyone in the frame.

With that shot finally checked off the list, she'd have to race off very soon to the location for the bridal party portraits. 'Are you sure you don't want to come with me?' she asked Charlie.

'You don't have to babysit me, Stevie,' he said, looking like a catalogue model as he adjusted a cufflink. 'I know you have to work. I'll take Fred for a walk and play with him for a while, then head to the reception pre-drinks and find someone to chat to. Aunties love me.'

'I'm sure they do.' Stevie smiled, and kissed him on the cheek.

'Sorry to interrupt,' Johnno said, having trotted up the steps as the group dispersed, 'but are we heading off for photos now?' His voice was flat, and Stevie thought with shame of the last time they'd seen each other, under the unforgiving fluorescent lights of the pizza shop. Johnno also seemed rather unforgiving, which was going to make for a long afternoon.

'Yep, we'll be on our way in a few minutes. Johnno West – this is Charlie Jones. My assistant-slash-date.'

'Nice to meet you, mate,' Charlie said, offering a dazzling smile along with his hand. Johnno made some gruff sounds as he took it.

'Johnno, I know I wasn't in the best of form the last time we saw each other. You know how hangry I can get waiting for a pizza. Can you forgive me? We're stuck with each other for the rest of the night, so please don't be mad at me.'

He nodded. 'Truce.'

'Is Sarah here?' Stevie asked.

'Nah, didn't want to hassle Gav for a plus one late in the game,' Johnno said casually.

Charlie raised an eyebrow. 'Wait – John West? Like the tinned fish?' He giggled.

Johnno forced a laugh. 'Not my parents' finest hour.'

'At uni his nickname was the Salmon,' Stevie interjected, trying to lighten the mood.

'Not the Tuna?' Charlie asked.

'Nah, that was my best mate, Tom. He was the one pulling all the good sorts, the Tuner, while I was just battling my way upstream.'

'Adorable,' Charlie said. 'I suppose I'd better let you two get on with your duties.' He pulled Stevie in for a kiss that felt more ostentatious than necessary. 'I'll see you at the reception, babe.'

The reception was at the town golf club. The links were far from manicured. The greenskeeper did his best and the greens were impeccable, but the fairways were crunchy expanses of the beiges and browns that made up most of the western Queensland landscape these days.

But up at the clubhouse, alongside the river, the lawn was green and the beers were flowing. Arrangements of everlasting daisies studded the tables. Strings of fairy lights flickered on as the sun began to dip over the river.

The family photos were done and Christine and Gavin were mingling with their guests, never losing touch with each other. Stevie snapped a few frames; they stood back-to-back, each deep in conversation with other guests, but their fingers were secretly entwined behind them. Quietly Stevie stepped into a lull in their conversation and guided them away from the crowd.

'I want to try something quickly, while we still have the light. Do you trust me?'

'Depends if you're going to let me drive that thing,' Gavin said as they approached a golf cart. 'I've seen you drive, Stevie.'

'Gav, that was in college. But if you want to take the wheel, be my guest. I'll navigate.'

They zoomed sedately to a spot Stevie had cased the day before. It was off the fourth hole, a spot the greenskeeper must have picked out for his morning smoko break. A rustic bench was set in a clearing on the riverbank, gum trees arching overhead.

'Okay, you two just take a seat here,' Stevie directed. 'I'm going to back right up to get a nice wide shot. Don't feel like you have to pose, just keep turned slightly towards each other. Consider it my gift to you, a chance to actually be alone together before the party cranks up. If you want to have a little kiss, I won't tell anyone.'

Stevie paced back. Just as in her trial run yesterday, the sky had erupted into a hot riot of pinks. The water was still, pooling reflections of the gums and sky. She squeezed off wide shots, a few perfectly symmetrical, a few off-centre, some so zoomed out that Christine and Gavin looked like tiny dolls at the bottom of the frame with that sky endless above them.

Through the viewfinder she watched their gentle chat. Gavin rubbed Christine's shoulder as she wiped away a tear, still with a huge grin on her face. *What a bittersweet day this must be for her*, Stevie thought. Gavin ducked in to kiss Christine, and Stevie caught it. She moved back a little closer while they were distracted, and withdrew from her camera bag a cap gun she'd stolen from little Seb. She aimed it at the larger gum tree to the couple's left and fired.

The crack shattered the evening's stillness. In split seconds captured by Stevie's rapid shutter speed, a flock of galahs roused themselves from the gum tree and took flight across the sky, now bruising purple. Christine and Gavin turned first in shock, then delight, taking in the birds' deafening squawks. The shot might not work out, but Stevie had a hunch she'd nailed it. She just prayed there'd be no bird droppings rained down upon the bridal couple as she ran back towards them.

'Okay, you two – this time I'm driving. Or do you want to argue with my little friend?' she menaced, brandishing the cap gun with a giggle.

Stevie held a rueful hand over her glass of red wine as the waiter passed, conscious not to get too relaxed while she was still working. Charlie was exercising no such restraint. Stevie finished some last bites of roast potato and rich local beef, keeping an eye on the MC for the signal that the speeches were coming.

Leaning back to enjoy the last sip of her wine, Stevie felt a callused hand on her shoulder. It was, of course, Johnno, who had clowned around through all the bridal party photos, saving her from having to use her usual jokes.

'Stevie, have you got a line on when the speeches start? I need to duck out to the little boys' room before my big moment,' he said.

'You're good, Johnno. I've got eyes on the MC and, besides, the maid of honour will be up first anyway with a tear-jerker. Just crack a couple of serviceable jokes and the room will be yours.'

Charlie was watching their conversation shrewdly. 'Best man speech? Good luck, mate,' he said to Johnno. Stevie had never heard the word 'mate' sound like such an insult.

'Sorry, Charlie, I'm monopolising your date. How's your

night going? Are you managing all right out in the backwoods? I hope all the inside jokes don't get too boring for you.'

'Not at all. It's so wonderful to see Stevie in her element.' Charlie draped a possessive arm around Stevie's shoulder. 'Another bite, babe?'

He'd lifted the forkful of food to her mouth before she knew what was happening.

'Thanks, babe,' she swallowed.

Johnno looked nauseated.

Everything they were saying was ostensibly polite, so why did it feel like the air was full of blades? Johnno's hands caught Stevie's eye, folding and refolding a wad of ruled paper. She realised he was actually nervous.

'You'll be great,' she said gently. 'Remember to smile for your close-up.'

He almost jogged out of the marquee. A minute or two later, Stevie got the nod from the MC and left the table to get her camera out again. Given how emotional the ceremony had been, Stevie expected some moving speeches. The bridal party would be passing a microphone around at the head table, so Stevie secured a spot in front. She was going to get in a week's worth of squats trying to stay out of the sightlines of the guests behind her, though that would raise other challenges since no bride enjoyed a low-angled shot.

The MC introduced the maid of honour, who unfolded seven pages of single-spaced notes and placed a lace handkerchief within easy reach. *Lucky for Johnno*, Stevie thought. This would be a long one.

'Christine? It's my honour to stand here as your maid of honour. We've been through so much . . .' she began, before her voice cracked and the tears started. Luckily Stevie had got some early frames, because her handkerchief was now soaked and the ugly crying would not be welcome in the wedding album. Johnno tried to creep subtly in to his seat, prompting a look of daggers from the maid of honour; he sheepishly passed her his hanky.

Fifteen soggy minutes later, the MC introduced Johnno.

'Evening, ladies and gentlemen. As you can see, I'm the best man. Now, I'm going to keep this speech like a miniskirt: long enough to cover the essentials, short enough to keep your attention.'

As Johnno reeled off classic tales of their uni hijinks, Stevie saw him relax into the speech. He had an easy grace that somehow made even the filthiest anecdotes palatable to prudish aunts. She captured Christine in stitches, Gavin looking concerned, friends and family laughing. And the close-up she'd promised Johnno was easy: side angles of his tanned face, by turns animated, consternated and quietly smiling. With a slow shutter speed, his hands were a gesticulating blur, while his eyes were warm but still. Most blokes looked better in a tux, and Johnno was no exception.

As he finished with a toast to the bridesmaids, the crowd roared and whooped for him, and Stevie raised her glass with them. Charlie waited a beat before lifting his own.

'I didn't think I'd ever do this again,' Christine started, with a cordless mic over the bridal table. Johnno was back in his seat, enthusiastically applying himself to his beer, and Stevie was working an angle from the side of the marquee that took in a swathe of the guests' rapt faces looking at Christine.

'I thought I'd get married once, and spend the rest of my life with Sean. When Seb and I lost him, I figured that was my supply of love used up,' Christine continued. 'But just as I learned when Sebastian was born, there's no limit on our capacity for love.

As Seb grew, I found I could love him more and more. Even when I thought my heart was so full it would burst, it would swell a bit more the next day. And then when I met Gavin, I slowly realised that romantic love was something I could have again.

'Sean will be part of the rest of my life, just as I thought on our wedding day. He's here with us today . . . maybe looking down on us, but also in the kind and wonderful family who raised him, who are so generous to be celebrating with us today. We're forever bound together by our shared love of Sean, and now Sebby, and I'm so grateful for that.'

Sean's mother was smiling and nodding through tears, her husband rubbing her shoulder and clearing his throat. Stevie felt a lump in her throat, and even Johnno looked like he had something in his eye.

'When I realised that Gavin could make space for the role Sean would always have in our lives, especially for Sebastian, I knew I could get married again. I know people have said how unlucky, how unfair life was that I could lose Sean and be widowed at a relatively young age. But I know I'm lucky. To know love, and to have my heart swell a bit more each day. Maybe what's unfair is that I get to have two soulmates.

'Gavin, I love you. We love you. We're so lucky to have you in our lives, to welcome you into our family.'

Stevie still wasn't used to feeling all eyes on her when she was out with Charlie. Even stranger than everyone looking at them, however, was seeing her regular workplace – raucous bush weddings – through his wide city-boy eyes. As soon as the band started up, he'd pulled her onto the dancefloor, and the camera strapped to her wrist hadn't seen much action as he twirled and dipped her. He'd loosened his tie and was looking devilishly rakish; gliding past in Gav's arms, Christine fanned herself and winked at Stevie.

When the telltale riff of 'Eagle Rock' started up and trousers began to hit the floor, Charlie looked around in bewilderment. 'What's . . . happening here?'

'Do they not have this tradition where you're from?' Stevie giggled.

'Tradition is a generous way to describe a room full of pantsless men. Can we really do this in a post me-too world?'

'I always found it more tragic than threatening, as displays of masculinity go,' Stevie said. 'It's harmless.'

'Am I expected to join in?' he asked, looking alarmed.

'Whatever floats your boat, babe.'

He shook his head and pulled her away. 'Get me out of here.'

'That's an occupational hazard, I'm afraid,' Stevie said as they took a seat.

Charlie checked his phone before looking back and draping an arm around her. 'Are you all done?'

'No,' she said. 'Once everyone's zipped up again I'll need to take some more shots on the dancefloor.'

'I think I'll head back, then. Check on Fred. You can just come when you finish up.'

'No, stay! These are my friends, Charlie. We can dance all night.'

'Not if you're working. And anyway, I want you all to myself.' His pout was exaggerated for dramatic effect, but the guilt it prompted was real.

'But there's still people I wanted to introduce you to. Let me show you off. It'll be fun.'

'Nah, babe. I'm beat. See you back at the motel. I'll be waiting.' He kissed her and cleared out.

'Psst, Stevie.'

Stevie had just ducked back into the marquee after a solid half-hour of shooting on the dancefloor. She scanned the tables to place Johnno's voice. It was coming from the seat she'd been in earlier.

'I'm trying to protect this dessert for you, but the vultures are circling,' he stage-whispered, side-eying a plump aunt who happened to be passing. 'Take a load off.'

'Thanks,' Stevie said, sinking into the seat next to him. She still had a bit more work to do, but it felt good to get off her feet for a moment and cross her heeled sandals on the opposite seat.

Johnno nudged over a plate with a sunshine yellow slice of citrus tart. 'Nearly time to down tools?' he asked.

'Pretty much,' she responded thickly, swallowing a bite. The sugar was just what she needed. 'I caught little Seb's moves on the dancefloor before he had to go to bed. Might be good to get a few more of the guests letting their hair down.'

'So where's Charlie?'

'He's gone back to the motel. Taking care of Fred.' Stevie tried and failed to hold back a note of disappointment from her voice.

'I guess you two are pretty serious? Congratulations, Stevie.'

'Thanks?' *I don't recall asking for your blessing*, she thought, prickling.

'He's very smooth, isn't he?'

'How do you mean?' Her voice was light but carried a warning he couldn't miss. 'Well-groomed? An easy conversationalist? Impeccable manners?'

'No, he's great,' Johnno backtracked.

'If there's something you want to say, just spit it out,' Stevie said.

Johnno was flushed, and she could see him decide not to let it go. 'Just doesn't seem like the type I thought you'd go for. What does he know about the bush?'

'He knows nothing about the bush, Johnno. And you know what? That's really quite refreshing. What are we basing my "type" on, anyway? The last relationship I had, seven years ago? It didn't work out, as you might recall, and I haven't had a lot of options since then. So why not try something different?'

'It's just *very* different,' he said. 'And it's like you think you have to act different, be different, to be with this guy. "Oh, *babe*" and fawning over him and letting him bloody feed you. That's not who you are.'

'And you're the expert on who I am?'

'I know you, Stevie. I was there when you were trying on scenes and personas like dress-ups in college. The grungy music girl, the wild party girl, the country wife for Tom. The brash single girl who doesn't care what people think. Even now, on your Instagram, it's like you're always composing the perfect image of who you think people expect you to be. When you've never needed to change at all.'

'So you think I'm just a big fat fake?'

'That's not what I'm saying.'

'That's exactly what you're saying.'

'I know you, Stevie,' he repeated. 'I don't know why you hate me for it.'

'I never said anything about hating you,' she relented. She thought about apologising. But the longer she looked at his maddening, stubborn face, the more her anger returned. 'Forgive me if I find it a bit rich, being lectured on my romantic choices, while you're going out with a teenager your mum picked out for you. Have you told her you're planning on bailing back to London when things get too hard here? Or are you keeping her in the dark like your family?'

'Sarah's not a teenager, as you're well aware. And you really showed the merits of maturity when you met her at the pizza shop the other day, Stevie. You made it hard for me to explain to her why we're friends, after that performance.'

'What explanation did you come up with?' she asked. 'Because it doesn't really feel like we are friends, right now.'

'You're obviously very busy,' he said, standing up. 'I'll leave you to it. Better go make sure Gavin's glass is full.' And he hightailed it out of there, fists clenched.

Instagram post by @StevieJeanLoveStories:

ALEX & STEPH, August 2019: You know and love them from your TV screen, but there's even more romance between these two that never made it on camera. Until now! Thanks to my lovely assistant, Charlie, who doesn't believe in Instagram so I can't tag him, for making it a night to remember.

20

Kicking her boots under her seat in the QantasLink departure lounge of Brisbane Airport, Stevie tried not to check her phone again. Paula had already texted twice with photos of Fred vegging out – Stevie was going to be on the road for a couple of weeks, so Fred was on an extended holiday at Paula's. Their flight to Cairns wasn't due to board for another fifteen minutes and Charlie would waltz in any minute with a sheepish grin, she told herself.

Pulling the Network Six-branded folder out of her carry-on bag, Stevie ran through the paperwork again. There was a time line for the next four days, from the charter flight from Cairns to Alex's family property, through to the rehearsal dinner, the big day, and a recovery knees-up before the long journey home. There was a list of wedding guests, on which a Network Six assistant had flagged notable attendees to make sure she captured them. The *BB* producers were hoping to ignite some last-minute drama and had insisted on inviting all the girls Alex had rejected.

Six and *Ladies Day* had even supplied Stevie with a mood board of the kind of photos they wanted: willowy brides with mermaid hair staring wistfully out over rolling green hills; elegant tables of guests in black tie under starlit skies; starlets with smudged eye-liner and cut-off shorts skipping in gumboots through festival sites mushroomed with white tents. All well and good, but Stevie had a few ideas of her own.

She pulled out the notebook where she'd jotted ideas over a few beers with Alex and Steph a couple of weeks earlier. Alex had drawn her a mud map of the property, and Stevie had marked in the special spots he'd mentioned. She compared it to the aerial photographs Network Six had supplied, with squares and circles superimposed to indicate the reception marquee, the dancefloor, the tent village, the mess hall for crew, the vans for make-up, hair, and the editing team. They might have to be sneaky, but there should be time to get the personal shots Alex and Steph wanted without alerting the production team, and still cover off everything on the *Ladies Day* brief.

'Sorry, babe,' Charlie panted, rolling up with a sleek suitcase and holding out a bunch of roses. 'Client emergency.' He shrugged apologetically, sliding into the seat next to Stevie and planting a kiss on her cheek. His phone rang, and he frowned at the number before silencing it and pocketing the phone. 'They can wait. I'm all yours for the next four days.'

Stevie looked down at his pristine loafers and tiny bag.

'You brought some old clothes, right? Alex said he'd take us out to see the new calves and there's rain predicted, might get a bit muddy . . .'

'I'm ready for anything, Stevie. I'll carry your gear, carry you through the mud, whatever you need. It'll be an adventure.'

Stevie beamed back at him. 'I'm so glad we're doing this. You'll have the best time, promise.' He kissed her just as the PA dinged with the announcement that their flight was boarding. Between their thighs she felt his phone buzz again with another call.

He offered his hand and led her onto the flight.

A couple of hours later the chartered plane landed bumpily on the landing strip at Athelton. The flight had been rough, packed with production crew and an elderly aunt of Steph's who'd scored a ride. She had been noisily sick as the prop plane dropped and bobbed over a patchwork of paddocks, fields and bush below.

Carrying her gear bag along the landing strip to a row of waiting hired Land Rovers, Stevie felt her excitement building. The hues were elemental: bruised purple storm clouds, blood-red earth, views all the way to the horizon. *Yes, this will do very nicely.* Stevie felt a little shiver of anticipation at the conditions. 'Isn't it magnificent?' she breathed.

'I bloody hope dinner is better than whatever that was they served on the flight,' Charlie grumbled. But even his pissy mood couldn't deflate her.

'Are you hangry?' she teased. 'Don't worry, the feasts here are legendary. Although according to the schedule we'll have meals delivered to our tents tonight. We can put Six's catering to the test.'

Charlie grunted, the wheels of his fancy suitcase grinding in the red mud. At the sight of him, even with a heavy mood on his brow, a perky production assistant waiting at the cars lit up. She looked twenty-five, tops, and was smoothing her hair beneath a headset and smiling as they approached. Waving them over with a clipboard in one arm, she cried, 'I'm guessing from the gear you must be Stevie? I'm Pandora.' She offered her hand to shake but all of this was delivered to Charlie, who perked up a bit now someone was flirting with him. 'And you are . . .?' she asked.

'Charlie. Stevie's assistant,' he said, shaking Pandora's hand.

She was just indicating that they follow her into a Land Rover when a four-wheeler roared up. Alex was holding his hat with one hand and steering with the other. He parked and ran over to hug Stevie.

'Alex, this is Charlie,' Stevie introduced them.

'Great to meet you, mate,' Alex said, extending his hand. 'Pandora, would you mind taking Stevie and Charlie's bags back to their tent? I'd love to give them a little tour on the way. But we'll have to beat the storm.'

Pandora looked disappointed, but loaded the bags into the back and headed off.

Alex grinned once Stevie and Charlie were sat on the back of the quad bike, and gunned the engine. 'Hang on.'

'Is this sa—' Charlie's nervous question was swallowed by the roar of the engine and the wind whipping their hair as they took off. Stevie filled her lungs with humid, earthy air. When she saw the panic on Charlie's face though, she gave Alex a gentle pat on the back to slow him down. With the bike running slower, Alex filled Stevie in on how manic the past week had been with the network setting up the wedding venues and broadcast equipment.

'Your parents must be loving having a bunch of city slickers getting in the way,' Stevie said.

'Just wait, they'll tell you all about it,' Alex said.

'When are the guests arriving?' Charlie asked. The open paddocks were giving way to the mini-civilisation Network Six had set up, and the homestead was just visible a few hundred metres away. On their left, a row of tents came into view.

'Most people will get here the day after tomorrow,' Alex explained. 'Although a few people they want to film are landing in the morning. That includes Camilla and Shandi, which will be fun.' Both women had last been filmed tearfully boarding the flight to leave Athelton after Alex had told them he'd chosen Steph. 'I mean, they're lovely girls. I still feel bad they didn't enjoy the experience of the show. That said, I have no regrets about how things turned out,' he said.

He swung the four-wheeler in next to a tent. A little sign said 'Stevie Harrison', and their bags were neatly piled in front of it, beside a beaming Steph holding a bottle of champagne aloft. She hugged Stevie and kissed Charlie on the cheek.

'You must be Charlie. I've heard so much about you,' she said warmly. Alex put a proud arm around her and Stevie wished her camera wasn't in pieces in her bag.

'I'm guessing you're both beat after the flight,' Steph said, 'and I know they'll be dropping off your dinner pretty soon. We just wanted to leave you a little welcome present.'

'It's so special to be here with you both,' Stevie said. 'Thanks for making time to see us in – it must be crazy.'

'Well, we wanted to tee you both up for a little tour of the place in the morning,' Alex admitted. 'We'll have to get going early though, sneak out before the producers are up and nosing around. That okay?'

'What time's sunrise?' Stevie asked.

'About five forty-five,' Alex said.

'We'll meet you here at five fifteen,' Stevie said. 'I can't wait to see the light. Wear something you don't mind being photographed in.'

Steph kissed her on the cheek, then straddled the bike behind Alex before he took off towards the homestead.

Charlie was taking off his mud-caked loafers, looking bereft. 'Do we really have to get up at five am?' he moaned.

Once he'd showered and returned to the tent to find the caterers had delivered bowls of steaming curry and rice, Charlie was in a much better mood. 'Aw, isn't this nice?' he said, finding a hand-written note on a scrap of paper tucked into his bag. It was from Pandora, offering her assistance at any time of the day or night, along with her mobile number.

'Delightful,' Stevie said drily. 'Make sure you zip up the door all the way, okay? There's a few creepy crawlies around these parts.'

'Yes, ma'am. Now, as your dedicated assistant, is there anything I can help you with?' He sat behind her on the bed and started rubbing her shoulders.

'More of that would be very helpful, thank you,' she said, melting into the massage. She'd already packed a small bag for the morning, a workhorse camera body and lens to see what the morning light brought. 'Lucky I already set the alarm. We'd better get an early night.'

Charlie was slipping the straps of Stevie's singlet down over her shoulders. He leaned over and turned out the lamp. 'I suppose it's not all bad out here with no phone reception and nothing to do . . .'

'Nooo,' came Charlie's moan of protest when the alarm started bleating at 5 am. It was pitch dark inside and outside the tent.

'Come on, tiger, just throw on some clothes,' Stevie cajoled. 'Alex will be here in fifteen minutes.' She dressed, grabbed her gear and unzipped the tent, praying that Alex would bring coffee of some description. She heard the rumble of an old work truck approaching as Charlie finally emerged from the tent, looking sleep-tousled and adorable.

Blearily pulling on the shoes he'd left outside on the tent's small deck, Charlie suddenly gave a high-pitched squeal and leaped about five feet in the air. The loafer he'd hurled away in fright landed on its side, and from it sheepishly hopped a green tree frog.

'Always a good idea to shake your boots before sticking your toes in.' Stevie tried not to laugh, sensing Charlie was not in the mood to be teased. At least he was very much awake now, and Alex and Steph had missed his little freak-out.

'Come on, you two,' Alex called from the truck, idling with the lights on low. 'We need to get out of here before anyone from the network wakes up.'

Stevie and Charlie piled into the back seat of the dual cab and they trundled eastward, the first gilded crack of dawn peeking over the horizon. Steph poured coffee into chipped enamel mugs, which Stevie and Charlie accepted gratefully. As they drove, the sky lightened by tiny degrees of grey, and as their eyes adjusted to the gloom, they could just make out the country rushing by outside the windows. The dry grass was bejewelled with pearls of dew.

They must have driven for thirty minutes, none of them very chatty, before Alex stopped the truck. They were on a dirt track that sloped downhill towards a patch of gum trees.

'We can walk from here,' Alex said, leading them onward. Steph took his hand. 'Wet season, grass would be waist-high here.' Even in the dry season, there was still some grass around them, and sounds of munching and snuffling hinted at happy cattle nearby.

'Sounds like bloody Jurassic Park,' Charlie whispered to Stevie. She had taken her camera out of her gear bag and slung it over her shoulder, ready. After a short descent a waterhole was revealed, the rosy sky reflected in calm waters ringed with ancient rocks and eucalypts.

'It's perfect,' Stevie said, lifting the camera to her eye as Alex and Steph turned at the sound of her voice. 'For the benefit of Charlie, who's not a *Bush Bachelors* fan, can you explain the significance of this spot?'

'It's where we had our first kiss,' Alex said. 'Not that you would have seen that on the show.'

'This big softie kept trying to get us time away from the camera crews,' Steph explained. 'One day Shandi and Camilla were having a spat over something and the crew were so excited. They were like sharks smelling blood. And Alex grabbed my hand and whisked me out here. It was stinking hot, middle of summer, and we went swimming and . . .'

'I almost feel sorry for them that they didn't get it on film.' Alex smiled. 'In my head, it was the most beautiful moment. Maybe it wasn't. But now it's just ours and we can remember it how we want.'

Stevie nodded in understanding. Even though they weren't dressed in their wedding finery, this was the moment they wanted to capture and keep for themselves, before the circus took over.

'Well, you're not man and wife yet, but shall we do a few portraits here?' Stevie had been quietly taking shots all the while Alex and Steph had been telling the story of the place, the red sky shot with gold behind them. Over the next forty-five minutes she kept them talking, sharing sweet memories and their hopes for the future. When a couple of cattle wandered down to drink at the waterhole, Stevie got some final shots of the couple with a placid beast.

The sun was fully up, the light flattening, by the time they walked back to the truck. Steph unwrapped a tea towel of warm boiled eggs, which they peeled and ate with slabs of buttered bread. They had completed their secret mission just in time: as they packed up their food, they heard a small plane descend and land on the property.

'Here comes trouble,' Alex said, looking up through the

windscreen. He started giving Stevie and Charlie a tour, but within a half-hour, a helicopter buzzed overhead at the same time as a fleet of vans sped up to them. Camera crews piled out and started filming as the chopper hovered and landed.

'What's going on?' Charlie asked, and Pandora appeared with her clipboard to usher him out of the shot. From the helicopter spilled two glamorous women, high heels first.

'Oh God,' said Alex and Steph in unison as Camilla and Shandi minced their way towards them. It was an ambush. Stevie wished she had some popcorn. Alex squeezed Steph's hand and walked over to greet the women.

'Alex!' Shandi squealed, her voluptuous curves barely wrapped in a floaty silk dress. Her blonde hair was whipped every which way by the helicopter taking off again behind them. Next to her, Camilla, an auburn-haired ice queen in a structured sheath dress, twinkled her manicured fingers in a little wave to Alex. He kissed each woman on the cheek and welcomed them back to Athelton. There were three camera operators shooting the reunion from various angles, and one of them turned to train a lens on Steph for her reaction as Shandi wrapped a hand around Alex's bicep.

Stevie had been so caught up in the drama she hadn't noticed Charlie's agitation. 'They're not going to film us, are they?' he hissed.

'Don't see why they would,' Stevie said.

'Did you get the release forms?' Pandora asked. 'Obviously it's not about you guys, but the cameras are going to be rolling for the next couple of days. We can't risk missing anything good.'

Alex was leading Camilla and Shandi over to Steph. There was a flurry of air kisses and death stares until Camilla looked in Stevie and Charlie's direction and did a double take.

'Charlie?'

21

'What are you doing here?' Camilla asked, genuinely bamboozled.

'Do you know her?' Stevie asked, confused. But Charlie's attention was focused on the cameras inching closer and closer to capture his reaction.

'I do not consent to being filmed, you cannot use this footage,' he was saying. And then, to Camilla, 'I'm sorry, have we met?'

'Are you serious?' came Camilla's incredulous reply.

'What is going on?' Stevie, Steph and Alex asked in unison.

'Search me,' Charlie said. 'I don't know this girl.'

'Unbelievable,' Camilla spat, turning on her heel. Shandi put an arm around her and they hobbled off together towards the production crew's tent.

'Is he serious about not signing the release?' a furious producer was asking Pandora, who was frantically flipping through her clipboard.

'Charlie,' Stevie asked. 'What was that?'

'I genuinely have never met that woman,' he said, pulling her away from the scene. 'She must have mistaken me for someone else.'

'Someone with the same name?'

He shrugged. 'I don't know what to tell you. But I swear it's a misunderstanding. Stevie, have I given you any reason not to trust me?'

Stevie paused, thinking of the man she'd seen power walking away from her down James Street. Maybe Charlie had a doppel-ganger? 'This is so weird' was all she could say.

'Let's not let it derail us. I'm finally getting to see you work and you're amazing – that's what's important. The way you managed Alex and Steph this morning, keeping them moving and relaxed and so focused on each other . . . You're so talented, Stevie.'

'I've had a fair bit of practice,' she said, but the truth was she had spent years refining her technique with couples, and Charlie's flattery landed in the sweet spot of praising something she was proud of.

'You guys okay?' Alex approached cautiously.

'Just a misunderstanding,' Charlie said, but Alex was watching Stevie's face.

She nodded. 'All good.'

'Good,' Alex said. 'We're going to have to head back to the homestead to get ready for the rehearsal dinner. I'm sorry to cut our tour short, Charlie.'

'No problem,' he replied. They piled back into the work truck and Alex and Steph chatted lightly until they dropped Stevie and Charlie back at their tent.

That night Charlie begged off the dinner with a headache, but Stevie couldn't afford to miss the opportunity to meet so many of the key players ahead of the wedding. The night passed quickly, Stevie meeting Alex's and Steph's parents and the wider family. She thanked Alex's parents for their hospitality.

'Can't wait for the bloody vultures to piss off,' Alex's red-nosed dad said with the frankness of most of a bottle of red wine, 'but at least we're not footing the bill.'

The Network Six crew were filming at the rehearsal dinner, but seemed most focused on Camilla and Shandi. A producer was constantly whispering to them, but thankfully Camilla didn't have any further outbursts about Charlie. The cameras were also trained on Alex and Steph, so Stevie naturally featured in the action as she talked to various family members.

'Stevie, can we get you speaking to camera briefly?' Pandora asked. 'The viewers will be seeing a bit of you as the wedding photographer, so it would be great if you could introduce yourself.'

Stevie had dressed and done her make-up with care, knowing she might be filmed. But by this point she had had a couple of glasses of wine. She was tipsy enough that she felt quite confident going in front of the camera. 'Where do you want me?'

Pandora guided Stevie in front of a simple background and pointed out a mark for her to stand on. 'Just look down the barrel of the lens like you're looking at a friend, and tell us a little about who you are and why you're here,' she instructed.

'I'm Stevie-Jean Harrison,' she started, and for some reason the face she imagined speaking to was Johnno's. It worked though, and her face relaxed into a smile. 'I feel pretty weird being on this end of the camera, because I'm here as Alex and Steph's wedding photographer. I shoot a lot of bush weddings, but this is my first with a camera crew. It's gotta be the best job in the world, getting to capture people's most special day, telling their love stories, in the most beautiful country in the world. Really, these are the relationships that keep regional Australia alive. So as you watch Alex and Steph's wedding you might see me here and there, taking photos.

But hopefully I'll fade into the background for you, and for them, because I want them to be fully focused on each other, relaxed, thinking of all the reasons they love each other, having a day they'll never forget.' She paused. 'Was that all right?'

Pandora nodded. 'You got that?' she asked the cameraman and the guy holding a fuzzy boom microphone over Stevie's head, who gave a thumbs up.

'Are you a romantic then, Stevie?' the bloke behind the camera asked. 'Are you married?'

'I'm not married,' Stevie said. 'But of course I'm a romantic – how could I not be? That said, I've kissed a lot of frogs before finding any-one resembling a prince. I was starting to think I'd met all the blokes in Australia and there was no one for me. But . . . yeah, there might be someone.' She grinned. 'Okay, that's got to be enough, surely?'

'Yep, you're free,' Pandora said.

Stevie said her goodnights and headed back to the tent.

'You feeling better?' she asked Charlie, handing him a piece of cake she'd wrapped up at dinner.

'You're so sweet.' He smiled, tucking in to the cake. 'Yeah, I'm feeling much better. C'mere.' He opened up his arms and enfolded her. She nestled in. 'Everything all set for tomorrow?'

'I should run over the time line one more time, check my gear, wash my face.' She stifled a yawn.

'You've had a long day, babe. I'll set the alarm and we can get some sleep,' he said. Stevie's eyes were already closing.

Stevie woke with a start but it was still early, with plenty of time for her to get ready before starting her work shooting Steph and the bridesmaids getting ready. Already the tent city was a hive of activity, with black-clad Pandora clones racing around with their clipboards and headsets.

The day went off without a hitch, despite the producers' best efforts to ignite a dramatic meltdown between Alex, Camilla and Shandi. Shandi clearly had her eye on the best-looking groomsman and Camilla also seemed distracted, but Stevie didn't even see her look in Charlie's direction. Charlie proved himself a helpful camera assistant and Stevie enjoyed having someone else to lug her gear for once.

Late in the evening, Stevie finally put her feet up and beamed as Charlie brought her a slice of cake and a glass of champagne.

'You've earned these, babe,' he said, and she was feeling so pleased with how everything had gone that she let him feed her a forkful of cake. 'I knew you worked long hours but I had no idea how intense this would be. You're incredible.'

The bubbles were deliciously cold and Stevie could feel them going directly to her head. 'I think we did good today,' she said, reaching out her fingers to play with the collar of Charlie's dress shirt.

'Can I assist you with anything else, babe?' he breathed. Stevie was vaguely aware of a camera by the next table but Charlie was already kissing her, and it was very nice.

'Mmm. I should probably get a few last photos on the dancefloor,' Stevie protested what could have been seconds or hours later. Charlie eventually freed her from his embrace, but not before peppering kisses over her neck and shoulders.

The Network Six cameras got their last shots of Stevie-Jean Harrison whirling on the dancefloor with toddlers and great-aunts, in the thick of the action as young and old danced the night away. They caught her proud grin as Alex and Steph hugged her in thanks before they stole away from the party. And she was radiant as she winked at the camera. 'Best job in the world.'

22

Things had been tense since Johnno arrived back at Haven Downs a week ago. Even though he'd made Sarah get up at 2 am to leave Brisbane after Kate's cranky call, making sure he'd be home by mid-morning, Kate was implacable.

'Good luck,' Sarah had murmured as Johnno dropped her home. Their night in the motel double bed in Toowong had passed restlessly, both of them hyper alert to the other's tiniest movements, but neither confident to make a first move. Johnno had felt paralysed, weighed down by everyone's expectations about what he should do – not just Sarah, but his parents, his friends . . . It just didn't feel quite right. When he finally drifted off to sleep, it seemed like the alarm was going off seconds later. But he'd been on the other side of the bed, gently spooning Sarah, his chin tucked into her shoulder and her hands holding his.

'I'm sorry it put a damper on our last night away,' Johnno apologised through the open driver's side window. Standing outside, having collected her bag as he idled the engine, Sarah was tall enough to be at his eye level.

'No need to apologise,' she said. 'But make it up to me soon, okay?

See you at tennis?' Johnno felt a rush of affection for her and reached out to tuck a stray strand of blonde hair away from her face. Before he knew what was happening, they were kissing. It was gentler than the mauling after their first date, either because she didn't want to spook him, or maybe just because she was sober this time. Johnno felt aware of every sensation, the mechanics of teeth and tongues and lips, but the fact that he'd kissed her without agonising over it was the most reassuringly natural development between them in weeks. He broke away gently, had to clear his throat before he could speak.

'Yeah, see you at tennis.' The smile Sarah gave him was dazzling and he matched it. It was only at the Haven Downs mailbox that he remembered what he was coming home to, and the smile faded. He half-expected Kate to be waiting on the verandah for him, arms crossed tightly across her chest, looking at her watch and tapping a foot impatiently. But he didn't even see her for dinner that night.

Rod was laid up with the bad back that had plagued him in recent months, another strain on their resources when they were already missing Cam.

'You and Kate are going to have to pull together this week,' Rod said. 'There'll be the feeding each day, and we're due to get some more bales dropped off the day after tomorrow.'

Johnno nodded. 'Righto.'

'There's rain on the radar,' Rod continued. 'Cloud building up until Friday, when it looks like we might actually get some showers. We'll see, but I'd be keen to have you move the heifers out of the windmill paddock. You know how it gets boggy.'

The next morning Johnno met Kate at her cottage. She was sitting on the front verandah as he pulled up, and when she saw him, she pulled on her boots and grabbed her hat.

'Ready to crack into it?' he asked. 'I brought coffee . . .'

At her nod he poured her a cup in the thermos lid, and she held it between both hands as he drove. And aside from the occasional shout to get his attention, she maintained a stony silence with him all week. They hauled hay, dropped feed from the ute as stock cantered behind them, checked fences and bores, found and fed poddy calves. And they spoke about six words to each other. Like the barometric pressure building inexorably towards the rain that was forecast for that day, they were building towards something. And just as the parched earth cried out for moisture, they both knew something had to give.

They were moving the heifers as Rod had requested, getting started far later than they'd intended to. The morning's feed had been a comedy of errors. First the gate got stuck, then the starving mob swarmed the ute and Johnno lost control of the hay. He had to try to wrestle the bale back from the dozens of hungry sets of teeth trying to tear into it. Then Rabbit caught a whiff of a wild dog and bolted, and it took nearly an hour to get her back.

Now the clouds wrapped around them, dark and dolorous. Johnno and Kate had left the work ute in their destination paddock and were on motorbikes to herd the mob. They only had to drive them a few hundred more metres through the gate, but the cattle were unsettled and antsy, like they were jazzed by the weather as well. Kate's working dog Ziggy was rounding up the stragglers when the first bolt of lightning flashed. Seconds later came a boom of thunder so loud it seemed the sky might crack in two, and all hell broke loose. Fat drops of rain began pelting them, and spooked cattle ran in every direction.

—

It took some coaxing, but the flame from the newspaper Johnno had found behind the seat of the ute finally caught on the damp leaves and sticks he'd gathered. The camp fire was still far from a done deal – the wood they'd been able to gather was wet from the storm earlier – but hopefully the damp didn't go too deep and it would smoke for a bit before catching. Johnno kept breathing on the flames to keep them alive, cupping his hands protectively around the tiny blaze like he was back at a school desk with Jim Dyson trying to copy his spelling test.

'Couple of tea bags, tin of beans, four pieces of bread, a muesli bar, two apples,' Kate said, counting out the contents of her esky. 'There's plenty of water at least, but the dogs will be going hungry tonight. Christ, what a shitshow.'

'Aw, come on. It's not so far from the old days when we used to camp out in the school holidays,' Johnno said, looking up from his little fire to see that it was getting dark fast.

'Just without the cute packed dinner from Mum, the warm dry swags and the marshmallows,' Kate scoffed.

'I'll rig up a tarp over the tray of the ute in case there's more rain, but if it gets too cool you can sleep in the cab,' Johnno said. 'The dogs'll be right for a night. We'll be up as soon as it's light, and I've got an old billycan we can use to make some tea. Bit of fencing wire to make a fork and we'll have toast and beans – a proper cowboy dinner, eh?'

'Yeah, all right,' Kate grumbled, but he could sense her mood lifting, finally.

It was well and truly dark by the time they'd set up the tarp, settled the dogs and checked what blankets, rags and food they'd have for their night out. Johnno had radioed to the homestead that they wouldn't be back until morning, Rod gruffly muttering that they'd be cold and hungry, but agreeing it was better than getting bogged trying to rush home.

After wishing his folks goodnight, Johnno found Kate tending the fire, the flames leaping twice as high and licking at a steaming log. 'Now we're cooking with gas,' he said happily, pulling out his billy and filling it with water from the cooler.

'Just needed a bit of tough love,' Kate said. 'You can't baby a fire, just gotta give it a chance to burn what you need it to.'

Johnno bit down the urge to argue. At least she was talking to him. 'So how much longer until Cam can get home?'

'Another week, last he reckoned. I tried to get him on the two-way before but no dice. And my text hasn't gone through. He shouldn't be too worried about me, though.'

Kate had set up the fire so there was a clear spot for the billy to nestle between two logs, and Johnno set it there to boil. He pulled his big esky closer to the flames and sat down wearily. 'What's it like, being married?' he asked. 'I mean, does it feel different to when you were going out?'

Kate started. 'Jesus, things aren't moving that fast with Sarah Childs, are they?'

'God no,' Johnno cried, the terror in his wide eyes making Kate laugh again, not without some relief. 'Just a general philosophical question. It doesn't really feel like I'll ever have that.'

'You will,' Kate said. 'It's hard to define . . . Getting married doesn't change anything tangible. I s'pose it means something real in terms of the law, and money. People say it's just a piece of paper, but there's something more to it. You don't necessarily feel it when you wake up that first day after the wedding. But it's a kind of security, peace . . . You know that for all the stuff that will happen to you, all the hard stuff you'll have to deal with, this person will be with you.'

'That sounds pretty good,' Johnno said.

'I wouldn't recommend rushing into a wedding in search of that feeling,' Kate said drily. 'I don't know if it's the same for everyone. And there would be people out there who feel it without having to get married. But to me it was like an extension of how I felt when I met Cam. Like something was settled, so life could really start.'

'You old romantic.' He grinned.

'Piss off.' She threw a handful of mud just to the left of his head. He knew it would have connected if she'd wanted it to. 'It's not like I went out with that many blokes,' she continued. 'But I just remember it as this constant niggling. All this energy that would get burned up worrying, "Does he like me? Do I like him? Is this what it should feel like?"'

'That's familiar.'

'And then I met Cam, and all that wasted nervous energy just stopped. Like, oh, *this* is what it should feel like.'

'You just knew?'

'I mean, there was excitement and I'm probably remembering it now as easier than it was.' Kate flicked the wet mud off her fingers. 'But for the most part I was sure he felt the same way, and it just made all that stress and insecurity seem silly. At a certain point you just have to trust that it feels right, that it can be that easy, and just enjoy it.'

Johnno thought about how much of his recent days was spent agonising over what to do about Sarah, or what to text her. Or reliving that night outside the motel with Stevie, trying to figure out what had made her pull back, whether he should have pushed harder.

'So how is it going with Sarah, really?' Kate asked.

Johnno sighed. 'She's so sweet. And she makes me laugh, and

makes me feel good. Except when something reminds me how young she is and I feel ancient!'

'You poor blokes have it so tough.' Kate rolled her eyes. 'How's the . . . y'know?'

'Yeah, we haven't . . . y'know.' Johnno stuttered, and Kate raised her eyebrows. 'It just . . . hasn't felt right.'

'No chemistry? That's not a good sign, little brother.'

'Ugh, it's so weird talking about this with you. There are moments of chemistry, but I think the vibe is too brotherly. I keep getting all up in my head about what it means if we hook up and then I leave her high and dry. Can't exactly ghost the girl from next door.'

Kate nodded. 'That's not dumb. But . . . it just sounds like your brain is doing all the work. And in my experience . . . you know it's real when your heart and your other bits don't wait to give your brain a chance to get involved.'

Johnno's brain immediately started playing its well-worn high-lights reel of the night he'd grabbed Stevie and dropped his pie. He groaned. The billy lid started rattling as the water finally came to the boil.

'Ah, you know the feeling,' Kate said, as he busied himself grab-bing the billy off the fire with a set of pliers so he didn't burn his hands. 'And it's not Sarah you feel it with.'

'No,' he admitted, lifting the billy lid and dunking in their two tea bags. 'I think I've been hoping that it might develop with Sarah. But the person I don't have to force it with isn't interested.'

'How do you know?'

'There have been . . . opportunities, and she's stopped things before they could go anywhere.'

Kate rolled her eyes. 'We're talking about Stevie, right? Yes, Johnno, you're that obvious,' she said as he looked at her in surprise.

'She's with someone else,' he said.

'So are you,' Kate shot back. 'And I wouldn't be so sure she's not interested. Have you told her how you feel?'

He let this hang for a moment, the absurdity of a woman asking a man from western Queensland whether he'd taken an opportunity to be emotionally vulnerable, and they both cracked up laughing.

'No, not explicitly. But I've flirted with her. She can't have missed the fact I can't take my eyes off her whenever I see her. And . . . I kissed her, a few months back. After a big night and lots of beers, when she stayed in town after a job here. I thought it was finally happening. But she cut it off.'

'The plot thickens. I knew something must have happened,' Kate said, prompting a quizzical look from Johnno. 'Did she kiss you back, or did she stop it straight away?'

He winced; it felt wrong to be talking this through with his sister. But who else was he going to process it with? Not Sarah, certainly not Tom, and Rabbit still wasn't talking back.

'She kissed me back. I was sure she felt something. It was like a school dance make-out, you know? Where you could have been pashing for hours? But without the braces and bad technique.' They both giggled. 'But yeah, nah, she laughed it off and sent me home. But what do you mean, you knew something had happened? Because I was moping around?'

'No, it was her performance at Ladies' Day. Her reaction when you got knocked out – it was just a bit odd. You probably don't remember it.'

He shook his head. 'That evening is a blank in my memory.'

'She was quite upset . . . She was fronting like she was cranky about something someone said, but I got the feeling she was thrown by how she felt when you got hurt. You know it was her who called Paula to take you to the hospital?'

Johnno vaguely remembered feeling confused in Paula's back seat. 'I guess I never put that together.'

'Gawd, what a pair you are. Well, what are you going to do about it?'

'She's seeing this Charlie bloke – I'm not a grub,' he protested. 'Besides, the more pressing issue is Sarah.'

Kate threw her head back, laughing at his dilemma. 'No wonder you're so bloody delighted to be stuck out here cut off from everyone,' she teased. 'Now, are you going to pour me a cuppa or what?'

Every last skerrick of bean sauce had been mopped up with fire-blackened toast, and both Johnno and Kate were glad their etiquette-strict mother hadn't been there to see how they'd eaten with no plates or utensils. Johnno had opened the driver's side door so they could hear the late-night country music show, twangy old-fashioned songs that crackled with the thick fuzz of AM radio. They were boiling another billy to make one last cup of weak tea before trying to sleep.

A soft rain was falling. Not enough to threaten the fire, although it was slowly soaking their clothes. But it was comfortable enough and neither wanted to disturb the tentative peace that had formed between them.

'These old songs are something else,' Johnno said. 'You'd never know if they were recorded last week or in the thirties.'

'Life doesn't change much for the old cowboys,' Kate agreed. 'Whether your dog's died, your wife's left you or the rain won't come, it's the same misery, decade after decade.'

'What a life to look forward to,' Johnno joked. He grabbed the tea bags that had been drying on a rock near the fire, added them back to the pot, and rinsed out their enamel mugs. 'But seriously, Kate – I've been thinking a lot about this. Mum and Dad have it all wrong. It shouldn't be me taking over Haven Downs.'

Kate was sitting on a low esky, craned forward looking at the fire with her elbows on her knees and her chin in her hands. She looked up across the fire at Johnno. 'What are you saying?'

'I'm saying we need to go to them, together, with Cam, and tell them the people who should be taking over management of the property have been here all along.'

Kate was quiet.

'Don't tell me you haven't thought about it,' Johnno said. 'I bet you know exactly what you'd do. From tomorrow morning until September next year and ten years down the track, if you were in charge.'

'I do,' she said simply. 'But they haven't listened before. Why would they listen now?'

'Because we'll make them listen,' he said. 'Have you costed your plans? Do you have numbers?'

'Just some back-of-the-envelope stuff. For starters, if we bought a Droughtie bull to put over the Angus herd, that'd inject more hardiness in them while we ride out this drought. We'd need a loan from the bank, but if my projections are right, we'd have it all paid off within two years.'

'That's perfect,' Johnno said. 'We'll get it all drafted out, then when Cam gets back you can go over it all with him. And then we'll sit Penny and Rod down in a couple of weeks so they can start getting used to the idea before it all goes to the lawyers.'

'And what are you going to do? They'll be gutted to see you go again,' Kate said.

'Well, I'd love to stick around, if you'll have me,' he said. 'There are a few ideas I want to put to you, around water management and trialling some small crop rotations to regenerate the soil a bit. If you let me clean up the old barn, I could use that as my base, get out from under Mum and Dad's roof for all our sanitys' sake. And you can use me for labour in the meantime.'

'You're serious? You're not going to change your mind on this?' Kate asked. 'We can't wait much longer to start having kids, so we need to be able to make long-term plans.'

'I know,' he said, 'and I'm sorry if my indecision has kept you from doing things you wanted to do. I'm not going to change my mind. My old boss in London was holding a position for me but I've told her I'm not coming back. I should have done it a long time ago.'

Kate nodded.

'If I'm honest, I could never really see myself doing what Dad does. I love the land and the animals, but the day-to-day is grinding me down. I feel like I can be making more of a difference at a planning level, and the stuff I've started looking into, regenerative and holistic farming practices – I think it can really make people's lives better out here. I'll need to do a lot more research but I reckon I could get into some consulting work.'

'Well, you don't have to ask me twice,' Kate said. 'And I won't make you spit swear, but how about a cuppa and a handshake to seal the deal?'

They'd both woken at first light after an uncomfortable sleep, but the continuing soft rain and the afterglow of their productive night's conversation cancelled out any morning grumpiness. With the dogs and the bikes safely on the back of the ute, they'd headed home, letting the morning news bulletins do the talking. When Johnno dropped Kate back at her cottage, she nodded and gave him a tight-lipped smile.

'Thanks, Johnno. I'll let you know when I have something drafted and we can chat about it from there, hey?'

'You bet. Give my best to Cam when you talk to him.'

He walked into the homestead, muddy and stinking of smoke but purposeful. Penny and Rod looked up over their instant coffees as if noticing it too.

Johnno caught his mother's whisper as he stripped off his soggy work clothes in the laundry. 'I knew it would sort them out, a night camping.'

'I'll run that washing, Mum,' he called back to the kitchen. 'Just gonna have a quick shower, then I'll take care of it. Don't you touch it.'

'Okay, love,' she called, and he heard the smile in her voice, his father's grunt in response.

That night their Sunday roast wasn't as boisterous as usual, with Cam still away, but it was more relaxed and convivial than it had been in weeks. Penny nattered away with all the news from her elder daughters and their kids. She and Rod were planning a trip to Brisbane to visit Sandra and her brood, which had grown with the arrival of twins a few weeks earlier.

'We'll be back two weeks today,' Penny said as they all scraped the last of the custard and apple pie from their bowls.

'Don't run the place into the ground while we're away,' Rod grumbled.

'All right, I'll cook the roast that night you get back,' Johnno said. 'Cam will be here and we'll have the whole gang together again.' Kate shot him a grateful smile.

'Fine by me,' Penny said. 'Now, I'm going to leave it to you two to wash up. Alex and Steph's wedding is on TV at eight-thirty.'

'Mum, don't tell me you're still a *BB* tragic,' Kate teased.

'Go on, Kate. I know you're obsessed as well,' Johnno said. 'I'll wash up.'

'Whatever you did to him out there last night, I like it,' Penny stage-whispered. Rod harrumphed but quietly followed them into the lounge. Johnno knew he had a soft spot for the show as well.

Johnno was just scrubbing the last stubborn spots on the roasting tray when Penny called out. 'Isn't this your friend, Johnno, on the TV? The photographer?'

He wandered into the lounge still wearing the pink rubber gloves, trailing dish-soap bubbles. 'What are you on about, Mum?'

And there was Stevie's face on the flatscreen. She was rosy-faced, a couple of wines deep if he knew her at all, but she was radiant. The camera cut to shots of her working the room at a dinner, not formal enough for a wedding; it must have been the rehearsal. She was kissing cheeks and giggling with young and old, the Harrison charm at full wattage. Johnno had met Alex through friends once or twice and recognised his parents, too.

'She looks well, doesn't she?' Penny clucked. 'Would you bring me a cuppa, darling?'

'Just a sec, Mum,' Johnno said, as the camera cut back to a tight shot of Stevie, looking down the lens with a mix of shyness and good humour, with text flashing up to identify her as the wedding photographer. Stevie was telling the camera about her job.

'I'm not married. But of course I'm a romantic – how could I not be? That said, I've kissed a lot of frogs before finding anything resembling a prince. I was starting to think I'd met all the blokes in

Australia and there was no one for me. But . . . yeah, there might be someone.' The glittering *Bush Bachelors* logo twinkled on screen before a commercial started shouting at them.

'Ooh, is she going to get a storyline? Johnno, bring the chocolate,' Penny shouted.

'I'll take some popcorn,' Kate said, winking.

'You're all mad,' Johnno said. But he rushed to finish the washing-up and make his mum's tea so that he could keep watching. Setting a block of Toblerone on the coffee table, he flopped into a recliner and started flipping through a book to feign lack of interest, as Penny and Kate oohed and squealed at Alex's former flames disembarking from a helicopter to confront him.

'Ah, there she is,' Kate said. 'And that must be—'

Bloody Charlie, Johnno thought dejectedly. He had to admit they looked good together.

'But how does she know him?' Penny was asking.

'He's acting like she doesn't,' Kate said, 'but look how shifty he is!'

Johnno realised they weren't talking about Stevie, but the tall redhead blinking out from under bombshell lashes.

The cameras focused on the girl's reaction rather than Stevie's, and Johnno wondered what had happened next. He and Rod soon gave up any pretence that the show didn't have their full attention. They watched as the wedding unfolded, with occasional glimpses of Stevie capturing the action and Charlie carrying her gear. After Stevie backed down the aisle shooting Alex and Steph's joyous walk out as husband and wife, the Six cameras caught Camilla pulling Charlie aside and into what looked like a production tent. He emerged a few minutes later and jogged after Stevie, while Camilla took a few more minutes to come out, smoothing down her dress.

'Oh my God,' Kate said.

The light shifted and the action moved to the reception, Alex giving a heartfelt speech that brought Steph and his mum to tears. Stevie even looked like she was wiping her eye as she crouched down to take photos of him in action. But the show's focal point shifted unexpectedly away from the speeches and again found Camilla pulling Charlie outside.

This time the crew were able to keep them in sight, and though they hovered far enough away that Charlie and Camilla weren't aware they were being filmed, a boom mic picked up their discussion. The editors had even subtitled the eavesdropped conversation so viewers wouldn't miss a treacherous word.

Johnno watched in horror, along with most of Australia, as Charlie made it very clear he did indeed know Camilla in the most intimate sense. After some heated conversation, when he assured Camilla that his relationship with Stevie was fading, and he dodged Camilla's questions about why he hadn't contacted her, she relented and melted into his arms.

'That rat!' Penny shouted, banging her teacup on the coffee table in disgust.

But the worst was still to come, when Charlie, cool and unruffled, swept an unsuspecting Stevie off her hard-working feet with a glass of champagne. He fed her cake and she kissed him like she was the luckiest girl in the world. Johnno felt sick, and then his phone buzzed with a text from Sarah.

OMG. Your friend Stevie just got cheated on, on national TV. (Monkey emoji, eggplant emoji, crying emoji)

'Oh God,' Kate said, looking up from Facebook on her phone. 'People are going off. Stevie's a meme! I wonder if she knew what they were putting to air?'

Instagram post by @StevieJeanLoveStories:

YASSOU! I'm off the grid for a destination wedding. Can't wait to see @_Tallulah_Swift_ and @DeclansDecks all dolled up. Hope I don't make an ass of myself.

23

Stevie was sitting side-saddle on a donkey that was picking its way along a cobbled street on a Greek island, with no idea that her face was becoming recognisable across Australia. She handed her phone to the farmer she'd hired the donkey from, trying to explain via charades and some very terrible Greek that she wanted him to take her photo. When he finally handed it back, he'd saved his number with a heart emoji, but thankfully he'd got a shot as well. Stevie knew it would look fantastic on Instagram, her straw hat, sandals and white linen dress striking against the village's whitewashed buildings and olive trees. The reality of being sweatily perched on an animal that was somehow both viciously angry and too lazy to move was less picturesque, but no one needed to know that.

As she cut her losses and hopped off the donkey, Stevie congratulated herself for her travel planning. She'd allowed herself a full two days to relax and explore before the destination wedding she was shooting on Wednesday. Sure, things were a little tighter on the way out, with a complex patchwork of ferries, buses and flights to get back to Brisbane with a night's rest before a Saturday wedding booking near Mungindi. But that would be fine.

For now she still had the rest of the day to herself on Sifnos before meeting the bride and groom, Tallulah and Declan, for a drink in the evening. She'd even done a cooking class the day before, and hiked out to the remote church where the wedding would be held. It was going to be spectacular – a tiny, ancient stone chapel out on a wind-buffeted cliff, starkly white against the azure shades of the sea.

'Efharisto,' Stevie said, thanking the farmer as she popped her phone back into her bag. Posting the picture would have to wait until she had some wi-fi, most likely when she got back to Athens for her flight home. She hadn't bothered organising a local SIM card for her phone and had switched off roaming, having been burned before by astronomical data charges. Besides, a few days unplugged from the world would do her good. It already had.

As her sandals trod over ancient stones and she breathed in sea air laced with the fragrance of rosemary, smoke and coffee, Stevie forgot about editing work and spreadsheets. She forgot about speeding fines and her accountant. She forgot about housemate interviews, about Jen not wanting to see her, about 22-year-old girls making her feel inadequate and old.

If the walls of this village could talk, they could tell the stories of generation after generation, dating back to early civilisation. For centuries people had loved and laughed and fought and celebrated here; they had haggled at the market, swum and fished in the ocean, picked olives, shared wine and bread. They had shaded their eyes from the same blinding glare of the sun bouncing off the white walls of the village. It felt petty to worry about ten years of ageing while breathing in centuries of history.

The dry heat and flat light of midday reminded Stevie of the westernmost parts of Queensland she had visited. But where those plains stretched out in red ochre desert tones, here the earth and stone were more muted in colour. Everywhere the leaves of olive and rosemary trees gave the eye green relief, as opposed to the occasional grass or scrubby tree in the outback. What both places shared above all was a sky that seemed like it went on forever, an uninterrupted mythical blue no painter could tame on canvas.

'Ómorfi gynaíka' came an appreciative shout from a man sitting outside a cafe as she passed. The catcalling in Greece was next level, but Stevie was enjoying the attention. It reminded her of her early days in New York, how her nerves at travelling alone in such a big city were eased when she walked down Broadway and men called out things like 'Now that's a tall drink of water' and 'I'd like to take you home to meet my ma.'

There really was nothing better than travelling solo, Stevie thought. That same sense of boundless freedom she'd felt those months in New York was growing in her now. She wondered if it was the contrast to her life at home that made it feel so exciting. To go from everyone knowing your business to being utterly anonymous on the street. Free to do anything you wanted, free of expectation, in a way she never could be in a community where the Bush Telegraph existed.

Sometimes Stevie wondered what her life might be like now if she'd ignored the end of her visa and stayed on in New York. Paula would have missed her, but who else would really care? She might be working in fashion or magazines, running a gallery or helping out on film sets, clinking cocktails with glamorous friends, dancing with beautiful men in dark dive bars. Well, the last one wasn't so far from reality, at least.

As much as the colours and geometric shapes of the island grabbed Stevie's eye, she found herself training her lens on people going about their days. First she framed a lovely moment as a tourist couple walked down an alleyway hand in hand; then she noticed an old woman sitting in her doorway, a million stories carved into the lines of her face, hair wrapped in a kerchief. She took a shot of children putting out a saucer of milk for stray neighbourhood cats; zoomed in on a man releasing pigeons on a rooftop. At the open-air seafood market, she took photos of young men carrying buckets of octopus, a portly gent singing loudly as he deboned fish.

On a pebbly beach she stripped off her dress and ran into the ocean, her sun-warmed skin sizzling against the waves. Inspiration simmered in her mind as she floated in the surf. Later she sipped ouzo as she sketched out ideas for new projects, types of work she could diversify into, and places she wanted to travel to. All those conversations about the future with Charlie had been swirling around her head. But here, thousands of kilometres away from the world she knew, it felt actually possible that she could make a fresh start.

She looked back through her camera at her photos from the day and jotted down the stories she'd imagined for her subjects. Technically it was no different from writing the love stories she used to caption her wedding couples on Instagram. But oddly these stories of people going about their normal days seemed more profound. Stevie found herself thinking back to Nina and Trish, the way they'd find small ways to brush each other's hand in passing, or the way Nina watched Trish speak with rapt attention. The tiny hallmarks of a love grown over decades, expressed in daily habits and gestures rather than grand speeches or fancy outfits. And how those lives and loves were the ones that held together the bricks and mortar of their towns and communities. Stevie wanted to tell *those* stories. And she had a feeling they'd feed her soul more than perfect wedding after perfect wedding.

But first there was another perfect wedding to shoot. She arrived ten minutes late to the bar, where Tallulah and Declan were already deep in conversation with a woman bearing a clipboard who could only be a wedding planner.

Tallulah unfolded herself from her seat into the most statuesque, tanned blonde Stevie had ever had the chance to shoot. She could have been a model; she definitely got sent free bikinis to post to her Instagram, where 400,000 people followed her. Declan was equally tanned, a hint of chest hair peeping out from his deeply unbuttoned linen shirt. Stevie stifled a giggle imagining Johnno's hirsute cleavage in the same outfit. This was one ridiculously good-looking couple.

After the requisite air kisses, they got down to business. The wedding planner gave Stevie an itinerary for the following day. Everything was timed down to the minute.

'You will not be late, yes?' Stefani ordered Stevie.

'Absolutely not,' Stevie said.

The ceremony was to be simple, with no bridal party. Only Tallulah and Declan's family and about twenty-five friends would be in attendance. They'd been lucky (or Stefani had earned an impressive fee) to secure the Church of the Seven Martyrs for the ceremony. The iconic chapel was only opened a few times a year, and even this small wedding party would fill it. After the wedding, Stefani had allocated an hour and a half for photos of the couple, timed beautifully for the sunset, Stevie had to admit, before dinner at an oceanside taverna.

'And then we party,' Tallulah said. 'Dec's pulled some strings and got one of the best DJs from Mykonos to play for us.'

'I didn't think there were any clubs on the island,' Stevie said.

'There aren't,' Declan said. 'And the noise restrictions are sick. So we've got a superyacht for everyone – and we can take it out far enough that no one on Sifnos can hear or complain. It's going to go off.'

'Our little gift to thank everyone for coming.' Tallulah beamed.

The day went off without a hitch. The weather was clear, the sky unmarred by a single cloud, the waves flawless beneath it. The church was a white beacon on the golden rocky outcrop, capped with a blue roof. Tallulah was stunning in a figure-hugging lace dress.

'Oscar,' she'd purred proudly when Stevie arrived to find her being zipped into it by Stefani.

'De la Renta,' Stefani clarified, unnecessarily.

Tallulah's loose waves tumbled over her bare tanned shoulders and were capped with an elaborate gold crown. 'Dolce,' she explained as the hairstylist carefully arranged it among her gleaming tresses.

'Yep, and Gabbana, got it,' Stevie cut off Stefani. There were Christian Louboutin gold sandals, Paspaley pearl drop earrings, and a long, lace-trimmed veil trailing from the back of the crown. She was a vision, Stevie had to admit, and Declan's white tuxedo, clearly custom-made, was the perfect counterpart. His Italian leather loafers and her pristine scarlet soles weren't immune to the dust of the rocky, winding pathway to the church, but the composition was exquisite. In the golden light of afternoon, the wind picked up to give Stevie dramatic shots of the veil and Tallulah's hair flying against the burnished backdrop.

Stevie took thousands of shots, each more beautiful than the last. As well as the wide shots capturing the church and the landscape, there were the rustic interiors of the chapel, the Orthodox priest in his own finery, the emotional guests, and then sunset portraits of Tallulah and Declan canoodling in the streets and olive groves like something from a very expensive catalogue. Stevie had switched to a flash for more modern shots at the reception dinner, capturing the vibrant food and flamboyant servers under string lights as a fairly famous singer-songwriter played acoustic guitar. They pushed the tables back for the first dance and used a sabre to cut a cake nearly as tall as Tallulah.

And then the bride had slipped away for a costume change, emerging in a breathtakingly tailored backless ivory jumpsuit, her hair tucked up into a different crown. 'All aboard,' she cried, leading the wedding guests out of the restaurant, across the sand of the beach and down a jetty to the waiting party boat.

Stevie felt like they were in a film. Paper lanterns glowing orange floated around them. She couldn't have got a bad angle of Tallulah if she tried, as Tallulah skipped along the gangplank, sandals dangling in one hand while she pulled Declan along with the other.

Soon they were motoring out into the bay, the waves lapping gently as the lights of Sifnos shrank away behind them. And then the DJ started up, the music impossibly loud. Stevie fluttered around taking photos that wouldn't look out of place in high-society pages. Everyone was gorgeous, dripping with jewels and designer fashion, and drinking straight from magnums of French champagne. After Stevie had done a lap and shot all the guests in decadent revelry, Tallulah took her hand.

'Stevie, darling, you've been wonderful. But now it's time for the camera to go away. I'm going to take this, okay?' She took the camera from Stevie's hands and clipped on the lens cap as Stevie acquiesced meekly. 'Let's pack all your gear away below decks.' And she led Stevie downstairs to a luxurious wood-panelled room where guests were congregating in small groups. The camera gear was tucked into a cupboard where Stevie also saw a box of guests' phones, and Tallulah handed the key to Declan, who pocketed it.

'You'll get it all back when we dock,' Declan assured Stevie, who was so caught by surprise that she watched all this unfold unquestioningly. 'We just want everyone to be able to relax and fully enjoy themselves without having to worry about winding up on Instagram, you know? And that includes you, Stevie.'

'That sounds amazing,' Stevie said. 'But when are you planning to dock back on Sifnos? I've got to get the early ferry out tomorrow. Can't miss my flight.'

'You'll be fine, lovely.' Tallulah smiled all her perfect teeth at Stevie and caressed her hair.

'Now, let's get you some party favours.' Declan rubbed his hands together excitedly. On a mirrored table there were enough lines of coke to make a mob boss do a double take, and bowls of pills like candy. Stevie was no stranger to a few recreational substances, but it had been a couple of years since she'd partaken and she wasn't sure of her tolerance.

Tallulah handed her a glass of vintage champagne and said 'You'll love this' as she placed a small pill on Stevie's tongue. *Well, I'm basically on holiday*, Stevie thought. *What's one last night of fun?*

Feeling like Alice in Wonderland about to go down the rabbit hole, she threw back the champagne and swallowed. The music was pulsing through her whole body and Stevie was ready to dance.

24

A savage beam of sunlight was boring directly into Stevie's eyelid and she woke with a start. She sat up abruptly and it took a couple of minutes for her to figure out where she was. A hotel room . . . Greece . . . Tallulah and Declan's wedding . . .

'What time is it?' Stevie scrambled for her phone, but it was dead. A clock radio blinked 8.47 in red, each second-long pulse echoed by an insistent pounding in her head. The ferry back to Athens was leaving at 9.30. Stevie flew into the bathroom, avoiding eye contact with the mirror. Even after a steaming shower her eyes were panda-ringed with last night's eyeliner. She struggled into a pair of skinny jeans and tried to remember how or when she'd got back to her room. Sunglasses made life slightly less painful as she threw clothes into her bag and pulled on her boots. *Ready. Just need my camera bag.*

Stevie's blood ran cold as she had a flashback to her gear being locked away by Tallulah. It wasn't here. It was 9.10 and it would take ten minutes to get to the ferry port. *Oh God!*

Racing down to reception, Stevie checked out and was halfway out the door when the receptionist called, 'Miss, there is a bag here for you.'

'Tallulah, you crazy bitch,' Stevie whispered as she read a note in looping cursive, tied to the handle of her gear bag.

Thanks so much for capturing our day, Stevie. Can't wait to see the pics – get home safe, you party animal xxxxx

Stevie ran over cobblestones to the ferry port. The wind was blowing hard and when she got to the ticket desk, pulling euros from her pockets, it took her a minute to understand why the girl behind the counter was shaking her head. She pointed out the window at savage waves, and then to a sign that read, 'All ferries cancelled due to rough conditions'.

'But I have to get back to Athens for a flight,' Stevie tried to explain. 'Oh God, oh God.' The girl waved her away and Stevie slumped into a chair.

'Heeey,' croaked a very stoned man in a fedora sitting opposite her. He had taken off his shoes and had a huge backpack next to him.

'Hi,' Stevie said dismissively.

'Get comfortable, my friend,' the man said with a Dutch accent. 'They say the forecast is bad for the rest of the day. There might not be a ferry until tomorrow morning.'

'But I need to leave today,' Stevie said, panic rising in her throat. If she didn't get to Athens by mid-afternoon, she'd miss her flight.

'Nothing we can do, may as well relax.' He smiled, pulling his hat over his eyes and slumping down into the seat.

Stevie rummaged through her bag for the Lonely Planet guidebook she'd brought. She needed to talk to someone and had no language to do so. She had no way of finding Tallulah or Declan, and her phone was dead. Flipping through the book, she found a list of basic phrases and went back to the counter to argue with the girl there, but she'd put up a sign saying 'Back in thirty minutes' and was clearly napping behind it.

Maybe I'll just have a little rest, Stevie thought, *and the weather will clear.* She sat back in her chair, looped the handle of her gear bag around her arm and closed her eyes behind her sunglasses.

'Hey, Stevie.' A voice startled her awake. Her neck had seized up and she had no idea who this man was, smiling at her.

'We met on the boat. I'm Jimmy?' he said. 'We danced together for like three hours?'

'Nice to see you,' she choked out, her voice thick with the pack of cigarettes she now remembered smoking the night before.

'Bit dusty, hey?' Jimmy asked.

'Just a bit,' she said. 'You haven't seen any bacon and egg rolls around here, have you?'

'Nah, but there's a guy selling octopus sticks a little ways down the street.'

Stevie gagged at the thought. 'What time is it?'

''Bout three-thirty,' Jimmy said. 'The website wasn't updating with ferry times so I figured I'd come down here and see what's what. I'm supposed to be flying out of Athens in a couple of hours.'

'I've already missed my flight,' Stevie said blankly, the reality setting in.

'Chin up,' Jimmy said. 'Maybe you can get on my flight. I had a chat to that nice girl behind the ticket desk and she said there should be a ferry in an hour if the wind keeps dropping like this.' He sat down next to her, pulled on a huge pair of noise-cancelling headphones and started watching *Gossip Girl* on his phone.

Stevie lifted one of the cans off his ear. 'Do you have a phone charger I could borrow?'

Her phone battery had crept back up to 80 per cent while Stevie napped fitfully, until there came a PA announcement in Greek and a flurry of activity.

'Ferry's on.' Jimmy clapped his hands. 'We're in business. Get your ticket and I'll mind your stuff.' Stevie smiled at him gratefully, and even the ticket bitch was nice to her. Now she just needed some wi-fi to start figuring out a new flight.

But there was none in the ferry terminal, and none on the ferry itself. Once they disembarked in Athens, Jimmy offered her a ride to the airport, and only there did she finally manage to get some service on her phone. It shuddered to life and vibrated for a full five minutes as notifications poured in.

'Wow, mate,' Jimmy said. 'You're running hot. Come wait in the lounge with me. I'll have a chat to the hosties and see if there's a seat on the flight for you.'

Stevie followed him blindly as she tried to weed through the notifications on her phone. There were hundreds of emails, which seemed a bit high for the five days she'd been offline. Five thousand alerts from Instagram? That couldn't be right. Her text and voicemail boxes were full, but she couldn't access them without roaming. What was going on?

'Stevie,' Jimmy called impatiently. He was talking to a woman in a red suit and silly hat behind the service desk. 'The flight's booked out. There's only a seat in business class for nine thousand dollars, otherwise you have to patch together three flights via London, Dubai and Singapore.'

'Holy cats!' Stevie said. She didn't have that much on her credit card. 'When does that one arrive in Brisbane?'

'Both options only get you to Sydney. Business class with me will get you there by midday on Friday. The other option will take until Sunday.'

'Okay, I have a job five hours' drive from Brisbane early on Saturday. I'm going to have to find nine grand. Can she put a hold on it and I'll sort out the money asap?'

'We're due to board in ninety minutes. Is that going to work?' Jimmy asked.

'It'll have to,' Stevie said grimly. She opened WhatsApp on her phone.

She tried calling Charlie. The app made it look like he was online, but it rang and rang and rang until Stevie hung up. She opened a message to him: *I've hit a snag getting back from Greece and need some help. Can you call me urgently? xx*

A little bubble appeared like he was typing back, then disappeared.

Are you there? Stevie wrote. His profile picture blinked to offline.

'What the . . .?' Stevie muttered. But she didn't have time to waste. She knew she had about six grand available on her credit card but she'd need more. She really didn't want to make Paula anxious, and knew she'd struggle with the technology to make a quick transfer. She had to assume Charlie wouldn't get back to her. She was going to have to risk going against Jen's request not to contact her.

Stevie's heart thumped as she dialled the number. She'd just give it three rings, then give up. Maybe she could call the bank and request some credit? But Jen picked up on the second ring.

'Stevie! My God, are you okay?'

'Oh Jen, thanks for taking my call, I'm sorry to bother you. Wait – how do you know I'm in trouble?'

'I've been trying to call you since it aired,' Jen said. 'I didn't think you should be alone.'

'Since what aired?' Stevie asked. 'Jen, I'm really sorry to ask this of you, but I'm stranded in Athens. I need to borrow some money fast to book the only flight that's going to get me back in time for a job on Saturday.'

'Wait, you don't know?'

'Know what?'

'Stevie, when did you last speak to Charlie?'

'I just tried calling him but he didn't pick up. My phone's been off for five days, I still haven't been able to look at my texts and calls. But look, I'm running out of time – can you help me with about four grand? Just until I get back and move some money around?'

'Okay. Yes, you'd better just get back as quickly as you can. Right, what do you need? Do you want me to just book the flight for you and we'll figure out the rest later?'

Stevie could have wept, such was her relief at hearing Jen swing into action.

'Jen, the only seat left is business class. It's obscene. If you can transfer me four grand I can put the rest on my credit card.'

'Okay, whatever you need. Honey, you didn't get insurance?'

'Do you even need to ask?' Stevie hung her head. 'We can talk later about the thousand ways I've messed this up.'

'Right, I've just made the transfer – you should get an email. Can you purchase there at the airport?'

'That's what I'm going to try. Can I call you back and let you know how I go?'

'Yep. Send me an email before you take off with your flight

details and where you need to get to on Saturday. I'll see what I can do from my end to help.'

'I don't deserve you, Jen.'

'No, you don't. Off you go. And . . . just stay offline till you get back, okay? We can figure it out together.'

Stevie pushed away her curiosity at whatever ominous news Jen was hinting at and raced up to the service desk. Jimmy sprang to her side and finally things were going right. The seat was booked, she was checked in, her bags were taken care of. Her heart rate finally steadying for the first time in what felt like two days, Stevie felt weary down to her bones, and like her hangover was still seeping out through her pores.

'You'll get a good sleep in business class at least,' Jimmy said.

'All my life I've wanted to fly business and now it's going to be wasted on me.' Stevie laughed wryly. She remembered Jen's instructions. 'Hey, I've just got to send an email before we board, okay?'

She tapped out an email to Jen with the flight number, noting that it would land in Sydney and if Jen could book her a connecting flight to Brisbane and put it on her tab. If she could sleep on the flight, get straight back to Brisbane and prep her gear and fuel the car, she could leave at 3 am and make it to the wedding on time. It was going to be ugly, but she could make it.

Jimmy had guided her into the queue to board their flight. After she hit send, Stevie was puzzled to see a number of names she didn't know in her inbox. One she did know, though, was Lily Taylor. She knew she shouldn't, but she opened it.

Stevie, I hope you don't mind me reaching out. I hope you're doing okay with everything. But I had to let you know – he did the same thing to my friend Betsy. Whatever he tells you, however he tries to explain it, don't listen. He seems to have a pattern of stringing girls along, then ghosting them, three and four at a time. Let me know if you'd like me to put you in touch with Betsy (there's kind of an informal support group for his exes) and take care of yourself. L xx

What was this nonsense? And then Stevie saw the subject line: *Charlie*.

'Hey babe, is this you?' Jimmy was asking, pointing at a meme on his Instagram.

'Sir, please switch off your phone as you leave the terminal,' an airline attendant said wearily.

'Just a sec,' Stevie pleaded, trying to get her fuzzy head around what was on Jimmy's screen. It was a picture of her, her cheeks flushed and lit like she was on TV – oh God, it was from the *Bush Bachelors* broadcast. And then there was a picture of Charlie . . . And then a picture of Charlie with his arms around Camilla . . . And then he was kissing Stevie.

'Ma'am,' the attendant said curtly, and Jimmy snatched back his phone.

Stevie trudged onto the most luxurious flight of her life and enjoyed exactly none of it, her anxiety building about the storm she was about to fly into.

25

Stevie's eyes shuddered open as the plane's wheels bounced on the tarmac in Sydney. It had been nearly a full twenty-four hours since they'd left Athens. The initial leg had been excruciating. Then there was a discombobulating stopover in Dubai, where she and Jimmy had walked for miles in an endless shopping mall, squinting under fluorescent lights. Stevie had obediently avoided opening anything on her phone except Jen's reply email, which included details of the flight booked to take her back to Brisbane. As the next plane cruised towards Sydney, Stevie had surprised herself by sleeping soundly for hours. Perhaps those business-class seats were worth the price tag.

The turnaround for her flight to Brisbane was tight, so her goodbye to Jimmy was rushed. She hugged him tightly. 'Thanks for getting me out of Athens. I don't know if I could have done it without you.'

Jimmy waved her away. 'Look me up and buy me a drink next time you're in Sydney, okay?'

'Only if you promise never to tell me what I did on the boat the night of the wedding,' Stevie agreed, before racing off to her connecting flight.

By the time she finally landed in Brisbane, Stevie had lost track of how long it had been since she woke up in Sifnos. As she pulled her bags off the carousel, Stevie felt approximately six hundred years old. She was just making her way towards the cab rank when one of the dozen drivers waiting for a fare stepped forward with a sign that had her name on it. Stevie's jaw dropped, and as the driver lifted their cap, she realised it was Jen.

Stevie burst into tears immediately.

'Oh, Stevie, it's all right,' Jen said, pulling her into a hug.

Stevie's apology came out as a series of hiccupping sobs and a wave of tears on Jen's shoulder.

'Let's get you home.'

The sun was setting as Jen drove. The radio was shrieking the eighties pop songs Jen always somehow found on the radio. Once Stevie had composed herself a bit, Jen turned down the volume slightly.

'How are you feeling about the drive in the morning? You'll have to make an early start,' Jen said.

'Yeah, actually I'll set my alarm now,' Stevie said, then realised she'd have to turn her phone on, which she'd been avoiding. 'I'm scared, Jen. I don't want to know, I don't want it to be real.'

'But you have some idea of what to expect?' Jen asked.

'I saw an email from Lily, of all people. She said Charlie had done a similar thing to a friend of hers. Not that I'm sure exactly what he's done . . .'

'Do you want me to tell you first, or do you want to just switch on your phone? Do it like ripping off a bandaid, get it over with?'

'Tell me,' Stevie said grimly.

Jen gave her the broad strokes of what had aired on *Bush Bachelors*, the immediate backlash to Charlie's dog act, the social media campaign to find and shame him.

Stevie groaned. 'I'm a laughing stock.'

'Actually . . .' Jen said, 'you're kind of a hero.'

'What?'

'I mean, yes, there are a few slowmo supercuts of you to really depressing Adele songs, and some mean memes. You should look up what the *Betoota Advocate* posted about you – that was pretty brilliant.'

'This isn't helping, Jen,' Stevie said.

'But then this kind of movement started . . . A bunch of girls came forward and said Charlie had done the same thing to them. And so many of us have been there. Dudded by blokes when we dared to hope for a bit of romance. So this whole "I stand with Stevie" hashtag took off.'

'Ugh. So glad I can be a figurehead for all the other sad old spinsters out there.'

'You went viral, bitch! There's probably a bunch of emails in your inbox with producers trying to get you on board for *The Bachelorette*. You'll definitely be able to get laid off this whole thing, if you want to.'

Stevie sunk down into the seat, groaning. 'I definitely can't look at my phone now.'

Jen pulled into the driveway behind Stevie's Pajero and it was just like old times as they tramped up the stairs with Stevie's bags. But then Stevie unlocked the door, and the dark house echoed back at her.

'Come in for a wine? Ugh, I can't believe I just said that – I'm never drinking again,' Stevie said. 'But truly – stay for a cuppa? We haven't caught up with Jessica for ages.'

Jen put down Stevie's bag in the hallway. 'I don't think that's a good idea.'

'Sure you don't want to help me go through the marriage pro-posals in my inbox? Not even all the photos of Fred that Mum's sent over the past week?'

'Not this time. Andrew's expecting me,' Jen said. Stevie could see she was still hurt. Maybe their friendship would never be the same again. 'I'm glad I could help you get home safely.'

'Thank you, for everything,' Stevie said, tears starting again. 'I'll pay you back as soon as I can.'

'Good luck tomorrow,' Jen said.

Stevie closed the door behind her and the tears kept flowing.

Stevie wanted nothing more than to collapse. But she knew if she didn't prepare for the next day's wedding before going to bed, things could easily fall apart. She unpacked her gear bag and started down-loading files from Tallulah and Declan's wedding. As the images flickered across her screen, Stevie caught intriguing glimpses of her shots of life in Sifnos, but she didn't have time to get distracted.

Stevie took out fresh memory cards and started piecing together her kit for the next day. Next, she headed out to fuel her car and thanked God she'd left Fred at Paula's place, then felt a rush of guilt that she'd even had the thought. She should be taking care of her own dog. She'd treated him as an afterthought and yet he was probably the only one who wasn't disappointed in her now. She would have liked to take him to Mungindi, but it would have made the past few days even harder if she'd had to worry about him overstaying his welcome at a kennel. She vowed to treat him when she got him home again.

With the car ready, her bags packed and her plan for the morn-ing hastily sketched out, Stevie showered and crawled into bed. She'd avoided her phone all afternoon but now she had to set an alarm and it couldn't be put off any longer. When she switched the phone on, it danced for minutes with a chorus of beeps and vibrations, and Stevie felt her heart rate quicken as the number of notifications climbed higher and higher. Eventually it was still. She took a deep breath, set her alarm (and a back-up alarm) for the morning and decided to start with the texts.

There were voicemails from numbers she didn't know. Stevie decided to leave those for later, or possibly never. There was a series of messages from Paula; in reverse chronological order they went from high anxiety down to blissful obliviousness:

STEVIE ARE YOU ALRIGHT

Darling please let me know you're ok.

Stevie, I know you're out of the country but have you seen Bush Bachelors yet?

(with a photo of Fred in front of the TV) We're watching you on BB!

There were messages from Jen, from a few clients and seemingly everyone she'd ever met. She scrolled past a number of missed calls from her dad. There were a lot of people sharing their 'concern', when she hadn't heard from them in months or years. It was ghoulish, the way people came out of the woodwork when you were publicly shamed, congratulating themselves that their own lives weren't so messed up.

One name was glaringly absent from her inbox: Charlie's. Absolute radio silence. Not a word of explanation, or apology, or even acknowledgement of her existence.

It was just so bizarre. He had been the one who pursued her so ardently, the one who was so demonstrative and romantic. She hadn't put any pressure on him; they'd talked about the future, but they were all conversations he'd started. What was in it for him to build up her hopes and then destroy them? What did he get out of stringing her along? And it sounded like she was just one of many.

The dark part of her brain was chanting these questions over and over, urging her to call Charlie and beg him to explain, repeating all the worst things she believed about herself as reasons why he would do this. *You're old, you're sad, you're strange, you're broken, you're hideous, you're alone, you'll always be alone, who could love you?*

Finally she made herself look at the texts from unknown numbers – a few were old acquaintances who'd dropped out of her contacts, rubberneckers. A few were clients, checking she'd still be able to do their gigs. Some were from journalists and producers trying to get her to share her side of the story. Their tone was casual but thirst bled through.

The texts soon seemed innocuous compared to the firehose of garbage opinions, jokes and judgement on social media. Faceless trolls shared a litany of unsolicited thoughts about her looks, her decisions, her dating history.

Of course a guy that looked like that would be cheating on a bush pig like her.

Chicks r so dumb.

Maybe if she lost a few kilos I'd give her a sympathy root.

Stevie made herself close the apps, silence the notifications and put the phone facedown on the bedside table. But even with a pillow jammed over her head the words and images swam around her brain, circling the drain, driving her insane. *Bush pig. Slut. Idiot. Ugly. Old. Dumb bitch.*

When the alarm shattered the silence at 2.30 am, Stevie was already awake. She wasn't sure she had slept at all, but she had to get on the road.

—

Stevie made good time on the five-hundred-odd kilometres to Mungindi. She allowed herself a stop at South Star for old times' sake, parking outside the bakery to grab coffee and a pie for breakfast. All the landmarks of the town seemed to have some connection to Johnno. Even the pies were his favourite.

Stevie felt wretched when she thought of that night months ago, when he'd kissed her outside the motel. What would her life look like now if she'd let things play out? Would it be her setting the Bush Telegraph's chins wagging about young love? *Don't be an idiot, Stevie*, she told herself. It would have flamed out as soon as the mystery was gone, all those years of wondering finally put to the test. How could any hook-up live up to that? It'd probably be a total dud and then the friendship would have been ruined.

Amid the hordes in her inbox there had been a single text from Johnno. *Charlie's the biggest dickhead I've ever seen. I hated seeing you treated like that. There's so much better out there for you, Stevie. x*

Stevie cringed as she imagined him sending it. He had probably watched the show with Sarah. They had probably laughed about it together.

It looked like recognition flickering across the face of the young bloke behind the counter at the bakery when Stevie ordered. Did he remember her from that night with Johnno? Or from TV? He wouldn't be the last one. Probably most of the people at the wedding she was headed to would have seen it. *Oh God, oh God.*

Stevie started up the Pajero for the last leg of her journey. It was 9.30 by the time she got to Mungindi, and she headed straight for the house where the bride, Sally, was getting ready with her girls. The sky was clear and the sun was beaming down already. Stevie felt almost woozy with fatigue, a bad sign considering how many hours of work lay ahead. *Time to put on the show*, she thought to herself, striding into the house.

'Good morning, ladies. Where's our beautiful bride?' she boomed.

Sally was wrapped in a floral robe, sweating slightly around the hairline of a lacquered beehive do. The ceremony was a relatively early one, and Stevie was concerned about the three-hour gap before the reception that she'd have to fill shooting portraits when she hadn't scoped locations. She'd shot in this area before, but she knew Sally had seen those photos – the previous bride was Sally's sister, so she couldn't get away with recycling too many set-ups.

Stevie just tried to keep moving. Every time she let herself take a quiet moment the words started swirling around her head, and she thought she heard people talking about her. Her eyelids started to feel like they were weighted and she wondered if she could sneak away for a nap without being noticed. Not bloody likely.

The reception was like her phone come to life: an endless stream of unsolicited opinions and messages. She wasn't sure which was harder to take, the curiosity or the sympathy. She had a lot of older women offering to set her up with their sons. A lot of younger women offering up their similar experiences. A lot of lewd looks from the young blokes. And the old ones, come to think of it.

She gritted her teeth and smiled. *Just get through today*, she told herself. *You can fall apart later.*

26

Johnno's phone was ringing with a number he didn't even know he had saved.

'Paula?'

'Johnno, I'm sorry to call you out of the blue. But I heard you might be driving up to Brisbane and I was hoping you could help me with something.'

'Yeah, I'm heading up tomorrow for a meeting. You okay?'

'I'm fine,' Paula said. 'But I've had Fred for nearly two weeks now and he's pining for Stevie. And she won't let me come, but I know she's in a bad way. Do you think you could take Fred for me and just make sure she's all right?'

Johnno stifled a groan. Every time he thought of Stevie he wanted to cringe: how brattily she'd acted the last few times he'd seen her; how he'd agonised over what to text her after her TV disaster and how she'd never responded; how limp and unassertive he was every time he was faced with her.

'Johnno? You there?'

'Yeah, Paula.' He sighed, knowing he was never going to say no. 'That's fine. I'll be on a pretty tight turnaround so I can't spend a lot of time with Stevie, but I can definitely take Fred for you.'

'That's wonderful, thank you,' she said, and he could practically hear her beaming down the line. 'Do you mind just calling in to my place on your way out of town? I'll make sure everything's packed up and ready so it won't slow you down.'

Johnno hadn't been to Stevie's house before, but Paula had given him the address. Fred had been pretty good as far as passengers went. The doleful looks he was shooting from the back seat were easy enough to ignore, and when Johnno stopped for fuel, he leaped from the cab to pee and was back before Johnno had poured out water for him. If he had one complaint, it was Fred's complete lack of conversation, which unfortunately allowed Johnno's thoughts free rein to torture him.

His mind was a looping relay of worries, each one handing the baton of his attention to the next. Would he and Kate be able to put the plan to their parents in a way Rod and Penny could understand? Would his plans for his new business have any chance of success, or was he just going to fail spectacularly and disappoint his parents again? Would he be able to locate his big boy pants and work out this thing with Sarah before either of them got hurt? What on earth was he going to say to Stevie? And on, and on, and on.

He scanned the radio tuner, finding nothing but ABC AM. A rugby league game was just starting and Johnno turned up the volume on the commentary until it drowned out his brain. Fred whimpered and put his paws over his ears.

The Queenslander was silent as Johnno grabbed Fred's stuff and opened the ute door for him. Fred bolted up the stairs until he could go no further, whining and shaking with a full-body tail wag as he scratched at the lattice doors. Johnno trudged up behind him, wondering why Stevie was taking so long to open the door.

'Stevie,' he called through the lattice, but still she didn't emerge. He juggled Paula's care package, trying to retrieve his phone from his pocket. He dialled Stevie's number, and told himself if she didn't pick up within fifteen rings, he'd put Fred in the backyard with some food and water, and give up. She answered on the fourteenth.

''lo?' came a croaky voice, thick with sleep, or sedatives, or both.

'Stevie? You right?' He heard bedclothes rustling and Stevie clearing her throat.

'Johnno? Sorry, I'm not one hundred per cent at the moment.'

'Clearly. Look, are you home? I'm at your front door. Your mum asked me to drop Fred off to you.'

He heard her hauling herself out of bed, coughing with the phone held away from her, and possibly muttering some profanities. 'Just a sec,' she said, before hanging up.

A full five minutes later she finally unlocked the door, and Fred nearly bowled her over. She was barefoot and wearing sweats, pale and shivery, hair scraped back into a messy topknot. As someone who felt he had a well-considered opinion of her beauty, Johnno had to admit she looked terrible.

Her voice was cracking as she told him, 'I'm afraid I can't offer you much by way of hospitality.'

'No stress,' he said, determined not to get sucked in to any damsel-in-distress act. 'I won't keep you.' But as he went to hand her the basket of food and treats Paula had packed, he saw the light in her eyes flicker and she visibly reeled. He threw the basket down and caught her as she staggered. 'Right, let's get you back to bed.'

'I'm fine,' she said, frowning, but her voice was weak.

He guided her back down the hallway, in search of her bedroom, as Fred whined and skittered around, his anxious claws tap-dancing on the polished floorboards. It wasn't hard to find Stevie's room, as it was the only one in the house that seemed furnished. 'You here by yourself?' he asked, trying to keep Stevie focused.

'Yeah, Jen's gone,' she mumbled. 'S'posed to be interviewing housemates but haven't been up to it. Also, it makes me want to slit my wrists.' She laughed hollowly, and it turned into a cough. He helped her sit down on the bed and she crawled back under the covers. The blinds were drawn and it was like a musty little cave.

'Have you seen a doctor?' Johnno asked, taking in the empty boxes of painkillers and half-full water glasses on the bedside table.

Stevie shook her head. 'Seems to be some sort of virus. My throat is killing, my head weighs a ton. I'm just trying to sleep it off.'

'When was the last time you ate something?' he asked.

Stevie was lying back on the pillow, eyes closed. She shrugged.

'Right,' Johnno said. *There goes the afternoon*, he thought. 'You rest, I'll get Fred fed and go to the chemist and see if they recommend any drugs for you.'

'S'okay,' Stevie said faintly, already drifting off. 'I'm fine.'

When he was sure she was out to it, he pressed his broad hand to her forehead. It was like a furnace. 'Bloody hell, Stevie,' he muttered, tiptoeing across the unfamiliar floorboards even though nothing would have woken her. Looking for food in Stevie's kitchen was a fool's errand, and by the look of things she hadn't washed up in at least a week. A pile of bills was teetering on the kitchen bench next to a plate of toast crumbs. Luckily there was still a big bag of dog food in the pantry, and Johnno shook out a few handfuls into the bowl he found on the back deck. As he rinsed and filled Fred's water bowl, he started making a mental list. He'd have to try to reschedule his meeting at the bank for the next day.

'Come on, old girl,' Johnno said, hoisting Stevie upright and into a chair in the corner of the room. 'I just need a minute to change your sheets, and then we'll get some food into you. Drink this.'

She sucked on the Hydralyte, eyelids still heavy, barely aware he was there as he stripped her bed. At least she was getting some fluids, he told himself. The bed remade, he went to guide her back in. She was on fire in his arms.

'You should change into something cooler,' he said.

'I'll have a shower,' she said, but she was unsteady on her feet.

'Just put on a nightie or something for now, hey?' he said gently. 'I'll be back in a minute.'

When he returned with a tray of soup and an array of over-the-counter pharmaceuticals, he was relieved to see she'd shed the jumper and trackies for a singlet and shorts. He forced himself to look away from her body and set down the tray on the bedside table he'd cleared.

'You're still burning up. The chemist said these should help.' He held out a handful of pills and a glass of water. Once she'd swallowed, he got her sitting up in the bed, and he fed her soup by the spoonful. It seemed to give her strength immediately, and he wondered again how long it had been since she'd eaten.

'I'm not a baby.' She giggled.

'Oh, would you rather feed yourself?' he asked.

'No, this is nice,' she said. She was getting drowsy again, and he put away the bowl and spoon. 'It's so hot,' she said listlessly, tugging at the pillows.

He wet a washcloth in the bathroom and returned to her side, pressing it to her face until it came away warm.

The drugs were making her giddy and childlike, confused as well as sleepy. 'It's so weird that you're here. I was thinking about you. Did I call you to come?'

'No, your mum asked me to. She's worried about you.'

'Just a little flu,' Stevie said. 'I feel better already. You wanna spoon?'

'No, thanks.' Johnno smiled.

'Sure?' she asked with a grin.

'Yes, I'm sure. You're disgustingly sick.' He laughed.

'Worth a shot,' she said.

'Go to sleep, you pest,' he said, getting up to take the tray out to the kitchen.

'Love you, Johnno,' she mumbled, drifting off to sleep. And those three words rolled around and around in his head.

You're pathetic, he told himself, throwing the dirty bowl into the sink.

—

Stevie woke, disorientated. She felt like she'd slept for a year, but at least her head didn't feel like it would explode when she lifted it off the pillow. Light was trickling through the blinds and a bird was chirping faintly; she judged it was early morning. Her sheets smelled clean, although she did not, and the room was much tidier than she remembered it being. Flashes of memory came back to her, foggy with fever: Fred racing through the door, Johnno sitting by her bed. Johnno?

Stirring, she realised he was right there, asleep on his back, fully clothed on top of the doona, as far away from her as he could get without falling off the bed. He was a fidgety sleeper, a trace of a scowl on his face, an arm thrown up the way babies sleep.

She was still too disoriented to think about why he was there, what this meant. She just knew her fingertip ached to trace the shapes of his face, his collarbones, his chest. *Well, THAT would be crazy*, a distant rational part of her brain told her.

He stirred and rolled away onto his side, and she gently inched across and curved her body to mimic his. His breathing stayed steady and slow, so she let herself close the millimetres between them, let herself mould her body to his back and softly drape her arm over his waist. He shifted just the tiniest bit, relaxing back against her. It felt like puzzle pieces clicking into place, like a key sliding into a lock. Stevie breathed him in, drifting back to sleep.

—

Dappled sunlight through the blinds hit Johnno's eyelids, but he was able to shift slightly and keep dozing. He was drifting in that sweet, submerged state of not-quite-yet-awakeness, when it doesn't matter where you are or what time it is. He felt cosy, in sheets that smelled fresh and unfamiliar, cradled in the warm weight of some-one breathing gently behind him. His fingers were intertwined with another soft hand, and he unconsciously pulled the arm around him tighter.

As his mind floated towards the surface of consciousness, his body became more aware of the curves of the one enveloping him. He was clothed, but where his shirt had ridden up over his hips and torso he felt smooth skin warm against his. A long, bare leg was thrown over his own, and he reached down to trace its shape: up along a straight, smooth shin, over a bent knee, to the gentle curve of the back of a thigh. The leg hooked him closer and he ground back gently, his jeans starting to feel restrictive. Were those the points of nipples he was feeling through the back of his shirt? Was that a hand creeping to his waistband?

Johnno was suddenly wide awake, breathing heavily, painfully aware that he had a raging hard-on in Stevie's bed. He was 90 per cent sure she was fast asleep and unaware of the effect her unconscious spooning was having on him, and he was worried that if he rolled over to check he wouldn't be able to stop himself from doing something inappropriate. The poor thing was sleeping off a terrible fever and here he was imagining molesting her.

So he gently unravelled her leg from his, tugged down his shirt and, finally, not without some regret, untangled her fingers from his and placed her arm back along her side. He eased himself to the edge of the bed, his feet against the cold, bare floorboards completing his rude awakening.

Time for a cold shower, mate, he thought, allowing himself just a few seconds to look back at her sleeping face, dappled with sunshine, and to tuck a strand of hair away from her still-warm forehead and behind her ear. He heaved himself off to the bathroom with a sigh as she slumbered on.

—

The room was mid-morning bright when Stevie woke to Johnno opening the window. She smelled tea on the bedside table, a curl of steam rising from a cup there.

'Time for you to eat something, sleepyhead,' he said. 'How are you feeling? Can you sit up?'

'Think so,' Stevie said, pulling herself upright against the pillows, hoping her nipples weren't on show. *Relax*, she told herself, *he'll be too busy trying not to gag from the stench of you to be checking you out.*

Johnno sat in the chair by her side and handed her a plate of toast, thickly buttered with barely a suggestion of a scrape of Vegemite. *It doesn't mean anything*, she told herself. *Anyone could accidentally intuit your Vegemite preferences perfectly.*

'Wait,' he said. 'You should take some more of these first.' She left the plate on her lap and he handed her a glass of water, opening his palm to drop the pills into hers. He took back the glass after she drained it, went to hand her the teacup, then paused and blew on it first. Stevie thought it might have been the kindest thing anyone had ever done for her. She didn't usually take sugar but the sweetness he'd added was perfect, the toast was perfect.

'This tastes like the best meal I've ever had.' She laughed. 'How long was I out?'

'You've probably slept about fifteen hours, I think,' he said. His hair was still a little damp from the shower and he smelled of soap and boy and coffee, a scent she wanted to bottle and covet forever.

'I feel a million times better. Wait, you've been here all that time?'

'Oh, yeah,' he said casually. 'Just had to make sure my buddy Fred was settled back in. I will have to head off in the next few hours, though. If you're okay,' he added.

'Of course. You've already done too much,' she said, wondering where exactly this pang of disappointment was coming from. 'I must look terrible. Do you mind sticking around while I have a shower?'

'Course,' he said, taking the plate of crumbs from her and pulling back her sheets. Stevie felt exposed in her little shorts and a singlet, but he wasn't looking anyway.

Under the hot water, lathering her hair, Stevie felt newborn. Her joints were still a little sore, her skin hypersensitive to the beads of water rolling off her. A sudden memory flashed into her mind, of her limbs wrapped around Johnno, his backside grinding back into her, her nipples growing taut against his back. *Oh God*, she thought, *you absolute pervert. Maybe it was just a dream?* But there was no denying it any more. She was imagining Johnno West naked and, worse, enjoying it.

Get it together, Harrison. She could hear his voice in her head, laughing at the very idea that she was crushing on him. She'd always felt like their brains worked in a similar way, although she shuddered now to think he might be able to read the lascivious thoughts she was having about him. He had been taking no such notice of her half-dressed form.

And yet, he was here. He'd stayed the night. He was taking care of her, and it felt somehow . . . right. Stevie's mind was bolting, imagining a string of Sunday mornings in bed with perfectly prepared toast and tea and Johnno next to her in the sheets. She imagined opening her front door and him standing there, smiling. She imagined nights next to him on the couch, mornings of him kissing her goodbye through her rolled-down window. She imagined all the hours that Charlie (*goddamn Charlie*) had wanted to spend glued to her side, all the time she'd spent second-guessing and wondering how she was supposed to act with him, and how easy it would feel if it were with Johnno.

Oh for God's sake, came her interior monologue. *Did it take him going out with a 22-year-old or making you Vegemite toast for you to realise you're in love with Johnno West? You stupid, stupid girl.*

The shower suddenly felt too warm, and Stevie turned it down and let the cold blast over her as she tried to stop the spinning sensation in her head. She dried herself, arms and head feeling heavy again as she dragged a comb through her hair. The only clothing within reach was a strappy silk nightie hanging on the back of the bathroom door, and she pulled it over her head and reeled back to the bed. Johnno must have heard her hit the mattress, and his head appeared around the door.

'You decent?' he asked.

'Yeah, just feeling a bit dizzy again,' she said.

'You still need more rest,' he said.

She lay back against the pillows, let him pull the sheet up over her. She shut her eyes to try to stop the spinning, and he brushed back the hair from her face with rough fingers, averting his eyes from the silky straps on her shoulders.

'What did you do to yourself, Stevie-Jean?' he said quietly.

'I just burned the candle a bit too much at both ends,' she said, eyes still closed. 'Jen moved out. Things got out of control. Partied a bit hard in Greece, stuffed up the flights to get home, did the Mungindi wedding running on empty. I could feel myself getting sick as I came home – that's why I didn't pick up Fred.'

'You have to take better care of yourself,' he said, and there was a note in his voice that made her open her eyes and fix them on his.

'Why are you here?' she asked.

'I told you. Your mum called me to get Fred and drop him off. I was coming to the city anyway.'

'Did she ask you to stay?'

'No, but she would have if she'd seen the state of you.'

'Johnno . . .' She tried to find the words, and nothing seemed to fit. 'I've been a bloody idiot.'

'Don't think about all that stuff, Stevie,' he said. 'It'll all blow over before you know it.'

'It's not just that,' she said, horrified to feel a tear leaking out of the corner of her eye. 'I've been an idiot about you.'

'About me?' he said, stiffening.

'All the time you were right there, and I didn't see you for what you are. Too caught up in my pride and distracted by the idea of a fresh start, a different life. I didn't think love could be so easy, so simple . . .'

He paused, brow furrowed. 'And now you think I'm just some dumb bogan you can settle for when the flashy bloke leaves you high and dry?'

'That's not what I meant, not at all,' she said, mortified. 'There is nothing dumb about you. You notice everything, you take care of people, you're kind and hilarious and you look so good in a suit. I just mean the way it is between us. There's no drama. I'm never guessing at what you're thinking, I'm not trying to figure out what the right response is, it just makes sense . . .' She trailed off, knowing the words coming out of her mouth were falling far short of the feeling of revelation she'd had in the shower. She could see Johnno's shoulders hitching up, his face stony, her cause lost.

'I know it's too late now,' she said, looking down at the sheets she was kneading with her fingers. 'You're too good, I'm too broken. You're with Sarah. You deserve to be happy. I shouldn't have said anything. Just . . .' She took his hand, trying to get him to meet her eyes. 'Just know that I see you now, and I'll always kick myself that it took me so bloody long.'

He stroked his cool thumb against her hand, cleared his throat and pulled his hand away. 'You've had a rough few days, Stevie, and you're not yourself. It's okay,' he said, and she closed her eyes again, felt the tears trickling down her cheeks. He had set out all the boxes of pills on her bedside table, along with a big glass of water. 'Everything you need will be here, okay? Just cancel all your plans for a few days and get as much sleep as you can.'

She kept her eyes closed, listening for the creak of the chair as he stood up. She felt him kiss her brow lightly, then heard him walk down the hall. Fred tiptoed in and, after giving her hand a reassuring lick, settled down next to her bed. Johnno was gone, the pillow was wet and she was tired, so tired.

27

Johnno stood in Stevie's kitchen, clenching and unclenching his fists. His heart was pounding and his blood felt hot with an anger that gave him a rare insight into why other blokes punched things. He leaned his forehead against the doorframe and focused on slowing down his breathing.

Figure it out later, just get out of this house, he told himself. He washed up the last crumby plates in the sink, filled Fred's water and food bowls, then threw his dirty clothes into his bag. He dialled Kate as he pulled the locked door shut behind him, ignoring Fred's quiet whines from inside the house as his boots clomped down the stairs.

'Johnno, how'd you go with the bank?' Kate answered, all business. It was a relief to have a rational conversation unclouded by emotion.

'I got caught up and had to miss the appointment. I'm on my way there now to see if they'll squeeze me in.'

'What happened? You'd been planning that meeting for weeks.'

'Paula rang me and asked me to drop off Fred at Stevie's, and when I got here she was really sick. I had to stick around for a bit to make sure she was all right – there's no one else around.' Johnno kept his tone flippant.

'Oooooh,' Kate teased. 'You had to nurse her back to health? Bet you hated that.'

'She's off with the fairies, talking some real rot. I had to get out of there,' he said, unlocking the Cruiser and starting the engine. 'Anyway, how's everything back on the place? Did Cam get home?'

'Yeah, he turned up yesterday arvo.' Kate paused, listening to Johnno's indicator ticking. 'Look, are you all right? You sound all worked up.'

He sighed. 'Things got a bit weird with Stevie.'

'Did you hook up?' Kate asked breathlessly.

'No. I'm telling you, she was so feverish she was basically hallucinating. God knows how long she'd gone without eating before I arrived.'

'So what's the problem?'

What *was* the problem? Was it the nauseating rush of lust and shame, the same queasy feeling as when he'd eaten too much junk food at the Royal Show in Grade Seven and then gone on the Cha Cha?

Was it his stung pride? Feeling like her second choice, her back-up plan, her consolation prize? Like he was just the life raft for her to cling to after Charlie had betrayed her and her life had fallen apart? Did she think he would just drop everything the second she decided he was worth her interest? What did she know about his life, what he was going through, where he was heading? How would they even make any kind of life together?

Was it the bitter slap of the timing of it all? Or maybe it was the guilt he felt when Sarah Childs' sweet face popped into his head after every thought of her had been crowded out by Stevie's mesmerising arse and the silky straps slipping off her shoulders.

Was it the jarring shock of experiencing Stevie's desire, conscious or unconscious, when he had spent so long convincing himself he had to give up on her?

Was it wanting desperately to believe what she said and knowing that it was just her fever talking?

'Johnno. You there?'

'Yeah, I'm here. Look, I've gotta focus and find a park at the bank, try to summon some charm. Whatever happens, I'll see you tonight.'

'Sure. You don't want to try to catch Mum and Dad at Sandra's place while you're there?'

'Nah, I'll wait till we're all together. Ring ya later.'

'Righto,' Kate said, and hung up.

Johnno groaned, knowing she'd go straight to Cam to speculate on what had happened, and that he'd be in for an inquisition as soon as he got back to Haven Downs. But first he had to grovel his way in to see the loan manager at Westpac, and find out if his and Kate's plans could get off the ground.

The following Sunday afternoon Kate was sitting on the kitchen bench while Johnno finished studding a big leg of lamb with garlic cloves and rosemary stalks.

'Here, can you drizzle a bit of oil on here for me?' he asked her, and she obliged. 'Now salt.' He massaged the oil and seasoning into the meat and washed his hands before putting the tray into the oven. Rabbit took up a sentry post in front to make sure the lamb didn't escape.

'Right. Should be about two hours – six-ish. What time did Mum say they'd be here?'

'About five,' Kate said.

'We'll get a bit of cheese out in case they're early,' Johnno said. 'What about Cam?'

'Said he'd be here in an hour.'

'Great. How are you feeling?'

'Ready. Well, Cam and I will run through it all again when he gets here. But I think it's a solid proposal . . .' She trailed off.

'It is, and you're going to sell it that way,' Johnno said. 'No "I think", no room for doubt. You've done the research, we've run the numbers. It makes sense for the land, for the business, for all of us.'

'So why am I so bloody nervous?'

''Cause it's your future. Of course you care. But we're not asking their permission, okay? We're adults talking about the best way to solve a problem. And I'll start things off by letting them know I'll be stepping back, so then you and Cam offer the solution for how things can run.'

When Cam arrived they had a dress rehearsal of sorts. Johnno had been worried Cam wouldn't take it seriously, but he kept the smart-arse comments to a minimum and managed to ease Kate's nerves.

'Right, you two,' Johnno said. 'Go home and shower. I'll get everything ready here. Cam, make sure you iron your shirt this time, okay?'

'Yeah, yeah,' Cam said. 'Just don't overdo the lamb or we'll all be cooked.'

Rod and Penny's wagon swung into the garage a little after five. Rod immediately set out on the four-wheeler to do a quick check of the paddocks closest to the homestead, while Penny shouted after him to be quick. As Johnno brought in their bags from the car, Penny fluttered around, giddy with stories about how the twins were developing and who they looked like.

'All good for dinner at six-thirty, Mum?' Johnno asked.

'What a treat,' she said. 'I'll just freshen up.'

Even over the roar of her hairdryer he heard Rod come in with a clatter of the screen door and bark at him to get himself cleaned up for dinner.

Finally everyone was around the table, Cam putting a steady dent in the cheese platter that Kate was too anxious to even pick at.

'Place is looking good,' Rod conceded gruffly. 'Nice bit of green about after that rain.'

'Kate had it all under control. I had to spend a few days away,' Johnno said. He placed the roast in front of Rod to carve, shooting Kate an encouraging smile.

'Again? Off showing Sarah Childs a good time, were you?' Rod teased drily. Penny's face lit up.

'No, I had a few meetings,' Johnno said. 'We've been doing a bit of research, putting together some ideas for this place.'

'We?' Rod repeated.

'Dad, Mum, we need to talk.' Johnno sat down at the table with the others. Kate took a deep breath, and Cam reached out to top up all the wineglasses around the table. 'I know you've always expected me to take over the reins here. And I'm honoured that you'd put the future in my hands. But it's because I want our family and our property to have a sustainable future that I can't be the one to run it.'

Rod looked up from carving the lamb.

'What are you saying, John?' Penny asked quietly.

'I'm not the right man for the job,' Johnno said. 'My heart's not in it. You, and Haven Downs, deserve better. And there's a much better person right here, ready to step up and run the show. Kate – along with Cam – has been here keeping things ticking over for years. They want to raise their family here and they've put together some really good plans that they're going to talk you through.'

'And what about you? Are you taking off again?' Rod asked.

'Oh, John,' Penny said.

'I'll be here to do whatever labour Kate and Cam need for the next year at least. I've got a few business ideas I want to explore, but I'd like to keep this as my base, if you're happy to have me. I was thinking I could set up a bit of a workshop in the shed, move out there, and I'll earn my keep.'

'Hmmph,' Rod said.

'Dad, we've run some numbers,' Kate started. 'With a Droughtmaster bull we could build some hardiness into the Angus herd. If we try some more drought-tolerant pasture mix in one of the paddocks, that would improve the soil quality and help run the cattle. It's an investment but it'll pay for itself before long.'

Rod was silent, but at least he wasn't shooting her down.

'Show him the figures, Kate,' Cam said. As Kate warmed up and expanded on her ideas, Johnno moved around the table serving everyone. He'd had no doubt Kate would be able to make a convincing case, but he was impressed by how calmly and clearly she was articulating her argument. Cam was hanging back, letting her do the talking, but Johnno saw his hand on Kate's under the table, giving her strength. Occasionally he'd chime in to reinforce something she said.

They're a real team, Johnno thought. Equals, working towards their future, each contributing from their strengths, complementing and boosting the other. So much more than the sum of their parts. He thought of Sarah, the flimsiness and unbalance of their relationship, and he knew he had to bite the bullet and talk to her soon to sort things out.

By the time Johnno was bringing out dessert – ice cream with Milo, he was no Penny – the table was littered with empty wine bottles. Kate and Rod had their heads bent together over a sheet of numbers, Rod scribbling with a biro.

'Well, let's give it a go,' Rod said, reaching out to shake Kate's hand, and then Cam's.

Cam rubbed Kate's back and she turned to kiss him. 'You did it,' he whispered in her ear, and she grinned.

I want that, Johnno thought.

Late the next morning the air conditioning of the tractor cab wasn't as soothing as Johnno had hoped. Cam had predictably produced a celebratory bottle of rum after dessert and it had turned into one of the rare nights when Rod got out his old Johnny Horton records. There had been a rowdy game of 500; there might have even been dancing around the lounge room. There had definitely not been enough sleep, and Johnno had drawn the short straw of working this morning while the others slept off their hangovers.

His resolve to clear things up with Sarah was weighing heavy, too. What did Stevie used to call this feeling? The HOGs. Hungover guilts. Bloody Stevie. *Get out of my head.*

A text wasn't going to cut it with Sarah. Even a call was poor form. He'd never hear the end of it from his mum. He'd have to do it face to face. Not at tennis. Somewhere they could be alone, no witnesses. Maybe they could go shooting again? No – he didn't have much relationship experience, but he was pretty sure break-ups and firearms were not a good mix. Finally, he tapped out a message.

Sorry I've been quiet lately. Dad's been up me to clean up some old junk in the swampy paddock. Wanna come over and light some stuff on fire tonight?

The ringing of his phone startled him. Surely she couldn't tell a break-up was coming just from that?

'Johnno, mate. How ya going?'

'Joe? Can't lie, I'm a bit dusty,' Johnno said.

'Big night?'

'Few too many rums with the old man and my sister. Bastards are still in bed.'

'That's rough. Can you talk a minute?'

'Yeah, sure. What's up?'

Joe explained that he and Connie were looking to expand the lines of local produce and smallgoods at their store. 'We've had more tourists coming through, and they love anything local. Are there any producers out your way we could talk to about supplying us? Anything gourmet or just really good quality?'

Johnno thought for a minute. 'Yeah, there's a few that come to mind. What about olive oil, some cheeses? There's a great little company making beef jerky just outside Toowoomba. And I've heard there are some people blending teas down near Bogga.'

'That sounds perfect,' Joe said.

'Would you guys sell flowers? There are some girls growing natives out here – they'd probably stand up all right to being transported over your way.'

'Interesting. I'll see what Connie thinks. Might be a better fit for the gallery; they're selling lots of crafts out of there.'

'I'll look into it and shoot you an email with a few contacts,' Johnno said.

'Bewdy, mate. It's so hard to find anything online. All this amazing stuff right under our noses and we have no idea. Someone needs to teach them how to sell.'

'Yeah,' Johnno said, his brain chugging into gear. He barely heard Joe say goodbye as he ended the call.

28

Stevie slept through most of the next week. In her disorientated waking minutes, her thoughts tortured her. She cringed every time she thought of how Johnno had dismissed her when she tried to tell him how she felt. Even if he did think she was incapacitated by illness, he couldn't have got out of there any faster. Was the idea of them really so repellent to him? What had changed? Because she was pretty sure he'd been flirting with her earlier in the year. Things must have become serious with Sarah.

And then she'd heard him on the phone to someone as he left, his voice floating back through her open window, so casual about it all. As far as he was concerned, Stevie was off with the fairies and talking rot. He was probably laughing about her with Sarah Childs right now. Those phrases had taken up residence in her mind along with those from the social media trolls, echoing through her listless dreams.

Fred didn't leave her side. He watched over her, licking her hand to wake her up when he needed food. When she seemed stronger, he dropped his lead at her feet, as if he knew the fresh air would help clear her head. *If you can't take care of yourself,* he seemed to say, *at least take care of me.*

Her phone was like a live bomb; every time it buzzed, she flinched. After a particularly insistent barrage of vibrations, Stevie finally picked up a call from Paula. The role reversal was complete – now it was Paula's turn to listen to Stevie crying down the line.

'I know it doesn't feel like it, but you'll survive this,' Paula was saying. 'Have you found a housemate yet?'

'I've got some applicants but I can't bring myself to respond,' Stevie said, starting to cry again. 'I can't replace Jen.'

'I know you're not telling me everything, but I know you need the money, Stevie. You've been too sick to work, so you're not earning . . .'

Stevie had had to cancel an elopement and a big weekend wedding, which had both been booked for many months. She'd had some awkward conversations with upset brides who assumed that Stevie was too embarrassed after the *BB* scandal to show her face. Stevie had rung around all her contacts in the industry to find replacement photographers to cover both events, so the couples weren't inconvenienced. But there would be the matter of their deposits, which they'd be asking to have refunded once they were back from their honeymoons. Stevie couldn't remember how her contracts were worded around cancellations, and the ring-around had left her too exhausted to think clearly.

'Every time I sit down at the computer to try to catch up on the edits people are waiting for, my head spins. The phone won't stop ringing. Brides are comparing notes in my Instagram comments about how long they've been waiting for their albums. Which mingles nicely with the trolls. It's just all too much.' Stevie sighed. 'Why did Charlie do this to me, Mum?'

'I'm pretty sure it wasn't about you, honey,' Paula said gently.

'I don't think I can live with not knowing,' Stevie wailed. 'It's making me crazy.'

After a pause, Paula said, 'I've had a lot of time to live with not knowing why. I'm not saying it's easy. But you can only make peace with your part in it. What other people think, feel, do – that's out of our control. If you did everything you could to make things right, that's all you can ever know for sure.'

'We're not just talking about Charlie any more, are we?'

'I had to take responsibility for my part in what happened with your father. He showed me who he was, but we still pushed on hoping things could turn out differently. Now you don't talk to your dad, and that makes me so sad.'

'I hate what he did,' Stevie said.

'But it's just that – something he did. He's still your dad. We all make mistakes.'

'And how,' Stevie grunted.

'But what would I know? I can't even figure out how to turn off the dating app on my phone.'

'You haven't taken down your profile?'

'I don't know how! And you wouldn't believe the photos some men have the temerity to send.'

Oh God, Stevie thought. *This is my future. I'm going to be fielding dick pics in my sixties.*

'One minute I'm having a perfectly civilised chat with a Roger from Roma. The next he sends a photo – I can't even describe it. Hang on, I'll send it to you.'

'Mum, no. I don't need to see it.'

'It's terribly stunted and in desperate need of some pruning. I can't believe anyone would share a photo of something in this state. These men have no self-respect.'

'Mum!' Stevie squealed as a message preview popped up on her screen. 'Wait. What am I looking at here?'

'Right? He's got the nerve to call himself a keen gardener.'

From somewhere deep inside a laugh fizzed up through Stevie, piercing the hurt and overwhelm that had been weighing her down, until she was gasping through uncontrollable giggles and feeling something like her old self. 'You're mortally offended because Roger sent you a picture of his roses and they're not up to scratch?'

'What did you think I was talking about, darling?'

After yet another message that her voicemail was full, Stevie bit the bullet and listened to them, huddled on the floor with Fred for support. As well as teary brides chasing their final photos and distant cousins 'checking in' after seeing her on TV, there were a number of messages from slick-sounding producers. One was particularly insistent.

'Stevie, it's Rick Cross again from Network Six. I'm going to be in Brisbane this week and I'd really like to meet with you – I think you'll be very interested in what I have to discuss. Call me, please.'

Judging by Stevie's emails and the other messages, Jen had been right about the producers wanting to capitalise on her fifteen minutes of fame. It was too mortifying to countenance. Until she finally answered a call from her accountant.

'Stevie, I've been trying to get hold of you for months.'

'Sorry, Todd, it's been hectic.'

'Have you been opening your mail? Emails?' he asked.

'. . . Yeah, mostly.'

'Not the ones from the tax office, I'm guessing, or I would have heard from you sooner.'

'What do you mean?' Stevie asked.

'You're behind on your BAS, and unless we can get the paper-work together in the next week, you'll be audited. Either way, there's a big bill to pay for the taxes you've missed.'

Stevie's stomach dropped. 'How big?'

'Depending on what rabbits I can pull out of hats, if you ever give me your up-to-date accounts, you're looking at about eight grand.'

Eight grand. Plus the four she owed Jen for the flights. The ten on her maxed-out credit card, not to mention the slew of bills wait-ing to be paid. Stevie groaned.

'Come in to the office tomorrow. Bring every receipt, every scrap of paper you've got. I'll block out two hours and we'll crack into it.'

Stevie hung up the phone, feeling shell-shocked. She'd hadn't left the house in more than a week, hadn't walked Fred, was living among piles of dishes and dirty laundry. She thought with shame of how tidy Johnno had left everything and how quickly her mess had returned.

Her phone rang again. She picked up, hoping Todd had found a miracle fix for the tax situation. 'Stevie? Rick Cross.' *Oh God.*

'Look, mate, I'm not interested. I've had enough attention to last a lifetime,' Stevie said.

'I can understand that,' he said smoothly. 'But I just want to make sure you know what you're turning down. What I can offer you is a hundred-thousand-dollar opportunity, not to mention the sponsorships and gigs that our talent tend to attract long after their show is off the air.'

'A hundred grand?' Stevie repeated.

'Let me buy you lunch tomorrow,' he said.

A meal couldn't hurt, and she'd have to drag herself out to the accountant's anyway . . .

'Where should I meet you?'

Stevie walked into the restaurant right on time, and before she could tell the hostess who she was there to meet, a tall man in a suit was approaching her with his arm outstretched.

'Rick Cross,' he said, shaking Stevie's hand warmly and flashing a lot of very white teeth. 'It's so great to meet you, Stevie. Thanks for coming.'

He guided her to a window-side table with a hand on the small of her back, and Stevie was glad she'd taken the time to blow-dry her hair and pick out a silk dress she hadn't worn in a while.

'You look lovely,' Rick said, as if reading her mind. 'Cocktail to start? Or a nice cool rosé?'

'I wouldn't usually have a cocktail at lunch,' Stevie said, 'but it's been a long morning.'

She'd spent a full two hours with Todd the accountant and left feeling like a penitent schoolgirl. There weren't many schoolgirls who had to figure out how to pay an $8000 tax bill, though. 'I'd love an icy gin martini, couple of olives, just a little dirty.'

'Aren't you full of surprises?' Rick beamed. 'That sounds so perfect, I believe I'll have one too.' He was highly skilled at restaurant ordering as well as small talk, and it was only after he'd confidently ordered them a feast that Stevie realised she hadn't even seen the menu.

Two frosty martinis were set down in front of them, and as they clinked glasses Stevie remembered, a little too late, the handful of cold and flu tablets she'd taken at breakfast. *Oops.*

'That's a strong drink,' Rick said, wincing.

'No playing around, that's what I love about a martini,' Stevie said. 'Speaking of which, Rick . . . I'm happy to take advantage of your hospitality here, but I suspect you need to cover off on some business. Right?'

'There's no rush,' he said. 'But I do have an offer for you, and I get the feeling you don't want to beat around the bush.'

'Pun intended?'

'Definitely. Look, Stevie, you're a smart girl. You've got a great look, and a great story. You were on screen for a total of three minutes, and the country fell in love with you. You're real, and people connect with that.'

Stevie rolled her eyes.

'You can be as cynical as you like about what we do. We're in the entertainment business and, yes, we're manufacturing drama. We choose our on-screen talent with the express purpose of creating conflict. We set up situations, clash personalities, ply people with alcohol to lower their inhibitions, and feed them gossip and ideas so they react. It's not Shakespeare, but you know what? We get a lot more eyeballs than the theatre.'

The waitress placed a steak in front of him, fish in front of Stevie, and a mass of side dishes between them. She poured out wine for both of them that Rick had evidently ordered as well. Rick sniffed his glass, tasted the rich pinot, and gave the waitress an approving nod. He took a bite of bloody steak before continuing.

'Thing is, we have all these tricks to make drama, but we've only developed them out of necessity. When there's something real, we don't need all the smoke and mirrors.'

'You expect me to believe that if I say yes to doing a show

with you, there will be no producers manipulating me behind the scenes?' Stevie asked.

He laughed heartily. 'I can't make a guarantee like that. But what I'm saying is, every few years there's a bit of reality TV magic when we can put someone on screen who's not there trying to create their fifteen minutes of fame.' He paused and changed tack. 'You watched the season where Alex and Steph met, right?'

Stevie nodded, her mouth full of green beans.

'We didn't even get the half of their story on camera, and it was still the best relationship we've ever put to air. You remember how it felt to watch that?'

She nodded. 'I just don't think I could let go like that on camera. I'd get all awkward.'

'So be awkward,' Rick said simply. 'I'm not asking you to fake something you don't feel. Just react like you would if you met these blokes as wedding guests. Take the piss out of them. Laugh at them when they're idiots. Get to know them.'

Stevie chewed thoughtfully.

'We've never done this before, Stevie. We're talking about upending our franchise to structure a season around you, our first Bush Bachelorette. You'll have the best-looking group of blokes you've ever seen following you around like puppies. You'll have a glam team making sure you look as fabulous – or as natural – as you want, at all times. And you'll be paid very, very well. But we have to jump on this while everyone is still dying to know what happens to the sweet wedding photographer who got dicked over on *BB*.'

'Suppose I was actually considering this, Rick. Which is a stretch, given the experience I've had the past couple of weeks since you and your team aired my humiliation on national TV without a word of warning.'

'We did try to call you,' he said weakly.

'Sure,' Stevie said. 'Exactly how well paid would I be? And when would this circus get started?'

Rick pulled out a leather folder, opening it to reveal a substantial contract. He took Stevie through the upfront payment, the ongoing residuals from re-runs and streaming, the clauses for spin-offs and other potential roles with the network. He explained the major sponsors that were interested, the ads and appearances she'd be expected to do for them. The teaser marketing campaign they'd have to shoot within a month, before the show started production early in the new year.

'We've got our call-out for studs ready to roll,' Rick said. 'All we need is for you to say yes.'

The waitress cleared their plates and refilled Stevie's wineglass again. She couldn't remember ever reaching the bottom of it, but she felt truly relaxed for the first time in weeks.

'Dessert?' Rick asked, raising a wicked eyebrow. 'You don't have to decide today. Sleep on it, talk to your friends and family, but don't leave it too long. These things go cold quickly, but there's potential here to do something really special. Now – the deconstructed tiramisu or the pavlova? Eh, let's get both.'

Stevie had to admit he could make anything sound delicious.

Stevie woke with a pounding headache the next morning. Rick Cross had put her in a cab, handed the driver a crisp fifty and told him to keep the change. After struggling up the stairs and grappling with her keys, it was still very much afternoon when Stevie collapsed into bed. But despite a hangover, she felt the best she had in weeks.

As she flicked the kettle on to boil, Stevie spotted Rick's contract on the counter. It must have been forty pages: definitely post-coffee reading. After some cereal (Vegemite toast brought back too many memories) she tidied the house, took out the rubbish, put on a load of washing and slowly, painfully, worked through the pile of mail she'd been ignoring. Among the bills was a postcard from Evie and James on their honeymoon, and a card from Millie and Blake announcing they were expecting a baby. They'd worked fast.

'Okay, how are you tackling the day?' Paula asked on their now regular morning call.

'I've made a spreadsheet of all the bills I have to pay, which is daunting but I have to face it,' Stevie started.

'You do.'

'There are four jobs I can invoice for, so that's my first task. That should bring in at least eleven grand. And then there are another four clients I can invoice once I finish some editing, probably a couple of hours each.'

'Great plan, darling. I'm heading out to take George a cake, but let me know how you go. I'm proud of you.'

Midafternoon Stevie took a break to walk Fred. Before she got back to her computer, there was one thing Stevie needed to do. She had drafted and deleted about twelve different grovelling apology texts to Jen but nothing seemed right. It wasn't that Jen wasn't talking to her, but that when she did, it was stiff and polite, which was worse.

'I've got to get her back,' Stevie said to Fred, who panted his approval but wasn't much help with crafting a message. Eventually she just rolled the dice with *I miss you. Can I take you out for dinner tonight?* Then she tried not to watch the screen. She turned it face-down and kept editing.

She surfaced a few hours later, having finished the final images of a 400-shot set. It wasn't her best work but it was fine, and it was finished. She started uploading the files to the sharing site she used and set up access for the bride and groom. While she waited for the upload to complete she flipped her phone over and was delighted to see a text back from Jen.

OK. But I want Chinese and you have to take me to my favourite place.

Stevie knew the exact grotty, sweltering shop in West End Jen was referring to, and while she always put on a show of hating it, there was no place on earth she'd rather be.

'You're on. I can pick you up at 6.30 if you want a lift. Wine or beers?'

'Beers. I'll meet you there.'

Stevie emptied her recycling into the wheelie bin with a clatter. A voice came from a man leaning against her fence. 'Sounds like a lot of empty bottles in there, mate.'

Stevie did a double take. 'Dad? What are you doing here?'

'You never answer my calls or my messages, kid. What was I supposed to do?'

Stevie kicked the ground. She didn't want to invite Mark in but it felt wrong to have this conversation on the footpath in full view of the neighbours. Brisbane wasn't that much bigger than her home town when you got down to airing family laundry alfresco.

'Come in for a cuppa, then,' she said finally. On the verandah, Fred sniffed him cautiously. Stevie sipped tea while he helped himself to a beer from the fridge. They made small talk, catching up superficially on the years Stevie had been leaving Mark's texts and calls unreturned. It was easy to fall in with his larrikin charm.

'I saw you on TV,' he said. 'One minute I was beaming with pride – "that's my girl on the telly!" Next thing that bloody goose did what he did and I just wanted to knock his block off.'

'You and me both,' Stevie said.

'Did you want to knock my block off, too?' He pitched it as a joke, but Stevie was tired of pretending this was a lighthearted chat.

'I didn't want to talk to you after what you did to Mum.'

Mark dropped his head. 'I messed up, Stevie. If I were you, I wouldn't forgive me either.'

'She lost her home, her history. How did you let things get so bad?'

He leaned back in his chair, rubbed his stubble with a scratchy sound. 'Everyone always thought I was an outsider. I wanted to prove I could do it, so I didn't want to admit when things started going wrong. I really thought I could fix things without anyone realising. Right up until I realised I couldn't. I was so ashamed, I had to walk away – but I couldn't face her, couldn't face you. Then I lost it all.'

All the years she'd held him at arm's length, he'd loomed in her mind. But he was just a man. A man who got it wrong, in ways she felt all too familiar with. A man who'd always covered up his fears with tall stories and bravado, and taken the easy way out. He didn't have all the answers, but there was a lesson here, if she was strong enough to take it.

'Life's too short, Stevie-Jean. You've got to face your mistakes – it's never as bad as you think. As long as you can share it, it won't kill you. It's only when you try to struggle through on your own that things get hairy. Got any more of these?' He peered into the empty beer bottle.

She gave him the last one, and listened to a few more tall tales before she showed him the door.

Stevie made sure to be early, nabbing a table in the front and nervously necking a stubby while she waited for Jen. No matter the season, it always felt like the height of summer in this tiny restaurant. She'd never had a meal there without sweat dripping down the back of her calves, and this evening was no different. The beer bottle sweated in her hand, the label lifting off, and Stevie tried not to pick at it.

If Jen was surprised to see her there early, she was kind enough not to make a fuss about it.

'How was your day?' Stevie asked.

Jen sighed. 'Long. Work's a disaster at the moment.'

'Tell me about it,' Stevie said, and then she listened while Jen talked through the office politics, staff shortage and lack of resources she was dealing with. They ordered, and the food came out fast: a steaming whole fish covered with a tangle of green onions and chilli, greasy noodles, green vegies. They dug in with chopsticks, sharing everything, and Stevie asked the waitress to bring more beers.

'Want to see some photos of our boy? He misses you.'

'Hell yes,' Jen said, grabbing Stevie's phone. When she'd scrolled through all the pics, she said, 'Well done, I knew you could keep him alive.'

'He might have kept me alive,' Stevie muttered. 'And how's the wedding planning going?'

Jen looked up. 'It's not, really. Well, not for me. I'm pretty sure Andrew has at least a couple of Pinterest boards. I just haven't been able to feel excited about it.'

'That's normal,' Stevie said. 'It's a massive thing to plan. Have you got a date in mind?'

'September next year,' Jen said.

'If you haven't booked a photographer, I'd be honoured if you'd let me do it. As your wedding gift.'

'Well, you might be hopeless at a lot of life stuff but I really could've used your expertise on weddings over the past few weeks. The whole industry's an absolute rort, isn't it?' Jen gave a hollow laugh that turned into a little sob. Stevie was choking up too.

'Aw, Jen, I've missed you so much. I know I have to get used to living in a house without you, but not having you at all is too hard.'

'I know,' Jen wailed. 'It sucks.'

'No, you were right,' Stevie said. 'I was way out of line, and I had been for a while. I'm really sorry, Jen.'

'Thanks, Stevie. It's gonna happen for you, you know. We're just a bit out of sync at the moment, and that's okay. But I had to pick myself this time.'

'How's it been going, living at Andrew's?' Stevie asked.

Jen drained the last of her stubby, and Stevie handed her another. 'Well, he's a lot neater than you. It's been a weird role reversal having someone complain about my mess.' She grinned. 'But it's been nice. You know how particular Andrew can be about things. But he's really made an effort to give me a chance to put my own stamp on things.'

'I bet he's loving having you there, and you'll be good for him,' Stevie said. 'Loosen him up a bit.'

'Did you get someone else in my old room yet?'

Stevie shook her head. 'Not yet, but forget that. I want to hear your engagement story. All the gory details, please.'

Jen smiled at her, and told the story. She'd obviously had some practice, enough retellings to family and friends to have the narrative refined. The dodgy breakfast that had set up Andrew's food poisoning for the day; Jen's insistence that they traipse all over Paris anyway. The champagne Andrew had struggled to keep down while he set out a beautiful picnic with a view of the Eiffel Tower, and how she'd worried he might vomit on the vintage blanket borrowed from their Airbnb. How his hands shook when he offered up the ring box.

'It was a comedy of errors,' Jen said, laughing, 'and I'll never forget a moment of it.'

'Sounds perfect,' Stevie said.

Jen smiled again, but then said, 'Righto, Stevie. Cut this out.'

'Cut what out?'

'I know you have goss. How have you been going with everything?'

Stevie sighed. 'Honestly? I've been in a bad way. I was pretty down after you moved out. The stuff people were saying about me online really started to get to me, then I got really run down and crook after the Mungindi wedding. Had to cancel on a couple of clients, which always feels terrible. And now all the tax stuff Andrew kept nagging me about has come back to bite me, and I'm in a bit of trouble with money. Don't worry, I'll pay you back first,' Stevie added hastily.

Jen waved her away. 'Just pay me back when you can.'

'Dad showed up on my doorstep today, too.'

'How did that go? I'm guessing he wasn't invited.'

'No. You know I have a habit of leaving him hanging, so I suppose he felt like he had no alternative. Maybe I've been a bit hard on him. He obviously didn't intend for things to turn out this way, just was too proud to ask for help.'

'Well, imagine that. Ignoring the hard things doesn't make them any easier. Now where have I heard that before?'

Stevie punched her in the arm. 'Do I have to say you told me so?'

Jen smiled. 'I'll let it slide. But what about Johnno?'

'What about Johnno?' Stevie asked, looking down at the fish skeleton that remained of their dinner, trying to find pockets of meat that they'd missed.

'Well, he texted me last week and told me to check on you, for one thing.'

'He did? Ugh.' Stevie uttered a low moan of shame.

'What happened?' Jen asked.

'Mum asked him to drop off Fred and check on me. I don't know if she was trying to play matchmaker or just playing dumb—'

'Paula, that dark horse,' Jen interjected.

'Anyway, when he turned up I was in rough shape. I think I had a pretty bad fever at that stage. I don't actually remember him arriving, but I must have let him in. He basically stayed and nursed me for a couple of days, got me drugs, made sure I ate, changed the sheets . . .'

'Oh Johnno. What a lovely bloke he is.'

'Right? I think I might have tried to feel him up in my sleep when he was dozing on my bed. It's all a bit fuzzy in my memory. But it made me realise I wanted him – like, really wanted him – in a way I didn't know I did.'

'I bloody told you, Stevie-Jean.'

'Yeah, yeah. Anyway, I basically told him I was in love with him and he just patted me on the head and said I wasn't in my right mind. And then he couldn't get out of there fast enough. It was mortifying.'

'Hold up. In love with him? Stevie, really?'

Stevie sighed and shrugged. 'What does it matter? I'm smitten and he's moved on. It'd be funny if it wasn't so tragic. He was right there in front of me, and I don't know why I couldn't see it until it was too late.'

'Surely it's not too late?'

'No, it is. Maybe he was keen a few months ago, but I guarantee he's not any more. At any rate, I'm off blokes for a while. No good ever comes of it.'

'We'll see,' said Jen. 'Well, what about the other stuff? Are you getting things under control?'

Stevie nodded. 'Slowly. I've moved past the denial stage and I'm trying to sort things out. I really don't know if I'll keep shooting weddings. I'm thinking it might be time for a change. Move overseas for a bit, get away from everything. Or . . .' She paused.

'What?' Jen asked.

'I'm not seriously considering it, although I do keep having dreams about what I'd do with the money.'

'Did they offer you a TV gig?'

'The first ever season of *Bush Bachelorette*.'

'I would watch the hell out of that,' Jen exclaimed. 'But I don't know if it's what you need right now.'

'It's definitely not what I need right now. Aside from the dozen hot blokes trying to win my heart, and the hundred grand starting salary.'

Jen inhaled sharply. 'That's a lot of money.'

'Isn't it?' Stevie said. 'Could solve a few problems.'

New post in 'Neighbourhood News' from The Bush Telegraph:

GUESS WHO: A local girl made good who we love to follow on Instagram hasn't been posting lately . . . Maybe something to do with a rather public, rather embarrassing incident. I hate to say I told you so . . .

However, our favourite, very single snapper might soon be back on our screens in a big way. My sources suggest she's considering a deal to meet her match on TV. Lock up your bachelors and don't hold your breath for your wedding photos . . . LOL, Mabel

29

Muscle memory kicked in as Stevie guided the Pajero around the curves of the driveway into Mossdale. It had been years, but a shadow of the old anticipation she used to feel driving into Tom's family property rose up in her. In those days there would be a nervy mix of wondering how she'd fare with his parents, perhaps a tummy rumble knowing a good country feast was imminent. Now, of course, an even more volatile cocktail of emotions was in play. Shaken and stirred.

Stevie had kicked her virus and regained her strength. She was eating properly, keeping booze to a minimum and keeping her head down to get through this rough patch at work. The back beat of her mind was a looping cracked record of questions she didn't know how to answer – *Can I get out of this debt? Am I doing the right thing taking the* BB *money? I've already been humiliated on national TV once; will it happen again? At least I'll get paid for it. Or should I just sell all my gear and leave the country? Have I ruined things forever with Johnno? Can I get out of this debt?* And on, and on.

Breathe. She was trying to take things one day at a time, and she knew the best thing she could do today was a solid professional job shooting Tom and Lily's wedding. She was just going to have to put aside her personal issues and get it done. Forget about the history with Tom, forget about the insecurities Lily dragged up, forget about having declared her feelings to Johnno only to have him summarily reject them. Stevie cringed at the memory. *No, better not to think about that at all, ever.*

Parking amid a gridlock of four-wheel drives, Stevie took a few deep breaths before grabbing her gear, Fred's bowl and lead, and heading to the familiar house. She could hear a hive of chatter and activity in the kitchen, and her nerve faltered. So she ducked into the laundry for a second to compose herself – and came face to face with June Carruthers, who was apparently doing the same thing.

Stevie had seen Tom's mother briefly a few times in the years since the break-up, and they were always cordial, but it had been a while. This was the first time they'd seen each other since Bruce's death.

'June, I'm so sorry, I just needed a moment before seeing everyone,' Stevie started.

'Me too,' June said, taking Stevie's hands. 'It's good to see you. I'm glad you're here, if that's not too weird to say.'

Stevie felt her eyes watering. 'I was so sorry to hear about Bruce, June. I'm sorry I haven't been in touch more.'

'Don't worry, love,' June comforted her. 'It's been tough on all of us, especially Tom. But it is what it is. There's no use feeling bad about it. We're lucky to have Lily with us now, and having everyone here to celebrate feels right.'

'Gonna be an emotional day,' Stevie said gently.

'Without a doubt.' June smiled. 'Got my tissues ready. It's funny, I know Tom hasn't cried much since Bruce, and he might today. But Lily is the one who's really tightly wound, like she's taken on the weight of carrying us all today. I haven't seen her like this before. She's usually so calm.'

'I get the impression she likes to be in control,' Stevie said.

'That's an understatement. Well, let's just hope it all goes smoothly for her sake. I wouldn't like to be responsible for disappointing her,' June joked.

'Is it okay if I tie up my dog around the back of the shed?' Stevie asked, brandishing his water bowl. June nodded. 'I'd better start setting up, then. The garden is looking amazing, by the way.'

'Thanks, dear. Now, you get out there and meet the celebrant. Tom's around somewhere. Lily doesn't want any of us to see her till she's ready. Come and have a piece of cake with me when your work's all done tonight, okay? We'll catch up.'

'I'd love that. Enjoy the day.' Stevie kissed her on the cheek and June squeezed Stevie's hand as she left the room.

Stevie braced herself to see Tom or Johnno (with Sarah?) and for any number of other potential awkward run-ins. But her stroll across the lawn that June had lovingly manicured through the drought was blessedly free of confrontation.

—

Tom was straightening Johnno's tie in the bathroom. 'Bloody hell, mate. Aren't you supposed to be taking care of *my* outfit? Best man, my arse,' he ribbed.

'Yeah, yeah,' Johnno said. 'Given how late I am, I need all the help I can get.'

Tom fussed at the tie while Johnno eyed his stubby of beer across the room. It didn't seem like Tom would be too impressed if he reached for it.

'So, do I have to break the news to Lily that your plus one is a no-show?'

The blood drained from Johnno's face. 'Mate, I'm so sorry. With everything that's happening it slipped my mind. I'll tell Lily.'

Tom laughed. 'Too right you will. You know how long it took us to whittle down the guest list. What's the story, anyway? I thought things were going well with Sarah?'

Johnno winced. 'She's a lovely girl. Better than I deserve. My heart just wasn't in it.'

'Break-ups are the worst. How did you do it? You didn't ghost her, did you?' Tom asked.

'No, Dad, I did it in person. It was awkward as hell but that was kind of our default setting, so we survived it. I think we might actually manage to be friends. Eventually. I'll leave that ball in her court. Oh God. Tennis is going to be uncomfortable.'

'You're sweating.' Tom laughed. 'Go on, finish your bloody beer, we need to get out there.'

—

Stevie took in the flat cloudless sky, the rose bushes and gardenias that encircled the lawn with fragrance. It was only October but it felt like midsummer. The sun beat down harshly, and the guests slowly massing on the lawn were wearing hats of all kinds with the black-tie tuxedos and gowns Lily had insisted upon.

Tom and Lily were skipping the church in favour of a simple late-afternoon ceremony in June's garden. Per her discussion with Lily, Stevie was going to focus on candid shots of the ceremony and reception. Lily didn't want a lot of posed portraits or any shots of her getting ready. Stevie would get her first glimpse of the bride at the same time as all the other guests.

As everyone took their seats Stevie was on high alert for familiar faces she both wanted to see and wanted to avoid. Jen and Andrew were due to arrive any minute, and she had a feeling the Bush Telegraph would have wangled an invitation somehow. Kate West had waved to her before taking a seat next to her husband, and Connie and Joe's kids were running around with Christine's son, Sebastian, while Gavin tried to keep up. But of course it was Johnno's broad shoulders Stevie was really scanning for as she hovered at the back of the crowd.

The seats were full by the time she finally spotted him walking out of the house with a reassuring arm on Tom's shoulder. They were deep in quiet conversation and didn't look up as they took seats in the front row next to June. They kept chatting until the celebrant cleared her throat and waved for Tom to take his place, at which point Johnno shook his hand animatedly and gave him a little pat on the bottom as he stood up. Stevie told herself she would have been watching closely enough to capture that moment at anyone's wedding.

There was a collective intake of breath, and everyone swivelled. Lily looked incredible. Slinking down the aisle to a recording of a ukulele ballad, her skin was glowing and tan and there was plenty of it on display. Her silk slip dress was luminescent, her makeup was simple and timeless, her hair fell in glossy waves. A white orchid the size of a saucer was tucked behind one ear, offsetting her architectural gold jewellery. She carried a trailing wild bouquet of dark greenery and sprays of tiny orchids and star jasmine. She even smelled expensive. *She wouldn't look out of place in the pages of* Vogue, Stevie thought.

Lily had no bridal party, but a gaggle of designer-clad fellow law students in expensive haircuts stacked her side of the seating arrangement. Tom was transfixed as Lily made her way towards him, and Stevie captured the adoration on his rapt face. This was a wedding that would look stunning in black-and-white. Lily's instincts had been bang-on.

Suddenly the song began to skip, repeating the same notes over and over again until the celebrant finally dived at the CD player and stopped it. Stevie saw Lily's shoulders tense, but luckily she'd reached her destination and no one noticed the music stop. They were too focused on the joy and excitement on Tom's face when he took Lily's hands in his.

'Dearly beloved,' the celebrant began. A middle-aged woman in a boxy suit, Monica had briefly introduced herself to Stevie before the ceremony. Stevie hadn't thought much of it when the celebrant confided that this was only her second wedding and she was quite nervous. But her voice kept wavering over the dinky PA system long after Stevie expected her nerves would have abated.

Stevie continued shooting the ceremony as Monica slowly dug herself into a pit of despair. She managed to call Lily 'Lucy', and Tom 'Tim' and 'Terry'. Lily barely reacted, a smile plastered on her face throughout, but Stevie thought she caught an eye twitch at 'Terry'. Nevertheless, Stevie knew she was getting beautiful photos, and once it was over to Tom and Lily for the vows, their genuine emotion had a chance to shine without Monica's stiffness. Stevie noticed how Lily gently encouraged Tom, who'd started to choke up a bit. Tom watched Lily with open adoration as she spoke her vows clearly, with the projection she'd honed in the courtroom. They were a great fit.

'Tom and Lily, I now pronounce you husband and wife.' Monica nailed the dismount, and the crowd went wild. Tom swept Lily backwards into a Hollywood kiss, and Stevie knew it would be one

of the stand-out images of the day. The toe of Tom's freshly polished RMs had caught the hem of Lily's dress, though, and as he
dipped her back up she narrowly avoided flashing a (no doubt magnificent) nipple. The couple giggled nervously and Monica hastily
cued up the CD player for the song they'd walk back down the aisle
to as a newly married couple. But instead of the Beatles song listed
in the order of service – 'Something' – it was 'Yellow Submarine'
that came bouncing from the speakers. Tom and Lily shrugged and
went with it. The guests sang along; it was a ridiculous moment but
one none of them would forget.

After Lily and Tom had signed the registry, wellwishers sur-
rounded the happy couple. Stevie got some crowd shots and images
of family and friends hugging. Jen gave her a supportive wave.
She captured Johnno briefly embracing both Tom and Lily before
he stepped away to give others a chance. Stevie felt a tug at her
heart to see him in black tie, his hair just at that sweet spot before
being too long, his jaw clean-shaven and tan against the starched
white collar. He caught her eye and she tried to walk away, but he
caught up with her.

'Poor old Monica made a meal of that, hey? Good thing the
bride's so chill and put her at ease,' Johnno joked.

Stevie laughed in spite of her nerves. 'So there's no bridal party,
but you're still the best man. How'd you swing that?'

'I'm just that good. Just wait for my speech,' he said.

God, what was she supposed to say to him now? The conversation faltered.

'How have you been, Stevie?' he asked gently. 'You're back
on track?'

She hung her head. Of course he was thinking of what a disaster
she was. 'Nothing like a bit of soul-searching,' she said sarcastically.

'I'm figuring out where to go next. I think I need a change in direction. They've actually offered me my own season of *BB* – a Bush Bachelorette for the first time, can you believe it?'

Johnno laughed, and then realised Stevie wasn't joking. 'You're gonna do it?'

'The money they're offering is insane, and I need it,' she said. 'Besides, I've already been humiliated on national television once. May as well get paid for it.'

He frowned, but when he didn't speak Stevie found herself babbling on. 'Even if it goes terribly, I can just take the money and leave the country, for good this time. But who knows, maybe I'll meet my soulmate!' she finished brightly, the smile never quite reaching her eyes.

'You've really thought about this,' Johnno said, and she nodded. 'Well, good luck to you, Stevie-Jean. When you're hobnobbing with all the celebrities in Sydney, at least I'll be able to say I knew you before you were famous.'

A silence yawned between them, but neither seemed able to walk away. Johnno was fiddling with the order of service in his hands. *Is he nervous?* Stevie wondered.

'Well, you look much better than the last time I saw you,' he finally said.

'I'll bet,' she said, with a harsh little laugh. She breathed deeply, focused on keeping her spine straight, and said the words she needed to. 'Thank you, for all that you did. I'm sorry I made a mess of things.'

'It's okay,' he said quickly. 'You were really out of it.'

This is your chance, she thought. *Don't take the easy way out.* 'I know I was sick, but I remember what I said,' she said. 'I meant it. It wasn't a mistake.'

'Don't worry about it, I'm over it,' he said quickly. 'You've always had it right. We've been through too much as friends to muck things up. It's not worth it. Look, I'd better go and check on June.'

Stevie nodded and watched him go, the pounding in her chest only abating slightly as he disappeared from sight. *That's that then,* she thought sadly. *Just because Sarah's not here doesn't mean anything. But I did all I could do. Time to let it go.*

Feeling tears springing to the corners of her eyes, Stevie slipped away in search of a quiet spot. Rounding the shed to find Fred for a cuddle as her vision blurred with tears, she slumped down onto the concrete before realising they weren't alone.

'Ciggie, love?' came a woman's raspy but warm voice.

Stevie could only nod. Her carcinogenic guardian angel tucked a dart between her lips and cupped the flame of an orange plastic lighter for Stevie to draw back on.

'Bit much, isn't it?' the woman said, and again Stevie nodded.

The first drag made her head spin. She looked over at the woman, who was looking out into the garden. She couldn't be older than her early forties, and seemed uncomfortable in an expensive matronly dress.

'Don't judge the outfit. My daughter insisted on it,' she said, reading Stevie's glance. 'I haven't been this covered up in years, but we had to make the right impression for this crowd. How do you know the happy couple, love?'

'I'm the photographer,' Stevie said, offering her hand. 'Stevie. I also . . . went out with the groom for most of my twenties. Not awkward at all.' She smiled.

'Jeez, he does all right for himself, old Tom. Well, you didn't make a scene during the ceremony so I'm guessing you're not trying to win him back.' That raspy laugh came again. 'I shouldn't be here, you shouldn't be here, but I've got some perfume and breath mints so no one will bust us. Christ, if my girlfriends could see me now. Like a naughty little schoolgirl.'

They laughed together.

'I'm Cynthia, Cyn for short. Lily loves that.'

'You're from Lily's side?'

'I'm her mum.'

'Oh!' Stevie said.

'Not what you expected?' Cyn asked.

'Not exactly,' Stevie admitted.

'Lily's done a very good job of removing every trace of her upbringing from her new life,' Cyn said.

'I'm sure that's not true,' Stevie said.

'No, she had to.' Cyn was matter-of-fact. 'She's a smart girl – she knows what it takes to get ahead. Just makes things a bit awkward for her when she has to invite her daggy old mum to try to mix with her new friends.'

'Weddings are always stressful, I think. Different people try to deal with that stress in different ways. Lily's way seems to be being super prepared.'

'That's one way to put it,' Cyn said. 'I was worried she'd blow a fuse with that celebrant, but she might make it through yet. She's got a bit of her dad's temper in her, much as she tries to hide it.'

'Is he here? Lily's dad?'

'No, love. He's in Wacol. Got a few more years on his bit yet.'

'Oh. I'm sorry,' Stevie said.

'Honestly, he's spent more time there than he ever did being a dad to Lily.'

'Well, I'll package up some photos for Lily to take him so he can see how beautiful she looked.'

'That's a nice idea. So, if you don't mind me asking, how come it's not you with Tom's ring on your finger?'

'That's a conversation for another cigarette.' Stevie sighed.

Cyn pulled out two more from her pack and handed Stevie her lighter.

'Just not the right fit.' Stevie shrugged after a deep inhale. 'He knew what he wanted his life to be and expected me to fit into it. I had no idea what I wanted to do, but I didn't really want to be a farmer's wife. Now I'm no one's wife, and I still have no idea what I want to do.'

'I reckon he probably learned a lot from you, but Lily's also good at telling him what their life should be.'

'They're much better matched than we ever were,' Stevie admitted.

'So who are you moping over, then?' Cyn asked.

'The best man.'

'The best mate?'

'Yep.'

'You don't do things by halves, do you? He seems fun, though – I like him.'

'He's pretty great,' Stevie said sadly.

'You're telling me he's not up for this?' Cyn asked, sweeping a broad sketch of Stevie's form with her cigarette like a laser pointer.

'It would seem not.'

'Ah, he'll come round. Just making you sweat for it a bit, I reckon.'

Stevie sighed as she stubbed out her cigarette. 'Right, I better get back to it.'

'Aren't you going to take my picture?' Cyn teased her, contorting her curves into a pin-up pose. Stevie raised the camera to her eye and snapped a series of fun portraits.

Fred started to yap excitedly as Jen appeared. She ran over to give him a cuddle and a scratch.

'Sorry to interrupt,' she said. 'I just need to inhale your smoke for a minute or two.'

'Want one?' Cyn offered.

As Jen wavered, Stevie said, 'No, she's quit.' But Andrew had already barrelled around the corner.

'I knew it,' he roared.

'It's not what it looks like,' Stevie and Jen shouted in unison.

'I'm out of here,' Cyn muttered.

'You're not still smoking?' Andrew asked.

'It's killing me on an hourly basis, but no, I haven't had a puff since we got back from Europe,' Jen said. 'There may have been some incidental passive smoking, but I have plausible deniability on that.' Andrew gave her a hug.

'Can I borrow Jen for a minute?' Stevie asked.

'You know I can't compete with you, Stevie,' Andrew said.

'Who said anything about competing? You got the girl. I'm sorry I never congratulated you properly, Andrew. I'm really happy for you both.'

'That means a lot,' he said.

'You don't need my blessing,' Stevie said.

'No, but I'd still like it.'

She gave him a hug. 'You got it.'

'Come find me when you're ready.' Andrew winked at Jen.

She and Stevie sank down to sit on the concrete, Fred nuzzling between them.

Jen leaned her head on Stevie's shoulder. 'You okay?'

'I will be,' Stevie said. 'I gave it one last shot with Johnno, and he said he's over it. But I tried.'

Jen gave her a hug.

Stevie sighed. 'What if you're my person?'

'Whoa, plot twist. I know you just got rejected, but I did not see that coming.'

'No, I mean what if you're my platonic person.'

'Oh. Yeah, I guess I always figured I was.'

'But you have Andrew. You'll be off having babies and stuff soon. What if you're my person, and I'm not *your* person?'

'Stevie. You've seen enough weddings not to subscribe to the "one perfect day" bullshit. Why would you think there's one perfect person who's going to fix everything for you?'

'So . . . Andrew's not your person?'

'You're both my person. My people. It takes a village, et cetera. Andrew is the person I'll build a family with; you're the person who makes me laugh.'

'Why don't I have a village?'

'You do, you idiot. You've just been carrying on like a pork chop and neglecting them.'

'No one knows me like you do.'

'You're not that much of an enigma, mate.' That made Stevie laugh. 'You expect everyone to leave when they see the real you because you think it's what you deserve. But that's just when the good stuff starts.'

30

'You're not serious?' Lily shouted into her phone, failing to keep a shake out of her voice.

Tom's eyes were wide and Stevie tried to pretend she wasn't there. Lily had taken a call from the caterers while they were shooting a few quick portraits. 'I'm going to put my husband on, he'll be able to give you directions,' she said. Lily shoved the handset at Tom. 'The caterers are at the wrong property. They should have been here hours ago – there's no way they can get dinner out on time.'

Lily stalked away to blow off steam while Tom talked the caterers through how to get to Mossdale, and Stevie continued to pretend she was invisible.

'Everything okay?' Stevie asked when Tom hung up. Lily had walked a fair distance away and seemed to be doing a deep breathing exercise.

'They'd been trying to ring for hours but Lily's reception is patchy out here. Should be able to get here and get set up within the hour, but they'll be serving dinner much later than we'd planned.'

'Have you got drinks?' Stevie asked.

'Plenty,' Tom replied.

'Then you've got nothing to worry about. Why don't I give June a ring and see if there's something we can scratch up to line people's stomachs in the meantime? Give you a few minutes with Lily.'

'That'd be great. Thanks, Stevie,' Tom said. He started walking in Lily's direction, then paused and turned back. 'Stevie?'

'Yeah?'

'She's got a lot going on today, you know? She's not quite herself.'

'Don't worry about it,' Stevie said. 'I've been to a few weddings, remember? Seen much worse, I promise you.'

Tom smiled and jogged off, while Stevie dialled the house and asked for someone to find June. June agreed to search for some easy appetisers and put her cousins and nieces to work. She said she'd also send Johnno to let the bar staff know they'd be working hard for the evening, and to put out some games and change up the music to something that might get people dancing early.

Lily and Tom returned, composed, just as the sun was starting to drop. Stevie took some last portraits, dreamily backlit in the dusty field as the sky splintered into wild colours. But she had an even better feeling about the long-range shots she'd been able to sneak in after calling June, of Tom comforting Lily and making her smile. By the time they were walking back into the reception the last of the light was fading.

'Lily!' Cynthia waved from the dancefloor. She had removed her heels and appeared to have been having a dance-off with the youngest of the wedding guests. 'Little buggers are wearing me out,' she stage-whispered, pulling her shoes back on. She collected a champagne flute from a nearby table and flagged down a passing waiter to top it up before slumping back into a squatter's chair and lighting a cigarette.

'Hard to find a perch around here, isn't it?' came a voice from the neighbouring seat. The woman removed an enormous hat decked with fake flowers before Stevie recognised her. 'Mabel,' she said, holding out her hand to Cyn.

'Cynthia,' Cyn responded in a mock-posh accent, dangling her own hand limply between them. 'Mother of the bride.'

'Mum. We talked about this – have you been drinking water?' Lily said.

'Yes, darling,' Cyn said, waving around a fag tipped with a tremulous centimetre of ash as she leaned back in the chair. 'I'd bloody kill for something to eat, though.'

Lily gave an exasperated groan, and Tom quietly offered to go and find Cyn some food.

'I'd love a bite too,' Mabel called to his retreating back. Cyn was singing along to the INXS song that was playing and Stevie was taking a few pictures of her and Mabel looking very relaxed when Mabel started to sniff.

'Cynthia?' Mabel said. Cyn was still singing quietly, with her eyes closed. 'Cynthia!' Mabel shouted, slapping at Cyn's chest where cigarette ash had ignited the rayon and started to smoulder.

'Mum!' Lily shouted.

Cyn screamed, shooting out of the squatter's chair. 'Stop, drop and roll!'

Quite an audience had gathered by this time, and they watched as Cyn threw herself to the ground. Soon she was laughing uncontrollably and attempting, it seemed to Stevie, to do the worm. Stevie felt slightly guilty for having photographed the entire sequence of events, but her real regret was not switching to video.

Cyn's performance had been enough to distract everyone from the sky bruising with storm clouds. At the first deafening crack

of thunder there were genuine screams, and then another round
of squeals as fat raindrops began pelting down. Lawn games were
thrown down and hats abandoned as guests raced for cover in
the marquee. Lily was trying to help Cyn, who was still hacking
through a laughing fit, to her feet. When she finally got vertical,
Cyn raced off towards the house.

Lily stood stock-still, turning slowly to take in the debris strewn
across the lawn, the exodus towards the marquee, a sheet of water
sliding off the top of the bar tent to soak the brave souls still waiting for a drink.

'Lily,' Stevie shouted.

The rain was soaking into her hair, weighing down the beautiful waves, and making her dress cling to her. Still, she didn't move.

Stevie sensed a different kind of storm brewing. She touched
Lily's arm gently. 'Let's take a moment,' she said, drawing Lily
away. The only place she could think to take her was June's laundry,
where they came upon Cyn wriggling into a satin dress that showed
off all the curves her suit had hidden.

'Oh Mum,' Lily sighed.

Cyn shrugged. 'Lucky I brought a backup. You right, love?'

'Am I right?' Lily repeated, her voice rising in pitch. 'Let's see.
The celebrant got our names wrong for the entire service. We
walked back up the aisle to a children's song. I flashed a nipple.
We have a leaky tent full of drunk guests trapped with nothing to
eat. I look like a drowned rat, and my mother managed to light
herself on fire. I've been better, Mum.'

'Yeah, I might see how June's going in the kitchen,' Cyn said,
mouthing 'good luck' to Stevie as she raced off.

Stevie guided Lily to sit down on a stool and found a mirror
for Lily to fix her hair. 'Look, Lily, I know it's not quite what you'd

imagined, but you're doing really well. The caterers are finally here, so the food's just a bit delayed, and June's helping them work out some snacks to keep everyone going in the meantime.'

Lily sighed heavily and narrowed her eyes at Stevie.

'Do you want me to go and get one of your girlfriends?' Stevie asked. 'I'm sorry if this is weird. I just wanted to give you a bit of space to vent, if you need it.'

'Stevie, I'm not going to lose it.'

'It's fine if you want to. I know you're probably used to everything looking perfect. I know it's hard when you have a plan and it feels like it's fallen apart.'

'I know you think I'm a brat who can't handle not getting my own way.'

'Not at all,' Stevie said, wishing she'd never tried to do this.

'That's not who I am,' Lily said, her manicured fingers fiddling with her teeth. From between perfectly painted lips she drew out a false front tooth. 'This is who I am.'

'Now that's a party trick,' Stevie said.

'I grew up in a housing estate in Inala. I've seen my dad more often in a jail visiting room than at my own dinner table. I got in a punch up with a bitch from Darra in Year Eleven netball and Mum couldn't afford the dental surgery to save the tooth. I saved every cent from my job at Macca's to get a false one so I wouldn't have to interview for uni scholarships with a missing front tooth.

'I never expected special treatment. I earned everything the hard way. I studied harder, I worked more hours. I bought every piece of designer clothing myself on lay-by until no one could tell I came from anywhere different to all these other Ascot molls. But every time I smile, there's a bit of Inala hiding under the surface.

'I'm not ashamed of where I come from. My mother gave up everything to make sure I had every possible opportunity. And I'll do the same for my kids. But don't think for a second that I take any of this lightly.'

Lily was breathing hard after this little speech. Stevie was speechless. How could she have read Lily so wrong? She reached out to pat Lily's arm, which shuddered slightly as the tears began.

'I just wanted one perfect day.'

'I think the horse might have bolted on perfect, Lily.'

'No shit,' Lily said, and she broke into a wicked giggle. 'Oh my God, did you see what Mum changed into? I think she set herself on fire on purpose.'

'Forget perfect,' Stevie said. 'That's not what this day's about. It's about you and Tom, the way you take care of each other. And you are so right together. The way he looks at you, the way you put him at ease. That's better than perfect.'

Lily sniffled.

'You wouldn't ever have got to meet Bruce, would you?' Stevie asked, and Lily shook her head. 'Does Tom ever talk about him?'

'I've tried,' Lily said. 'He just hasn't been able to go there yet.'

'He will,' Stevie said. 'I'm sure he'll talk to you about it. And I'm not trying to lord it over you. But you need to understand that Bruce was hilarious. It's a tragedy that he's gone, and the worst part is that his name makes everyone so sad now. Because Bruce was the life of every party. He was the biggest prankster this side of the border. He brightened every room he walked into. That's why it was such a shock when he went the way he did.' Stevie was getting choked up now. 'You can give them the same lightness. They're lucky to have you.'

Stevie held out a hanky, and Lily dabbed at her eyes. 'C'mon, let's get you back out there.'

They ran back towards the marquee, hand in hand, in the pelting rain. All eyes were on Lily as she took her place at the head table, her dress blotched with wet patches, her hair bedraggled. At that moment a scream went up from the side of the marquee, where a three-tiered wedding cake was on display.

'Susie, no!' Connie shouted, but her three-year-old had already excavated two generous handfuls of the bottom tier of the cake and was ecstatically biting into one of them.

The room held its breath, everyone swivelling to see Lily's reaction.

'It's not such a bad idea, really,' Lily said, and cracked up laughing. The relief that swept through the room was like a storm breaking, and the guests burst into laughter as well. Stevie got as many shots as she could of the dampened guests throwing their heads back. She also made sure to capture young Susie, her face covered in icing but without a trace of guilt.

The teenage waiters began drifting into the marquee with silver platters held aloft. They were dressed in their fanciest black outfits and bow ties and acting as they'd been briefed to, like they were serving fine diners, but their trays were loaded with party pies and sausage rolls that June had managed to find in the coldroom.

Lily grabbed a pie. 'Got any sauce?' And the crowd cracked up again.

Tom caught Stevie's eye, mouthing a *thank you*.

'All right, tuck in everyone, we'll get you fed somehow,' Lily said, and the applause was deafening.

—

Stevie was crouched down at her gear bag switching memory cards when Mabel bailed her up.

'You've had your work cut out for you today.'

Stevie gave a tired smile. 'I dunno, none of us will forget this wedding in a hurry.'

'You'll make them look fabulous. You always do.'

'Thanks.' Stevie sighed. 'It's a far cry from a masterpiece, but I'm good at it'

'Pfft. Who's talking about masterpieces?' Mabel scoffed.

'I want to tell a story that matters,' Stevie said urgently. 'And damn it, I want a big love story of my own. I thought I was too late to get either one. I tried to stop wanting it. But I do want them. And just because I'm older than I thought I'd be when I got them doesn't mean I'm going to let go of the dream.'

Mabel laughed. 'A story that matters? Darl, you've been telling it this whole time. All those love stories, and the places they bring to life. There's nothing that matters more. You think you have to be young and dumb to fall in love, or make great art? Rude. I'm doing my best work and I'm in my seventies.'

That got a smile out of Stevie.

Mabel continued. 'You know what the young ones have over us? They don't know what they don't know. They don't know failure and loss, they don't know what the future holds, so they're confident in their convictions. We've been knocked around a few times by the world and we know how easily things can be lost. Don't let it make you too scared to take a chance.'

There was a roar from the guests, finally fed and extremely well lubricated, as Johnno walked up to the podium.

'I'd better get back to it,' Stevie said, gathering up her camera and kissing Mabel on the cheek.

Stevie watched Johnno play up to the crowd, strutting like a boxer entering the ring for a title fight. She knew then that he was nervous, understanding as she did now that he acted like a clown the most when he felt unequal to the situation. He was carrying a fat stack of cards with handwritten notes. She knew that however casual the speech appeared, he would have worked hard on it for weeks out of his love for Tom.

Johnno cleared his throat at the microphone. 'G'day, I'm Johnno West.'

There was a pop and the PA system died. All power to the marquee seemed to short out, and the string lights blinked out one by one.

—

The rain pattering on the canvas was quickly drowned out by the guests' growing hubbub in the near-darkness. Johnno grabbed a candle and wolf-whistled loudly to get the room back under control.

'Well, bugger. Can everyone hear me?' he shouted.

They all cheered.

'Looks like we're doing this the old-fashioned way,' Johnno said, and he threw the cards of his speech over his shoulder.

'As the best man, my job here is pretty simple. I roast the groom, get you all laughing, and then I toast the bridesmaids. But we don't have any bridesmaids, and I think we've all had plenty of laughs already today without me piling it on to poor Tom and Lily.'

Lily rolled her eyes.

'I will say that for all they've been through today, they still look like they've stepped off the cover of a bloody magazine. Ladies and gentlemen, put your hands together for Lily, what a stunning bride, and this bastard who gets to look at her every day for the rest of their lives.'

The crowd whooped and tapped their glasses with their forks, and Tom duly pulled Lily in for a kiss to more cheers.

'Now, I've been to quite a few of these dos in the past year. I've done a few of these speeches. I've got a mate who's been to even more than I have,' Johnno continued, his eyes finding Stevie, who was crouched in front of him, and giving her a wink. 'It's heady, isn't it? This feeling at a wedding? Kind of glowing from the inside. All that love and emotion we keep under wraps so we can get on with work and life day-to-day . . . Suddenly we're wearing it on our sleeves and blowing it into our hankies. It's all right, Mabel, let it out.'

There was a honking blow and lots of laughter.

'Weddings bring up a lot of feelings we don't let ourselves examine most of the time. Love, yes. But also sadness, and grief, as we remember those who aren't there to celebrate with us.'

June's eyes were shining, and Tom put his other arm around her.

'Weddings make us think about the big milestones of life, and how we're keeping up, or not.'

Stevie caught his eye at that. She wasn't even pretending to take photos any more.

'Weddings give people an opportunity to celebrate with their families, to show off their great taste, to look beautiful. Sometimes it makes the bystanders feel like they're not measuring up. Sometimes even the people at the centre of it feel like they're putting on a show, faking the perfect life, the perfect love, the perfect day because they think that's what a wedding should be.

'And if you'll pardon my French, that's bullshit.'

He heard a laugh bark out of Stevie, along with the rest of the crowd. She was crying.

'It's a long way from what we know makes for a solid marriage,' Johnno continued. 'Marriage, and love itself, isn't about the big day. It's the everyday. It's not about the spectacle, the pretty words, the pretty pictures. It's about showing up and being there for the ugly stuff, and loving it anyway.

'And, as I've learned, it's not about waiting for everything to be perfect. Life's too short to hold yourself back for the day when you're richer, or thinner, or you have things more together. We have to enjoy what we have, while we can. Even when life is tough, when the rain doesn't fall or we lose someone we love dearly.'

He was waving the candle around wildly for emphasis, the flame flickering. The rain was falling harder outside, but his voice carried strong and clear.

'We're all just groping around in the dark, trying to find our way, do our best. Everything might be dark and damp, but you have to find the sparks of love and joy in the small moments. You gotta cup your hands around those sparks and protect them. Breathe life into them gently, until they grow into leaping flames.'

Kate's voice carried across the tent as she heckled, 'I've seen you try to light a fire, Johnno, ya bullshit artist!'

He grinned, and the crowd laughed again. 'Yeah, yeah,' he said. 'Not every spark builds into a fire that will sustain you, and that doesn't mean you can't enjoy it for what it is while it warms your hands. You can't force it.' He thought of Sarah, and wished for better for her. He thought of Tom and Stevie all those years ago, limping along and making each other miserable when the flame had flickered out.

'Then some fires rage out of control and burn everything to the ground, and you have to start all over again.' He could see tears rolling down Stevie's cheeks, and it took all his self-control to stay where he was and finish.

'But the best ones grow slowly, fed with kindness and care by two people working together. They're a safe point you know you can find your way back to, even when you get off track for a bit. And in turn they keep you warm, and nourish your family, and even your broader community.

'Tom and Lily, they've built a nice little fire. She's a bit green, and he's a bit wet, but they're making it work. Even this rain can't stop them.'

Lily raised her champagne flute to Johnno; Tom rolled his eyes.

'Together they're warming up this place in a way it's needed, badly, after a couple of dark years. I know Bruce is looking down, feeling very proud of these two and how they've handled today. Thanks for the rain, Bruce – it's nearly as good as having you here.'

There was much rustling and sniffling as everyone reached for their tissues and hankies.

'You don't need a hopeless bastard like me to wish you good luck, Tom and Lily. You're gonna be just fine. But all the same, know that all of us here are warming our hands at the fire you're building. We're all standing around you, to block the wind and help you burn stronger every day. Would you all join me in raising your glasses – to Tom and Lily!'

'Tom and Lily,' chorused the crowd. There was an almighty ripping sound and a sheet of water hit the ground as half the roof of the marquee collapsed under the weight of the collected rain. There were shrieks as the guests rushed to the dry side of the tent.

Everyone was pressing in on Johnno as he walked away from the podium, wanting to shake his hand and slap his back. He kept looking back at the spot where Stevie had been, but she was gone, and he slowly shook off the wellwishers to try to find her.

—

Stevie had raised her glass to Tom and Lily with the crowd. Johnno's words had cracked something open in her, her skin felt raw and exposed, alive to the slightest breeze. Her face was a mess and she was frantically trying to wipe away the tear tracks of eyeliner and mascara from her cheeks as she raced to the edge of the marquee to find some privacy. She knew her face was red and her eyes were swollen from crying, and she dreaded him seeing her like this when it felt like finally, maybe, there might be a chance he could love her back.

At least the blackout would hide her redness somewhat, she thought thankfully, as she finally found a balled-up tissue at the back of her camera bag and gave a honking blow cloaked in the anonymity of the dark.

Unfortunately, it was at this exact moment that the lights flickered back on, and Johnno was somehow in front of her.

'Hark, what's that sweet sound?' He grinned. 'Is it the trumpets of angels? No, just the nose trumpet of a beautiful strumpet.'

'Don't look at me, I'm hideous.' She was laughing and crying at the same time and it was not helping the snot situation.

'You're definitely going to have to work on your dainty crying before you star in the next hit reality TV show,' he said.

'Oh God,' Stevie wailed, wandering further out from the shelter of the marquee. The rain on her face brought cool relief.

'Stevie, you're not going to be the next Bachelorette,' he said gently, following her and cupping his big hands around her shoulders.

'I need the money,' she sniffled. 'What's worse, I already signed the contract.'

'Well, I know a pretty sharp young lawyer who could take a look at that and give you some advice.'

'Who?' Stevie asked, looking out into the night, resisting the deep need she felt to melt back into his chest.

'The new Mrs Carruthers. Besides, I don't want you getting your head turned by fifteen gorgeous idiot blokes with sixpacks who have nothing better to do than get drunk, fight among themselves and fall hopelessly in love with you.'

'Why?' she asked the darkness.

'Because *I'm* hopelessly in love with you, you deadshit,' came his voice at her ear. 'And I'll never have a chance if you develop a taste for rock-hard abs.'

'Don't you dare fuck with me, Johnno West,' she said. 'You know how I feel about you. It's not a joke.'

'I've never been more serious about anything in my life,' he said, and he slowly spun her around, hands brushing down her arms to draw her waist to his. 'We've wasted enough time already.'

And he kissed her, hard and long, the tears on her cheeks replaced by raindrops. They kissed until the rain drenched their hair and each felt the other smiling, and giggles bubbled up between them.

'Jesus, you're a sight.' He grinned at her, and she punched him in the arm.

'What are we going to do now?' she asked, as he wiped mascara from below her eye with a rough thumb and tucked a strand of damp hair out of her face.

'We're going to dance, and drink, and stay up as long as we can without ripping each other's clothes off,' he said.

'But what about after tonight?'

'She'll be right,' he said, taking her hand.

And Stevie believed him.

An unnatural squeal split the night sky. Stevie and Johnno looked up as fireworks began to pop and fizz above the marquee.

'That's a bold move, letting off illegal explosives after everything that's gone wrong today,' Johnno said.

'Quick, I need to get photos of this,' she said, already pulling the camera from her shoulder.

Instagram post by @StevieJeanLoveStories:

LILY & TOM, October 2019: In my experience shooting weddings, the big day doesn't always go to plan, but this one really took the cake (actually, it was a toddler who took the cake, but I digress). I won't use the word 'disaster', but this couple had a wedding they'll never forget. They still looked absolutely stunning and more in love than ever. The best man will tell you it was his speech that brought the house down, but the storm might have had something to do with the marquee collapsing. Luckily everyone was too busy dancing in the rain we've been praying for to worry about getting a little wet. There was a bit of magic in the air. Congratulations, Tom and Lily.

31

As the first rays of the new day's sun cracked over the horizon, a kookaburra stirred. Perched on a high bough of a blossoming gum that towered over June Carruthers' garden, she'd been sheltering throughout the night as the rain continued to beat down. But it was quiet and clear as the sun began its rise, and she shook out her wings and took a deep inhale, like a rock star preparing to belt a power ballad to an audience of adoring fans. She opened her throat and let rip with her laughing song, the loudest she'd ever sung, like she'd been training for it.

Back at ground level, the kookaburra's impressive song was not a hit for those with sore heads after a long night of revelry. Stevie-Jean Harrison stirred from a deep slumber as the trilling laughter drilled into her brain. She breathed in deeply, taking in the singular smell of swag canvas pulled over her head and, beyond it, the wonderful aroma of rain on long-parched earth. Stevie's head was thumping, but her body was perfectly cosy and resisted the kookaburra's attempts to tug her into consciousness. As her eyes cracked open, she tried to piece it all together: single swag, soft, well-worn sheets, no sign of undies (ooh), an arm draped around her waist, mouth like a desert . . .

An arm! Connected to the shoulder and the torso and ultimately the heart of Johnno West, who loved her! Stevie let the
movie screen of her mind triumphantly replay the memory of the
previous evening, particularly enjoying the part where Johnno
called her a deadshit and then kissed her in the rain. And the part
where he grabbed her hand on the dancefloor and pulled her out
into the darkness to kiss her again, and the part where he led her to
the back of his Landcruiser ute, where he'd rolled out his swag and
they'd nestled under the canvas as it muffled the raindrops. And all
the parts after that . . .

They'd decided to keep that night just for themselves and played
it cool among the other wedding guests until people started staggering off to bed and they wouldn't be missed. In hindsight Stevie
was sure they'd been less than subtle. She couldn't help following
Johnno with her eyes, and neither of them could stop smiling.

But with the morning came the light, and there wouldn't be
much more chance for them to hide. Still, it was only early. Soft
rain was beginning to patter on the swag again and Johnno's slow
breaths behind her ear were lulling her back to sleep. She snuggled
into him and he held her closer.

The sun was higher in the sky, albeit dulled by rain clouds, when
the canvas of the swag was ripped dramatically back a few hours
later. Stevie and Johnno squinted to behold Kate, who'd exposed
them with a flourish like a magician yanking the cloth out from
beneath a fully set table. Fred was at her side with an accusing look.

'Aha!' she cried. 'I knew it.'

'Steady on, Kate,' Johnno groaned.

'You're lucky it's raining. Everyone's headed into the house and the marquee in search of coffee. But they're looking for you both. Morning, Stevie.'

'Morning, Kate,' Stevie said. 'We'll be out in a second.'

'Mm-hmm. Well, it's about bloody time, you two.' She threw the canvas back over their heads and walked away chuckling.

Stevie groaned quietly. The extra hours of sleep had dulled her headache but not vanquished it.

'Well, good morning,' Johnno said, his lips deliciously at her neck and below her ear.

Now Stevie really didn't want to get up. 'I'm sure it's a lovely day,' she said, 'but I'd really like to just stay here for at least another day, you know?'

'Mmm, I know,' he said, his hands roaming up her rib cage and over her breasts. 'Good thing Kate didn't pull the sheet back as well.'

'Yes. Well, we might not be so lucky next time,' Stevie said. She rolled over to face him and he pulled her in for a lazy kiss. Stevie could feel him smiling under her lips, and she knew she was too.

'Feels like bloody Christmas morning,' he said happily. 'I just want to show everyone my new toy. If you're ready for that?'

Stevie smiled. 'Ready as we'll ever be, I think. Although strolling in wearing last night's dress feels a bit over the top. Do you have a spare shirt I can borrow until I can slink back to my car and change?'

'Yeah, hang on,' he said, wiggling into his boxers and sliding out of the swag. He returned a couple of minutes later with a gingham shirt, and Stevie pulled it on and emerged from the swag.

'I like that,' Johnno said.

'What?' Stevie asked, pulling her hair up into a topknot.

'I could get used to seeing you in my shirt,' he said, and kissed her forehead. 'You look gorgeous. You are gorgeous.'

'Stop,' Stevie said, meaning the exact opposite.

Stevie knocked at the back door and kicked off her muddy boots. She'd squirmed into jeans and a T-shirt in her car. She felt changed somehow. Like anyone could see from looking at her that she was different. It wasn't just the sex, although she did feel like all her limbs were looser. There was a warmth in her chest that seemed to grow every time she thought of the way Johnno had looked at her.

The screen door swung open and Stevie looked up to see June's smiling face.

'Come in, Stevie love. I'll make you a cuppa.'

Stevie hugged her.

'I missed you last night,' June murmured over Stevie's shoulder. Stevie kept June locked in the hug so she wouldn't see the blush taking over her entire face.

'Yeah, I needed a bit of an early night,' Stevie said.

'Gosh, I hope there isn't something going around. Johnno said the same thing. We can't have all you young ones getting sick.' June led her into the kitchen and put the kettle on. 'Go sit down. Do you still take milk?'

Stevie nodded. Rounding the door into the lounge room, Stevie felt like a criminal facing a jury. The room was packed. Tom was sitting on an armchair with Lily draped across his lap. Kate and Cam were eating toast at the table, along with Penny and Rod. Cynthia was looking a bit green around the gills and tapping a cigarette box on the table. Jen and Andrew were working on the crossword in

Country Life, sprawled over the carpet. Mabel was enthroned on the settee, mid-conversation with two of Lily's law school girlfriends. And Johnno was leaning against the piano, mug in hand and a puppy-dog grin at the sight of her. Mabel definitely caught the wink Johnno shot across the room at Stevie.

'Morning, Stevie,' they all chorused.

'So nice of you to join us.' June giggled, handing Stevie a cup of tea.

'Oh God,' Stevie said.

'Sorry.' Johnno shrugged. 'They all guessed.'

'This is mortifying,' Stevie said.

'It's about bloody time, is what it is,' Jen said, and everyone cracked up.

'But we do have to figure a few things out,' Mabel said. 'Where are you going to live? Or are you going to do long distance between Haven Downs and Brisbane? Johnno, you need a proper job. And Stevie, are you going into television?'

'Yes, when can you send me the contract to check?' Lily interjected. 'We're off to the Maldives in a few days, so can you email it to me asap?'

'Why don't you take a week's holiday, Johnno?' said Penny. 'Kate and Cam have things in hand at home.'

'Um, thanks, Mum. That'd be good, if it's all right with you, Dad?'

Rod harrumphed in a way that they took for agreement.

Stevie tried not to think about how many people were now involved in her fledgling love life. At least her mother wasn't here.

As if reading Stevie's mind, June said, 'I hope you don't mind, Stevie, but I invited your mum to come out today. I've not seen her for so long and I thought she might enjoy catching up while every-one's here.'

Stevie laughed. 'That's a lovely thought, June.' She crept over to Johnno's side and looked around the room. *A chain-smoking social worker, a nosy septuagenarian, a couple of farmers, my ex-boyfriend, my mum . . . Holy shit. This is my village. My people.*

'I feel like they're all waiting for me to make a speech or some-thing,' she whispered to Johnno. 'This is weird.'

'I really am sorry,' he whispered back. 'Everyone looked at me when I walked in and I just cracked into a grin and they knew.'

'What about Tom?' Stevie asked.

—

That had been Johnno's main concern too. While everyone ribbed Johnno, Tom had slipped out of the room. Johnno followed him as quickly as he could. He found Tom in his old bedroom, sur-rounded by the tarnished trophies and faded posters of past glories and obsessions.

'Mate,' Johnno started, his hands raised in surrender.

'Don't even think about apologising,' Tom cut him off. 'I don't know why I didn't see it sooner.'

Johnno shrugged. 'If I'm honest, I never thought I had a real shot with her.'

Tom shook his head. 'No, you two always got on like a house on fire. Did you like her then, when we were together?'

'I always loved her. But nothing ever happened when you were together,' Johnno said.

'Oh, I know,' Tom said. 'If anything ever had happened, I would have bloody well noticed you acting like this.' He laughed.

'You're not mad?'

'Have you seen my wife?' Tom asked in response, and Johnno could see his friend's heart swell at getting to use the word 'wife'. 'Just be good to her. I think you can manage that.'

'It's all I want to do,' Johnno said.

—

'Tom's okay,' Johnno said, and Stevie exhaled.

'They do raise a few valid points though,' she said. 'How are we going to make this work, with you at Haven Downs and me . . . I don't even know where I'll be.'

'Well, let's take it one step at a time. Can I come and stay at yours for the next week or so? Or we could go to the coast or something? Just do all the boring stuff I've been dying to do with you: eat breakfast, read the papers, sit on the couch, go back to bed . . .'

'Sounds good to me.' Stevie smiled.

When Paula's car eased in to a park outside the yard, Stevie ran out to hug her.

'Hello, darling,' Paula exclaimed. 'Are you all right? You didn't have a breakdown at the wedding, did you?'

'I'm fine,' Stevie said. 'I'm great. I just wanted to let you know before you get inside, I'm, er . . . Johnno and I are together. As of last night. I haven't been holding out on you, I swear.'

Paula hugged her again. 'As long as you're happy, I'm happy.'

Stevie looked back at the car. 'No George?'

'We're not joined at the hip, Stevie.'

'I suppose you're getting ready to move back to Avalon?'

Paula shook her head. 'I told him I wouldn't be moving out there. It feels a bit too much like trying to rewrite history. And it puts a lot of pressure on a very new relationship. Besides, I quite like being on my own.'

'So you broke up?' Stevie asked.

'Oh no. We're going to keep dating. Take a bike ride every now and then.'

'Mum!'

'I'm just teasing you, Stevie.'

Johnno, sick of waiting for Stevie to come back inside, had come out looking for her. Not wanting to interrupt their conversation, he crept up and put an arm around Stevie's waist, as Paula was continuing.

'Look, I love Avalon. It was our home. I'll cherish my memories of growing up there, of what my family achieved there, and seeing you grow up there too. I'm interested to see what the future holds for it, how George's plans take shape. But we never really own land. We're just taking care of it for a while.'

'I like that, Paula,' Johnno said.

'And I'd like to hear a bit more about your plans, Johnno.'

'You're in luck, there's a bit of a group brainstorming session going on inside.'

'Just look after each other,' Paula said, steering things serious again. 'Be honest, be open, be kind, have fun. The rest will be fine.'

Stevie watched Johnno wind up to make a joke. Then he swallowed, and said simply, 'I will. We will.'

Paula gave him a hug. He never let go of Stevie's hand.

New post in 'Neighbourhood News' from The Bush Telegraph:

YOU CAN RUN BUT YOU CAN'T HIDE: Rumour has it the heat was getting too much for Charlie Jones, and he's headed to London for a fresh start. Entertaining as he was, I'm happy to see the back of him. And don't you worry, I'll be putting my contacts in Old Blighty on high alert to make sure he doesn't pull any more stunts. The blue-rinse mafia is global.

LOL, Mabel.

32

Eight days later – eight blissful days of boring activities made magically riveting by doing them with someone you love – Stevie had just waved goodbye to Johnno, shocked at how the sight of his tail-lights made her almost want to cry, when her phone rang.

She was emotionally stable enough to have stopped screening unknown numbers, but she still answered cautiously without identifying herself.

'Is that Stevie-Jean Harrison?' came a brisk young woman's voice.

'Who's calling?' Stevie asked.

'You might not remember me, but it's Pandora . . . I'm a producer at—'

'Network Six?'

'Well, yes, I was working there when we met. But I was pretty grossed out by what they did to you. I basically gave notice the day we got back from north Queensland. I'm so sorry for my part in what happened.'

'Um, thanks.' Stevie wondered where this was going.

'Look, I'm calling because I've started working with some new people. You know Cath Summer?'

Stevie did not.

'Independent production company, mostly features and documentaries,' Pandora continued. 'I'd been stalking Cath for years. There are so few women who make it to the top in this industry and she's just a legend. When the opportunity came up I jumped at it.'

'Good for you,' Stevie said, still unsure what any of this had to do with her.

'Cath's working on this project about the ongoing drought and how it's affecting the economy and culture of small towns. We were having a few wines and I was telling her about you, and she's really keen to meet with you.'

'Me?'

'Yeah. I showed her your Instagram, your whole theory about how small towns live and die depending on young people falling in love. She loved it, reckons it's the narrative into the story we've been searching for. Anyway, we're in Brisbane for the next few days and I'm hoping you can meet us for a coffee? Just to talk through some ideas. No pressure, but I think you'll love Cath.'

Stevie felt like she'd contributed about ten words to this conversation, but all she had to add at this point was 'Okay'.

'Okay? Oh, Stevie, that's great. Have you got a pen? This is the hotel Cath's staying at. Meet us in the lobby bar at four pm tomorrow. We'll have a few drinks and a chat.'

What did she have to lose? Network Six's $100,000 was already a fading memory, thanks to Lily's advice and some uncomfortable phone calls with a very cross Rick Cross. Stevie was finally feeling more on top of her editing backlog after a mammoth effort during her days at the coast with Johnno. She'd invoiced enough to cover the tax bill and most of what she owed Jen, although there was still some credit card debt to sort out. But Stevie was also feeling increasingly like her future was diverging from wedding photography.

She and Johnno had been having a lot of conversations about the future. They both wanted to find jobs or businesses that could support them in the bush, something that would give back to the regional communities they loved while making the most of their skill sets. They'd agreed to do some research and brainstorm together when they met up in a week's time.

The next day Stevie arrived half an hour early for her meeting with Pandora and her boss. She wanted to give herself time to get settled, compose her thoughts and write some notes. Remembering (vaguely) Rick Cross bundling her into a cab, she was also determined to keep a clear head for this conversation. She sat at the bar with her notebook and ordered a mineral water and some olives. Her phone buzzed with a good luck text from Jen. She sent back a kiss emoji, then put the phone away. By the time Pandora approached her just before 4 pm, she was engrossed in her notebook.

'Stevie, thanks so much for meeting us,' Pandora said. She looked much more relaxed without the headset and clipboard Stevie had last seen her wearing, and was accompanied by a small woman with bobbed grey hair, enormous round red-framed glasses and a Marimekko-print smock dress. She could have been fifty or seventy; the twinkle in her eyes was twenty-five, tops.

'I'm Cath.' The older woman smiled, extending her hand. Stevie shook it. 'We've got a booth booked over here, grab your things and join us.'

Stevie slid in to the banquette seating.

'I love coming back to Brisbane these days,' Cath said conspiratorially.

'Where are you usually based?' Stevie asked.

'Sydney, but I grew up here. It's a helluva lot more fun to visit now than it was even ten years ago. Can I get you a drink?'

'Just another mineral water would be lovely, thanks.'

'Panda, would you grab the waitress? Get her to bring some of those truffle fries, too.' Pandora left to order and Cath leaned across the table. 'So, Stevie. Pandora's given me a bit of background on the set where she met you. I must confess I don't watch a lot of commercial reality shows, but I did see a cut of your scenes from the wedding special. That Charlie was a scoundrel. And I'm guessing the network tried to get you to do more on-camera stuff for them?'

'They did,' Stevie said. 'I nearly signed on for a series of *Bush Bachelorette*, and I've only just managed to extract myself from that. I'm a bit out of my depth when it comes to the world of television, so you'll forgive me if I'm cautious with you.'

'Of course,' Cath said. 'Can I ask – what happened to Charlie?'

'That's the million-dollar question. I never heard from him again, which seems like a blessing now. I was overseas when the show aired and had no idea what had happened until I landed home. It was pretty rough, dealing with the public spotlight for the first time over such an embarrassing episode.'

Cath shuffled along the seat as Pandora slid back into the booth next to her. 'How did you feel when they offered you the starring role?'

'Honestly?' Stevie said. 'I was packing my dacks about it. I only said yes because I needed the money. I was at a pretty low point. But I'm more sure than ever that it's not for me – I don't need to be in the spotlight. I'd rather be behind the scenes, telling the stories.'

'And what's your background with that?' Cath asked. 'Obviously your photography work is all about managing people on high-pressure days, working quickly to understand the narrative of their love story and how to make them comfortable so you can capture the best of the talent.'

'Exactly,' Stevie said, a little surprised at how well Cath got it. 'I studied communications, but I'm self-taught as a photographer. I love the storytelling aspect of the work, and I've been thinking about shifting my career more into that space. How do you know so much about wedding photography?'

'I don't,' Cath said. 'I was basically describing the role of a producer on a documentary. Of course, there's additional research before the shoot. Sourcing talent, preparing them so that when it comes to actual shooting we can keep things as tight as possible. Your experience working this way and your visual creativity appeal to me. But above all that, I'd love you to think about being involved with our project because you know the people we're telling this story about and for. I think you can help us tap into an authenticity that's critical for this project.'

Stevie's mind was racing. *Me, a documentary producer?* 'Can you tell me more about the project?'

Pandora jumped in. 'We've got interest from one of the major broadcasters and a streaming service for a limited-run documentary series. It's about the human impact of the drought, trying to bridge the gap of understanding between viewers in the city and the people living the reality on the land.'

Cath continued. 'To work, it has to look beautiful, which is my specialty, and it has to be character-driven. We need the faces and the voices of the people coping with drought on properties and in small towns. We need to find them, and then we need them to be comfortable enough to really open up on camera. I know that kind of vulnerability is especially hard for people from the bush. So that's why this research phase is so important, and the people we choose to work with.' She held Stevie's gaze as she said this last line.

'We're looking at doing a three-month shoot across at least three states, but ideally more,' Pandora said. 'Then three months for editing and post, and broadcast around autumn next year.'

'I'm hoping to find six main perspectives, or characters, to follow,' said Cath. 'My favourite cinematographer is on board as DOP so it's going to be gorgeous – working with her alone could be a great learning experience for you, Stevie.'

'And what would my role be?' Stevie asked

'Research initially – scouting for talent and locations, introducing me to people you think would be good to tell these stories. We'd have you do pre-interviews, drawing out the stuff we'll want to dig into when it comes to shooting. Then I'd want you to be on set for the shoot. You'd be a kind of go-between linking the talent and the crew. I'd also be open to you being on camera, or interviewing talent, if you want. But we'd want to get you some media training first, get you comfortable.'

'It's definitely a project that appeals to me,' Stevie admitted. 'Will there be a lot of oversight or guidance? It's going to be a bit of a learning curve for me and I would want to make sure the project turned out well. I'd feel a big responsibility to any talent I brought in that they're going to be represented fairly and know what will go to air.'

'That's fair,' Cath said. 'We wouldn't expect you to be an expert at the role straight away. And I've always enjoyed mentoring young producers, if you'd be interested in something like that?'

Stevie nodded, and Pandora looked achingly jealous.

'I know it's a lot to consider, so take your time,' Cath said. 'I've drawn up a rough agreement of what the research stage could look like for you, and how you'd be compensated. We can adjust it based on how you want to approach the role. But we'd really love to work with you. And if there's anyone else you think we should consult with, I'd love to hear your thoughts.'

Stevie thought of Johnno's vision of a network to upskill and promote regional small businesses. She thought of Joe and Connie and the impact they'd had on their town. She thought of Nina and Trish. She thought of Mabel and her network of spies and gossip and matchmaking. She thought of what they could do with access to a platform like this.

'I'll do that. Can I come back to you with some ideas in a week?' she asked.

Ideas marinated in Stevie's brain all the way home. Before she told Johnno about it, there was one other person she wanted to run it past. She leashed up Fred for a walk and dialled a number as she set out into the evening.

'Mabel speaking.'

'It's Stevie.'

'How are you, darl?'

'I'm good. I'm great. What are you up to? Can you chat?'

'You know me, Stevie. I'm always up for a chat. Just getting tarted up for bingo tonight, but I can talk for ten minutes or so?'

'I've been approached to get involved with a documentary project about the drought, and it sounds like a pretty legit opportunity.'

'Do you want me to do some background on it? Not my usual bag, but I can look into it.'

'No, that's okay. But I thought I might suggest that the producers consult with you on it as well.'

'Me?'

'Yeah. They want to follow people who show the human face of the drought, what it means for small towns. They liked my theory about how love stories keep good people in the bush. And no one knows better than you how important good matchmaking can be to a small town.'

Mabel let out a big belly laugh. 'You were impatient with my methods for a while there, but I knew you'd come around. Sure, tell them to give me a call. And that reminds me – have you heard from Charlie Jones lately?'

'Not a peep,' Stevie said.

'I expect it'll stay that way,' Mabel said. 'Word on the street is he's been run out of town. No great loss.'

Stevie agreed.

'One last thing – your Johnno hasn't got back to me about this, so tell him to pull his finger out. I have some ideas for potential suitors for young Sarah Childs.'

'Okay, I'll tell him,' Stevie said.

'So, you've decided to take it?' Johnno asked. He'd arrived back at Stevie's place and they'd been filling each other in on their respective opportunities.

'It's everything I've been looking for,' Stevie said. 'The first few months of research are flexible enough for me to finish off the weddings I had booked into next year, the pay's good, and Cath's going to mentor me and help me get some training so I really learn the ropes properly.'

'That's great. Why do I hear a "but" coming?'

'Well, there'd be three months on the road for the shoot.

I'd need to make sure Jen could take Fred. And I'd be without you.'

'Would they let you bring an assistant?' he asked.

'They might,' she said slowly, thinking about it. 'But it wouldn't be a holiday – I want to take this really seriously. And what about your plans?'

'I've got more research to do too. It would actually be great to tag along with you and get into some different markets to see what's out there.'

'Are you still thinking about the small business network idea?'

'Yeah. I think I could test some ideas and start building a frame-work. I need to find some keen, small-scale innovative producers to start the network first. Then I'd give them some training in ecommerce and set them up to sell online. What I could really use is someone to teach them about using social media. Maybe someone like you? We'd be a good team . . .'

'Are we moving too fast?' Stevie asked. 'What if you get sick of me, or realise I'm a terrible mess of a human being?'

'You? A mess?' Johnno's mock doubt made her laugh. 'Well, liv-ing in each other's pockets travelling around the country on a film shoot for three months will help us figure out sooner rather than later if we drive each other insane.'

She had to admit he had a point, even if it was a depressing one. 'I guess then we'd know if we had a future without wasting too much time.'

Johnno laughed. 'Stevie, I've wanted this since I was nineteen. Don't talk to me about wasting time. I'm pretty sure we're going to be fine.'

'But that's a lot of expectation. What if I disappoint you when you see what I'm really like?'

'Has anything disappointed you so far?'

Stevie blushed. 'No. Everything's been even better than I thought it could be.'

'See? It'll be right.' He pulled her into a hug. 'You've been so caught up you don't even know what day it is, do you?'

She racked her brains as to what he could be talking about, came up blank. 'I know it's twenty-three days since you told me you loved me, and I think it's November . . .'

Johnno walked away into the kitchen. He came back a few minutes later wearing a conical party hat far too small for his enormous head, bearing a chocolate cake studded randomly with Smarties and blazing candles, and quietly singing happy birthday.

As he sat down next to her, Stevie grabbed his chin where the elastic strap of his hat was straining, and kissed him.

'Steady on,' he said. 'You have to blow out the candles first and cut the cake. You only get to kiss the nearest boy if you touch the bottom.'

She blew out the candles, took the knife he offered and held eye contact as she sliced powerfully right down to the plate. A kiss ensued that was so delicious the cake was almost forgotten.

Eventually he finished cutting her a slice and served himself one. They munched away happily.

'Did you make this?' Stevie asked with a mouthful.

Johnno grimaced. 'I decorated it. But I had help with the baking. Mum sends her love.'

'I can't believe I forgot my own birthday. Thirty-two. Bloody hell. Where did you think you'd be when you were thirty-two?'

'I was never really sure. I could never picture myself running the farm, but I couldn't see myself in an office either. I didn't think I'd still be in London, but I wasn't sure. If I pictured anything, it was all out of focus except . . . I hoped I'd be with you.'

'You big softie,' Stevie teased, although her heart felt like it had swelled another size. She was learning that Johnno was quite full of these earnest declarations, and she realised it wasn't easy for him to be vulnerable without the armour of a joke. It made her want to share something equally scary.

'I didn't let myself admit it for a long time, but I think a part of me always hoped we could figure things out together,' she said. 'Like you say, I was never quite able to picture the future, but there would be little flashes, scenes, of a life I hoped to have. It's funny, for all the weddings I've seen I never really thought about having one myself. But I do have this image of a big king-size bed and Sunday morning sunshine and a tangle of little kids trying to nuzzle their way into the sheets. And sometimes I pictured you there, king of the kids.'

He was quiet for a long time.

'Sorry, that's a totally psycho thing to say,' Stevie back-pedalled.

'No, not at all,' he finally said. 'I do really want to be a dad. I reckon we'd make an amazing family.'

'Well, we have to get through the documentary shoot without killing each other before we can do that,' Stevie said brightly, trying to lighten the suddenly serious mood. 'And you've got your business to get off the ground. And we've got to work out where to live. Get Fred and Rabbit to get along . . .'

'That's true. We've got a lot to get through in the next year. We'll have to get married before we start having kids – Mum would kill me otherwise.'

Stevie laughed. 'If that's a proposal, it's pathetic. You know I expect a giant diamond, you on your knees, all the clichés.'

'Excuse me, it's a done deal,' he said. 'Oh, come on. You remember what you promised me that night at uni. I've been counting down. Happy birthday, Stevie.'

CODA

Brisbane, 2007

'Last drinks' came the shout from the front bar at the Royal Exchange hotel, fondly known to its devotees as the RE.

'Quick, get one last jug!' Stevie nudged Johnno towards the bar and he dutifully returned with a jug of XXXX beer.

Stevie sighed happily. Early into her second year at uni, she was no freshman, but being in this pub still brought back the sense of wonder she'd felt as a seventeen-year-old with a fake ID. Not that she could hold her alcohol that much better now, but those early days were so thrilling, so many excited young people shouting and smiling at each other through the gentle buzz of beer drunkenness and Pearl Jam covers. It felt like a little whirl-wind romance was around every sticky corner, and often one was – or at least a pash.

Johnno poured Stevie a schooner, swaying ever so slightly on his bar stool. The night had disappeared in a happy haze of pool, dancing, gossip and silliness. 'Drink up, Stevie, the bouncers will be through here in a minute to turf us out,' he warned.

'Yes, sir.' Stevie saluted and sculled the schooner, refilling it half-way before looking around the room. 'Where did everybody go?'

'Probably Subway,' Johnno said, and she nodded in agreement.

'Stupid friends. Eating stupid sandwiches.' Stevie would actually love a stupid sandwich but given her strict budget – she'd come out with $25 in her pocket – she'd just have to wait to get back to her room and make some two-minute noodles. Actually, that meant no cabs, either.

'Johnno . . .' She drew out his name with a winning smile.

———

'What do you want, Stevie-Jean?' Johnno let his voice sound exasperated, like the twinkle in her eye wasn't the best thing he'd ever seen.

'Do you want to get us a taxi back to college?'

He considered this for a moment; the queue for cabs outside, his own fiscal position, and the months he had waited to be alone with this girl. 'Let's walk. We can have an adventure,' he said. She cracked a wide grin – he knew she couldn't resist the word 'adventure'.

They drained their beers, thanked the bartender and spilled out into the street. It was a close and steamy Brisbane night. The stars were out, only the brightest ones managing to compete with the streetlights. Moths drunkenly crashed into each other in the haloes of fluorescent globes, and the air vibrated with cicada song.

Along the dark Toowong streets, a tall girl in shorts weaved along the footpath next to a sturdily built boy with messy hair. They shared a companionable silence punctuated by occasional bursts of singing.

'Where's Tom tonight?' Johnno finally asked, praying his voice sounded careless.

'Who cares,' Stevie grunted. 'I haven't heard from him since New Year's. He's probably scoping the freshers for my replacement. She's in for a treat,' she muttered.

'What a dickhead,' responded a delighted Johnno.

'Shoulda brought my bike,' she said ruefully. 'When does the adventure start?'

'Shhh . . .' he hushed her. 'Okay, this way.' He grabbed her hand and pulled her down a side street, guiding her down a steep drive-way into an apartment complex.

'Ohhh, look at that pool,' Stevie whispered, and he nodded. The gate was locked.

'I'll boost you over,' he said, cupping his hands to make a step for her to vault the fence. Stevie managed to stick the landing and watched as Johnno scaled his way in.

'I didn't bring my togs,' she said.

'Jocks will do,' he said, stripping off his shorts and polo, and she followed suit, slipping into the water in her bra and undies.

The water was bath-like, warmed all day in the sun, and the air was sharp with chlorine. Still, it was a relief to be immersed after a long clammy night.

Stevie sighed a delicious sigh. 'Is this what you do with all the girls?' she asked.

'No!' He laughed, and he thought he caught a little smile from her. 'Okay, so we can be quiet and chill here for a while, or we can make a racket and run to the next pool and hope no one catches us. What do you wanna do?'

They were facing each other, two heads floating above water-distorted bodies, hair slicked back.

'I can be quiet,' she whispered, 'but I really wanna do THIS!' and she splashed water in Johnno's face.

'Hey!' came a shout from a balcony overlooking the pool.

'Shit,' said Johnno. 'Go time.' They grabbed their clothes and he boosted her back over the fence, and they ran out into the street, soaking wet and barefoot in their undies, laughing uncontrollably.

'Okay, I know another place,' Johnno said, pulling on his shorts. 'But you're gonna have to be stealthy this time.'

—

Creeping through the streets towards St Lucia, they ended up in another unit block. Down a side passage, Stevie watched Johnno put a finger to his lips as he opened a door. They emerged into an unlit pool area, the air thick with the creamy fragrance of frangipanis.

This time she slipped into the water soundlessly, Johnno trailing behind her. She moved her own way in the water, ignoring Johnno but acutely aware of his presence. It was like they were in an unspoken competition not to break the silence.

The trees above them rustled with possums. A bat flapped across the sky, casting a silhouette across the full moon. Stevie could feel the night building inexorably to something; her limbs were being guided like tides under the moon. She set her elbows on the pool's edge and laid her cheek on the tiles, which were still warm from the afternoon sun.

Without a sound Johnno's hands appeared on the tiles either side of hers. He laid a kiss at the corner where her neck met her shoulder, so softly she wondered if she'd imagined it.

Slowly she turned, inevitability setting its own pace, the space between their lips disappearing millimetre by millimetre.

—

Johnno felt like his hands had been made to span her hips and draw her closer. From the tentative first contact of the kiss, they both inhaled in relief that the tension had broken, before taking the kiss deeper. His hand cupped her jaw and his fingers stretched up into her hair; all these motions he had imagined a thousand times, finally within his reach. He wanted to laugh with disbelief at his luck. It could have been minutes, hours, maybe even days.

'Stevie,' he whispered. It was as if the words broke a spell. She drew back slowly, faintly panting, and looked at him like he was a new person. But the longer she held her silence, the more Johnno's grin faded. *Oh God, no.* 'Stevie, I'm sorry, did I read that all wrong? You looked so beautiful . . . I just . . .'

'I think we should get home, don't you?'

He followed her out of the pool and they dried themselves with their clothes before dressing in silence, suddenly bashful. As they walked the last blocks back to college, he held her hand silently, trying to construct the sentence that would somehow get her back in his arms, help her understand how much this night had meant to him and how much he wanted to make her happy, not just tonight, but always.

'We drank a lot of beers tonight, huh?' Stevie said as they reached the entrance to Women's College. She took both his hands in hers and tried to meet his eye as he looked determinedly at the ground.

'I can't help this crush I have on you,' he said.

'But it would kill me if I messed up our friendship, and your friendship with Tom,' Stevie said. 'I don't want to not have you in my life.'

'Stevie, what if we could . . . We could be so good together,' he stammered. 'I can't get you out of my head. Every time I see you, I just wish you were with me.'

She leaned in and kissed him slowly, deliberately, a goodbye. Even so, there was a moment he felt her breath hitch and knew it could have ended a different way – but his pride was pricked, his bravado was gone.

'I'd be a terrible girlfriend, Johnno,' she said. 'I already am – you've seen me. And you should have someone beautiful, someone who makes you laugh and takes care of you and gets you off your arse to do all the amazing things you're supposed to do.'

He was silent.

'But if we're thirty-two and still single, we can marry each other, okay?'

'Promise?' he said.

She laughed and kissed his cheek. 'Sure. But we will never speak of this. Night, Johnno.'

He watched her walk through the glass doors of the college, turning for one last look at him as she unlocked the door, giving him a little nod. He started the long, slow walk back to Leo's, already calculating how many days and hours it would be until her thirty-second birthday. 2019 had a good ring to it.

ACKNOWLEDGEMENTS

There's a lot more complexity to the question of ownership and care-taking of land than this, but it is important to me to acknowledge that, as Paula says: *We never really own land. We're just taking care of it for a while.* I wrote most of this story on the Gadigal land of the Eora nation, picturing the beautiful country of the Kamilaroi, Mandandanji and Bigambul peoples, which Stevie and Johnno call home.

I'm the first to admit I'm a townie bogan with little to no firsthand experience of living and working on the land, but my roots and time living in regional communities left me with an indelible impression of the resilience, ingenuity and good-heartedness of the people who live and work in the bush. The parties and relationships I knew I could get right; the business of farming I needed some help with. I'm indebted to my early readers (and early besties) Emily Pullen and Bec Tickell for their insights and notes. If anything, this story undersells the innovation and creativity coming out of rural and regional Australia, but I hope it piques your appetite to learn more.

Johnno's breakthrough business idea was realised by the fabulous network Buy From The Bush; of course it took a couple of brilliant rural women to make it happen.

On the technical side, big love to my beautiful writers group, talented authors Sarah Percival and Emily Usher. Endless gratitude to my teacher and mentor Emily Maguire. I'm thankful to my superstar agent, Clare Forster at Curtis Brown, who thankfully had her own days at B&S balls and Duchesne College and recognised the world of this story.

My deep gratitude to my publisher Nikki Christer at Penguin Random House, who fell in love with this story, championed it and edited it to make it shine. Thanks to Amanda Martin for kind and whip-smart editing, and all the PRH team for their work on packaging this book and sending it out into the world. Thanks also to Jessica Howard for bringing a photographer's eye and a country girl's heart to the manuscript and saving me from a few howlers – her beautiful *Bush Journal* is well worth a subscription. Thanks to Pi James and Mel Davey for reading early drafts and for their wonderful support. And to iconic authors Rachael Johns and Rachael Treasure for taking time out from their own much-loved books to read and endorse this one.

This book is for my mum, who taught us to love books and take fierce pride in where we're from. For Dad, who taught us to work hard and not take life too seriously. And for Elle, my constant inspiration, who could probably write a better book if she decided to – thanks for always pushing me to be better, and for the wedding that started this story.

For beautiful Neicey, the best auntie ever, who taught my sister and me to cook, to eat cake for breakfast and that you don't need a man to live well, and who had her own big love story in the end. I wish you could have read this book. We miss you so much.

For Dot, who brings laughter and colour and loud banging noises to all our days and taught me the value of every possible writing minute. Thanks for giving me the mother of all deadlines to finish drafting this story, by being born. And thanks for sleeping like an angel so I could keep writing and reading.

And, above all, for Davo, who fulfilled the promise of a lifetime of fairytales, rom-coms and books that left me obsessed with that mysterious thing called love. You saved me from ever having to use Tinder – you gave me the meet-cute to top all meet-cutes. Once we found each other, life could really start. Thank you for your support and kindness, for laughing at my jokes and forgiving me all the evenings of ignoring you so I could work on this.

Like Stevie, I learned that just because you've aged out of being a prodigy, it doesn't mean you can't create something. Maybe all those years of not writing helped make me a better writer, somehow. But if you're reading this, beating yourself up for not meeting your goal – it's never too late to start.

Discover a
new favourite

Visit **penguin.com.au/readmore**